This could all go terribly wrong, terribly fast.

Her arms were trembling from the strain, her hands hurt, and her fingertips were likely bleeding by now. How could she have misjudged the location of the balcony from the roof so badly?

Charlotte reached for the railing with her foot.

Something warm grabbed her ankle. She stifled a scream.

"Miss Parnell," came a hoarse whisper. "Stop trying to kick me."

Viscount Moncreiffe? What in the world was he doing out here? The viscount's bare hand slid farther up her leg beneath her skirt. Her mouth fell open in surprise. She heard the crunch of his boots as he shifted position and reached over the railing. He patted her hip. "I've got you. Let go."

"What?" Nothing but space—a vast, wide open, empty space—stretched out beneath her.

What could happen? Worst ca[se] end up hanging upside down, skirts [ ]iving him a fine view before [ ]

If that happen[ ] [ ]g-stones below[ ]

With one [ ] [ ]tays were too tight for a c[ ] [ ]e let go . . .

Other **AVON ROMANCES**

Shirley Karr

Confessions OF A Viscount

AVON BOOKS

An Imprint of HarperCollinsPublishers

AVON BOOKS
An Imprint of HarperCollins*Publishers*
10 East 53rd Street
New York, New York 10022-5299

First Avon Books paperback printing: December 2006

To my sister Sandy, the best publicist in all of Texas. Here's hoping your kids will stop doing things that make your hair turn gray, sis.

In loving memory of Spider, our feline alarm clock and lap-warmer for seventeen years. Miss you, kitty.

Chapter 1

Alistair, Viscount Moncreiffe, peered into the window of the optician's shop, caught by the glint of sunlight on the gleaming metal body of the eyepiece on display. With growing interest, he read the placard that described its polished glass attributes. Its magnification was much higher than any eyepiece he currently owned. His set of three eyepieces for his telescope was adequate, but he was tired of adequate.

The cacophony of the city, the cries of street vendors, clatter of passing hackneys, all faded as he imagined what he could do with an eyepiece like that. How much farther into the night sky he could see. Perhaps even find undeniable proof that, contrary to what so many people

1

believed, Ceres and Pallas were indeed asteroids, and not planets.

A swift tug on his arm brought him back from the Andromeda nebula.

"I'm *so* sorry to have kept you waiting, dear," a woman said, tucking her arm through his as she continued walking.

Bemused by the most innovative way any female had sought an introduction, Alistair allowed himself to be towed along by the celestial being at his side, a young miss with sun-kissed blond hair and sky blue eyes. The swell of her full bosom was shown to advantage in her fashionably low-cut gown.

She gave a tinkling laugh, tossing her curls. Her smile was dazzling as she looked into his eyes.

Her direct approach was such a refreshing change from the simpering debutantes who'd practically drooled on his coat sleeves at the Knickersons' rout last night, Alistair decided to play along. "You are forgiven, darling, as your timely arrival kept me from spending an inordinate sum on a new eyepiece."

He hid a grin as her step faltered. She quickly recovered, though. "That's just as well, since your old one does the job quite well." She continued walking at a spanking pace, both hands wrapped around his arm as they dodged an orange cart and stepped in unison around a flower girl.

This was intriguing, but where was her chaperone? Footman, maid, outraged male relative . . . "Who—"

She cut him off. "I saw the most darling bonnet at the modiste's just now." She paused only long enough to show off her straight white teeth in a vacuous smile, then continued. "It was a straw poke bonnet, adorned with grapes and feathers and even an ostrich plume. Can you picture how adorable it would be?"

Alistair pictured how it would droop and disintegrate under the slightest bit of rain. Judging by the clouds looming on the horizon, threatening to block the sun, it was just as well she hadn't bought it.

The mysterious miss paused in her chatter long enough to furtively glance over her shoulder. She nibbled at her bottom lip, making it plump and red as a cherry.

"Who—"

She cut him off again. "So happy you agreed to accompany me this afternoon, darling. I love Auntie to death, but she can be rather a sourpuss at times, especially when her gout is acting up."

The last words were said over her shoulder as she stared at the street behind them. Alistair cast a glance behind them as well, but saw nothing untoward, just the usual collection of pedestrians, shoppers, and vendors crowding the sidewalk.

They reached the corner, and Alistair allowed the woman to gently steer them toward the alley. Once around the corner, she picked up the pace even more.

"Just a couple more doors down," she said, her voice now breathy from the effort of walking so fast. She patted his arm and looked over her shoulder. She came to an abrupt halt, staring back the way they had come, her hands falling to her sides.

They were alone in the alley, save for a cat eating its dinner near a pile of rubbish. The orange tabby looked up, a skinny mouse tail waving from between its jaws.

Alistair grimaced and turned his attention back to the young woman. "This has all been very entertaining, but who are y—"

She was gone.

Alistair swept his gaze around the alley. The only other living being in the vicinity was the orange tabby, now busily washing its face after its meal.

Voices drifted from the open door of a shop a few feet away. Alistair poked his head inside and peered past bolts of fabric stacked haphazardly, threatening to spill into the narrow passageway, which was littered with scraps of fabric and thread. He was about to step inside when the modiste's assistant appeared from behind a curtained doorway, her arms overflowing with a rainbow of silks and velvets.

After a startled moment, she dropped a quick curtsy and motioned with her head. "Beg pardon, m'lord, but the entrance is 'round the front."

"Yes, yes, of course. Thank you." He gave her a nod, retraced his steps, and hurried around to the shop's street entrance.

Though he loitered in the late afternoon sunshine near the dressmaker's for a half hour, he saw no one leave who resembled the mysterious miss with the bouncing blond curls. Several fashionable young women entered with their chaperones, but the only person to emerge was an old widow, leaning heavily on her cane.

With a glance at his pocket watch, and one last regretful look at the dressmaker's shop, Alistair hurried home to prepare for the Gatwicks' ball.

Pity. She was the most intriguing encounter he'd had

in all of London during his reluctant participation in the Little Season, and he hadn't even discovered her name.

Alistair stood next to his friend Nick and eyed the crowded ballroom with distaste. Beyond the swirling mass of humanity, the night sky was visible through the open balcony doors, beckoning to him. Clouds from this afternoon had cleared off, and the moon was in its last quarter, leaving the sky almost as dark and clear as it could get in London. Perfect for astronomical observations.

Father and Grandfather had other ideas, of course. Caring nothing for how few clear nights London offered in the autumn, both had insisted he attend this ball—each for quite different reasons.

But Alistair knew how to play their game. Just as he had done at so many other social functions, he'd entrusted his coat, hat, and the haversack containing his telescope and journal to a footman's temporary care when he'd arrived at the Argyle Rooms. As soon as both relatives had seen him mingle, he would claim his belongings, climb up to the roof, and be able to get in a few hours of observation before he made a return appearance in the ballroom before the trip home.

"Come along, there's someone I'd like you to meet."

Alistair stifled his groan and narrowed his eyes at his friend. "Not you, too, Nick. Bad enough my father keeps bringing every lightskirt to my attention, and Grandfather every marriage-minded miss. Thought I was safe from all that nonsense with you."

Nick shook his head, his gold earring winking in the

light cast by the many chandeliers. "Give me some credit. I'm introducing you to a man, not some miss."

Alistair rested his hands on his hips. "I know you sailors are known to have some odd appetites, but I do not—"

Nick threw his head back and laughed, and grabbed Alistair by the elbow, pulling him along. They plowed through the churning crowd, dodging the dancers and duennas, and pulled up short at the staircase, where more new arrivals had just been announced.

"Blakeney, you're a sight for sore eyes," Nick said, clapping a gentleman on the shoulder.

The man grinned as he turned. "Well, look what the wharf rats dragged ashore." He and Nick continued their boisterous greeting, much to the sniffing disapproval of a matron who entered behind Blakeney. Alistair tugged the two of them away from her.

Like Nick, Blakeney was dressed appropriately for the occasion. And just like Nick, there was nothing untoward in his appearance or demeanor, yet there was something about him that declared he didn't quite belong amongst polite society. Alistair liked him immediately.

Introductions formally performed, the three headed for the refreshment table.

"How is it that you know this old salt?" Blakeney took a swallow of the weak punch and frowned. Nick retrieved a flask from his coat pocket and splashed some into each of their cups, earning a smile from Blakeney.

"Nick was the school chum always getting us into trouble." Alistair nudged Nick when he was stingy with the alcohol.

"Somebody had to be the one." Nick took a swig straight

from his flask before tucking it away again. "Heaven knows it wasn't you, always arguing with the teachers, or Tony, busy teaching the bullies a lesson. Though you were both willing to go along with my ideas."

Alistair tasted the doctored punch. Much better. "And you, Blakeney? I take it you know Nick in his capacity as common sailor."

"There is nothing common about me or my ship," Nick huffed.

Blakeney emptied his glass in one swallow. "Let's just say Nick saved me and Charlie from having to swim a time or two."

Nick winked.

Realizing Blakeney was likely referring to work Nick had done for the Home Office during the war with Napoleon, sneaking his brig past the French blockade, Alistair settled in to hear a good yarn or two.

"Do you see him?"

"Not yet, Aunt." Charlotte scanned the sea of dancers as she and Aunt Hermione stood at the entrance to the ballroom at the Argyle Rooms, hardly sparing a glance for its famed elegant décor. Her brother's tall form should be easy to spot, if he was in the ballroom as he'd said he would be. If he was off on a secret meeting without her . . . He'd assured her he'd meet them at the ball, completely ignoring Charlotte's protests at being left behind to help Hermione.

He'd rarely left her behind when they were working together in Paris, but it seemed all bets were off since they'd come to London.

As soon as her aunt had duly admired the Grecian lamps and painted ceilings, they stepped into the crowded, noisy ballroom. Steven was nowhere to be found amongst the colorful mass of swirling dancers.

Charlotte forced her fists to unclench as Hermione's friend came forward to greet them.

"My, don't you look lovely," Lady Durrell gushed after she'd greeted Aunt Hermione. Charlotte pasted a smile on her face as Lady Durrell nudged her son at her side. "Doesn't she, Elliott?"

"Yeth, Mama. You look ethpecially charming tonight, Mith Parnell."

It took all of Charlotte's willpower not to snort. She'd previously met the dandy at another ball, and knew his lisp was just as much an affectation as his seven fobs. The more he drank, the less he lisped. Aunt Hermione flashed her a pointed look, but Charlotte shook her head. Thirty thousand a year or no, she would not encourage the silly young earl.

Lady Durrell remained oblivious to Charlotte's disinterest. "You looked just as lovely at your cousin's wedding breakfast last week. Do you know when she and Lord Glavin will return from their wedding journey?"

Charlotte tried to not think of Marianne at all—it was her cousin's fault that Steven was set on marrying her off. Just because Marianne was two years younger, Steven worried that Charlotte soon would be considered "on the shelf." As if that mattered to her. She had more important things to do than worry about getting leg-shackled.

Luckily, Aunt Hermione stepped into the conversation,

and Charlotte swept the room again, searching for a sign of Steven. There he was, coming out of a side room. Since he'd actually made an appearance, she felt almost in charity with him again. Almost.

A few excruciating moments later, she and Hermione were able to work their way toward Steven. He greeted their aunt with a kiss on the cheek, oblivious to Charlotte's close scrutiny. As soon as she saw him up close, she recognized that look in his eyes, the same look that was always there when he was working. Blast. He'd left her out of it, after he'd promised not to.

Well, if he was going to break his promise, she felt no compunction against breaking hers as well. She need stay only a little while, and then she could slip away. When Aunt Hermione had announced the location of tonight's ball, it had seemed like a gift, an opportunity not to be passed up.

Steven leaned close to give Charlotte a kiss on the cheek, and whispered in her ear. "See anyone you like? I'll arrange introductions."

Just because Marianne had gone all silly at the prospect of marriage did not mean that she felt the same way. In fact, a husband would only get in the way of her work. She gave a disdainful sweep of the gentlemen present in the ballroom.

Her breath caught. There he was, the gentleman she'd accosted on the street this afternoon. He was easily visible despite standing amidst a group of men. Taller than his companions, with his wavy light brown hair no longer hidden by his hat, though she couldn't see his sparkling blue eyes from this distance. His elegant clothes were well-tailored to his trim form, though he was far from being a dandy.

She took a half step to the side, almost hiding behind Steven. Should she plead a headache and make her escape before he saw her?

As though he sensed her staring at him, he lifted his head, sweeping her side of the room. He froze, and then gave a small smile of recognition as he locked gazes with her.

Blast. Now what? If she left the ball, he might seek out Steven, ask questions that she didn't want her half brother to hear.

Well, the gentleman had gone along with her outrageously forward behavior this afternoon, so he must possess a healthy sense of humor. She'd just have to arrange an introduction and give him some silly excuse for her earlier actions. And keep her brother out of it.

All in the line of duty, of course. And do it quickly, before he left his group of friends and started toward her.

If their conversation required the privacy of waltzing together, well, that was just a sacrifice she'd have to make. Remembering the feel of his muscles beneath his coat sleeve, and wanting to feel them again, had nothing to do with it.

"No, sorry, I don't see any prospects here," she said. Aunt Hermione dragged Steven into conversation and introduced him to a particularly vapid-looking brunette just then. "I'll be right back," Charlotte whispered, and slipped away before anyone could stop her.

* * *

Blakeney had left to greet someone or other, and Nick had wandered off with a widow who wanted to make merry, effectively abandoning Alistair to his fate amongst the matchmakers in the ballroom.

He looked beyond the couples forming the quadrille, to the wallflowers and their duennas seated against the far wall. Was there anyone he had not danced with before, who would not expect an offer after being partnered in one country dance?

Wait, back up. There she was. The miss from this afternoon! He smiled, but she did not return it. He was about to go to her, but was detained by Clarke and Dorian and other fellows of The Royal Society. While TRS was committed to the advancement of science in general, many of its members had banded together to study astronomy.

"Moncreiffe, I say," Dorian said, clapping him on the shoulder. "Tell us of your visit with Herschel and his forty-foot telescope. Is the view really as sharp and clear as everyone claims? I have a guinea riding on your answer."

"I did not have another telescope with me worthy of making a comparison, but I assure you the view exceeded all my expectations." Normally eager to converse with fellow members of the Society, Alistair couldn't help a pang of regret. Now the young woman was nowhere in sight. He'd missed his opportunity.

Clarke claimed Alistair's answer could not settle their wager, and the topic quickly spiraled from telescopes to betting books.

"My lord, may I have a moment?"

Alistair stepped away from his companions' jovial bickering and smiled at his hostess, who suddenly stood before him. His smile widened at the sight of the mysterious blond miss standing next to Lady Gatwick.

"Viscount Moncreiffe, may I introduce Miss Charlotte Parnell?"

Chapter 2

⁓◦⦿◦⁓

The blonde blushed prettily and batted her eyelashes as she rose from her curtsy. No spark of recognition flared in her eyes. Her smile was correctly polite and did not falter as she made the briefest of eye contact before resting her gaze on his cravat.

Alistair was certain it was her. Unmistakable blue eyes. He decided, again, to play along with her game. After performing the niceties, and both women looking at him expectantly as the quadrille ended, Alistair led Miss Parnell out as the orchestra began a waltz.

Perhaps she wasn't playing a game this time. Did she really not recognize him from the street? It was on the tip of his tongue to ask about their initial encounter.

"Oh, la, my lord," she said as they took their positions for the dance. "You're so tall, I scarce can reach your shoulder." She batted her eyelashes again.

Alistair had opened his mouth to speak, but closed it in surprise.

She glanced to her left as a couple passed by, the lady's crimson skirts brushing Miss Parnell's pale blue velvet gown.

"Such a shocking display of flesh," she said, half to herself. She looked up at Alistair. "But isn't that a most darling reticule?"

Miss Parnell continued with her vapid commentary on the dancers they passed. Alistair began to fear she was just as empty-headed as she appeared. Had someone coached her into her brazen behavior this afternoon? Surely such a silly creature could not have come up with such a tactic by herself.

To her credit, she danced divinely, following his lead easily, as if they'd partnered each other often. Her subtle scent of rosewater teased his senses as they moved across the dance floor.

He adjusted his hand at her waist, feeling her lush curve beneath the smooth velvet of her dress. Her gown was quite proper, the light color typical of a young miss, the neckline cut low enough to give a hint of her charms yet high enough to still be decorous. But their close proximity during the waltz, and the advantage of Alistair's height, gave him an excellent view of her bosom. He couldn't help noticing a freckle on the inner curve of her left breast, a perfect little dark circle on her creamy flesh that rose and fell with her every breath. Her voice had become breathy from the exertion of the dance and the effort of talking nonsense nonstop.

With a start, he realized she had stopped talking. Feeling a slight twinge of guilt, he raised his gaze to meet hers. Her blue eyes sparkled, and for an instant he thought he saw a gleam of satisfaction. But she batted her lashes, and the vapid smile was once more firmly in place.

"Isn't the dry weather lovely, my lord? My aunt predicts it will still be clear for Lady Bainbridge's Venetian breakfast in two days. Aunt's hip is never wrong when it comes to predicting rain."

Clear skies meant great observations, if he could get out of the city, or at least up onto the rooftops. If he could get away from his father and grandfather.

"The dry weather should increase the longevity of that bonnet you were admiring this afternoon."

Her step faltered, and he tightened his grip on her hand and waist to help her stay upright. He hid his satisfaction at her momentary astonishment, though he wasn't sure if her reaction was for the way he'd practically picked her up off her feet, or for drawing attention to the elephant in the room between them.

"Yes, about this afternoon . . ."

He eased his hold, letting her support her full weight again. "Yes, Miss Parnell?"

"I . . . I wanted to thank you, for going along with, ah, my little game." She batted her lashes at him. "I'm afraid I outpaced my maid, and there were some people on the street that I did not wish to see me walking alone."

He'd wager a guinea there wasn't an ounce of truth in her statement. "And walking with a perfect stranger was a better alternative?"

"Mmm, perfect, yes," she murmured, so quietly he barely heard her. She raised her gaze to his and met it full on, looking as though many words wanted to tumble from her lips all at once. "Yes, it was," she said at last, in a normal tone of voice.

"I do hope it's not a practice you indulge in often. Could have been quite dangerous for you, were I a different sort of person."

"Yes, of course you're right, my lord. I believe I learned my lesson." She cast her eyes down, but Alistair wasn't taken in. There was still something else going on. Perhaps he could tease it out of her upon further acquaintance. He hid his smile at the prospect.

Just then they danced past the potted palm in the far corner, where Alistair noticed his father standing with a woman in a flesh-colored gown that upon first glance made her look as though she were nude. Father had his arm around the woman's waist, and she was so close she was practically inside his coat. He winked at Alistair just before he bent his head to kiss the woman's throat.

Alistair quickly turned so Miss Parnell would not see his father's disgraceful behavior. He took a step back, making sure there was proper distance between himself and his partner. He had no intention of being stiff-rumped like his grandfather, but had sworn that he'd never embarrass the family like his father. Sometimes it seemed he'd spent every day of the last twenty years balancing the fulcrum between his grandfather's nearly puritanical ways and his father's descent into debauchery.

Miss Parnell cleared her throat. "So, are you as delighted as I at the prospect of continued dry weather?"

"Yes, I am enjoying the weather very much," Alistair replied, disappointed at the return to mundane topics.

Should he press her for more information, or let her grow more comfortable in his presence first?

Miss Parnell continued in a similar vein, discussing how much rainfall was predicted for the month, how she hoped it would hold off for the outdoor amusements scheduled during the Little Season.

She paused mid-sentence, her gaze focused on the balcony door. Alistair followed her gaze, just in time to see Nick and Blakeney slipping outside. Miss Parnell's eyes narrowed, her lips pursed, but just for a fraction of a second. Then her bland smile was back in place.

Hmm. Most women tended to either swoon in ecstasy at the sight of Nick or frown in disapproval.

"Will you be attending Lady Bainbridge's Venetian breakfast, my lord?" She fluttered her lashes at him again.

"I have not made up my mind yet."

She took a shorter step than the dance called for just then, which brought her body into brief contact with his, her velvet skirts brushing against his breeches.

It could have been an accident.

"I do hope you'll be in attendance," she said, her breathy voice pitched low.

Alistair kept his polite mask in place. Now *this* was behavior with which he was all too familiar. "I shall have to consult my appointment book." It seemed only fair that if she wanted to pursue him as though her intent was to make a match, he could press for details and find out what she really was doing. After her innovative behavior this afternoon, he hoped she wasn't doing something as ordinary as concealing an assignation.

The dance took them past the row of wallflowers, where Grandfather sat deep in conversation with a matron and what appeared to be her daughter. Grandfather tried to catch Alistair's eye, but he pretended not to see, and instead returned his gaze to Miss Parnell's freckle.

Her sudden intake of breath made him look up. He caught her staring at a woman in red, the same one they'd danced past earlier, slipping up the stairs, arm in arm with a male companion.

When he glanced back, Miss Parnell's smile was dazzling. The music ended, and he escorted her back to their hostess. How soon could he partner her again, without causing undue speculation about his motives?

"I do hope your schedule permits you to attend the breakfast," she said. As Alistair bowed over her hand, her fingers squeezed his, and her smile grew even more vapid.

He gave a noncommittal murmur and made his exit.

Perhaps he was misreading the whole situation, and everything was in fact the way it appeared on the surface— Miss Parnell was merely a silly miss on the hunt for a husband. In which case, he should avoid her at all costs.

Duty done, both relatives having seen him, he was now free, at least for a few hours. He made his way to the footman in the hall to collect his haversack and coat.

The footman with whom Alistair had entrusted his telescope was nowhere in sight. A bran-faced youth who appeared too young to be out of the schoolroom jumped up from the footman's bench as he approached. "Beg pardon, my lord," he said, his face turning bright red. "We, er, had to move some things from the cloakroom, so your haversack is in the, er, the small salon." He gave directions to a room at the back of the building.

Alistair thought it odd to move the guests' belongings so far from the front entrance, but shrugged and wound his way through the hallways to the indicated room, sidestepping the occasional couple seeking some privacy.

As he turned the knob to open the door, he couldn't help glancing over his shoulder. No one else was in sight. No one, that is, but a particularly ugly piece of statuary standing guard in the corner.

The salon was lit only by a small fire and one candle on a side table. Shadows flickered across the walls. It took his eyes a moment to adjust before he spotted his haversack on a chair by the window. He hesitated another moment, searching the dancing shadows. In the tidy space, nothing seemed to be out of place. Not one coat or hat or other item belonging to another guest graced the room.

He eyed his haversack, ten steps away. With a last look to make sure the door to the hall was wide open, he strode across the room.

The click of the door closing sounded like a cannon blast.

"Good evening, my lord." Her voice was silky soft, but the look in her eyes was that of a hound that had just cornered the fox in its den.

Not again. "Good evening, Miss . . . ?" Alistair had his back to the window, one hand snagging the haversack strap, the other feeling along the windowsill behind him. With any luck, the window was unlatched.

"Miss Hewitt." She ran her fingers through her guinea-gold blond hair as she spoke, mussing the once carefully arranged curls. "Miss Christine Hewitt. You stood up with me at Almack's last week. We danced together again, just two nights ago."

"Ah, yes. My grandfather introduced us." He pushed against the wooden sill and managed to get the tips of his fingers into the tiny space at the bottom. Just a little more . . .

"His grace was very kind." She slid the sleeves of her gown off her shoulders, exposing a generous expanse of bosom. "I would very much like to further our acquaintance, my lord." She stepped toward him, breasts first, a feral light in her eyes.

"Terribly sorry, Miss Hewitt, but I just remembered a previous engagement." He shoved the window all the way up, ducked his head out to see if there were any rosebushes in the vicinity, and dove through. Just as he landed in the bed of petunias below, he heard the salon door slam back against the wall.

"Unhand her, you lecherous—" The older woman stopped in mid-screech. "Where is he?"

"Oh, Mama!" Miss Hewitt wailed.

Slinging the haversack strap over his neck, Alistair sprinted to the corner of the building and did not slow down until he reached the front entrance. He brushed off the worst of the dirt as a footman—a different footman— let him in the front door.

"If I may be so bold, my lord," the servant murmured, reaching up. At Alistair's nod, the footman plucked several errant petals from his collar and cravat.

Alistair glanced at his clothes in the better light of the hall, but saw no other visible evidence of his roll in the flower bed. His telescope seemed to have survived the fall intact, with no new scratches on the wooden case. After nodding his thanks, he strode for the staircase and the door to the roof.

The trouble with Miss Hewitt, he thought with a rueful shake of his head, was a pitiable lack of originality. Had she no idea how many times that particular snare had been set for him? When faced with parson's mousetrap or an undignified leap out a window, well, clothes could be cleaned. Or replaced.

Miss Parnell would never engage in such unoriginal behavior.

Plenty of misses engaged in subterfuge in the pursuit of a husband, and she *could* actually be seeking a suitor. But there was more going on behind those guileless blue eyes, under that mass of blond curls, than mindless pursuit of a match. There had to be. What else could explain the abrupt, brief changes in her behavior?

Perhaps she occasionally succumbed to the pressure all the young women must feel from their families, with the expense and expectations inherent in a London Season. A sort of dual personality, where her natural inclinations were stifled in order to meet someone else's expectations. Heaven knew he'd had to stifle plenty of his own inclinations.

He might go to Lady Bainbridge's breakfast after all, if only to further observe Miss Parnell. And her freckle.

Once up on the roof, Alistair set up his observation deck. It took only moments to attach his telescope to its tripod, spread a thin blanket, and retrieve his pencil and journal from his haversack. He kept his gaze at rooftop height or higher, not wanting the gas street lamps below to ruin his night vision. He sat down, legs crossed, and waited for his eyes to adapt to the darkness.

The light breeze had cleared away the last of the clouds from earlier in the day, leaving the stars bright, though he could make out only part of Via Lactea. This late in the year, he could barely see the teapot lid on the upper tip of Sagittarius to the south, though Mars had risen above the eastern horizon. Unfortunately, it was too late in the evening to see Venus or Jupiter.

He shifted to a more comfortable position. What other invitations had he received that had been issued by hosts with an easily accessible, well-placed roof? If he was doomed to spend the entire Little Season in London playing peacemaker between his relatives, he wasn't going to give up his observation time altogether.

Movement across the way, a white blur, caught his attention. It looked like a ghost creeping across the roof of the hotel next door. Ridiculous. Alistair got up on his knees and leaned forward, straining to see. Then he chided himself, peered through his telescope, and adjusted the focus.

The apparition crept closer to the edge of the neighboring roof.

Alistair blinked. Her fair hair and light dress appeared almost white in the faint starlight, but that was definitely Miss Parnell peering over the edge. He leaned out, and saw what she must be looking at—three balconies, of which the middle one was just below her and a little to the right.

The two buildings were close together, scarcely six

feet apart, and only a low hedge separated their gardens. Thorny bushes, if he recalled correctly, and they were a good four stories down.

Miss Parnell got down on her knees and leaned over. Suddenly she was swinging in the air, fingertips clinging to the edge, reaching out with one foot.

But she had misjudged the distance. She clung to the edge of the roof by her fingers, four stories up, the balcony just beyond her reach.

Blast. No wonder she had always left the breaking-in part to Steven—doing so in a dress was nearly impossible. Not to mention dangerous. Foolhardy, even. As Charlotte dangled by her fingertips, four stories up, she tightened her grip on the roof tile and looked over her shoulder, toward the balcony that had seemed to be right *there*.

Perhaps she should have waited a little longer for her eyes to adjust to the darkness, after the bright lights in the ballroom next door. But the window washer's ladder leaning against the hotel wall had been easy enough to climb. And no telling how soon Aunt would start looking for her, or when Steven would return. The rat. How dare he leave her behind, after all the work they'd done together?

Charlotte swung her left leg out, reaching for the balcony railing. Still too far. The breeze picked up again, swirling around her skirts, chilling her in places that had no business feeling a breeze.

She had just as much right to chase after the stolen snuffbox as Steven did. More, in fact. Hadn't she been the one to collect most of the information when they worked in France? All she had to do was bat her blue eyes, show a little décolletage, breathlessly hang on their every word, and most men became blithering idiots, blathering their deepest secrets. Or she chatted up maids, collecting servants' gossip.

Steven had no right to insist she stop serving her country and start serving a husband instead. And how dare he so cavalierly dismiss her theory that Madame Melisande was responsible for stealing the box?

She gritted her teeth and inched her left hand along the edge, then the right. When Madame Melisande had left the ballroom, heading upstairs with a paramour, she realized this might be her only chance to search the widow's room at the hotel next door to the Argyle Rooms. It was too good an opportunity to pass up.

Her fingers slipped on the roof tile. She scrabbled for another grip and tried to catch her breath. Her new maid had laced her stays too tight again. It took hardly any exertion to make her breathless, and she worried about spilling out of her gown altogether.

Annoying for her, but it had an amazing yet highly predictable effect on the male of the species. Suited her purposes, though, especially when she noticed that the viscount had noticed. He had the sense of humor to go along with her this afternoon, but he also had predictable male reactions to female charms.

And he had muscles. She'd bumped against him to gauge his reaction, but had been unprepared for her own response to contact with his tall, lean body.

Her breathless state was due entirely to her tight stays, not his flat abdomen and hard thighs and toned calves that owed nothing to padding. With all her silliness, surely she had put to rest any suspicions he might have had about her behavior, and convinced him she was just as empty-headed as any miss prowling the marriage mart.

She inched her hand to the left again, then the other hand. She reached out her left foot, searching for the railing, but encountered nothing but air. She had to be getting close.

Her dancing slipper slipped off her foot. It landed with a faint *thwap* on the stone patio, four stories below.

This could all go terribly wrong, terribly fast. Her arms were trembling from the strain. Her hands hurt and her fingertips were likely bleeding by now. How could she have misjudged the location of the balcony from the roof so badly?

More sounds. The rustle of fabric, a soft thud. Had someone inside noticed her climb past a window? No lights filtered through the curtains on any of the three balcony doors. She reached again for the railing with her foot.

Something warm grabbed her ankle. She stifled a scream and tried to shake it off.

"Miss Parnell," came a hoarse whisper. "Stop trying to kick me."

Viscount Moncreiffe? What in the world was he doing out here? The viscount's bare hand slid farther up her leg beneath her skirt, holding the back of her knee, above her stocking. His other hand slid up her right side, all the way to her hip. Her mouth fell open in surprise. She heard the crunch of his boots on the balcony as he shifted position, the clink of his fob banging against the iron rails as he reached farther over the railing. He patted her hip. "I've got you. Let go."

"What?" Nothing but space—a vast, wide open, empty space—stretched out beneath her.

"I'll catch you. Let go."

She heard confidence in his whispered command, felt the strong grip he had on the back of her left knee. What could happen?

Worst case, she'd end up hanging upside down, arse over teakettle, skirts over her head, and give him a fine view of her nether regions before he let go in shock.

If that happened, immediate death on the flagstones below was an acceptable option.

With one last shallow breath—her stays were too tight for a deep one—she let go.

Wind whooshed past her ears but her fall was mercifully brief.

Moncreiffe hauled her into his arms and up against his hard chest. He grunted upon impact and staggered back a step, but quickly steadied. She wrapped her aching arms around his wonderfully broad shoulders and buried her face against his neck and the cool linen of his cravat. She wasn't on solid ground yet, but this felt even better.

"Are you injured, Miss Parnell?"

She felt the rumble in his chest as much as heard the quiet question. "I'm fine, thank you," she managed between panting breaths. She inhaled his comforting scent, a mellow mix of spice, tobacco, and a hint of musk.

She lifted her head enough to look over his shoulder. The safety of the balcony floor was still a long way down.

Tall men, and their long arms, could be quite handy. "Not that I don't appreciate your assistance—I do, by the way—but why are you here? I thought you were still at the ball."

"I could ask you the same question."

His grip shifted, and Charlotte became aware of his right arm around her shoulders, the left under her knees. Her skirts had bunched up in her lap, revealing her stockings and bare knees. Was anything else bare? Well, it didn't really matter, since there was no one else around. Moncreiffe held her out from his chest, just far enough to look at her face, though in the darkness his was a pale blur.

Light flared behind the curtain next door, and suddenly the other balcony door swung open.

An older gentleman, in his late fifties at least, stood there, holding up a candelabrum, his arm wrapped around the waist of a woman wearing too much rouge and not enough clothing, clearly a member of the demimonde, a Cyprian.

"Father," Moncreiffe said with a nod, rather calmly.

Father? Charlotte squeezed her eyes shut, but not before she saw the wicked gleam in the other woman's eye.

"Alistair, my boy! If I'd known you wanted a room, I'd have—"

"No! No, that's quite all right, we, ah, just wanted a moment of quiet for, ah . . ."

The older man chuckled. "The bed's in there, not out here."

Moncreiffe coughed. He cleared his throat, then seemed to suddenly remember he was still holding Charlotte aloft in his arms. He set her down gently and gave her skirts a slight shake into place, then straightened to his full height.

Charlotte tucked her shoeless left foot behind her right, hoping no one would notice her missing dancing slipper.

He cleared his throat again. "No, we are not in need of a, ah, bed. We just—"

"Up against a wall can be good, too, but at your height, it'd be a lot easier with a Long Meg." He turned his broad grin on Charlotte. "Not that you aren't a most charming pocket Venus." He winked at her.

Charlotte felt her cheeks flood with heat.

"Sir! Miss Parnell is no lightskirt! She's . . . Ah, she . . ."

Both Father and Charlotte turned their gaze on Moncreiffe, while the Cyprian snickered into her hand. In the flickering light cast by the candles, Charlotte saw Moncreiffe's blue eyes gazing at her intently. They suddenly widened, just for an instant. He wrapped his arm around her shoulders and turned back to his father, his chin high in the air.

"Miss Parnell has just done me the great honor of accepting my marriage proposal."

Chapter 3

Charlotte felt light-headed.

"Married? At your age?" Father's eyes narrowed. "Don't be ridiculous. Bed the wench and be done with it."

Charlotte would have gasped, had she been able to draw a deep enough breath.

Moncreiffe tucked her against his side, his hand around her shoulder. "I'll thank you to speak more respectfully of my intended, sir."

Father held the candelabrum higher and leaned toward them over the balcony railing, examining Charlotte. Moncreiffe held his ground, and his grip on Charlotte. She stayed perfectly still, chin up, hardly daring to breathe.

At last the older gent backed up. With a harrumph, he grabbed his companion, who was obviously cold in her thin dress, and retreated back into their room, muttering imprecations about "that damn stiff-rumped duke's doing" as he slammed the door.

Charlotte had grown roots. Couldn't move if she tried. Never in all her years of working on the Continent had she found herself in such a situation.

Moncreiffe cleared his throat and took a step back, leaned over the railing as though judging the distance to jump to the ground. Finally he faced her. "I most humbly beg your pardon, Miss Parnell."

Her mouth fell open.

"I don't know what came over me. I just couldn't give him the satisfaction of thinking that I, that you and I, er . . ."

"Had a carnal relationship?" She had the satisfaction of seeing his Adam's apple bob, even above his cravat.

"Er, yes. He keeps telling me to, ah, sow wild oats, as it were. And I would *never*, er, not that you're not appealing, but . . ."

She folded her arms over her chest. "Keep digging. You're well on your way to China." His discomfort should have increased hers, but instead had the opposite effect. Her breathing almost back to normal now, she saw the humor in the outrageous situation.

He ducked his chin, his blue eyes sparkling, his full lips twitching as he held back a smile. Her stomach fluttered.

"The good news is, I doubt Madame Cyprian, whoever she was, will tell anyone of our encounter, and my father certainly won't. The last thing he wants is for me to become engaged. That would make my grandfather far too happy."

Sounded like a family situation she should stay far away from.

"I appreciate you playing along like that. You're very quick on your feet."

At least he hadn't made the mistake of saying "light" on her feet. She was trying to think of something brilliant and witty to say when Moncreiffe rested a hand on the railing and leaned toward her. "But I must confess to a great deal of curiosity as to why you were hanging from the rooftop."

Oh. About that. Hmm. She tossed the question back to him to stall. "And I am curious how *you* came to be out here, with such propitious timing."

Moncreiffe hadn't moved away. "I was preparing to make some astronomical observations from the roof next door when I saw a more earthly body in a precarious position." His teeth gleamed in the semi-darkness as he smiled. "And you, Miss Parnell?"

She gulped. His hand rested on the railing at her back. He stood close enough that she could feel the heat radiating from his body, remember the feel of it next to hers, inhale his scent. She could not let that distract her. Men became insensible, talkative creatures around her—not the other way around. "You're sure your father won't speak of our encounter?"

His lips twitched, silently acknowledging her diversionary tactic. "Certain of it."

"Then we should leave before anyone else discovers us and reaches the wrong conclusion." She ducked past his arm and reached for the door handle. She'd used several extra pins to hold up her hair in case she needed one to pick a lock, but fortunately, Madame Melisande was a trusting person, or just careless, and had failed to lock it. Charlotte hurried inside.

"You don't seem the usual type of burglar," he said, his voice barely audible.

She hadn't heard him follow her in, yet felt his presence at her side as strongly as if he were still holding her. They stood stock-still in the shadowy room, with the only light coming from the faint glow of the dying embers in the fireplace.

"We can't be seen together," she whispered, ignoring the urge to reach out and touch him again. "I'll wait a few minutes after you're gone, then go downstairs, just like the other hotel guests."

She walked toward the door but paused, feeling the heat and weight of his hand on her shoulder, and tingled as he leaned down to whisper in her ear. "I sincerely hope the rest of your evening is less eventful, Miss Parnell." He gave her shoulder a gentle squeeze before moving away.

The balcony door curtains fluttered as he passed. She heard the faint *clang* of his boots on the iron railing, and then he was up and gone from view, back the way he'd come, just as quick and agile as Steven when it came to climbing about on roofs. Gratifying to know her initial assessment had not been proven incorrect.

Charlotte stood frozen, staring at the empty balcony, reliving the moments in Moncreiffe's company. The encounter with his father could prove problematic. He did not wish Alistair to marry, but apparently the duke did. Too bad she didn't know the viscount's thoughts on the subject.

She gave herself a slight shake. What on earth was she doing, thinking about Moncreiffe and marriage, when she had gone to such lengths—not to mention risk—to be here, now, to search Melisande's room?

She made sure the hall door was shut and locked, did the same for the balcony door, then lit one candle from the glowing embers and began going through the courtesan's belongings.

Half an hour later, she sat back on her heels with a sigh of defeat and closed her eyes. No, she would not give in. Of course it wouldn't be this simple. She got up and made certain everything was back in its original position. She had found plenty of evidence if she were inclined toward blackmail—at least a dozen gentlemen would pay handsomely for the return of their tokens of affection. Melisande collected paramours the way other women collected shoes or gloves. But there was no sign of the object Charlotte was after.

Perhaps Melisande carried such a valuable item in her reticule, or on her person?

She'd have to bribe a maid, find out Melisande's schedule, follow the courtesan. Go to the same social functions, get close to her.

If she went alone, it might raise suspicion, not to mention possibly causing a scandal if she came to the attention of some busybody stickler for propriety, and Aunt Hermione and her gout were only good for a couple outings per week.

She'd need an escort. Steven was out of the question, obviously. He'd only be interested in finding her a suitor, and would ditch her while he went off on his own search, conveniently forgetting all about their successful partnership. The rat.

Suitor. Hmm. Marianne had been squired about by Lord Glavin to all sorts of events and outings while they were engaged. A husband was still out of the question, but a fiancé might be just the ticket.

She went still. Viscount Moncreiffe. He'd already brought up a fake engagement.

How could she let him know she would like to continue his charade, without him thinking it a ploy to actually lure him into parson's mousetrap?

"You sly puss," Steven said with a grin two days later, tossing the morning's paper onto the table in front of Charlotte. He waved dismissal to the footman stationed by the sideboard, so they were alone.

She swallowed her bite of egg on toast. "Beg pardon?"

Steven stabbed an article halfway down the page that contained all of the social announcements. "When were you going to tell me you snagged yourself a viscount? One that's heir to a dukedom, no less." He ruffled her hair. "Nicely done, poppet. Mama and your papa would have been so proud." He pulled out a chair and sat across from her. "Though to be proper, shouldn't they have come to me to discuss marriage settlements before making the announcement?"

Charlotte's fork clattered to the floor, unheeded, as she snatched up the newspaper. There it was, printed in black and white for all the world to see. *The Duke of Keswick announces the engagement of his grandson, Alistair,*

Viscount Moncreiffe, to Miss Charlotte Parnell of Bath.
It went on to discuss the two families, including Moncreiffe's father, the Marquess of Penrith, and listed information about her pedigree of which Charlotte had only a vague recollection.

"But marrying you off to the heir to a dukedom! I suppose we can forgive them their little oversight."

"I . . . we . . . it's not like that. We barely—" Charlotte gave up on an explanation at the sound of the door knocker. It was still far too early for any of Hermione's friends to come calling, even with this juicy tidbit to discuss.

The butler appeared in the doorway moments later. "A gentleman caller, miss," he announced, proffering the silver tray with a lone calling card.

Steven snatched up the card. "The bridegroom comes!" He pulled Charlotte's chair back from the table. "Where did you put him, Farnham, the drawing room?"

"Yes, sir, but the gentleman asked specifically for Miss Parnell." His disdainful sniff conveyed his opinion of the impropriety of calling at such an early hour.

Charlotte snatched back the card from Steven. "Surely you'll allow me a few moments of privacy with my fiancé?" She flounced out of the room without a backward glance.

"Five minutes," Steven called. "Then I'm coming in, and I'm not going to knock."

Alistair paced before the empty fireplace in the drawing room. Stupid, stupid, stupid. He should never have lied to his father, or at least not that particular lie. He should have known Father would confront Grandfather, believing it was the duke's influence that made Alistair inclined toward matrimony at the tender age of twenty-five.

He plowed his fingers through his hair, wishing yet again the two men would choose someone else to be the rope in their decades-long game of tug-of-war.

Because his father couldn't keep quiet and Grandfather couldn't resist rubbing success in his son's face, now all of London was privy to a private conversation. A conversation regarding a fake engagement. How did one go about asking a gently bred miss to declare herself a jilt?

Why, why couldn't he have thought of a better reason for being alone on a balcony in the dark—the balcony of a hotel rumored to be a favored setting for assignations— with Miss Parnell?

And why had she been dangling above said balcony in the first place?

He turned at the sound of the door opening. Miss Parnell stood still for a moment, as though reluctant to share the room with him. No sign of a chaperone. The footmen in the hall were stationed on either side of the drawing room doorway, their backs to him.

She was dressed for staying at home, in a modest sprigged muslin gown, her hair pulled up in a simple but elegant chignon instead of a mass of ringlets. He had been worried she might not even be up yet. After spending almost until dawn at his telescope, he was awake this early only because of his father's outraged roars upon seeing the newspaper.

Miss Parnell came forward slowly and gestured for him to be seated.

Alistair waited until she had settled on the sofa before taking an armchair across from her. "I do apologize for my early arrival, but I wanted to warn you—"

"About the announcement in the paper?"

Damn. "You've already seen it?"

"As has my brother. He'll be joining us in a few minutes, by the way. He was a bit affronted you did not approach him about the marriage settlements before sending off the notice."

Alistair pinched the bridge of his nose. Good thing he loved his father and grandfather so much, or he'd have murdered them both in their sleep long ago. He lowered his hand to his lap and leaned toward Miss Parnell. "I don't know quite how to say this, but—"

"Allow me to guess. Your father and grandfather had a row, your father let slip what you told him, and Grandfather sent off the notice without anyone else's knowledge, and now you want me to cry off."

This might prove easier than he thought. "The thing is—"

"Are you promised to someone else, Moncreiffe?"

Alistair shook his head.

"Are your affections engaged elsewhere?"

"No, but you see—"

"Do you wish to be married, my lord?" She was leaning forward now, hands tightly clasped, her expression intent. He could almost see the wheels turning behind her blue eyes.

He tried to choose his words carefully. "Eventually, yes. It is expected of me, part of my duty. But I had hoped that would not happen for several years at least."

"But your grandfather wishes for you to marry sooner rather than later?"

He nodded. "He thinks that would help ensure I do not become a loose screw like my father."

"Might your engagement make him just as happy as an actual marriage, at least for a while?"

Alistair leaned back in his chair. "What are you getting at, Miss Parnell?"

"My brother wishes for me to marry. Like you, I do plan to marry, but I hope to make it later rather than sooner. An engagement would please him much in the same way it would please your grandfather."

Alistair felt some of the tension leave his neck and shoulders. "Are you suggesting we indulge in a bit of subterfuge, Miss Parnell?" He held back a smile at the confirmation of his suspicions. This was no empty-headed miss before him, regardless of what she may have wanted him to think.

She batted her lashes. "At the end of the Little Season, our plan is to remove to my aunt's home in Bath for the winter. By then I think you and I will have spent enough time in each other's company to find we don't really suit after all." She rose to her feet, her hand extended. "Are we in accord, Moncreiffe?"

He grasped her petite hand in his. "I believe we are, Miss Parnell." They shook on their agreement. Alistair allowed himself to smile, for the first time in days.

Their hands were still clasped when the door burst open and a familiar, tall blond man entered.

He quickly shut the door behind him, depriving the

footmen of the chance to gawk at the proceedings, and stood there with his hands on his hips. "I thought the name in the announcement seemed familiar."

Miss Parnell hastily withdrew her hand. She cleared her throat and blinked several times, then smoothed back a strand of hair and faced her brother, hands loosely clasped. "Steven, Lord Moncreiffe and I were just, ah, discussing terms. We— Wait, you two know each other?" She shot Alistair an accusatory glare before turning it on her brother.

"A mutual friend introduced us the other night." Alistair tugged his waistcoat into place. "Had I realized the family connection, Blakeney, I would have sought your permission before pursuing a match with your sister."

Alistair's thoughts moved at lightning speed as he spoke the mundane platitude. Blakeney worked for the Home Office, as did Nick. *Nick saved me and Charlie from having to swim a time or two.* Miss *Charlotte* Parnell dangling from the rooftop, trying to sneak into the room beyond the balcony door, now made much more sense.

But the war was over, and had been for some time. What would two ex-spies be after in London?

Clearly, Miss Parnell was not working in complete harmony with her brother. Rivals, more like. At the least, she wanted to deceive him about the nature of her engagement.

Once again, two people were using Alistair as a pawn in their power struggle. By going along with her deception, he was playing right into her hands.

As he looked down at the pretty blonde beside him,

her lovely freckle hidden by her high-necked gown, he thought he might just enjoy being in her hands.

Besides, it appeared they had no one willing to serve as peacemaker, unlike Father and Grandfather.

"No harm done," Blakeney said, striding forward. "Perhaps we should adjourn to the library so we can discuss practical matters?"

Miss Parnell stepped forward and to the side, blocking Alistair's exit, unless he wanted to knock her over. "Actually, we were discussing plans for Lord Moncreiffe to escort the three of us to Lady Bainbridge's Venetian breakfast this afternoon."

"We were?" Alistair murmured.

"Not what it looked like to me," Blakeney said, folding his arms across his chest.

Miss Parnell raised her chin. "He's going to bring his carriage by at one o'clock." She stepped aside and raised her hand, palm down. "Until then, my lord."

Alistair took the hint and dropped a kiss just above her bare knuckles. "Until then."

Just when he thought Blakeney was going to challenge him, he moved aside at the last second to let Alistair pass through the doorway.

He reclaimed his hat and coat from the footman and walked home, deep in thought. With any luck, a false engagement to a pretty girl like Miss Parnell would keep away all but the most aggressive of the marriage-minded young women who'd been dogging his steps.

Would she realize he knew of her real intentions? What was she really after, that she wanted to get without her brother's cooperation?

And more importantly, should he help her, or try to stop her?

He needed to gather more information before drawing a conclusion. Miss Parnell, at the least, was worthy of further observation.

Introductions to Miss Parnell's aunt and then getting the foursome into the carriage prevented any private conversation with his temporary fiancée. He barely managed to be the one to assist her from the carriage when they arrived.

The Bainbridges' garden was decorated with paper lanterns swaying in the light afternoon breeze. An army of servants kept the dishes filled to overflowing with delicacies, feeding almost the same size crowd as had graced the ball at the Argyle Rooms last night.

Alistair had almost decided to spirit Miss Parnell away so they could talk, when he realized they were now the only ones seated in the dappled sunlight beneath the elm tree in the corner of the garden.

"I know what you're up to," he said softly to her as she bit into a pastry.

She dropped the pastry onto her plate. She swallowed and patted her cherry-red lips with her napkin. "I know I shouldn't have taken a second tart, but the first was so good."

He almost smiled. "Not that. In fact, it's refreshing to see a woman who doesn't pretend she eats like a bird. No, I meant I know why you want a fraudulent fiancé."

"You do?" She stared down at the pastry as though it had been the one to speak, not him.

"You're trying to do something without your brother's knowledge—something that required breaking into someone else's hotel room."

She held on to her plate with both hands and turned her blue gaze on him. "Do you see the half dozen or so daggers plunged into my back, my lord?"

A lingering glance over her entire luscious figure, and Alistair assured himself she was speaking metaphorically.

"Those are from the ladies who've congratulated me on my forthcoming marriage to you. Very determined ladies who had every intention of diligently pursuing a match with you for themselves. Let us not pretend that I am the only one who benefits from this arrangement."

He allowed a rueful grin. "I had noticed the sudden lack of handkerchiefs dropped in my path since the announcement appeared." He rested his arm on the back of her chair and turned toward her, leaning over just far enough to catch a glimpse of her freckle. He barely resisted the impulse to twine one of her curls around his finger.

Not only had she changed from the simple gown of this morning into something with lacy frills and a lower neckline, but her hairstyle was again a mass of pinned-up ringlets. He wanted to pull the pins loose, one by one, and let the curls dance around her creamy bare shoulders.

He cleared his throat. "Fair enough, I acknowledge we both benefit. I've already deduced your interest in this event extends beyond Lady Bainbridge's garden décor and gastronomic offerings, and not just to receive accolades for your triumph."

"My triumph?" Her puzzled frown put a tiny line between her eyes. His fingers itched to smooth it.

"My grandfather is a duke, my father a marquess, and I'm their sole heir. I'm considered quite a catch." He spoke with enough deprecating humor to tease an answering smile from Miss Parnell.

"You catch quite well, too." She flushed with color at the admission, but did not look away.

Alistair felt an answering warmth spread through him, remembering the feel of Miss Parnell in his arms on the balcony the other night. He hadn't wanted to let her go. Who knows how long he might have held onto her, kept her tightly against his body, had they not been interrupted?

He reached for her hand and turned her palm over to examine her fingers. "No lasting damage sustained from your foray on the rooftop?" All he could see were faint red marks, which for all he knew might have been left by juice from the tart she'd been eating.

"Nothing of consequence," she whispered.

At the breathless tone in her voice, he looked up. Her gaze was locked on their joined hands, where he was absently stroking her fingertips.

He patted her hand and sat back in his chair. "Your interest in this event?"

She offered her plate to a passing footman and brushed crumbs from her lap. "Everyone who is anyone is here. Being seen in public with you has cemented our arrangement. If anyone had any doubts about the veracity of the announcement in the paper, they were erased when you caressed my hands just now."

Guiltily, he looked up at the people strolling through the garden or standing in clusters, eating and gossiping.

More than a few heads turned quickly away, caught staring at him and Charlotte. "I was not—" Recognizing the futility in a denial, Alistair cut himself off.

Having had such intimate physical contact so early in their acquaintance—holding her aloft in his arms—had apparently decimated his usual reserve. If he kept this up, he'd be as licentious as his father. At least where Miss Parnell was concerned. He sighed. "Yes, everyone can see we are in fact engaged. But you were interested in this event before we entered into our agreement."

"Of course. As I said, everyone who is anyone is to be seen here."

He'd wager his last farthing that social standing was at the bottom of Miss Parnell's list of priorities. He quickly reviewed her actions since their arrival at the Bainbridge residence. After surveying the guests who'd arrived before them, she'd excused herself to the ladies' retiring room, and he thought she'd been gone an inordinately long time. Even for a woman. "You didn't break into anyone's bedchamber here, did you?"

"Break in? Of course not."

"Don't split hairs. Did you do here what you did the other night?"

"Fall into a man's arms, literally?" Smiling, she batted her lashes. "Nearly break my neck? Meet a courtesan face-to-face? No, I did none of those things today."

He wiped a tiny crumb from the corner of her mouth and tipped her chin up with one finger. "Miss Parnell."

She gave a small sigh of defeat. "I did not find what I was looking for the other night. I had reason to believe I would be successful here. I was not."

He glanced around at the crowd of people milling in the garden. Who, or what, was she after? He counted himself lucky she'd revealed even the fact that she was searching. Soon, he'd persuade her to confide in him in greater detail. "So. What do we do now?"

"We?" She gave a delicate shake of her head. "You are going to escort me to various functions, squire me about on your arm. The ladies will wish me ill, and sigh over you, but from afar. I will occasionally slip away to look for"—she pursed her lips in thought—"what I'm looking for, and then come back to your arm, with no one the wiser."

Alistair folded his arms. "So essentially you want me to be your escort and your alibi."

"And in return, I shall protect you from the marriage-minded masses."

He smiled at the image of the short, curvy blonde beside him fighting off hordes of women—her dress swirling about her shapely ankles, ringlets swaying, bosom heaving with exertion.

Having the pretty Miss Parnell on his arm would be no hardship. Their proximity would allow him the opportunity to wear down her defenses, find out what she was really up to. "What outing or event is to be on our social calendar next?"

Chapter 4

❧

A nother ball that night, as it turned out, held at the home of Lord and Lady Addington, one street over from the Argyle Rooms, and the hotel where Alistair had learned Madame Melisande was staying. He'd noticed the French widow, whose charms could be rented if not actually purchased, had become a common element in Miss Parnell's activities.

Madame Melisande had arrived at the Venetian breakfast shortly after Alistair's chat with Miss Parnell under the elm tree, and his fiancée had quickly excused herself to the ladies' retiring room again. She'd come back looking less than satisfied, moments after Melisande had reappeared.

"Unless you plan to depart from respectability," he whispered in Miss Parnell's ear as they made their way through the receiving line that night, "I'd like to know your interest in the courtesan." Aunt Hermione was just ahead of Miss Parnell, and Blakeney was only a step behind Alistair on the crowded staircase. The courtesan in question was five places ahead of them in the receiving line, and Miss Parnell was taking note of every person Melisande engaged in conversation.

Miss Parnell studiously ignored him and moved forward to greet their hostess on the landing, dropping a curtsy and complimenting the marchioness's sapphire blue gown. The two women discussed the gown and the modiste who designed it, and commiserated on the outrageous prices she charged for her work, but wasn't it worth it in the end?

Intrigued by Miss Parnell's change in demeanor, Alistair paid closer attention. The empty-headed miss was back—the persona she'd used to fob him off during their first dance together.

Their group stepped into the ballroom doorway, was announced, and entered the fray. From the corner of his eye Alistair noted several young women whispering behind their fans as the foursome passed by. More than one wistful look was tossed his way, and several full of venom were directed at Miss Parnell.

Miss Parnell's Aunt Hermione was oblivious to the undercurrents. "My, you are a tall one," the older lady gushed upon finding herself standing beside Alistair.

He smiled down at the diminutive lady. The top of her head barely reached above his elbow. Though she had never been classically beautiful, there was a handsome quality to her features, which lasted longer than simple beauty. Silver strands highlighted her once golden hair, framing her still youthful face. He was struck by the family resemblance with her niece, and realized for the first time that most men would probably not consider Miss Parnell to be pretty in the traditional sense, either.

"I trust I'm leaving you in good company," Blakeney said to Aunt Hermione, with a pointed glance to Alistair. "I see someone I must say hello to."

"Off you go." Aunt Hermione made shooing motions. She glanced up at Alistair. "If you wouldn't mind fetching me a cup of punch, young man, I'll be happy to sit among the chaperones while you two dance." Her eyes twinkled as she beamed at him and her niece.

Minutes later Alistair and Miss Parnell took their place in the dance lines forming. He was fully aware that the movements of the dance would afford her the chance to look over everyone in the ballroom without being obvious. It would also allow him to converse with Miss Parnell, and watch where her attention was drawn.

He saw Madame Melisande cross the room at the same moment Miss Parnell saw her. The widow soon entered into a heated conversation with a gray-haired gentleman, who thankfully was not Alistair's father.

"Neither of them look very happy, do they?" Alistair noted as they waited out their turn at the end of the dance line a few minutes later.

"He seems to be trying to placate her," Miss Parnell murmured.

"I wonder who he is," they both said at the same time. They shared a quick smile, then stepped into position in the dance, exchanging places with another couple, and began working their way back up the line.

The first time Alistair had slipped from a roof while attempting to get a closer look at the stars, his governess had insisted dancing be added to his studies once his ankle healed, in addition to the usual courses of Greek and Latin and estate stewardship. He had resisted and complained, to no avail. The agility and balance he'd gained from the extra practice had served him well over the years. It had even spared him much of the awkwardness that usually accompanied adolescent growth spurts.

He was doubly grateful now for those many hours of dance practice, because he found himself distracted by Miss Parnell's smile, or the graceful way she moved, rather than concentrating on his own steps in the dance. He moved by rote, so no one was aware of his preoccupation.

"My aunt undoubtedly knows who he is," Miss Parnell said when the figures brought them together again. They briefly held hands as they ducked under the arch made by the other couple in their square.

"Excellent." They spun away from each other and circled back.

Soon the music ended and he escorted Miss Parnell to her aunt.

"Which gray-haired gentleman?" Aunt Hermione replied, after Miss Parnell had taken a seat and made her inquiry. "There are so many of them." Aunt and niece shared a chuckle.

Miss Parnell described the gentleman in question, without resorting to pointing.

"Sir Nigel Broadmoor is a loose fish, someone with whom you should have no contact," Aunt Hermione pronounced with unexpected vitriol.

"Has he done you harm?" Alistair leaned forward to see her reply.

Aunt Hermione pursed her lips as though tasting an unripe lemon. "Last Season, he set his sights on my Marianne. Did everything he could to try to compromise her, poor girl, short of putting his hand up her skirt. Had she a larger fortune, I doubt we could have successfully fended him off."

"What would a fortune hunter possibly want with Madame Melisande?" Miss Parnell murmured.

"Fortune hunter, card sharp, all-around loose fish," Aunt Hermione said. "You steer clear of him, miss, do you hear me?"

"Yes, ma'am." Miss Parnell demurely folded her hands in her lap. She turned to Alistair, pitching her voice low enough that only he could hear her. "He doesn't seem Melisande's usual type of paramour."

"And you know her usual type?"

She nodded, almost absently. "Men like you, or your father. Wealthy. In a position of power. Preferably both." She propped her chin in her hand, tapping her bottom lip with one finger. "Sir Nigel is neither."

Alistair stared at her finger, wondering what it would feel like to trace her lip with his own finger. "Perhaps they are simply drawn toward each other. We cannot always control who we find ourselves attracted to."

"No, I don't think—" She cut herself off and turned to

Alistair, biting her bottom lip, as though reading the unspoken sentiment behind his words.

He waited, but she said no more. When the silence began to draw out, he returned to a question she had ignored earlier in the evening. Dealing with his father and grandfather, he'd learned that bluntness was usually far more effective than polite subtlety. "What is your interest in the French widow?"

She stared at her hands in her lap so long, Alistair began to think she wouldn't answer. At last she took a deep breath. He raised his gaze from the freckle on her bosom to concentrate on her reply.

"There is an object that's gone missing. It belongs to someone important, and it needs to be returned to its owner. I believe Madame Melisande took that object, or knows of its whereabouts."

"And your brother does not share in your belief."

"Steven dismissed my theory." Her lips momentarily thinned at the remembered insult.

While his friends Nick and Tony were as close to him as brothers, he had been an only child since the accident twenty years ago. Did brothers and sisters fight differently than male siblings? Trade insults, and then brush them off as easily as boys did? He doubted they'd resort to fisticuffs as often. Though the idea of Miss Parnell participating in a physical fight definitely seemed a possibility.

He tapped his chin. "I wonder if perhaps Sir Nigel somehow found out about Madame Melisande's activities."

Miss Parnell glanced at him, eyebrows raised, then turned back to watching the couple in question.

"Is the missing object valuable?" Alistair continued. "If money is to be made from taking the object, he's the sort who would want to be part of the scheme." He studied Sir Nigel, who was still near the potted palm, in animated conversation with Melisande. Miss Parnell's sudden gasp brought his attention back to her.

"He's got it!" she whispered. She nodded, smiling. "He found out what Melisande was doing, wanted to be part of the scheme, but she wouldn't cooperate, so he took it from her. She's just recently realized she no longer has it."

"No wonder you couldn't find it. By the way, what is it?"

She bit her bottom lip. "Only a very few number of people know about the . . . object, and even fewer people know that it's missing. If word got out, it could have disastrous consequences."

"Disastrous?" Alistair raised one eyebrow. "For whom?"

"En— Enormous numbers of people."

Knowing about the work her brother had done for the Home Office, Alistair was fairly certain she had almost said England. He sat up straighter, suddenly realizing that what he'd gotten himself into could have far greater consequences than damaging a young woman's reputation, as when his father had misinterpreted Miss Parnell being aloft in his arms on the balcony of a notorious hotel.

A woman as daring as she, who had accosted a strange man on the street, would not be easily dissuaded from her chosen path. Not to mention how calmly she had gone along with his bald-faced lie, unruffled even under his father's scrutiny. Informing on her to her brother would only compel her to commit still more daring and dangerous acts in defiance.

Even the extreme option, of them actually getting married, was unlikely to give pause to a woman who would climb up onto a roof in the dark and try to swing down onto a balcony while wearing a gown.

If he could not dissuade Miss Parnell from her quest, he now felt it his obligation, for God and country, to help her succeed.

He did not, however, feel obliged to share this realization with her.

"What are you two discussing so intently, hmm?" Aunt Hermione leaned toward her niece. "Setting a date for your wedding, perhaps?"

Charlotte felt heat bloom in her cheeks. "Aunt!" she hissed. Moncreiffe cleared his throat. Charlotte continued, forcing a calm tone. "As I explained to you, it is too soon for that. The viscount and I need to become better acquainted."

Aunt Hermione harrumphed. "Should have done that before you accepted his offer, miss." She leaned toward Charlotte's ear for a conspiratorial whisper. "Though with him being so easy on the eyes, not to mention heir to a dukedom, I can understand why you didn't wait." She straightened in her chair, a knowing smile gracing her lips.

Charlotte stifled a sigh. She hated to disappoint her aunt, and the old gel would be when they called off the fake engagement. But a husband was not in her future, did not fit into her plans. Just as a wife was not in Moncreiffe's immediate plans.

Aside from being caught in the apparent feud between his father and grandfather, she felt confident he was only going along with her subterfuge as a way to dispel the ennui that plagued so many gentlemen of the ton. The same ennui that made them such easy targets when she needed information from them, or needed to use them to further her plans.

She did not feel guilty. She was harming no one. Her conscience was clear.

The same could not be said for Steven, the rat. The someone he had to say hello to turned out to be Gauthier, whom they had often worked closely with in France—further proof that Steven had not declined the assignment, as he had claimed. "Wants to simply enjoy the Season, my arse," Charlotte muttered.

"Beg pardon?"

She batted her lashes at Moncreiffe. "Did you say something, my lord?"

He shook his head and returned his attention to the dancers on the floor.

Charlotte gave herself a mental shake. What was it about Moncreiffe that made it so easy for her to act the part of a breathless, giddy green girl encountering her first handsome man?

It wasn't as though she'd never kept company with attractive men before. Even the handsome, wealthy, and powerful Marquis de Archambault, a man known for his discriminating taste in women, had invited her into his bed on more than one occasion, before she'd left France. She had never been tempted to accept his invitations.

If Moncreiffe were to invite her, however . . .

She glanced over at his hands resting on his knees. A casual, utterly proper position. Innocent. She stared at his long, almost elegant, fingers, remembering the way they had felt against hers as he'd caressed her hands earlier that afternoon, in the garden as they sat beneath the elm tree. He'd know exactly what to do with his hands, put those fingers to good use, to pleasure a woman.

His lips, too. Just look at that gorgeous mouth, the charming smile. He would know how to kiss, warm and gentle, passionate and all-consuming. Not slobbering and clumsy, like Freddie Lawson, when she was twelve. Moncreiffe would make her toes curl, send shivers down her spine. The good kind.

What would he taste like? Sweet like sugar plums, or heady like a good claret? Rich and warm, like her morning chocolate . . .

She stifled a groan. She'd seen it in enough men to recognize the emotion in herself—lust. How lowering to discover she was just as susceptible to lusting after an attractive member of the opposite sex.

Well. Now that she had identified the enemy, she would be better prepared to fight it. And the way to win this war was to deny it battle.

Viscount Moncreiffe was only a means to an end. Just as she was for him.

"Do you think you could make some discreet inquiries, my lord?" Charlotte whispered behind her fan.

"About Sir Nigel?" He touched his bottom lip with one long, elegant finger. She wished he'd stop doing that.

"Check the betting books, see if he's come into any funds recently, or anticipates doing so in the near future, that sort of thing?"

She nodded, unable to form a coherent thought, mesmerized by the sight of his fingertip tapping his full lower lip.

He abruptly lowered his hand and clasped his fingers together. She cleared her throat. What had they been discussing? Oh, right. "See if you can find out who else Sir Nigel might be spending his time with."

Moncreiffe nodded. "See if he's had any unusual contact with people in positions of power?"

Charlotte kept her expression carefully neutral. Moncreiffe couldn't possibly know what was at stake.

He kept looking at her expectantly. She had the feeling he was baiting her, trying to trick her into revealing more than she intended. Wasn't that exactly what she had done, on so many occasions, to so many men?

She'd have to ask Steven to look into Moncreiffe's past. Much as it galled her to admit it, there were things that a single young man could do in London society that a woman could not. Although it wouldn't be too out of the ordinary for a newly engaged woman to make inquiries about her husband-to-be. Though, as Aunt Hermione had said, those things were generally done *before* accepting the offer of marriage. Not after.

Steven wended his way through the crowd just then and took the empty chair on the other side of Aunt Hermione.

"How is your friend?" Hermione asked, patting Steven on his knee.

"My what? Oh, ah, he's fine. Yes. Just did a bit of

catching up. Hadn't seen each other since Cambridge, you know."

Aunt Hermione soaked it up, obviously believing every word. Charlotte ground her teeth. The musicians struck up a waltz. She leaned forward, to see around her aunt. "Steven, I believe this is the dance you promised me tonight."

"I did? Yes, of course. If you don't mind, Moncreiffe."

Moncreiffe waved his hand in a magnanimous gesture, his blue eyes twinkling. How annoying that after such short acquaintance he saw right through her subterfuge, when her beloved blood relative, Aunt Hermione, accepted every word as gospel truth.

Moments later, Charlotte and Steven took their place among the dancers. "Enjoy your chat with Gauthier?" she said, pleased that her voice remained neutral.

"Don't be angry, poppet," he said, expertly leading them to the least crowded section of the dance floor.

At least Steven had the grace to not deny it. She fought to keep the anger out of her voice. "How could you leave me out of an investigation, after all we've done together? Haven't I proven myself enough?"

He looked pained, even though it had been several years since she'd last trod on his toes. "I've already explained, it has nothing to do with your skills and ability, or any supposed lack thereof." He took a deep breath and stared into the distance for a moment, as though hoping to draw inspiration from the potted palm in the corner. "Being back in England, watching Marianne get married, I realized I've been unfair to you."

"Unfair? Bloody right you have. I've put in my time, figured things out that had even you stumped, and yet you dismissed my theory about Madame Melisande out of hand. That hurt, Steven."

He shook his head. "I'm not talking about the case, poppet. It was selfish of me to bring you to France after Mother passed away, wrong to involve you in my work. Now the war is over, we're in London, you should have a chance at happiness. Lead a normal life, like Marianne."

She started to stutter a protest, but he forestalled her by tilting her chin up with one finger.

"You shouldn't be involved in dangerous work. I'd never forgive myself if harm came to you."

He hadn't seemed so concerned when he'd brought her to his tiny flat overlooking a Paris alley five years ago, or when he'd shown her five different escape routes to three different bolt holes. He'd been only too delighted to hear the news she gleaned from maids, mistresses, and shop girls.

She had thrown herself into their work, devoting herself to ferreting out every snippet of information, using her French lessons in a way that would have shocked her teachers speechless. Work had distracted her from her grief over losing her mother, and given her life purpose. Her existence had meaning, made a difference, like her father had. Much as she loved her mother, Mama had been a butterfly, flitting about society, pretty but accomplishing little.

Steven was still talking. "You should marry Moncreiffe and have babies. Be happy."

Charlotte almost groaned in frustration. "We've had this conversation before, Steven. What will it take to convince you that this work is what makes me happy?

Chasing clues, solving puzzles . . . *this* is a normal life for me." She wanted to continue to serve the crown, not get married. A husband would only get in the way.

But Steven's chin was set, her passionate plea falling on ears that had gone deaf as soon as they'd come to London, at least where her future was concerned.

She could be just as stubborn. "Did Gauthier have any new information?"

He let his breath out in a sigh. "You won't leave it alone, will you?" He meant his tone to be harsh, but Charlotte heard grudging admiration. After pausing long enough she thought he wouldn't answer, he spoke. "We think the . . . item . . . has been moved again. Tomorrow we're going to make some more inquiries. If I keep you informed about our progress, will you try pretending to be a typical London miss?"

She'd done nothing *but* pretend since coming to London. She pretended to enjoy endless shopping excursions on Bond Street with Aunt Hermione and paying morning calls that took place in the afternoon. Even her engagement was pretend.

She beamed. "I can agree to that."

And now Steven was going to keep her informed about his investigation. Perfect. However, she didn't trust that he'd tell her *all* his progress, so she'd keep an eye on him, just the same.

The next morning, Charlotte rummaged through the trunks in her room, deciding which outfit to wear for following Steven. Should she choose a maid's uniform, or housekeeper's? A shop girl's? Didn't really matter, so long as it was the attire of someone who could walk the streets without an escort, without raising any eyebrows or drawing attention.

She poked around the assorted wigs and garments until she banged her knuckles against something hard, long and narrow. The cane. She'd have to return that, along with the wig and dress she'd borrowed from the modiste's shop, before the assistant who'd helped her had the cost deducted from her wages.

Charlotte smiled at how she'd given Moncreiffe the slip that first day they'd met, walking right past him when she exited the shop's front door. He'd even tipped his hat, in deference to what he'd thought was an old crone.

Such a polite chap. How fortuitous that he'd paused to peer through a shop window when she'd thought someone was following her.

Only once before had she accosted a man on the street. The suspected traitor she'd been following down a Paris side street had suddenly doubled back. She'd hooked her arm with a beefy fellow just stepping into the street and sauntered right past her suspect.

As soon as they'd turned the corner into an alley, the fellow developed six hands, and it had taken her knee to his nether regions to convince him that *No* meant not in his lifetime.

She doubted she'd ever have to resort to such means with a gentleman like Moncreiffe. She sat back on her heels, the cane clutched to her chest. To be brutally honest, she doubted she'd offer even a token protest. The thought of his hands, roaming over her body . . .

Good thing their engagement was completely fictitious, merely for mutual convenience, so that kind of situation would never arise. Her ability to resist him, or rather inability, would never be tested.

She quickly dressed in a maid's uniform, scraped her hair into a tight bun and covered it with a mob cap, then gathered the costume to be returned, threw on an old cloak, and headed down the back stairs, out the garden gate, into the mews.

Steven was still eating breakfast, but she knew where he was likely to meet Gauthier. She had just enough time to drop off her burden at the modiste's shop before eavesdropping on them.

Chapter 5

Alistair slouched lower in the armchair and raised his newspaper higher as Sir Nigel walked past him at White's the next afternoon. As soon as he was out the door, Alistair shoved the paper aside, retrieved his journal and pencil, and recorded the names of the men with whom Nigel had exchanged more than banal pleasantries.

He'd never before tried to conceal his observations, if one didn't count deceiving the teachers at school when he was supposed to be studying something other than the night sky. Subterfuge lent an air of excitement to an otherwise tedious activity.

An extra guinea slipped to the waiter who brought Alistair's wine confirmed that all of the men with Nigel were his usual cronies. Also as usual, the waiter quietly added, Nigel had graciously allowed someone else in the group to pay for his meal and drinks.

If the man was expecting to come into money soon, he was being very circumspect about it. He hadn't even entered anything in the betting books in over a month.

Alistair checked his watch. Just enough time to go home, change clothes, have his phaeton readied, and take Miss Parnell for a drive, as they'd agreed last night at the ball, so they could discuss what he'd learned. Or the lack thereof, since he didn't think the information he'd gathered so far would prove to be of much value.

Even so, he was going for a drive in the park on a beautiful day with an intriguing woman—the perfect opportunity for intimate conversation to get better acquainted with his mysterious miss.

He picked up his pace.

"Let me take the reins," were her first words upon stepping out of the town house and seeing his high perch phaeton.

Alistair exchanged a knowing grin with the groom holding the horse. "Perhaps some other time." He gave her a hand up, admiring the way her dress clung to the curve of her hip as she climbed up to the seat before she sat and settled her skirts.

"I'm considered a dab hand," she said with the same eager tone as soon as he was seated beside her.

The bench was narrow, requiring that their legs touch. He had a bit more space on his side and could move over a tad, but decided he preferred the contact with Charlotte's rose-scented body, however incidental. He also liked the way the folds of her sprigged muslin skirt bunched up against his buckskin breeches.

Alistair nodded to the groom to let go the horse, then gave the reins a slap and pulled out into traffic. "I wasn't aware driving lessons were part of a lady's education these days."

"Steven taught me. Said one never knows what skills may come in handy." Her smile hinted there were a great many unusual skills that had been part of her education.

Alistair returned her smile, eager to explore the extent of her unorthodox learning.

Before traffic became any heavier, he shared with Miss Parnell what he'd learned so far about Sir Nigel. He spared a glance to witness her response to his findings, and had to force his attention back to his driving, away from her finger tapping her lush lower lip.

"Perhaps my theory is all wrong, and has been from the beginning." She let out a sigh big enough that he felt it against his side. "Sir Nigel has nothing to do with the object, and last night we were simply witnessing nothing more sinister than a lover's quarrel."

They turned into the park and down Rotten Row, joining the slow parade of vehicles. "It's early days yet," Alistair said, disliking the sound of defeat in her voice.

"No," she said, her voice laced with dejection. "Steven was right, and I was wrong. I should leave it alone, and just play at being a milk-and-water miss, like he wants." She let out another sigh that brushed her rib cage against his, her downcast gaze focused on the ground passing beneath the phaeton's wheels.

He had a hard time believing she would give up so easily. Even on their brief acquaintance, this seemed out of character for her.

Then he remembered how she had played the vapid miss when they first danced. He hid a smile. "It's a good thing you have no intention of treading the boards, Miss Parnell."

She gave him a wide-eyed innocent stare, which he returned.

After a few moments she gave him a rueful grin. "Too much?"

"If you really wanted to drive, all you had to do was say so." He did a quick check to make sure traffic was still flowing as slowly as usual through the park.

She opened her mouth, no doubt to argue that she *had* said so, but closed it when he thrust the reins into her hands. She sat up straighter and adjusted the reins in her grip, her teeth flashing in a smile. "He has such a sweet gait, does he not?" She pointed her chin at the bay gelding in the traces.

"Maxwell does, and he has a tender mouth, as well." Alistair forced his hands to stay flat on his knees so they wouldn't snatch back the reins. Everything was fine so far. No children or dogs playing nearby that could startle the horse, no reason to expect Miss Parnell to drive them into the Serpentine.

"I shall take extra care, then." The reins adjusted to her apparent satisfaction, she settled back in the seat, seemingly prepared to continue driving for the rest of their outing.

They rode in companionable silence for several minutes. Alistair tried to look everywhere at once, to spot anything that might upset Miss Parnell or the horse, and at the same time keeping an eye on her. Two little boys chasing a dog, shouting and barking, ran toward the carriage. Alistair tensed, ready to take back control, but she kept the horse steady with just a flick of the reins. The dog suddenly doubled back and chased the boys away from the vehicles.

"Please try to relax, Lord Moncreiffe. I'll have you know I haven't overturned a cart since I was ten." She flashed him a quick grin, then returned her attention to the crowded road ahead.

Alistair did not relax his vigil, but he did allow some of the tension to leave his shoulders. They continued along the crowded path, nodding at acquaintances, returning a waved greeting now and then. The looks of disappointment on several women's faces, misses and matrons alike, were almost comical. When he'd decided to bring Miss Parnell for a drive, he'd only thought of it as a chance to talk without being overheard, rather than it being a public outing with his fiancée.

While he was accustomed to women staring at him, he was surprised to realize two men on the path behind them were staring at Miss Parnell. Were they disappointed suitors? They were dressed well enough to blend in with the park crowd currently on parade, but something about them seemed a bit off. Like they'd be more comfortable in the company of Nick, or Miss Parnell's half brother, Steven.

But Nick had sailed on the midnight tide just before the newspapers printed the engagement announcement. Alistair shouldn't be surprised that her brother had set someone to watch over him with Miss Parnell, as a chaperone of sorts. If he had a sister, he imagined he would be quite protective, too, if she had just become engaged to a stranger.

Perhaps his imagination was simply being overly suspicious, thinking they were being watched. But the men had stayed just behind them, within one or two carriage lengths for the last complete round through the park, past all of the park gates, and had not paused to speak to anyone.

Then again, neither had he and Miss Parnell.

So focused on his thoughts, Alistair was startled when he heard his name called. Up ahead, two riders were threading their horses between the carriages, coming closer to the phaeton.

Clarke hailed him again. Miss Parnell slowed the horse and edged to the side of the path.

"Moncreiffe, well met," Clarke called as he and his companion reined in their mounts beside the phaeton. "See, I told you that was him," he said in a loud aside to the other man. "Dorian here didn't believe that was you, letting a woman drive your carriage." His fatuous grin showed far too many teeth.

"My fiancée was demonstrating her technique," Alistair replied.

"So the rumors are true," Dorian said good-naturedly. "Snared by parson's mousetrap. And so soon."

"But Dorian, lad, can't you see why?" Clarke doffed his hat and held it over his heart. "Moncreiffe, had I seen her first, I vow I would have fought you for the lady's favor."

From the corner of his eye, Alistair watched Miss Parnell's reaction. Judging by the amused smile on her lips, she didn't seem to mind the interruption.

"Well, Moncreiffe, don't keep us pining away any

longer." Dorian removed his hat as well. "Introduce us to your lovely bride-to-be."

Alistair cleared his throat. This was the first time in his life he'd made this particular introduction. "Miss Parnell, may I make known to you two friends and fellow astronomers, Mr. Clarke and Sir Dorian. Gentlemen, my fiancée, Miss Charlotte Parnell." He was proud his voice remained calm.

It was amazingly easy to refer to the attractive, mysterious woman at his side as his fiancée.

"Charmed, Miss Parnell." Clarke lifted her hand to drop a kiss on her gloved knuckles. He continued to hold her hand longer than necessary.

Alistair cleared his throat. Twice.

Clarke finally took the hint and let go. The twinkle in Miss Parnell's eye told him she hadn't missed his little display.

Dorian was not to be left out. "So pleased to meet the charming miss who stole Moncreiffe's heart," he said, just before bestowing a kiss on her knuckles as well. At least he let go promptly.

Miss Parnell took the attention in stride, gracefully acknowledging their tribute, without the preening he might have expected. She simply adjusted the reins in her grip again as soon as her hands were free.

Plenty of women had aspired to be his viscountess, banking on his future prospects, which would make his wife a marchioness and eventually a duchess. Somehow Miss Parnell seemed immune to such concerns.

But was she, really?

Or was this just more of her playacting, and she had no

intention of crying off by the end of the Little Season? He had considered that possibility when they'd first entered into their agreement, but decided Miss Parnell was in earnest about outwitting her brother and had no designs on becoming a viscountess.

It was too late to second-guess himself. "I hate to be rude, gentlemen, but you're cutting in to unchaperoned time with my fiancée."

"And precious time that is." Dorian set his hat back on his head.

"Aye," Clarke seconded. "To be sure, I would not let two brigands such as ourselves waste a moment more of it." He shoved his hat back on, bowed toward Miss Parnell from his seat in the saddle, and nudged his horse away from the phaeton.

"I do hope we'll see much more of you in the future, Miss Parnell," Dorian said, just before he followed Clarke back out into the crowded path.

A few carriages rumbled past the phaeton, then there was a break and Miss Parnell gave the reins a light slap, and Maxwell plodded on.

"Well, then," Alistair said, stretching one arm along the back of the bench, not quite touching Miss Parnell's blue velvet spencer. "What do you want to do next?"

"Wh-What do you mean?" Her fingers tightened just a bit, her thumb restlessly rubbing the leather rein.

"About Madame Melisande and Sir Nigel."

Her fingers stilled.

"If you truly think he has nothing to do with the missing object, are you going back to following her around, or have you another plan?"

"I'm not certain yet. I haven't had time to formulate a strategy." She spared him a sidelong glance, her blue eyes sparkling with good humor. "I've been a bit distracted."

Alistair leaned closer and lowered his voice. "I do my best," he whispered in her ear. He was inordinately pleased with the goose bumps that instantly rose on the exposed flesh at her neck, the tiny hitch in her breathing. This close, he caught a hint of her rosewater perfume. If he were to nuzzle her neck, kiss her just there, beneath her ear, he'd be surrounded by her scent.

Not wishing to draw undue attention from any passersby, he reluctantly leaned back. He couldn't help glancing at the road behind them as he did so. He froze. The two men on horseback were still there, two carriages back. They should have passed by while Clarke and Dorian had been annoying him.

"I don't wish to alarm you," he said, leaning close again. "But I think two men are following us. They seem far more interested in you than in me. Is there perhaps a jilted or unsuccessful suitor in your past, someone you'd like to tell me about?"

"Blast." Miss Parnell kept her eyes on the road ahead, her expression neutral. "Would one of them happen to look like he's borrowed the clothes he's wearing, and have curly black hair desperately in need of a wash?"

Under the pretext of adjusting his sleeve, with his arm still resting on the back of the bench, Alistair took another look behind. "An apt description. Friend of yours?"

"Only in that he's the reason you and I bumped into each other that first day."

"He's followed you before?" Still no cause for concern, Alistair reminded himself. Blakeney was exactly the sort of person to set someone watching his sister and not tell her about it, especially given his clandestine profession.

"I turned down several streets and went in and out of three shops to make sure I wasn't simply being unreasonably suspicious. I didn't become concerned until the second fellow joined him." Her gaze darted to Alistair, then back to the road. "I knew they wouldn't come any closer if I was with another man."

He took his eyes off the road ahead to stare at her. "Are you saying I was the lesser of two evils?" He was uncertain if he should take umbrage at her assessment of him being safe.

"When faced with the choice of devils or angels, I think it most wise to associate with heavenly hosts."

Alistair coughed. Was an angelic comparison worse than an unintentional insult, or better?

"I consider myself fortunate that you had stopped to peer through that shop window. By the way, what was it you were looking at?"

"An eyepiece for my telescope." He glanced over his shoulder. Both men were still there, two carriage lengths back, deep in conversation, as though they cared not a whit about Miss Parnell. "They seem to be distracted. Turn here, now! Let's see if we can get rid of them altogether."

"You're willing to let me drive out on the open street?" She turned the horse, leaving the park.

"Is there a reason I should not?" He itched to take back the reins, but forced his hands to remain on his lap. This exit was on the far side from where they had entered the park, which meant they would have to negotiate even more of London's clogged streets to get Miss Parnell back home.

"Steven wanted me to know how to drive, but he'd never actually let me do so in traffic if he were with me."

Alistair hoped he sounded convincing. "I trust you to know your limits, and that you will give back the reins before taking any foolish risks with me, my carriage," he spared her a smile, "or poor Maxwell."

Her quiet reply was lost in the clatter of a mail coach lumbering past in the opposite direction and the call of an orange vendor. It sounded suspiciously like "bleedin' miracle," but he couldn't be sure.

His heart only stopped two or three times, certain they were about to be killed, but each time Miss Parnell kept the horse and phaeton under control. He managed to keep his hands to himself as she made a few unnecessary turns, making sure they were not being followed, before driving unerringly to her town house. He was too tense to engage in idle conversation on the journey, and did not wish to risk distracting her, so his comments were limited to informing her that they seemed to have given their two followers the slip.

After what seemed like hours, she reined Maxwell in at the front of the town house. Alistair jumped down and jogged to the other side of the carriage, beating the footman so he could be the one to assist Miss Parnell in descending to the street.

Lifting her at the waist instead of just offering her a hand down was not forward behavior for an engaged couple, even if he did let his hold linger and slide across a tad more of her velvet-covered curves than absolutely necessary.

His friends thought him oblivious to his effect on the fairer sex, when in truth he was merely circumspect—he had no wish to raise unwarranted hope in any maiden's thoughts by responding to her flirtatious overtures. With Miss Parnell, however, there was no risk of her reading unintended meaning into his actions, since they were engaged in subterfuge together.

And to be successful in their deception, they had to act the part of a betrothed couple. She demonstrated her unspoken understanding of this by the way she rested her hands on his shoulders, letting her fingers slide through the hair at his nape.

By the gleam in her eye as he set her on her feet, and the way she patted the phaeton, he realized he'd made a grave mistake that afternoon. She would now expect to be allowed to drive his carriage again.

He almost groaned.

She said something, too softly for him to hear, so he bent down and turned his head, the better to hear her over the noise of the traffic.

"Thank you," she whispered, and kissed him on the cheek.

Stunned, he didn't immediately pull back. He wished he'd taken the time to shave again before their outing, worried her tender lips might have been scraped by his stubble. Her soft, delectable lips, currently curved in a sensual smile.

The footman cleared his throat.

They sprang apart. Alistair straightened to his full

height and offered his arm to escort Miss Parnell up the steps. He waited until they were exactly halfway to the door, out of earshot of the footman, groom, and the butler holding it open, before speaking.

"I've been invited to the Eccleston's rout this evening."

Miss Parnell raised her brows in polite query.

"Their town house is one square over from the hotel where Madame Melisande is staying. The view from their roof offers an excellent line of sight to her balcony."

"And you know this because . . . ? I thought astronomers gazed up at the night sky. Now it turns out you're a Peeping Tom?" The late afternoon sunlight hit her teasing eyes at just the right angle, making them bright and clear. Bottomless pools of blue, deep enough to drown in.

Alistair gave himself a mental shake. "Knowing what view is afforded by the host's roof is how I decide which invitations to accept."

"Wouldn't it be simpler to just stay home?"

He shook his head. "And deal with the displeasure of both my father and grandfather? That way lies madness."

Miss Parnell patted his arm with her free hand. "But how does the view from the Eccleston's roof help us, if you have to attend the rout?"

"Lord Eccleston is a member of The Royal Society. He'll not only give me permission to take my telescope up to his roof, he'll *expect* me to do so."

"So you make a grand public appearance, appease your relatives, then escape up to the rooftop?"

"I don't know about 'grand,' but yes, that's the general idea."

Miss Parnell gave a slight shake of her head. "Sir

Nigel may not be involved after all, but I still think Madame Melisande is very much in the thick of things. Rather than spying on her, I think it would be more productive if I searched her room again. She doesn't carry the item in her reticule."

Alistair felt his hair practically stand on end at the thought of Miss Parnell dangling from the roof. But he already knew her well enough to know that forbidding her to do so would be a waste of breath. "May I suggest a compromise? Tonight I will watch her, observe her schedule and that of her servants. Perhaps she will even take the item from its hiding place in order to gloat. Once we know her household's schedule, we'll be able to determine the safest time to search her lodgings."

He watched the warring emotions flit across Miss Parnell's delightful face, the urge to act *now*, versus the logical approach he'd presented.

She nibbled on her bottom lip and glanced out at the street. "Very well, then."

Good girl. Logic was always the best approach. Alistair nodded. "I'll see what can be seen tonight, and we'll discuss it tomorrow afternoon on another drive. I think we'll skip Hyde Park, however."

She gave him a small smile.

Just as they turned to go up the steps, a horse clattered up and the rider jumped down. Steven swept off his hat and the two men exchanged greetings before Steven turned his attention to his sister. "Have a good outing, poppet?"

"Delightful, thank you." She glanced between Alistair and her brother and back, a silent message in her bright blue eyes.

Right. No need to hang around and give Steven the chance to ask awkward questions, like plans about his sister's future.

Alistair bowed. "Until tomorrow, Miss Parnell. Good day, Blakeney."

"Tomorrow, my lord." She gave him a slight wave, and took her brother's arm to lead him indoors.

Alistair folded his legs and leaned his back against one of the chimney stacks of Eccleston's town house, blowing on his chilled fingers. He should have worn an extra shirt—there was more of a nip in the air at night this late in September.

He'd made his requisite appearance at the rout downstairs and participated in at least two dances, with very respectable, very married matrons.

Now that he was engaged, social events seemed far less crowded, with fewer women making demands on his time. It had been at least three days since anyone tried to trap him into a compromising situation. He hadn't realized how much the attempts had dimmed his enjoyment of social outings until he found himself actually joining in the laughter while dancing the energetic Roger De Coverly with Lady Eccleston. The only thing that would've made it more enjoyable would be dancing with Charlotte.

Even so, he had a purpose in attending tonight that had nothing to do with dancing, and he was eager to get to it. He'd paused downstairs long enough to prevent his father from upending the punch bowl over his grandfather's head—an attempt to interrupt the duke's soliloquy on morals—and forestalled further conflict by pointing out a widow making cow eyes at Father, which made Grandfather stalk off in a huff, before Alistair decamped to the roof. Lord Eccleston had personally escorted him through the attic and out the tiny door.

Now he sat, telescope at the ready, open journal on his knee, pencil in hand, his gaze focused slightly lower than the starlit heavens above.

The balcony curtains were still open in Melisande's room, and at least one candle lit. A maid had come in to turn down the blankets and add fuel to the fire, and left just a few moments ago. Perhaps he'd be in luck and Melisande would call it an early night, reveal whatever she had to reveal about the trinket Miss Parnell was so interested in, and he could get back to his observations. Much as he was enjoying the diversion with Miss Parnell, there would only be a few more nights of observing before the moon would rise too early and cast too much light.

He could always do as Dorian did, and get up in the predawn to search the skies after the moon had set. Alistair snorted. The only dawns he'd seen were those for which he'd not yet gone to bed.

To his left, the roof door opened, spilling a wedge of light onto the tiles. He rose up to a crouch. The door quickly closed again, and whoever had stepped outside stood there, motionless in the dark.

Lord Eccleston knew exactly where he was, and wouldn't need to let his eyes adjust to the darkness before moving.

The wind shifted, and a hint of the newcomer's scent wafted past him.

Rosewater.

"Over here, Miss Parnell," he called softly. He should have known she'd not be content to wait until tomorrow afternoon for his report. And he should have listened to his instinct that said to bring an extra blanket, to keep her warm.

He heard a soft rustle of fabric, her dancing slippers silent as she crossed the tiles. By the time he'd stood up and feeling had returned to his legs, she was at his side, one hand tentatively resting on his arm.

"See anything of interest?" she whispered.

Her face was but a pale blur in the darkness, her curves concealed by the folds of a dark cloak. "Can't see a thing," he replied without thinking.

"Beg pardon?"

He coughed. "No, nothing of interest has happened so far, but I have hopes that Melisande will be turning in early tonight. See how her chamber has already been prepared?" He set his hands on her shoulders and pointed her toward the window he'd been watching.

Charlotte quashed the tiny thrill at his touch and forced herself to focus on the task at hand, the real reason she was five stories above the ground, on a roof in the dark, again. With a handsome viscount. Even though said viscount still had his arm slung around her shoulders and stood so close his chest brushed her arm with every gentle inhalation.

Ahem. Task. Even when she squinted, she could barely make out the window in question, among so many others that also had a candle or two lit. She took in the view available, realizing how high and isolated they were atop

London's skyline. Exposed. "We shouldn't be standing in the open like this."

"I'm set up by the chimney stack, over there." He took her arm. "Mind the tripod. See the feet?" Following the blur of his hand, she saw three evenly spaced spots on the ground, glowing in the dark. "Phosphorous," he added.

They quickly settled on a blanket spread at the base of the chimney. Charlotte tucked her skirts in around her folded legs, careful to keep her light yellow gown covered by her dark cloak. Moncreiffe sat beside her, close enough she felt the heat radiating from his body. This was even better than the close confines of the bench seat in his phaeton—no horse to control, no hordes of prying eyes in the park to worry about. No men following her every time she set about following Melisande.

At least, she hoped there were no prying eyes.

Just hers and Moncreiffe's.

"Want to take a look through my telescope?"

"Yes, please," she said, ignoring the weight of her own spyglass tucked inside her cloak. She heard the rustle of fabric as he shifted, and the glowing spots moved closer.

"There," he said. He ran his hand from her shoulder down to her hand, then lifted it to the cold metal tube.

She leaned forward, closed one eye, and peered through the eyepiece. "It's a bit blurry."

"Must have bumped the focus ring. Not to worry."

She started to lean back, to grant him easier access, but he reached one arm around her shoulders, holding her in. His hand found hers again and guided it to the ridged knob so she could focus for herself, while he held the telescope steady with his other hand. She allowed herself a moment to enjoy the secure weight of his arm around her, the warmth of his hand on hers, though his fingers were a bit chilly. Then she bent to the task at hand.

"The view is amazing." Much wider field of view than her spyglass, she almost added. She could even read the time on the ormolu clock on Melisande's mantel. And since the scope was mounted on a tripod, her arms would not grow weary from holding up the spyglass.

"Does this make you a Peeping Thomasina?" She heard the smile in his voice. Moncreiffe still had one arm around her, and was so close when he spoke that she felt the warm puff of his breath against her ear.

She shivered. "Not at all. If I were gazing into some other window for my own entertainment, possibly. But I'm doing this for the prin—the principle."

"Ah. The . . . principle."

Blast. "Of course. We can't let Melisande get away with stealing the trinket. I have to get it back."

Stupid, stupid, stupid. She'd slipped up twice, and she was certain Moncreiffe hadn't missed either of them. There was no *we* in this investigation. There was just her, with a little assistance from Moncreiffe to disguise her actions, to serve as a distraction.

Problem was, he was proving to be more of a distraction to *her*.

Moncreiffe moved back a fraction, though he kept his arm around her. It helped ward off the breeze, which had been welcome when she first left the overheated ball-room but now seemed to come straight from the heart of winter. This high up, there was nothing to interrupt its flow, nothing to slow it down. Her fingers were growing numb, holding the chilly metal of the telescope.

This was good. Physical discomfort helped her concentrate. She moved the scope around a bit, looking through other windows in the hotel. Few of the curtains had been drawn against the darkness. The housekeeper was giving a dressing down to a cowering maid in the drawing room on the first floor, while a footman trimmed the candles in the ground floor salon's chandelier. Another maid and footman were visible in the doorway of a bedchamber's dressing room upstairs, doing . . . Oh, my. That didn't look comfortable at all.

Charlotte leaned back from the eyepiece and cleared her throat.

"Something of interest?"

"Not really, no." She coughed again, to clear the squeak.

Moncreiffe leaned in and peered through before she could move the telescope. He chuckled. "They're going to hurt themselves if they keep that up. Er, keep doing that. I mean—"

"I know what you mean." She was glad of the concealing darkness, since her cheeks must be flushed bright red. She'd seen people do that before, of course—couldn't be helped in her line of work. One occasionally saw things one didn't intend while conducting surveillance. But she'd never witnessed it in mixed company. She gave Moncreiffe a light smack on his arm, which was still slung around her shoulder. "Stop watching them."

"I'm not. I moved it back to Melisande's room. See?"

Charlotte leaned forward, too quickly, as Moncreiffe wasn't out of the way yet. They bumped heads.

"Are you all right?"

"Ouch. Yes, I'm fine."

"Let me see."

"See what? It's completely dark up here."

He removed his arm from around her shoulders, leaving a cold void. She barely had time to register that when she heard the sound of his hands rubbing together, and then they were upon her face.

The friction had warmed his flesh, almost scorching against her chilled skin. His touch was light, tentative at first, one hand on her jaw, the other landing on her ear before moving to her cheek. "Where did I hit you?"

She guided his fingers to her brow. "It's nothing. I'll be fine." She didn't lift his hands away, though.

First his fingertips probed her forehead and the surrounding area. She closed her eyes.

"There doesn't seem to be any blood."

"Of course there isn't. I told you, it's nothing." There was no reason for him to react in such a way to a minor bump. It was as if he was simply using it as an excuse to touch her.

Oh.

She sat perfectly still so as not to dislodge him.

He flattened the palm of his hand to her forehead, moved around a tiny bit. "I don't feel a bump forming, though it's probably too soon to tell." He kept one hand on her forehead, but the other slowly trailed down her cheek and cupped her jaw. The pad of his thumb ghosted over her mouth.

Her lips parted in surprise.

His other hand slid to one side, cradling her head, while his thumb continued to sweep back and forth over her bottom lip, ever so lightly, gently.

This was highly inappropriate. Very improper. She should tell him so.

She kissed his thumb.

The sudden inhale she heard was not hers.

She sensed him move closer, felt his breath on her cheek. He was going to kiss her. Replace his thumb, pleasant as it was, with his lips, which would be ever so much better. Those gorgeous, full but oh-so-masculine lips, were finally going to be on hers. She'd know how they felt, what he tasted like. She kept her eyes open, hoping details of his features would become visible in the darkness once he got close enough.

A tiny orange light appeared on a rooftop a few houses over, just beyond Moncreiffe's shoulder.

She stiffened.

So did Moncreiffe.

"We're being watched," she whispered.

Chapter 6

"**W**hat?" His tone held a growling hint of frustration. "What makes you think we're being watched?"

"Someone just lit a cigarillo, two roofs over. See?" She turned Moncreiffe's jaw away from her, toward his left shoulder, where the outline of a few chimney stacks was visible beyond because of the void it made against the stars in the sky.

There, by one of the voids, it came again. A faint orange glow that flared and then faded just as quickly.

"Could just be a spark from the chimney."

Reluctantly, she let go of his chin. "Would a spark fly back up like that?"

The smoker raised his cheroot, the orange light flared as he took another puff, then it swung down again, as he probably held it by his side.

"Wonder who he is." Moncreiffe turned back to Charlotte. "This afternoon I thought those two men in the park might be someone your brother had instructed to keep an eye on you—well, on us—but now I don't think so."

"What made you change your mind?" Of course Steven would not send someone to spy on her. He knew that she could fend for herself—he'd been the one to teach her.

"If your brother distrusted me to that extent, he would have insisted on accompanying us himself, or refused to allow you to go with me. There's also the fact that Melisande was riding her gelding in the park this afternoon, and she was shopping on Bond Street the day we met."

"You saw her back then?" Charlotte hadn't told Moncreiffe she'd been spying on the French widow when she realized there were two men following her.

"She entered a milliner's shop farther down the street, shortly after you took my arm."

So, even the grandson of a duke was not immune to the courtesan's charms? Charlotte gave him a pointed stare, the effect of which was, unfortunately, lost in the complete darkness.

The breeze carried the sharp tang of tobacco smoke after the smoker took another puff.

Amateur. Anyone who'd done any spying at all would know better than to do something so obvious, so stupid, that would give away their position.

Come to think of it, she'd seen Sir Nigel out on the balcony at one of the balls earlier this week, smoking a cheroot. Perhaps he was involved after all? She kept the excitement out of her voice. "Perhaps it *is* one of the men we saw this afternoon, and the smoker is doing the same as we are—watching Madame Melisande."

"Well, that would give more credence to your original theory about the theft." Moncreiffe shifted beside her, and a muffled thud came from the tripod as he moved it to a better angle for pointing the telescope at the other rooftop. "And it's highly unlikely anyone knew we were going to be up here." His voice grew more distant as he spoke while looking through the eyepiece. "You didn't tell anyone, did you?"

She tried not to be insulted. Moncreiffe was quite new at the spying business and could have no idea of her degree of experience in the field. "Of course not. Aunt Hermione thinks I'm lying down in one of Eccleston's guest rooms because of a headache."

"You don't have one, do you?" He sounded a bit worried, sincere rather than merely being polite.

She was touched. "Never had one in my life. But I often excuse myself because of them."

He chuckled. "I shall endeavor to remember that." His voice faded again as he bent back to the telescope. "I can't tell for certain if they're the same men from the park, but there are definitely at least two of them over there. They're passing the cigarillo back and forth."

"How disgusting. Let me look."

Once again Moncreiffe guided her hand to the eyepiece. This time she didn't try to adjust the viewing mechanism—there was nothing to see but the orange glow, still tiny even when magnified. No way to tell if it was in focus or not.

She straightened. "There could be a dozen men over there, for all I can tell. How can you see anything?"

"Sometimes it's what you can't see that tells you what's there. They're both standing, and from this angle, they're blocking part of Scorpius."

"Standing? They aren't trying to be surreptitious about this at all." Hmm. Maybe there was no *need* for them to be surreptitious. "How can we be sure they're not simply astronomers like you?"

"Well . . ." She pictured him tapping his chin in thought. "I know a member of the Society who lives close by here, but don't recall the exact location of his house in relation to this one." She heard him move the telescope back to its original position. "I suppose all we can really do is what we came here for. Watch for Madame Melisande."

They settled in again, waiting and watching, keeping an eye on Melisande's room as well as the smokers on the nearby roof, who seemed to have brought an endless supply of tobacco for their vigil.

After a while Charlotte realized Moncreiffe was not disturbed by the long silences between conversational gambits. In her experience, most men were in love with the sound of their own voice, or felt the nervous need to keep a dialogue going in mixed company, even if the topics were inane. "You spend a lot of time alone, don't you?"

"Not as much as I'd like to."

Her back stiffened. "Perhaps you should go, then. I can keep watch by myself."

"What? No, no, that's not what I meant." Even in total

darkness he talked with his hands, making them a ghostly blur as he gestured, occasionally touching her knee or arm to help make a point. "I spend so much time doing what other people want—and I'm referring to my father and grandfather, not you—it takes away from the things that are important to me. In accompanying them back to town, I missed being able to watch most of the Perseid meteor showers."

Fabric rustled as he unfolded then re-crossed his legs. "I suppose I became spoiled this summer, when I went on a two-month walking tour of the countryside. Observing is much more productive when you can get away from cities and their gaslights, and away from relatives."

She pictured him, his telescope carrying case balanced on his shoulder, a solitary figure walking a lonely dusty road by day, seated beneath the cold sky at night. "You were alone all that time?"

"Not at first. My friend Tony set out with me, but when we reached the Devon coast, he became enamored of a lady smuggler and stayed behind to woo her."

A female smuggler? How intriguing. "Your friend intentionally set out to seduce her? Not much of a gentleman, is he?"

"Tony may have *thought* that's what he intended, but deep down he's a good man. I attended their wedding last month."

"So he became a smuggler, too?" All the smugglers she knew were dependably undependable.

"For a short while, but they're both disgustingly respectable now. He helped her find a legal means for her gang to earn a living, and now the whole village has adopted him as one of their own. They make the most marvelous cheese." He patted her knee. "If they come to town, or we go down there, I'll introduce you to his bride. You and Sylvia would get along famously."

Sylvia the smuggler. Scratch that—Sylvia the *ex*-smuggler. Yes, they probably would get along, like two peas in a pod. Except Sylvia had left the pea pod and become respectable. Married.

Such a dire fate would never befall her. She wouldn't allow it.

But what was Moncreiffe thinking, suggesting he and she might travel together to Devon? Their engagement was a sham. They were only going to be together until the end of the Little Season or until she completed her mission, whichever came first.

She must be hungry as well as cold, given the sudden turmoil in the vicinity of her stomach.

Time to shift the conversation to more neutral territory.

"Steven taught me how to locate Polaris, to help keep me from getting lost at night, but I haven't paid attention to much else up there. What is it about astronomy that fascinates you?"

He took his time before replying. "As an adult, I'm trying to find proof for my theory that Ceres and Pallas are asteroids, not planets."

Planet or asteroid, comet or moon, did anyone but astronomers really care? Then the significance of his phrasing hit her. "And as a child?"

The odd huffing sound was Moncreiffe, blowing on his

fingers. Charlotte realized hers were icy, too, and tucked her hands under her arms.

"As a child, I was looking for heaven."

Heaven? She blinked. "Why?"

"Because I was a child." His tone was flippant, but there was a hint of pain beneath its surface.

She stretched her hand out. She was aiming for his knee but found his thigh instead. She spread out her fingers and softened her voice even more. "Why did you need to find heaven?"

His leg muscles contracted beneath her hand, as though he was preparing to flee rather than answer her query. When he finally spoke, there was a wistful note in his voice. "It was where the grown-ups told me my mother and elder brother and little sisters had gone, after they died in the carriage accident."

To lose so many loved ones, all at once . . . Her father had died when she was eight, her mother seven years later. The pain of each loss had been suffocating, a physical ache that still threatened to overwhelm her at times. She would not have survived losing both at once. "So you spent night after night up on the roof or out on the lawn, searching the skies, staring up at the stars. Wondering which one was heaven." She gave his leg a squeeze, admiring his strength of character. "How old were you?"

"Five."

Her heart contracted even further for the grieving little boy.

"My nurse was a Scotswoman, very practical. When she realized she couldn't persuade me to stay indoors on clear nights, she gave me a picture book of the constellations, and insisted my father buy a telescope for me. My first."

"Of many, no doubt."

"Not really. He consulted with William Herschel about the purchase and made an excellent choice. I've merely had to keep the lenses and mirrors polished, and change or add eyepieces over the years."

"So this is it, the telescope you've had since you were a boy?"

"No, I bought this one last year. My main telescope is at home in Keswick, in the Lake District, with an equatorial mount on the rooftop viewing platform. Doesn't travel well, I'm afraid."

He said some other things about angles and axes, and by the time he mentioned elliptical orbits, Charlotte's head began to swim. His tone was mesmerizing, though she understood little of what he said. The passion that crept into his voice betrayed the importance of the topic. She had better do some research if she was going to keep up with him. Being able to discourse about his passionate interest would make it easier to distract him from probing into hers.

"When we're done with your project and the Little Season is over, I'll finally be able to go back to Keswick. Will you be returning home to family in the countryside as well?"

"I'm not sure. Most of my family lives here, in London." Which was not exactly a lie. Aunt Hermione had rented the London town house, using Steven's funds, and they were her only family now.

Thinking about the losses they had each suffered, it

occurred to her this was something else she had in common with Moncreiffe—both had channeled their pain into a new endeavor. He had delved into astronomy, and after her mother's sudden death, she had found purpose in joining Steven in his occupation.

Traveling to Paris with Steven, joining his life and work there, had been a rebirth of sorts. If she had stayed in England, she'd probably be as sheltered and single-minded as her cousin Marianne.

Well, at least she didn't object to having the singled-minded part in common. Marianne had wanted to find a husband, but Charlotte wanted to find something a little bit smaller.

She peered through the telescope again. No sign of new activity in Melisande's bedchamber, though the footman and maid were still engaged. He must be a strong fellow indeed, holding her up against the wall like that for so long.

She blinked and cleared her throat. "Tell me more about the viewing platform you built, what it's like living in the mountains."

"You really want to know about me, beyond my usefulness in reaching your objective?" His tone held no bitterness or reproach, just a matter-of-fact statement that she was using him.

She disliked the thought of herself being cold and calculating. Then she remembered he was benefiting from their arrangement just as much as she.

Charlotte spoke slowly. "We should learn more about each other, as a betrothed couple would, because if anyone sees through our subterfuge, the jig will be over. My aunt asks questions about you, and I usually don't know the answer. Soon she'll become suspicious."

"Then I suppose we'll just have to spend more time together. Get better acquainted."

The words sounded innocent, but combined with the images she was viewing through the telescope, and given his close proximity and husky voice, they formed an altogether different connotation. She moved the telescope a few degrees to one side.

"What sorts of questions is she asking?" He'd turned his head, and his warm breath stirred the hair at her temple as he spoke.

She shivered. "Your favorite dessert, for one."

"Hmm. 'Tis a difficult choice, to pick just one. Can I tell you later, after I've had time to properly ponder?"

She almost laughed. "Yes, I think that would be acceptable."

The mention of Aunt Hermione reminded Charlotte that soon she'd have to make another appearance at the rout downstairs, before her aunt came looking for her. Much more time out on the roof, her cheeks would become ruddy from the cold, if they hadn't already, and Aunt Hermione might worry she had a fever.

Tucking her hands under her arms wasn't enough. She blew on her fingers, just as Moncreiffe had done earlier.

"Breeze has a bit of a bite, doesn't it?"

She heard the rustle of fabric again, then felt a rush of warmth as Moncreiffe wrapped his arm around her shoulders, this time enfolding her in his coat. She forgot to breathe. She felt his rib cage expand and contract against her side with his every breath, the silk of his waistcoat sliding against the back of her bare hand.

"Better?" He spoke so close, the tip of his nose stirred her hair, his breath a warm puff against her ear.

She nodded. What an intriguing way to warm one's ear . . .

She leaned a little closer, taking advantage of his warmth. He rubbed her arm, up and down, pulling her more firmly against his side. She'd been wrapped inside a man's coat before, but never with the man still wearing it. She felt Moncreiffe's beating heart, could almost hear it in the hushed quiet of the rooftops.

Her body chose that moment to reassert its need to breathe, and she inhaled. His unique scent was a subtle mix of spice, with a hint of musk. Not bay rum, but cloves and . . . anise?

"Getting any warmer?"

Not anise. "Which pocket is it in?"

"What?"

"Your licorice. Which pocket is it in?"

"And here I thought I was going to get away with being selfish, and not have to share at all."

She heard the smile in his voice. The hand holding his coat to her shoulder disappeared, so she reached up to keep the wool in place. His hand snaked into the coat pocket, brushing low against her right hip. She stayed perfectly still. A moment later she heard the crinkle of paper, saw a blur of white as he held out the offering just inches from her nose.

Their fingers brushed as she removed one of the three sticks left in the paper twist. Sweet, but with a sharp edge to the flavor. "Mmm. I haven't had licorice in years."

"Care for another piece?"

"No, thank you, don't wish to be greedy. I didn't bring anything to share." And she had only wanted to confirm her theory. Who'd have guessed the viscount carried sweets in his pocket?

More rustling, and Moncreiffe ate another piece before putting the paper twist back in his pocket. In the dark, the only way to make sure it went into the pocket and not on the ground beside them was to reach in like that, even if it meant brushing up against her again. At least, that's how she chose to interpret his actions. He hadn't shown any other indications of wanting to take advantage of the cover of darkness.

"Looks like we're going to get lucky."

"I beg your pardon?" Charlotte forgot that the coat enveloped them both, and nearly dragged Moncreiffe on top of her when she suddenly leaned away from him.

He straightened. "Madame Melisande has returned."

"You weren't looking through the telescope. How can you tell?"

"Because there's a flurry of activity. All the servants have returned to their duties, even the couple upstairs. Have a look."

Charlotte reached for the telescope again, but saw only a light blur. Blast. "I think I accidentally changed the focus again."

She stayed bent near the scope, so he wouldn't have to

remove his coat from around her. Purely for the sake of staying warm, of course.

"Got it. Yes, Madame Melisande has definitely returned. Looks like she's having a drink in the drawing room." Moncreiffe chuckled. "She must have been dancing with some unskilled partners. She's kicked off her slippers and is rubbing her toes."

With a slight huff of impatience, Charlotte pulled out her spyglass and trained it on the hotel. Very large, unskilled dance partners, judging by Madame Melisande's grimace. Charlotte aimed her spyglass higher. The bedchamber was just as before, ready to receive its mistress. The magnification on her spyglass was higher than Moncreiffe's scope, but the field of view was much narrower, so she kept the spyglass moving, sweeping the entire building and surrounding area.

A tiny orange light caught her eye. There, on the hotel roof. A brief flare as someone took a puff on the cigarillo, then it flew down to the roof and blinked out. Shadows moved.

She looked back to the other rooftop they'd been watching. It was now devoid of activity. How could she be so foolish and let herself be distracted?

"I don't believe it!" she hissed.

"What?"

"The other watchers—they're breaking into Melisande's room!"

"Wonder why they're doing it now, rather than earlier?"

"Maybe they got tired of waiting. With the way they

gave away their position so easily, I don't think they're professionals at this."

There was a brief pause, then Moncreiffe spoke again. "He seems to have had more practice at it than you."

"*He's* not wearing a dress."

"Longer legs and arms. He can actually reach the balcony."

Charlotte refused to think about her ignominious attempt to swing down onto the balcony from the roof, how she had ended up in Moncreiffe's arms. Literally. Although that had led to her current position, wrapped in Moncreiffe's coat, with his arm around her shoulders, so it wasn't entirely awful.

Candlelight in the bedchamber revealed the intruder's curly black hair and slightly disheveled clothes, though passable enough that he would have gone unremarked in most social gatherings. He rifled through drawers, quick and methodical, leaving things just as they had been, then moved on to objects on the fireplace mantel, lifting, inspecting, and replacing them. He pawed through the small jewelry box, holding up the various rings, necklaces, and ear bobs before putting them back. He found a stash of bank notes and coins, but put them back rather than pocketing them.

Charlotte clenched her fist. If she'd followed her own instincts, instead of listening to Moncreiffe, *she'd* be the one searching Melisande's room right now.

The intruder peered behind paintings, under the mattress and pillows, always careful to restore everything just as it had been.

"I'm guessing he's done this sort of thing before," Moncreiffe murmured.

"A few times."

Within mere minutes he had gone through everything in the room, just as Charlotte had the other night. He stood in the center of the room, hands on his hips, and turned in a slow circle. He started toward the fireplace, head tilted to one side.

"By Jove, he's got another idea."

"Shh." She didn't want to miss a single move. Perhaps he'd prove it wasn't there after all, and she hadn't made a huge mistake in waiting before attempting another search of her own.

The intruder touched the bricks around the fireplace, testing them, pushing, pulling. He knelt before the hearth and did the same with each stone. He fell backward as one came free in his hand.

Charlotte growled. *She* should have been the one to find the hiding spot.

The intruder quickly sat back up and peered into the gap he'd found. The lighting was too dim for her to see in, too, and then he moved, blocking her view entirely.

She gritted her teeth.

He reached in, then dropped something into his coat pocket, replaced the stone, and let himself out onto the balcony.

"Small enough to fit in a man's hand. Wonder what it is."

By the change in Moncreiffe's voice, he was looking directly at her. Not that he could see her face in the darkness.

"Doesn't matter," she ground out. "He has it, and he's getting away." Should she follow him with her spyglass, or try to get down onto the ground and follow him on foot?

She'd never get down to the street in time. She jumped up, throwing off Moncreiffe's coat, and hurried to the edge of the roof, trying to keep the shadowy figure in sight. Apparently the window washer's ladder that had eased her ascent to the roof a few nights ago was still conveniently placed—within seconds the intruder was on the ground, darting around the corner. He skidded to a halt. Another man had stepped out of the shadows, blocking his path.

"Bet he didn't see that coming," Moncreiffe said.

Light from the gas lamp on the street corner glinted off the pistol being pointed at the intruder's chest, held by . . . Charlotte squinted. "Is that Sir Nigel?"

"Same build, but can't be sure from this angle, with his hat brim casting a deep shadow like that." Moncreiffe came to stand beside her and tugged on her elbow. "Not so close to the edge, please, Miss Parnell. It's a long way down."

"But I need to see—"

"It will do you no good to confirm his identity between the third and second floor if you're dead when you hit the street."

She allowed him to pull her back a step from the parapet, but she kept her spyglass trained on the two men in the street below.

A carriage clattered up and halted beside the man with the pistol. The driver aimed a pistol at the intruder as

well. The intruder's shoulders slumped, and he reached
into his pocket and handed over the item he'd stolen from
Madame Melisande's bedchamber. While the driver kept
his pistol steady, the first man climbed into the carriage,
then they set off. It appeared to be an expensive vehicle,
with the trim painted a much lighter color than the dark
body. She couldn't make out any identifying marks, such
as a crest on the door.

The intruder's companion ran up to him just then.
Wild, wide gestures indicated a heated exchange, though
she couldn't hear any of it. They disappeared into the
shadows.

She wanted to scream in frustration. "Did you recognize the coach? Was it Sir Nigel's?"

"No, Sir Nigel doesn't own a coach. But I may know
whose it was."

Hope flared in her chest. "Whose was it?"

"What is the object everyone is after?"

She groaned. She should have known it would come to
this, should have known the viscount would not play
along forever.

His voice grew sharper as his patience waned. "This is
no game of Who's Got the Button, Miss Parnell. A man
just held another man at gunpoint. What is everyone after, that they are willing to risk life and limb, or inflict
bodily harm, to get it?"

"It's bigger than a button, I assure you."

Moncreiffe grasped her by the elbow, marched unerringly to the stairwell door, and pulled them both inside.
Dim light from the chandeliers below filtered up to the top

of the narrow staircase, seeming as bright as noon after the darkness on the roof.

Gone was the charming, easygoing chap who'd wrapped his coat about her shoulders. Moncreiffe's eyes sparked with anger, his full lips set in a tight line. "In what intrigue are you embroiled, Miss Parnell?" His grip on her upper arms was just short of bruising.

Her heart skipped a beat, but she kept her voice steady. "You were perfectly willing to go along with my efforts before, my lord. Nothing has changed since we entered into our agreement."

"Pistols were not involved then. It was one thing to aid you in outwitting your brother, a bit of sibling one-upmanship, quite another when pistol balls are flying instead of insults. What is at stake here?"

Charlotte bit her bottom lip. There was another emotion in his voice beneath the edge of anger. Concern. He was worried about her. "No one actually fired a gun. It was just a threat."

Moncreiffe backed her up until her spine was against the wall. He bent down until his eyes were level with hers, loomed in close enough for her to make out the narrow band of blue around his dilated pupils.

"What is at stake, Miss Parnell?" That was definitely concern, not just anger, with a tinge of fear. Fear for her safety.

He was worried about her?

That was her undoing. "A snuffbox."

His brows rose in disbelief.

"As I said, it's bigger than a button."

His eyes narrowed.

"A snuffbox stolen from the Prince Regent's private quarters."

He tilted his head back. "A snuffbox? All the subterfuge, the rooftop forays, being followed in the park, men being held at gunpoint. All that, for a *snuffbox*?"

"A *royal* snuffbox. Wars have been declared for less reason."

She had to give Moncreiffe credit. Despite his outrage, he'd kept his voice quiet. Servants passed by at the foot of the stairs without glancing up at them.

He dropped his arms to his sides and took a step back.

Charlotte took a deep breath, realizing only now that she'd hardly breathed while he'd been so close. She would not allow him to distract her again. "Whose coach did Sir Nigel get into?"

Moncreiffe seemed to debate whether or not he would answer. "I don't know."

Now was not the time for her to be angry, much as she badly wanted to stamp her foot. Onto Moncreiffe's instep. She grabbed his arm, to keep from smacking him, and kept her voice pitched low. "But you said—"

"I said I *may* know whose coach we saw. It was a distinctive design, even if they did conceal the crest on the door. There can't be very many like it. Add in the driver who's built like a whiskey barrel, and it should lead us straight to Sir Nigel and his accomplice."

She smoothed down Moncreiffe's sleeve. "Then we just need to visit the coach builders in town, find out who owns a fine carriage like the one we just saw. And hope it was built here in London, not somewhere else."

"*We* are not going. I will."

"But—"

"Be logical, Miss Parnell. I will inquire about a coach I saw and admired. Coach makers are going to fall all over themselves in an attempt to be helpful if they think they have a chance to earn my business."

Moncreiffe wasn't being arrogant or boastful, blast him. Merchants would indeed treat the grandson and heir to a duke far differently than they would treat plain Miss Parnell. "Ah, but think how much *more* helpful they would be if you are trying to find a particular coach so that you can order one just like it as a wedding gift for your affianced bride."

He opened his mouth to speak, but then closed it, snared by his own logic. He touched the tip of his index finger to the tip of her nose. "Round in your favor. Tomorrow I will compile a list of the finest coach makers in town and—"

She shook her head. "Have your valet or butler compile the list. I need you to go to the gentlemen's clubs again, see if Sir Nigel or any of his acquaintances change any habits, especially their spending habits. Observe their demeanor. He must be feeling quite confident by now, having stolen the snuffbox from Melisande, and her none the wiser."

Moncreiffe folded his arms across his chest. "You are giving me orders, madam?"

"I am the one with experience in these matters, so, yes." She had stared down heads of state. She would not be intimidated by the grandson of a duke, even if he did tower over her by a good eight inches or so. "We tried doing things your way tonight, to watch and observe—and observed the snuffbox being stolen right out from under us. Twice. I could have had it in my hands and completed this assignment. Now we go back to doing things my way."

He tilted his head to the side. "And if I refuse to go along? I could easily share your plans, your intentions, with your brother."

Having Steven know what she was up to would make things more difficult, but not impossible. "If you are so ungentlemanly as to renege on our agreement, you should know that I will find a way to proceed with my investigation, with or without your aid, with or without my brother's knowledge of my activities." She folded her arms as well. "But you must do as your conscience dictates, my lord."

"That's the hell of it," he muttered. He sighed. "I'll look into Sir Nigel and his friends further, and let you know as soon as I have anything to report. In exchange, I expect you to not do anything foolhardy in the meantime."

She refused to be baited. "Fair enough. I will expect you to call for me at one o'clock tomorrow."

"One?"

"To go shopping for carriages, of course. Any earlier in the day would only bring undue attention to our activities."

"Of course." With a rueful shake of his head, he reached out to straighten the folds of her cloak, and tucked a curl behind her ear. His expression seemed to hold a smoldering heat, like the banked coals of a fire late at night, but that was probably just the poor lighting in the stairwell. He trailed his fingertips down her neck before he dropped his arm to his side. "Slip your spyglass back into its hidden pocket and get back down to your aunt before she comes looking for you. I will see you tomorrow."

She refused to acknowledge the tingle that shot through her at his touch. "Until then, my lord." She hurried down the stairs without a backward glance.

Chapter 7

 ❧⟋⟍❧

Aunt Hermione, far from noticing Charlotte's pro-
longed absence at the rout, had been engaged in
conversation with a distinguished white-haired gentleman. "He still has all his own hair and teeth," Aunt
whispered, indicating the man who was currently fetching her a cup of punch.

"How nice for you," Charlotte murmured, taking her
seat. Her head swam with all that had happened up on the
roof and in the stairwell.

Rarely had she experienced such a dizzying gamut of
emotions in such a short time as she had with Moncreiffe just now. The usual tedium of waiting and watching changed dramatically with her increased closeness
with him, not to mention a heightened awareness of
Moncreiffe as a man. A man who'd almost kissed her.

And, unfortunately for her peace of mind, a man whom

she wanted to kiss. She'd wager his kiss was as eloquent as his speech, and just as passionate.

She was thoroughly disgusted with herself for allowing Moncreiffe to distract her and let someone else get to the snuffbox before her. Even more disturbing was the fact that her anger had quickly dissipated once she realized it meant she'd have to spend more time in his company.

She groaned. Focus on the task at hand. Tonight had yielded far more questions than answers.

Who were the men who'd been following Madame Melisande, and how did they know about the snuffbox? Who had stolen it from them after they'd stolen it from Melisande? Could those men be working for the Home Office, too, like Steven? If so, she didn't think much of their abilities, letting someone steal it right back.

Then again, they'd beaten *her* to it, so what did that say about her own skills?

Lord Q had told Steven how vitally important it was to retrieve the snuffbox, when he'd first given Steven the assignment.

Other people now knew about the stolen snuffbox. Did they realize just how important it was? The lengths the Home Office and their agents would go to in order to get it back? *Do whatever is necessary,* Lord Q had written.

Or was tonight's change of possession as simple as thieves fighting over loot?

No, a regular thief would have pocketed Melisande's money and jewels.

Well, she wouldn't make any more progress on the matter tonight. Tomorrow she would interview coach makers, confirm her suspicious about Sir Nigel, find his accomplice, and perhaps find out how the two of them fit into the plots swirling around the snuffbox.

Tonight, she had made a novice's mistake. She'd been distracted from her task by her companion. An attractive, intriguing companion with a fondness for licorice, but still . . . Unacceptable. It had been several years since she was a novice.

She was trying to prove to Lord Q that she could do the work just as well as Steven could, and without Steven's help. All these years, and the old man still thought it was Steven who'd retrieved so much information about the French to pass along. Steven kept her name out of his reports and only spoke of her as Charlie, he said, to avoid making her a target should things go badly.

Had nothing to do with him wanting all the congratulations, the adulation, all for himself.

Charlotte snorted.

But didn't *she* want to retrieve the snuffbox, alone, for the very same reasons? To finally gain recognition for her contributions, and receive the adulation, the approval?

She stared down at her folded hands.

The quintet of musicians in the corner struck up a lively tune. Too cheerful a tune, in fact, for her to contemplate such deep thoughts.

Moncreiffe had yet to reappear downstairs. He had probably gone back out to the roof, was now focusing his telescope on the skies, fully engaged in the research that was so important to him.

She could definitely see the appeal of astronomy as a hobby and all it entailed—sitting under the wide-open starry canopy in near total darkness until one's eyes adjusted to the lack of artificial light, revealing tiny details that went overlooked in the glare of day. Sitting side by side, conversing freely in the darkness. She'd dress in warmer clothing next time, though Moncreiffe had done his best to keep her warm.

Aunt Hermione spoke, yanking her back to the present. "What are you thinking about, miss?"

"Hmm?"

"You look a hundred miles away. Thinking about your young man? I saw him here earlier, but he seems to have disappeared."

"Oh, no, I—" She cut herself off at the sight of the tall, older gentleman approaching them, holding two cups of punch. Something about his confident yet relaxed bearing seemed familiar—a man who knew his place in the world but wasn't puffed up with his own consequence.

He did indeed have a full head of hair, pure white, quite distinguished, which made his eyes seem impossibly blue. The decades had etched lines around his eyes and mouth, but couldn't obscure the fact that he must have been breathtakingly handsome in his youth. To someone as old as Aunt Hermione, he must still seem extremely attractive. He looked expectantly from Hermione to her.

Aunt Hermione took the proffered cup and sat up even straighter, a girlish smile of delight on her face. "Your grace, may I present my niece, Miss Charlotte Parnell. Charlotte, I don't believe you've had the chance yet to meet the Duke of Keswick. Your future grandfa-ther-in-law."

Good thing she was sitting, as her knees surely had turned to jelly. She had half expected to meet Moncreiffe's grandfather eventually, but had pictured it quite differently. Moncreiffe at her side, for example.

"Charmed to finally make your acquaintance, Miss Parnell." The duke gave a proper bow, handed Charlotte the remaining cup of punch, and took the seat beside her. "I've been looking forward to the opportunity to speak with the enterprising young woman who succeeded in snaring my grandson."

"Snare?" By the twinkle in his eyes, Charlotte was almost certain he meant no insult. She took a sip of punch, which tasted vaguely of the licorice she'd eaten—a decided improvement over the insipid punch she'd tasted earlier.

"What method did you use to bring him to heel? He has managed to avoid any number of traps, imaginative and clichéd."

She wrapped both hands around her cup. "There was no trap involved, your grace, I assure you. Our engagement was entirely his idea."

The duke's eyes crinkled at the corners when he smiled, a more pronounced version of the same look when Moncreiffe smiled. "May I inquire as to how you two met?"

"He did not tell you?"

Keswick gave a tiny shake of his head.

It was always best to tell the truth as much as possible when engaged in lying. She lifted her chin. "I marched up to him one afternoon, bold as brass, tucked my arm in his, and had him walk with me down Bond Street."

The duke raised his eyebrows, his smile slipping a bit. "No trap, eh?"

She leaned toward him and lowered her voice to a conspiratorial whisper. "I had just realized I'd outpaced my maid, you see, and there was an unsavory looking chap following me, who seemed inclined to take advantage of the fact that I was alone. Enlisting the company of your grandson seemed the safer alternative at the time. I had no idea who he was until later." She gave a rueful grin.

Aunt Hermione was practically quivering on Charlotte's other side. The old gel must be dying to know what was being said between her and the duke, but manners prevented her from cupping a hand to her ear.

"A dire predicament, to be sure, Miss Parnell. I do hope you did not wound his masculine pride by pointing out the fact that he seemed 'safe'?"

"Alas, your grace, I did indeed make that mistake. But he seems to have forgiven me such an egregious breach of etiquette." She set her empty cup on the tray of a passing footman.

After the marquess's crude innuendo on the balcony the night Moncreiffe had announced their engagement, the duke's charm was a pleasant surprise. It was easy to see how Moncreiffe came by it so naturally. But she was astute enough to realize she had not yet passed all the older gentleman's tests. He may have sent the engagement notice to the papers to annoy his son, but she was sure he would still want to know more about her before he'd allow the marriage to take place.

It shouldn't matter if she passed his tests or not, since she had no intention of actually marrying into the family.

Yet something inside her wished for his approval. She'd never known her own grandfather.

"Has he made you aware of how he spends most nights, if the sky is clear?"

"You refer to his hobby of astronomy. Yes, we have discussed it. I'm looking forward to learning more."

The duke gave a slight nod. "It bodes well for the success of your marriage that you do not object to his mistress."

"Mistress?" She had not noticed Moncreiffe paying particular attention to any other females, but she was savvy enough to know that men had needs. Still, the idea of Moncreiffe bedding someone was a little unsettling.

"The stars, Miss Parnell. Alistair has been studying the night sky since he was a little boy. I doubt he will give up that habit, even for a wife."

That was undoubtedly the truth. Moncreiffe had yet to come downstairs. He was likely still out on the roof, staring up at the night sky. Was he warm enough, without her body heat to share?

The duke was giving her a considering glance from head to toe, though it was dispassionate rather than suggestive. He gave her another smile. "Though you may have some success in distracting him."

Charlotte kept her expression pleasant, though she couldn't prevent the bloom of heat in her cheeks.

"I see I have discomfited you. My apologies, Miss Parnell. That was not my intention."

"Not at all, your grace. I find your candor a refreshing change."

"As I do yours. I begin to see why Alistair was attracted

to you. He can't abide simpering ninnies." He leaned closer and lowered his voice. "Neither can I." He straightened. "Tell me, Miss Parnell, how did you manage to avoid the fate that befalls most gently bred English girls?"

"The fate of becoming a ninny?"

He nodded.

"I suppose we can blame my half brother for that. I've lived with him for the past five years."

"Ah, yes, after your mother's passing. Quite tragic. And your aunt so recently a widow herself at the time, unable to take you in."

Charlotte was intrigued that he recalled her personal history. She had assumed a secretary had researched her family tree and written the engagement notice to the newspapers, but it would seem the duke took a personal interest in his grandson's affairs.

She winced at her own poor choice of words.

"I understand your father worked for the War Office, and was awarded a baronetcy for his efforts before he died." The duke's tone was still polite, but managed to convey that a baronet was only slightly better than no title at all.

"It would seem your grace knows almost as much about my father as I do." She had made peace with her family's social standing, or lack thereof, years ago. Since she had no interest in obtaining vouchers to Almack's, she did not see it as a hindrance, though she was well aware many people would.

Their host, Lord Eccleston, stepped up to Keswick just then and begged a moment of his time.

"I have our enjoyed our chat, Miss Parnell." He took

her hand to kiss the air above her knuckles. With his familiar smile and sparkling blue eyes, she had an image of what Moncreiffe would look like in fifty years.

She shouldn't care what Moncreiffe would look like even fifty days from now, because their association would be at an end before then.

The prospect didn't feel as pleasing as it should have. "As have I, your grace."

Keswick would not be hurt when he learned that she and Moncreiffe had ended their betrothal. In fact, he would most likely feel relief, and plan for Moncreiffe to find a bride with more exalted ancestors.

He took his leave of Aunt Hermione in similar fashion, making her giggle and blush like a schoolgirl.

"I declare, you are a very lucky miss, marrying into that family." Aunt Hermione snapped open her fan and plied it vigorously.

Well, someone would eventually marry into Keswick's family, but it wouldn't be her. She had other plans. She couldn't resist teasing her aunt, though. "Thinking of marrying into it yourself?"

"Oh my, oh dear, no." She let loose another lilting sound that could only be called a giggle, continuing to fan herself. "No, I'm much too old for such silliness."

Despite the token protests, Charlotte couldn't help noticing that her aunt tracked the duke's progress as Lord Eccleston led him to a small cluster of people near the refreshment table and made introductions.

So, did the wind really blow that way, or was her aunt merely impressed by an impressive package—title, wealth, bearing, and a handsome face? Perhaps something would come as a result of her association with Moncreiffe after all.

She kept an eye open, hoping to see the viscount's tall frame stride into the ballroom, to no avail. Soon after Keswick left, Aunt Hermione declared an end to the evening, and they departed for home.

Feeling disappointment at not being able to dance with Moncreiffe was ridiculous, considering she'd been wrapped in his coat earlier, and they'd shared much more intimate conversation on the roof than they would have been able to in a dance.

But now that she knew what it felt like for him to hold her, she couldn't help wishing he'd do it again. Soon.

Steven was at the breakfast table when Charlotte came downstairs late the next morning. Aunt Hermione had already eaten and was ensconced in the salon, catching up on her correspondence, safely out of earshot.

Charlotte allowed the footman to fill her plate and teacup before excusing him from the room.

Steven watched him depart, then set down his cup, eyeing her warily.

She smiled brightly. "You would have been proud of me at the rout last night, Steven. I pretended to be just as much a ninny as any other London miss." The actual nature of her ninniness—being distracted from her task of watching Melisande—was unimportant. "I even engaged the Duke of Keswick in conversation."

"Did you now. And what is his grace like?"

She shook her head. "I've held up my end of our bargain. Now it's your turn."

He sighed and scooted his chair back from the table. "Very well. Let me refill my cup first." He moved to the sideboard and fussed with milk and sugar and the teapot until Charlotte thought she was going to have to hit him. Just as he was sitting down again, the butler entered, bearing a card on a silver platter.

"Yes, Farnham?"

"Beg pardon, sir, miss, you have a visitor."

Charlotte groaned at the delay.

Steven glanced at the card, then smiled at her. "You're in luck, poppet. Please send in Gauthier, Farnham."

"Very good, sir."

Moments later Gauthier shuffled in and was seated across the table from Charlotte, both of them on opposite sides of Steven, who sat at the head of the table, so they could converse in low tones. Charlotte brought the tea things to the table so the three of them could keep talking without wasting time for trips to the sideboard.

Gauthier nodded a greeting at her, ran his hands through his greasy dark hair, blew his enormous Roman nose on a pink silk handkerchief, and emptied half his cup in one swallow. "The good news is, our friends from Darconia are still in London, so we still have a chance of success."

Charlotte topped off his cup. "What's the bad news?"

"*Merci.* I am afraid that last night, they, how you say, gave me the fall."

"Slip. They gave you the slip." Steven sat back in his chair and shook his head. "You're losing your touch, old man."

"Insolent whelp. If you had accompanied me as we

planned, they would not have had such an easy time." Gauthier leaned toward Steven and gave a suggestive wag of his eyebrows. "How is the fair Mademoiselle Emily?"

Steven coughed and stared resolutely at Gauthier, who was only three years his senior, and refused to meet Charlotte's angry gaze.

She tapped her finger on the table. "You abandoned your post, a task assigned by Lord Q, in favor of engaging some woman's favors?"

Steven finally faced her. "No, of course not. I was, um, taking a page from your book, in fact. Emily is a maid at the palace, and I was . . . interviewing her."

"Interviewing."

He didn't blink. "Yes."

She'd just bet Emily was pretty, and poor enough that her dress didn't quite conceal all her charms. Charlotte drew breath to dispute his claim.

"*S'il vous plaît, mes amis*, do not fight. My head, it hurts when you argue." He tapped Steven's hand. "*Ma petite*, she is as skilled with her tongue as she is with a knife. You know you cannot win."

"We are not fighting, Gauthier. Perish the thought." Charlotte turned her dazzling smile from the Frenchman to her brother, losing the smile in the process. "So, what useful information did Mademoiselle Emily have to share?"

Steven cleared his throat. "At the fete last week, the night we think the snuffbox was stolen, she saw the two emissaries from Darconia standing by the fireplace early in the evening, where the box was on display on the mantel."

"Aha!" Gauthier slapped his hand on the table in triumph. "I was right!"

Steven took a deep breath. "She also saw Madame Melisande near the mantel before the snuffbox disappeared. It looked like she was checking her appearance in the mirror, but the snuffbox was directly below said mirror."

Charlotte resisted slapping the table. She did, however, raise her chin a tad higher in the air in her triumph.

"So it would seem you may have been correct from the beginning, poppet."

She couldn't raise her chin any higher and still see her brother or Gauthier. "If you finally agree that Madame Melisande stole the box, does it matter if the Darconians gave Gauthier the slip last night? Why not let them just go home to Darconia?" Let them leave, and not muddy things up any further for her investigation, since she knew the Darconians had been robbed of the box, probably by Sir Nigel. Surely they were at an impasse as to where to find the box now.

"Because we don't know for certain that Madame Melisande is the one who took it. If we find out she didn't, but in the meantime we've let the Darconians slip out of our grasp, we're going to have a lot of explaining to do to Lord Q."

As much as she wanted to prove that she was just as capable as Steven at completing the assignment, it was more important to get back the snuffbox. "Ah, but *I* am certain that Madame Melisande took it, though she no longer has it. The Darconians stole it from her hotel room last night."

Steven set down his teacup with precise movements. "And how did you come by this information?"

"I saw them. I was too far away to get the box myself."

Gauthier had gone still, staring at her intently.

Steven leaned closer to her and lowered his voice even further. "Where, exactly, were you?"

This was the part that could be interpreted incorrectly if she wasn't careful. "At the rout last night, I went up on the roof with my spyglass." No need to add any additional details. "Right after I saw the Darconians steal the box, they were held at gunpoint by another man who stole the box from them. I believe it was Sir Nigel."

Steven's eyes narrowed.

Gauthier cocked his head to one side, considering her statement.

Undaunted, she pushed ahead. "I have seen Nigel and Melisande together on more than one occasion. I think he may have stolen the box back for her. We should investigate him."

Steven shook his head. "If we investigated every man who spent time with Melisande, we would have to scrutinize half the men in London."

"What kind of gun was it?" Gauthier leaned his elbows on the table.

"I couldn't tell. Too far away, too dark."

"In the dark, so far away, how can you be sure it was Sir Nigel?" At least Steven wasn't asking why she had gone up to the roof.

"I can't, but the height and build were correct, and based on the interaction that I have witnessed between Melisande and Nigel, it would be logical for him to get back something that was stolen from her. We should investigate him."

Steven gave a slow nod. "Perhaps we—meaning Gauthier and I—should. You, however, promised to play the part of a London miss. Where was your fiancé when you were spying on Melisande's room?"

"You agree with me, don't you?" She reached an imploring hand toward Gauthier. She hated putting him in the middle like this, but she had no intention of answering Steven's question.

"Perhaps, *ma petite*."

Steven sighed. "We'll look into him, after we finish up with the Darconians."

"You're going to wait? No telling what he'll do with it in the meantime. He may not give it back to Melisande, especially if he discovers just how valuable it is. I've seen them arguing."

"We'll look into it, poppet, I promise." Steven had the gall to actually pat her hand. He turned back to Gauthier, who was busy dunking a buttered scone in his tea. "After the Darconians gave you the slip, you turned in early?"

Charlotte sat back, trying to calm her simmering resentment. How many times would she have to be right for them to give credence to her theories?

Well, fine. She'd just investigate Sir Nigel herself. Which had been her plan anyway. Let Steven and Gauthier chase after the Darconians—it would free her up to follow the real leads in the case. She buttered a scone and liberally smeared it with blackberry preserves. Delicious.

"Of course not, silly boy." Gauthier ate a bite of his scone. "I went to Lost Wages, my favorite gaming hell, and won fifty pounds." A look of bliss crossed his face as he swallowed the last of the scone. He kissed his fingertips. "You have no idea how bad London hotel food is, *mes amis.*"

"I'll pass your compliments to the chef," Charlotte said, thinking how accustomed to good food she had become in the short time since coming to London. Thank heavens she no longer had to eat her own cooking, or—God forbid—Steven's.

"You didn't come here to tell me you lost the people you were supposed to be following, or that you cheated at cards last night." Steven refilled his cup.

"*Moi*, cheat? Never. Unless the house, she is twisted, *n'est-ce pas?*"

Steven frowned for a moment. "You mean crooked."

"*Oui.* This house last night, she is very crooked." He glanced into his empty teacup. Charlotte filled it again. "But at this house, one can buy as well as play."

"Buy what?" She'd never heard of anyone shopping at a gaming hell before. Wagering possessions, certainly, but not selling or buying them. She thought most men hated to shop.

"Anything one's heart desires, *ma petite.* One need only give a description of the object one wants, prove one has the necessary funds to purchase it, and voilà, within a night or two it is there. Sometimes several of them to choose from, just like in a shop. They have an understanding for those who cannot purchase new, but who wish to keep up appearances."

Steven leaned forward, elbows on the table. "And did you express an interest in obtaining a snuffbox?"

Gauthier nodded. "Alas, my old one was lost when I traveled here." He grinned.

"It can't be so simple as to just buy back the snuffbox from a fence, could it?" Charlotte asked. If Sir Nigel was at low water, as Moncreiffe had suggested, perhaps there was nothing more nefarious to his plans than selling stolen property for a profit.

Lord Q had described the snuffbox as being inset with a fortune in small gemstones, quite valuable in itself, without considering it had been a gift to the Prince Regent from a female dignitary from the tiny principality of Darconia.

"If Madame Melisande knows of this gaming hell, that would explain why she took the snuffbox in the first place, a shiny bauble like that." Steven beat Gauthier to the last scone on the plate in the middle of the table. "It would have easily fit in her reticule, and even after cutting a fence in on the deal, would still fetch her enough to keep up appearances for another month or two."

With the scones gone, Charlotte put the lid back on the blackberry preserves. "Does Bow Street know about the extracurricular activities at this gaming hell?"

"I'm certain they do, poppet. And if they don't, there's no need for us to enlighten them until after Gauthier buys a slightly used snuffbox. And that should be . . . ?"

"Tonight."

"So soon? Marvelous." He cut the scone in half and gave part to Gauthier. "You see, poppet? You didn't miss out on anything with this case after all. Very simple and straightforward. Boring, even."

"Yes, I can see that." She snatched the just-buttered piece of scone from Steven and popped it in her mouth.

Business concluded, Gauthier began discussing his favorite dealer at the gaming hell, a buxom brunette. "I think she is the cousin of Melisande. Do you remember her, Vivienne, with the *magnifique* . . ." He gestured with his hands, indicating a woman with voluptuous curves.

Before he could become more specific in describing the woman's attributes, Steven held up a hand to silence him. "What are your plans for today, poppet?"

"I haven't decided about tonight yet. Aunt may prefer to stay in. But I'm going for a drive with Moncreiffe this afternoon."

"This afternoon?" Steven glanced at the clock, which showed not quite eleven. "You'd better hurry upstairs, then, if you're going to get dressed and ready in time."

She was about to argue that she did not require a ridiculous amount of time to prepare for a simple carriage ride, but realized she could put the time to good use. "Excellent idea. If you'll excuse me, gentlemen."

Both men stood, and Steven tugged her close to kiss her forehead as she passed. "See, I knew you'd come to like all this female folderol," he whispered.

She patted his hand, then dashed upstairs.

Once inside her bedchamber, she shut the door and leaned against it.

She hated lying to Steven, actively or by omission, but he'd left her no choice. If he had his way, the rest of her life would play out like the conversation over breakfast just now—concerned with her social calendar and the whereabouts of the man in her life, and little else.

Just like her mother. A woman who'd lived her life for one party after another, an existence as ephemeral as that of a butterfly, and having about as much impact.

The fate of the nation might not rest on whether she succeeded in retrieving the snuffbox—the prince could survive the loss, and Darconia was hardly likely to declare war on England over it—but *her* future was at stake.

Success in this assignment meant a more secure future for herself, working for Lord Q. A woman of independent means, not reliant on a husband or brother. Someone who made a difference. Like her father.

A glance at the clock told her she had just enough time to complete her errand before Moncreiffe arrived, but only if she didn't dawdle.

Now, which of her costumes was best suited for visiting a gaming hell?

Chapter 8

"**L**ooking for wagers regarding your lovely little bride-to-be?"

Alistair didn't look up from the betting book he was perusing at White's. "Good morning, Father. Bit early for you to be up and out, isn't it?"

"Could say the same for you." Penrith pulled out a chair at the table and sat down beside Alistair. "Stars were bright and twinkly last night, just the way you like them. Thought they'd keep you up until dawn. Or were you concentrating your efforts on other celestial bodies, eh?" He gave Alistair a playful elbow to the ribs.

Alistair closed the book, his finger marking his spot, and gave his attention to his father. The morning light streaming through the club's big bow windows showed every line of dissipation on the older man's face, and revealed there was far more gray than brown in his hair these days. Years of heavy drinking and late nights kept his blue eyes perpetually bloodshot.

"How I spend my nights is of no concern to you. What brings you here so early?"

Penrith grunted. "Couldn't take any more. Seems the old man likes that filly you picked, despite her father being a mere baron." He hailed a passing waiter and ordered wine. "Kept going on and on about the tête-à-tête he had with her last night."

The hair on the back of Alistair's neck stood on end. Miss Parnell and his grandfather had a chat last night at the rout, and she'd said nothing to him about it?

"What's that you're looking at, eh? Thinking of placing a wager of your own?"

Alistair quickly debated how much to say. "Not at all. I simply saw someone recently in a coach I admired, but I know he didn't own it, so I wanted to see if perhaps he'd won it in a wager."

"Haven't seen a coach change hands on a wager for a bit. Find anything interesting?"

"Not so far, and I've already checked the books at Boodle's this morning."

"Hmm. Who was in the coach? Perhaps I'd know the answer to your quest."

With his father's lifestyle and the company he kept, it was quite likely Penrith was more familiar with disreputable folks than he was. "Sir Nigel Broadmoor."

His father shook his head. "If that loose fish now has a fancy carriage, ten to one he stole it, not won it on a wager. Most likely it belongs to his crony Tumblety, and Nigel simply borrowed it."

Alistair frowned. "I've heard rumors about a Baron Tumblety. Something about him engaging in trade."

Penrith lowered his voice. "You keep a close eye on your baubles and trinkets if you ever find yourself near either one of them, you hear me, son? Or you'll likely find your watch fob up for sale at Lost Wages."

"I beg your pardon?"

Penrith shook his head in dismay before emptying his wineglass. "How did I manage to raise such a green lad?" He waved his hand, and a waiter came scurrying to take his order for a refill. Once they were alone, Penrith rested his hand on Alistair's shoulder and assumed the same attitude he had fifteen years before, when he'd painfully explained in crude details how babies were made, and how to not make them with the upstairs maids. Alistair braced himself.

"You see, son, not everyone is blessed with a head for managing their affairs the way we were."

Since Alistair knew perfectly well that the marquess's secretary handled his finances, and that Grandfather still kept him on a quarterly allowance, much as he did Alistair, he was inclined to suspect the value of the wisdom about to be dispensed.

"When fellows like Nigel and Tumblety find themselves in a bind, they don't have the wherewithal to bluff their way through it, like the rest of Society does."

Penrith so rarely played the role of father, Alistair felt obliged to go along. Besides, he'd almost forgotten what it was like to converse with one relative without hearing a harangue against the other. He rested his chin on his fist, his elbow on the table. "What do they do?"

"They pinch." He accepted the fresh glass of wine from the waiter, and waited until he was gone before continuing. "Nothing major, nothing to attract attention, mind you. People think they've merely misplaced their fan or fob or what have you. They think the maid or footman moved it and lost it, or that the butler miscounted the silver. They don't realize they've actually been robbed."

Alistair sat forward. "And what do Sir Nigel or Tumblety do with this booty? An extra fan or gewgaw isn't going to help them much when creditors and merchants pound on the door."

"They do if there's a few dozen people out there, pinching these baubles for them, so they in turn can sell them. How do you think I replaced my watch fob last year? The old man deprived me of my allowance, and I couldn't let dear Vanessa—or was it Giselle?—think I was at low water. I had to get another, quickly, and paying a jeweler's price for a new one was out of the question."

Since his father had lost the watch fob on a roll of the dice, Alistair was disinclined to feel sympathy in the first place. "So you bought a stolen fob from Tumblety?"

"Much as it shames me to admit, yes. And I don't ever want to see anything of yours show up at Lost Wages, so keep a sharp eye out. You never know who might be trying to filch." He took a deep swallow of wine.

"I always remember your words of wisdom, Father." Alistair finished off the last of his now tepid tea.

He believed it quite likely that Madame Melisande had intended to sell the royal snuffbox to Tumblety or Sir Nigel. But that didn't explain why the two men who'd been following Miss Parnell had stolen the box, or why

Nigel had stolen it back from them. How did Nigel know those other men were involved?

Ten to one, there was a great deal still that Miss Parnell had not confessed.

He tossed down his napkin, pushed the betting book to the center of the table, and rose.

"Where are you off to?"

He briefly considered saying he was off to look at stolen watch fobs, then thought better of it. "To find out who built Tumblety's coach, of course."

Charlotte ducked down an alley to avoid a large crowd of sailors coming her way on the street. Off in the distance, church bells tolled the hour. Noon. She had less than an hour to complete her task at the tavern before she would need to head home again to get ready for Moncreiffe's arrival.

A man detached himself from where he'd been propping up a doorway and sauntered toward her. "What 'ave we here? Fancy a bit of fun, ducks?"

"Some other time, per'aps." She picked up her pace.

"But this *is* a good time, love." He slung his arm around her shoulders, matching her stride for stride. "I just got paid," he cajoled in a gin-soaked voice. He jingled a few coins in his pocket.

She wrinkled her nose. Apparently the only time he washed his filthy dungarees or bathed was when he got caught in the rain. "No," she said more forcefully, and tried to shrug off his arm. Given the way she was dressed, she couldn't blame him for his assumption about her occupation. She kept walking.

"Come on, ducks, name your price, and we'll 'ave a bit of fun."

She stopped so abruptly he took an extra step before he faced her. She lifted the bottom edge of her skirt, just far enough to reveal the knife sheath strapped to her calf. "Tell you what, ducks, let's 'ave a race. I'll wager I can get my knife out faster than you can get out your pintle."

His face paled beneath the layers of grime, one hand subconsciously reaching down to cover his groin. "If you wasn't interested, you just had to say so."

She gave an exasperated huff, pulled her cloak closer around her, and once more strode toward the gaming hell.

She almost wished he'd given her an excuse to use her knife. Steven had taught her well. She was prepared for this life, for this work, whatever she encountered.

And she would prove it by getting back the snuffbox.

She reached the tavern without further incident and settled at a corner table, her back to the wall, where she had an excellent view of both entrances. One led to the street, the other to the kitchen and on toward what she supposed was the gaming area.

A red-haired woman who might be a serving wench sauntered up to Charlotte's table, one hand on her broad hip. "Girls off'n the street ain't allowed to ply their trade in 'ere, missy, so get yer arse out the door."

Charlotte pulled her worn cloak a bit closer around her shoulders, hiding some of the décolletage revealed by the low cut of her dark red gown. "That ain't the sort o' work I'm looking for." She checked that the table was dry and relatively clean, pulled a pack of cards from her reticule, and fanned them out across the table. She lifted one card and neatly flipped over the entire deck, then swept them up and shuffled them. "I 'ave a different specialty."

The serving wench harrumphed. "You'll be wanting to speak with Mr. Jennison, then. It's a bit early for 'im yet, but he should be along shortly."

"Mr. Jennison. Right. What's he like, then? Is he the owner of this place?"

"You'd certainly think so, the way he carries on sometimes. No, some rich toff owns this place. Jennison just runs the gaming rooms."

"That's good to know. I'm Susie, by the way."

"Ginny." After a glance toward the kitchen door, Ginny sat in the chair opposite.

Charlotte shuffled the cards as they talked. "So, any tips on what to say to Mr. Jennison when I meet him, or what not to say?"

"Well, don't expect 'im to look you in the eye. Wear something cut a little lower, and you probably won't even 'ave to show your cards."

Charlotte tugged her dress up a bit. "What about the owner? Is he a good man, pay everyone on time?"

Ginny shook her head. "Don't know nothing 'bout 'im, except Jennison gives out the wages every week, regular as clockwork."

The dim lighting and her heavily applied rouge made it difficult to discern if Ginny really didn't know about the owner or was simply reluctant to share such knowledge.

"I've heard there are some fringe benefits to working here," Charlotte ventured, fanning her cards out again.

"Aye?"

"Like maybe I can buy a real lady's fan, for a lot less than what the lady paid for it."

Ginny's eyes narrowed. "Mayhap. You'd 'ave to ask Jennison about such things. Me, I just serve the drinks." She gave a furtive glance over her shoulder, then flashed a grin. "Sometimes there are bonuses." She patted the elegant hair comb holding up her red tresses. It was silver, set with what Charlotte had thought to be glass rather than gemstones, and looked similar to one Aunt Hermione had lost when they'd first arrived in London.

She patted her own hair comb, an unadorned bit of brass. "Fair enough."

Three men seated near the fireplace shouted for service just then and banged their empty tankards on the table.

"Speaking o' drinks . . ." Ginny stood up.

"Thanks ever so much for your help, Ginny."

"No trouble at all." She went to her customers.

Charlotte scooped her cards up, slipped them back in her reticule, and glanced at the watch tucked inside. Oh, blast. Jennison would have to wait until later. She barely had time to get home and change before Moncreiffe was due to arrive. Steven couldn't know she had left the house.

She sensed someone watching her, and scanned the room. Her breath caught.

There, just inside the taproom door, stood Moncreiffe.

Their eyes locked, and she forgot all about the room full of people around them.

He looked away first, taking in the mixed clientele of young bucks, sailors, and vagrants filling the room, before returning his assessing gaze to her, his look of disbelief growing sharper.

Before it could become full-blown anger, Charlotte hurried toward him, and kept right on going, out the door, through the milling crowd and toward the carts rumbling past in the street.

"What in blazes are you doing here, in a place like this?" He caught her elbow just before she reached the street and spun her back toward him.

She refused to be intimidated. "Following a lead. What are *you* doing here?"

He muttered something that sounded like a Latin curse, tucked her arm in his, and they began walking. "Likewise."

Two sailors walking past pronounced their approval of her bosom.

Moncreiffe wrapped his arm around her shoulder, tugging her close to his side. "You shouldn't be in a neighborhood like this, especially dressed like that."

When she glanced up, he was looking straight ahead, but she was certain he had just been looking down her bosom. She clutched her cloak closed at her throat, hiding a smile. "This is the *only* way for me to be dressed when I'm in a neighborhood like this." Since his arm was around her shoulders, and she was dressed like a working girl, she wrapped her arm around his waist, making it absolutely clear she had already found a "customer."

He glanced down at her, and after a slight hesitation, caressed her shoulder with his fingers. Once more, he was willing to play along.

She gave his trim waist a squeeze in appreciation. Too

bad she hadn't thought to slip her arm under his coat instead of over it. "So tell me about the lead you were following."

Instead of answering her, he raised his arm and hailed a coach. An elegant, new coach, with the crest of the Duke of Keswick adorning the door.

The driver tipped his hat, and a tiger jumped down from the back to open the door and let down the step.

Moncreiffe spoke a few quiet words to the driver and then handed her inside. To her disappointment, he sat on the opposite bench, his back to the driver, rather than beside her.

She settled against the midnight blue velvet squabs, admiring the coach's pristine interior, the mellow scent of beeswax and new fabric tickling her senses. Even the glass on the lanterns sparkled.

They rolled along over the cobblestones with a gentle sway rather than teeth-jarring jolts. The only thing that would make it better would be to have Moncreiffe at her side. Though from this perspective, she could gaze upon him without being rude or forward, and trace with her eyes his classically handsome features which would make a sculptor cry. A painter would be better able to capture the intense blue of his eyes, the hint of red in his sensual lips, the tousled honey-brown hair that curled over his collar.

"Does your brother know what you're doing down here? It's a wonder he doesn't lock you in your room."

A sculptor would want to smooth out that scowl. "My brother is the person who taught me how to do such things as mingle with maids and chat up the doxies at dockside taverns, so locking me up would be rather hypo-critical of him, wouldn't it?"

Moncreiffe shook his head. "If you ever feel the need to do such a dangerous thing again, pray, ask me and I will accompany you. Day or night, just ask. It's a miracle you were not accosted."

"Oh, but I *was* accosted." She took some delight in his concerned expression, and rested her hand on his knee. "Rest easy, my lord, for I assure you that I can take care of myself, as well as any lecherous sailors foolish enough to cross my path." She lifted the right side of her skirt high enough for him to see the knife sheath strapped to her calf.

Moncreiffe glanced down, then made a strangled sound low in his throat.

She didn't usually make a habit of letting men see her stocking-clad leg, but both men this morning had shown appropriate responses. Quite gratifying, really, to know she had that effect.

She thought it prudent not to mention the fact that the leather confection had been made for her by Gauthier as a birthday present, custom fit. Or that there was a matching sheath and knife for her left calf.

She twitched her skirts back into place. "You were going to tell me about the lead you were following, that brought you to Lost Wages?"

He locked his gaze on her face. "This morning I discovered that Sir Nigel is known to be a fence."

One of the many qualities she admired about Moncreiffe was the way he spoke to her. Though not impervious to her charms—even he couldn't resist a quick glance now and then, and in this gown she could hardly blame him—he usually addressed her face rather than her bosom, as most men did.

"He mostly deals in small but valuable trinkets, and these items are rumored to change hands here, at Lost Wages."

Charlotte drummed her fingers on the velvet seat cushion. "That would explain his interest in the snuffbox. I wonder if Melisande stole it at his behest, or was she merely a thief acting on her own, and Nigel is her fence?"

"We still can't be certain it was Sir Nigel who ended up with the box last night. We have no proof yet."

"True." She nibbled on her bottom lip.

Moncreiffe tapped her knee. "Your turn. Why on earth did you come down here?" The *dressed like that* went unspoken this time, though he flicked his gaze to her exposed décolletage.

Drawing her cloak about her would only attract more attention to herself. "Steven and Gauthier—he's one of our associates—also learned about the stolen merchandise that moves through Lost Wages. They've expressed their interest to the proprietors of the establishment, and think they can simply buy the snuffbox here tomorrow night."

Moncreiffe's brows shot up. "So easily?"

She shook her head. "Nigel, or whoever ended up with it last night, stole the box from somebody who had in turn just stolen the box from another thief. They must realize the box holds more value than the precious metal and gemstones of which it is made. Unless they are complete lackwits, they will not sell it with the rest of their common plunder at a place like Lost Wages."

"Seems logical."

"The length of time it takes them to find a way to get the most money out of this trinket is the amount of time we have to get it back."

He nodded slowly. "So our next step is to confirm that it was indeed Sir Nigel we saw last night."

The coach stopped. Moncreiffe had apparently instructed the driver to go 'round back to the mews, where the tall hedges and garden gate concealed their arrival.

"I will call for you in an hour, as we planned," he said, handing her out of the carriage. "Or do we need to delay our drive, to give you more time to change?"

"That won't be necessary. I will be ready on time."

"You aren't sickening for something, are you?" Moncreiffe said as soon as he'd helped Charlotte up into his phaeton, after they'd exited the front of the town house.

"I feel fine. Any reason I should not?" She settled her pale blue muslin skirts around her knees, then gripped the handrail as Moncreiffe snapped the reins and they pulled out into the flow of traffic.

"I'm merely concerned that you may have caught a chill earlier. You look a bit flushed."

She self-consciously patted her cheeks, which were indeed a bit warm. "That's what comes of rushing upstairs and having less than five minutes to change before you arrived. Aunt Hermione needed to consult with me on some household matters, and I hadn't the heart to interrupt her."

He didn't need to know that Hermione had actually seen her in the scandalous red dress before she'd even reached the back stairs, and felt compelled to lecture her on appropriate behavior and wardrobe.

"Five minutes? I'm not sure whether I should be impressed at your speed or insulted by the lack of time you spent on your toilette preparing for our excursion."

Charlotte laughed. "If we were really affianced, you should be insulted. But since we are engaged in an investigation, you can be impressed."

"Consider me duly impressed, then."

The phaeton traveled along through the traffic almost effortlessly, Moncreiffe guiding the horse with a gentle hand on the reins. The same hands that had caressed her cheek in the darkness last night, up on the roof. This afternoon, those elegant long fingers were encased in fine kid gloves, soft as butter, no doubt. Would that she could have seen his face when he caressed her last night, what emotion his fathomless blue eyes might have revealed, seen if his heartbeat had quickened as much as hers.

They turned onto another street. With effort, she brought her attention back on task.

"If we can find the owner of the coach we saw last night, and connect him to Sir Nigel, then we should be able to prove Nigel has the box. How many coach makers are we going to visit?"

"None. I thought you might instead enjoy a drive through a neighborhood that used to be quite fashionable but has since fallen from favor."

She gaped at him. "Why the devil would you think I'd prefer that?"

"The purpose of going to the coach makers was to

discover the identity of the owner of the coach in which Sir Nigel departed last night. I have a list of them if you still want it." He patted his coat pocket, and Charlotte heard the crinkle of paper. "But what if I told you I have already discovered the owner's identity?"

"And he lives near here? Oh, this is marvelous." She patted his knee in appreciation. "However did you discover him so quickly? And who is it?"

"Baron Tumblety. I already knew that he was among Sir Nigel's circle of acquaintance—they are seen at White's together quite often. Tumblety exists on the edge of polite Society, as he has been known to engage in trade. It is even rumored that he is chief investor in a gaming hell."

Charlotte snorted. "If he's our man, down at Lost Wages they think he's a rich toff."

"We're getting close." Moncreiffe turned the horse onto a square lined with ancient oaks, their leaves turning yellow but not yet falling. Instead of governesses with their young charges in the square's park, a group of boys shouted and pummeled one another, and the only adult was a disinterested washerwoman, draping damp bed linens over the bushes to dry.

The wind shifted, carrying a hint of the Thames at low tide. The waterfront was not distant, far too close for this neighborhood to be fashionable.

"Would we not have more luck in finding the carriage if we went around back to the mews?"

Moncreiffe pulled a slip of paper from his pocket and compared the address written there with those on the houses they were passing. "I thought we'd have more luck if we found the correct house to begin with, before we tried tooling down the alley."

"Of course, my lord." Charlotte folded her hands together in an attempt to control her impatience and excitement. Steven had often commented upon her eagerness, praising her lack of maidenly reticence. He even claimed that her nose twitched like that of a hound that's caught the scent of her prey.

Moncreiffe would never make such an unflattering comparison, she was sure.

"Right. That's the one," Moncreiffe murmured.

Charlotte noted the nondescript facade, so much like its neighbors. Paint was peeling from the once-white trim on the pediment above the front door, but even in that detail it was similar to its neighbors. Only the dull brass house numbers on the mellow brick set it apart. No one appeared to be peeking out of the windows, nor was Nigel or Tumblety conveniently arriving or departing.

She counted the number of houses to the end of the row, before Moncreiffe turned the corner and headed down the alley. "We should not be doing this during daylight, in such a readily identifiable carriage."

"If we have occasion to come here again, I will borrow my grandfather's tilbury or gig." Moncreiffe slanted her a smile. "And each of us should wear a costume. Perhaps the duke's white wig from the last century for me, and a towering red wig for you, with a bonnet perched precariously on top."

She chuckled at the image his words painted.

Movement up ahead caught her eye. "That's it," she

whispered, struggling to sit still. "That's the carriage from last night." It was just being put away in the carriage house, the harness on the horses jingling in the crisp afternoon air as the coachman and tiger maneuvered everything into place. Like the trim on the house, the coach's paint was faded and peeling, but the inside of the wheels and other trim was yellow, contrasting sharply with the black lacquer on the rest of the body. A decade ago it must have been quite an elegant equipage.

"Whiskey barrel with two legs." Moncreiffe pointed with his chin at the rotund man with the whip in his hand. "Definitely the driver we saw."

"Pull up," Charlotte murmured.

Moncreiffe pulled on the reins to halt the gelding, still several houses up from Tumblety's. He looped one arm around her shoulders and leaned in close to whisper in her ear. "Just in case they wonder why we've stopped."

His warm breath stirred the fine hairs on her neck, sending a delicious shiver down her spine.

"Excellent idea," she murmured. She inhaled the warm scent of his shaving soap. She'd once cuddled in similar fashion with Gauthier to allay a suspect's suspicion, and they'd both struggled to keep from giggling.

Laughter was the furthest thought from her mind this time. She fought the urge to arch her neck, to invite Moncreiffe's kiss. His lips were so close to hers. Just a little turn of her head and they'd meet. She clenched her fist in frustration and slipped her gaze toward the stables.

The driver spit a long stream of tobacco juice and strode into the carriage house, disappearing from sight.

Moncreiffe waited a few moments, then clicked his

tongue, and the gelding obediently started, at a slow walk. Charlotte took a steadying breath. She had work to do.

As they rolled past, she tried to take in every detail of the garden, its fence, the gate, and the back of the house. She even stood up for a quick look, and grabbed Moncreiffe's shoulder in her excitement. "I saw him," she hissed, sitting back down, her heart pounding.

"Who, Tumblety?" They reached the end of the alley, and Moncreiffe turned the horse back onto the main street.

She nodded. "The study is up on the first floor, just over from the door leading down into the kitchen. I'll bet that's where he's keeping the snuffbox."

"In the kitchen?"

Charlotte opened her mouth to retort, but saw the glimmer of mischief in Moncreiffe's eye.

He quickly sobered. "Why do you think Tumblety has the snuffbox, and not Sir Nigel?"

"Why would Tumblety allow the use of his carriage if he were not in charge of their operation? And if I were in charge, working with a man like Sir Nigel, I wouldn't entrust him with the safekeeping of so much as a handkerchief."

"I agree. So what now?"

She took a moment to appreciate the tiny bubble of joy—it had been so long since a man had said he agreed with her. "When I stood up, I saw into the study, and there was a man sitting at the desk. You may call him Tumblety, but I knew him as Toussaint." Her heart was still racing from the shock of recognition.

"Knew him, how?"

"Let's just say that he and I have been after the same thing before. He even stabbed Steven once, because Steven got in his way."

Moncreiffe edged the gelding to the side of the road. Carriages clattered past in both directions. He glanced back at the way they'd come and gripped her upper arm. "Did he hurt you?"

The intensity in his eyes made Charlotte shiver. She shook her head. "Toussaint knew I would stay behind to take care of Steven rather than follow, so he got away."

"Do you think he saw you just now?"

"He was busy pouring a drink. I saw him in profile, which is why I'm certain of his identity. His proboscis is enormous." She held her hand out to indicate a nose the size of which would make even Gauthier's seem petite in comparison.

Moncreiffe dropped his hand from her arm, back to his lap. "All right, now that we've confirmed it was Sir Nigel who ended up with the box last night, and his partner is Toussaint or Tumblety, whichever is his true identity, what is your plan? Call in Bow Street? Tell Steven?"

She snorted. "He ignored my theory when I said Melisande was the one who stole the box in the first place. This morning he dismissed my suspicions of Sir Nigel and urged me once more to play the part of mindless miss. No, I'm leaving him out of it from now on, as he has tried to leave me out of it. *I* am going to be the one to take the box back from Toussaint."

She could already picture the look of shock on Steven's face when she held up the box in triumph.

Moncreiffe turned to face her, his knee resting against hers. "I can't have heard you correctly."

It's not like she had stuttered. "It's quite simple. Tonight, after Toussaint has gone to the gaming hell, I'm going to sneak into his study and steal back the snuffbox."

Chapter 9

Moncreiffe's blank expression made it seem as though he still hadn't heard her.

A carriage swept past, and the gelding whinnied a protest at being kept standing by the side of the road. Moncreiffe calmed him down.

Charlotte tried again. "I'm going to get the snuffbox, and complete the assignment while Steven is losing money at the gaming tables."

"That's what I thought you meant." Moncreiffe pulled off one glove and pinched the bridge of his nose.

It had to be a sin for a man to have such beautiful, elegant fingers. Charlotte compared her own much shorter, rather pudgy fingers. At least her nails were neat and smooth, now that she'd stopped biting them. She'd had no choice, what with Aunt Hermione threatening to soak her fingertips in vinegar while she slept.

Moncreiffe lowered his hand. "Telling you that your idea is madness, not to mention incredibly dangerous, would only goad you into attempting to steal the box on your own, wouldn't it?"

"Well, of course I'm going to steal it on my own. I just explained why I'm not going to involve Steven. He wouldn't listen to me anyway." Honestly, all the men in her life lately were proving to be incredibly dense. "And it's not madness. It makes perfect sense."

She repeated his last statement in her head. Oh, blast. Perhaps she was the one being dense. "You're actually willing to help me?"

He looked askance at her. "I'm certainly not going to let you try it on your own."

She stiffened her spine. "I'm perfectly capable of sneaking in and retrieving a small object on my own. I do not require your assistance, my lord." She folded her arms.

"Oh, don't poker up on me. I meant no insult to your skills as a burglar."

If he brought up her failed attempt to climb down to Melisande's hotel room balcony, she wouldn't be responsible for the consequences.

"I would worry the entire time you were embarked on your mission. Not for your own safety, of course, but for that of anyone you might encounter."

She looked at him from the corner of her eye.

"I'd be especially worried for any sailors who crossed your path. We aren't that far from the Thames, you know."

Blast those earnest blue eyes of his. They seared straight through her, whether brimming with concern or twinkling with humor, as they were now. She dropped her hands to her lap.

"Much better. I concede you have more extensive experience at breaking and entering than I do. What is your plan?"

A hackney driver shouted an obscenity at them as he drove past. He came so close, the phaeton rocked in the other coach's wake.

"May I suggest we get going, and I'll tell you along the way?"

Moncreiffe started the horse, and they joined the steady flow of traffic.

"Steven and Gauthier are expecting to meet their contact at the gaming hell shortly after ten tonight. That is our best chance for Toussaint to be there also, and since he'll be gone, his servants are likely to be lax in their duties. Sitting around the table in the kitchen, or helping themselves to his best claret, for example. It will be simple to sneak in, grab the snuffbox, and sneak out again."

"Not so simple. Do you know exactly where he's keeping the box? I doubt very much it's in plain sight on top of his desk."

Charlotte gave a negligent wave of her hand. "Men are boringly predictable when it comes to hiding their valuables. I shouldn't need more than a few seconds to locate it."

At half past nine that night, Alistair climbed out of his hired hackney four doors down from Miss Parnell's town house, as they had agreed.

A shadow detached itself from the shrubbery. In the

swaying light cast by the hackney's lantern, Miss Parnell stepped toward him. She wore a dark gray velvet dress and matching pelisse that absorbed what little light there was, and her black bonnet hid any hint of her blond curls. Her soft-soled shoes were silent on the cobblestones. "Good evening, sir."

"Good evening, miss," he said, glancing at the eavesdropping driver, and handed her into the coach. He shut the door and banged on the roof to give the signal to start. The coach rocked into motion, rattling Alistair's teeth as the poorly sprung vehicle bounced across every uneven cobblestone.

He rubbed his eyes. Had he really agreed to help his fake fiancée break into a gentleman's home?

Ah, but Toussaint was no gentleman, and Miss Parnell was determined to go through with her plan, with or without his help. He could not, in good conscience, allow her to undertake such a risk on her own. Nor did he have a snowball's chance in June of talking her out of it. She'd left him no choice but to assist.

And to be brutally honest, he could not quite quench the flutter of anticipation in his stomach, reminiscent of the thrill of finding and tracking the Great Comet five years before.

It was excitement, or he should have skipped the roast lamb at dinner.

He heaved a sigh. "You're certain you still want to go through with this?"

Miss Parnell responded by slipping her hand into his and giving it a slight squeeze. "Is this not the most marvelous feeling?"

He squeezed her fingers in return.

When they'd entered into their false betrothal, he hadn't considered how much they would touch each other. Her years on the Continent made her different from the other London lasses—bold in many respects, and very tactile. He'd noticed her reaction when he pretended to nuzzle her neck in the alley—more affected than she'd likely admit. Which seemed only fair, since the way she kept touching him was having an effect as well. If he wasn't careful, his enjoyment of their contact would endanger his bachelor status.

"The anticipation, the excitement. I've missed this." She squeezed his hand again. "You must be at your best, most observant and quick-witted, or the other party will gain the upper hand."

"I'm worried about the other party doing more than raising their hand. You're breaking into a man's home. Men tend to frown on that. They protect what's theirs."

"Oh, pish." Her other hand fluttered to rest on his knee.

Any other woman would do such only as part of a seduction attempt. Miss Parnell was simply conveying her excitement, he reminded himself.

"We will go through Toussaint's garden gate, and be in and out of his house in less than three minutes. The snuffbox will be mine, without Steven's assistance, and Lord Q will finally have to—"

"Lord who?"

Miss Parnell slipped her hand free of his. In an uncharacteristic show of discomfort, she cleared her throat and smoothed her skirts with both hands.

"Who is Lord Q?"

"He is the one who gives Steven his assignments." She let out a sigh. "Like most men of his generation, he believes women are best suited for looking pretty or giving birth. He has chosen to remain ignorant of my contributions to Steven's successful completion of his assignments. I intend to give the old goat irrefutable proof."

"So all this—this subterfuge—is just to prove an old gentleman wrong?"

"Of course not. It is vitally important that the snuffbox be returned to its rightful owner."

"And if you happen to benefit from being the person to retrieve said snuffbox, that is merely a delightful bonus."

"Nothing wrong with that, is there?" He heard the broad grin in her voice, even if he hadn't seen the flash of teeth.

Her excitement was contagious. They probably should reserve a room for him at Bedlam, but he found himself looking forward more and more to their adventure. The other night on the roof, he'd felt her need to *do* something, had felt it himself when he saw the snuffbox being stolen as they watched. Sometimes one had to stop observing and take action.

In the dimness of the carriage, Miss Parnell shifted on the bench seat. He missed her warmth at his side, but she had turned at an angle so their knees pressed intimately together. "I worked and trained with Steven for five long years. I know how to do this work. It's what I know best. It's what I *want* to do."

She rested her hand on his knee again. "You are at the beck and call of your father and grandfather, but eventually you will be free of their tether. Can you not understand why I want to have some measure of control over my own destiny? As a wife, I would be subject to my husband's will, even as I am now subject to my brother's will."

"And you think your path to freedom lies in working for Lord Q?"

"It's my only option." Her words were uttered with quiet conviction.

So, she'd misled him on at least one bit—she didn't plan to marry later, as she'd said, didn't intend to marry at all. With the tether that his grandfather and father kept him on, he did understand her dilemma. Working for Lord Q was her only hope at an independent life.

He folded her hand in both of his and gave her a reassuring squeeze. "Then tonight we will retrieve the snuffbox."

Her hand slid up his arm and to his cheek, and she leaned forward to drop a butterfly kiss on his jaw. "Thank you," she whispered against his neck.

Would she dare initiate such intimacies when they could see each other? Or was it only the darkness that made her so bold?

He inhaled the barest hint of her warm, rosewater scent, and felt the urge to gather her into his arms and discover just where she had applied the single dab of scent. Explore her lush curves.

The coach lurched to a halt, precluding any such explorations, or a test of his willpower.

Alistair climbed out and paid the driver. He turned to assist Miss Parnell, but she already stood on the sidewalk beside him. With a crack of the whip and jingle of the harness, the coach pulled away, and the two of them stood alone in the stark reality of the dark street.

Everything was the same as it had been this afternoon, yet looked different in the dark. Every shadow took on sinister overtones. He was aware of every sound, every echo. Even tracking the Great Comet hadn't stirred his pulse this way.

Doubts had plagued him all afternoon and into the evening, thoughts of all the things that could go terribly wrong. "Are you absolutely certain you want to go through with this?"

In answer, Miss Parnell tugged on his arm, heading toward the alley behind Toussaint's town house. He squelched his instinct to take the lead, understanding her need to do so. He stayed alert, ready to face whatever they encountered, do whatever necessary to keep her safe.

"I told you, we can't involve a third person, and we can't very well leave your gig and horse unattended. When we're done, all we need do is walk two blocks in that direction, and there will be any number of hackneys we can hail."

Alistair looked in the direction she pointed. True enough, traffic in the streets that way was still bustling, even at this hour, and likely would be until well after midnight. Three blocks in the opposite direction lay the waterfront, where the activity level depended on the tide, not the clock. He imagined he could even smell a hint of wet hemp and day-old fish wafting their way.

They hurried through the darkness, clinging to the

shadows down the alley. Miss Parnell paused as they reached the carriage house, her head cocked to one side as she listened. Alistair did the same, and heard nothing, not even horses in their stalls.

But of course—Toussaint would have been driven to the gaming hell, leaving the carriage house and stables empty.

She darted forward and tested the latch on the garden gate, which was locked from the inside. Before Alistair could even think to offer her a boost, she hitched up her skirts, found a foothold, and gracefully vaulted over the gate.

Once on the ground on the other side, she turned back to look at him, her eyes just visible over the top of the gate. *Coming?* She mouthed the word, keeping the silence they'd held since entering the alley.

With a glance back at the direction they'd come, he easily climbed up and over and dropped quietly to the ground beside her.

Rosebushes lined the graveled walk from the terrace door to the garden gate. Miss Parnell stayed on the grass, almost doubled over as she scurried toward the hulking black shadow of the town house. A sliver of light escaped from around the door leading down to the kitchen, but otherwise the house was shrouded in darkness.

Moments later, his heart pounding, Alistair pressed against the wall beside Miss Parnell, feeling the cold grit of the brick against his hands.

"You stay here, and whistle if anyone comes," she whispered.

"What are you—"

Before he could finish the sentence, Miss Parnell tucked the front of her skirts into the belt at her waist, revealing a pale strip of her thighs above her black stockings.

His breath hitched at the sudden, unexpected delight.

She would probably have slapped him, and rightfully so, had she noticed him staring, but she was intent on finding her first handhold and foothold on the rough brick wall, and then a second, and she kept climbing. She ignored the fragile-looking rose trellis and instead found handholds and footholds in the uneven brick.

His breath caught again, this time because her foot slipped. For an endless moment her leg swung in the air, far above the hard ground. He stretched up as though he could catch her. But she found another purchase and continued her ascent.

What seemed like hours later, she slithered over the balcony railing and disappeared from sight. Sweat pooled at the small of his back, and he was breathing as hard as if *he* had been the one climbing.

A rustling sound in the back of the garden caught his attention. He pressed his back against the wall and searched the shadows, straining his eyes and ears. Probably just a cat hunting its dinner.

Hunter and prey. Bad imagery to conjure up at the moment.

He squinted, hoping the excellent night vision that allowed him to see faint stars would enable him to separate the shadows in the hedge along the back fence.

Something larger moved. A dog, perhaps?

Up above, a candle flared to life.

"Run!" Miss Parnell's pale face appeared as she leaned over the balcony railing.

Like hell. He wasn't leaving her behind.

Something large and heavy fell from the sky, and hit the ground just a few feet away from Alistair. It turned out to be a man, who immediately got up with a guttural curse and ran toward the garden gate. Another man emerged from the shadows at the back of the garden, and the two got in each other's way as they both tried to climb over the gate at the same time.

Alistair looked up just in time to see Miss Parnell leap over the balcony railing and hit the ground with a grunt. She rolled over once and sprang to her feet. "Run, you daft man!" she called over her shoulder, already heading for the gate. Alistair sprinted after her.

"Thieves!" came the shout from a man stepping out onto the balcony. The candle he held aloft revealed his enormous nose. "Get back here!"

The first two men had just managed to clear the gate when Alistair bent down and boosted Miss Parnell over. A pistol barked. She yelped as she went over the top, and he heard a slight tearing sound. A torn dress was the least of their worries at the moment.

Hoping Toussaint didn't have a second pistol at hand, Alistair followed her over. He grabbed her arm to pull her to her feet, and they took off down the alley at a dead run. The other two men ran only a few yards ahead, their boots echoing loudly on the cobblestones. At the end of the alley they turned left, toward the busy streets.

Behind him, men shouted and cursed, and lit lanterns swung about wildly.

"This way!" Alistair tightened his grip on Miss Parnell's hand and tugged her to the right, heading in the opposite direction, hoping their pursuers would follow the much noisier pair.

She tried to keep up with his longer strides as they ran, one hand holding up her full skirts, the other securely in his grasp. When he judged their pursuers to be near the end of the alley, he pulled up short and hid behind one of the massive oak trees lining the square, shielding her between the tree and his body.

Two of the bobbing lanterns moved closer.

His lungs burning, Alistair tried to slow his harsh breathing. Miss Parnell buried her face against his chest, muffling the sound of her panting in his cravat. She hadn't cried out or complained. She hadn't even cursed at the disastrous turn of events, which was what worried him the most.

"This way, you fools!" Toussaint shouted, and the bobbing lanterns reversed direction.

Alistair risked a peek around the tree trunk, and saw four shadows heading after the first two men. "We'll give them a count of five to get a little farther away, and then take off again."

Miss Parnell nodded her assent, though she didn't lift her face or loosen her grip on his lapels.

The other men were now far enough away that Alistair could no longer make out their conversation, the light of their lanterns getting dimmer. "Let's go." Needing to keep hold of her in the darkness, he grabbed one of her hands, and they set off at a brisk, soundless walk. As soon as it was safe to do so, they would run, but now stealth was more important than speed. Once they had a safe distance separating them from the ruffians, he would let her rest. Find out what happened up on the balcony.

They encountered a rough patch of ground, and Miss Parnell grunted. Up until now she had been silent except for her labored breathing. Her grip on his hand was firm, almost painfully so at times.

Her continued lack of conversation was worrisome—he at least expected her to rail about her failure to secure the snuffbox. He remembered the report of the pistol, and his stomach clenched. Surely she'd have said something if she'd been hit. "Are you injured?" he whispered.

"'Tis nothing," she said, her voice tight. "Keep going."

After a few more blocks they turned another corner, with street lamps up ahead. Alistair headed straight toward them. She was noticeably limping now, but voiced no complaint or plea for a rest. She must have landed badly when he boosted her over the gate. Remembering her much shorter legs, he slowed his pace as much as he dared.

They drew a few stares from other pedestrians as they hurried past a brothel and a tavern, light and noise spilling from their doorways. Despite the cool night, perspiration beaded on her upper lip.

He halted under the street lamp at the intersection, as likely a place to catch a hackney as any, and whirled to face her, looking for any outward sign of injury. "What happened back there?"

Miss Parnell freed her hand from his and bent at the waist, resting her palms on her knees, and took deep breaths. "When I got up to the study, the fellow that broke into Melisande's room last night was already there, rifling through the desk. Toussaint came in with one of his henchmen, each of them holding a candle and a pistol."

Two men, each with a pistol. They could have easily fired a second shot. With better aim.

Muscles twitched in the center of his back. "How can you be sure it was the same man as last night? Melisande's room was dark. As was the alley tonight."

She straightened, hands now on her hips, though her chest still rose and fell with heavy breathing. Quite a lot of rising and falling, and he belatedly realized much of the movement was because she wasn't wearing stays. He forced his gaze upward.

From this angle, her bonnet's brim cast dark shadows upon the top half of her face, but the sweat on her upper lip glistened in the lamplight. "Same tobacco scent that kept blowing our way last night. Smelled it when he ran past me, almost knocked me over. Hoped he'd at least break his ankle when he hit the ground." Her breathing was still too harsh.

"Is yours broken?"

She held out her right foot, revealing a trim ankle, and rotated it. "See? I'm fine. Now all we need do is hail a hackney, and you can take me home. Tomorrow we'll figure out when to try again."

"Do that with your other foot."

With a sigh of impatience, she lifted her skirt and raised her left foot just high enough to rotate it before setting it down. She couldn't quite mask a groan of pain. "As I said, I'm fine."

Stubborn wench. "You're not fine, and this is no time

to play Twenty Questions. What is the nature of your injury?"

Color flared in her cheeks, but she kept her chin raised high. "If you must know, I think I may have bruised my . . . hip . . . when I went over the gate the second time."

Alistair winced. He'd thrown her too hard, given her too much of a boost. Though it was illogical, since he couldn't possibly see the bruise beneath all her clothing, he walked in a circle around her, needing to see that everything appeared normal.

Something glistened on the back of her skirt.

He tugged her closer to the street lamp and squatted down behind her, struggling to see details in her dark gray velvet skirt. There was a strip of white showing down near her knee, her shift visible through the tear he'd heard. More troubling was a narrow section of skirt in back that appeared black, from just below her hip to the middle of her thigh. Damn. He brushed his fingers against it, his gut twisting in dread.

She glared at him over her shoulder, fists on her hips. "Just what in blazes do you think you are doing?"

The warm, sticky dampness on his fingers made bile rise in his throat. He held out his hand, showing her the crimson stain.

"I believe you've been shot."

Chapter 10

"**O**h." The color that had risen in her cheeks suddenly disappeared.

Alistair straightened and fished his handkerchief out to wipe off his bloody hand. It couldn't be a life-threatening wound, since she was still standing there, seemingly debating if she should smack him for taking such liberty with her person. Seeing how pale she'd gone, he wrapped one arm around her shoulders.

"Fancy that." Her voice was a breathy wisp.

He was prepared for her to faint, or to shriek, or any number of typical reactions when one has been shot. He was not prepared for her matter-of-fact, "Well, I hope a hackney comes along soon."

"That's all you have to say?"

She huffed out a breath. "What would you have me say?"

He blinked. "Are you in pain?"

"Considerably more so than I was, now that you've so helpfully pointed out that it's not a bruise."

He glanced down at her backside again. The dark stain was getting bigger. "You're still bleeding."

"And here I thought I was just feeling a cold draft from the tear in my skirt."

He quickly folded his handkerchief. Since he couldn't see the actual wound, he let gravity be his guide, and pressed the handkerchief near the bottom edge of the bloodstain.

"What are you doing?" She spoke slowly, her voice low, the same tone one would use to depress the intentions of an encroaching toady.

He followed her gaze to his hand, cupping the left side of her derriere. "Trying to stop the bleeding."

"Oh. That is probably a good idea." She nodded, and almost lost her balance.

Alistair tightened his grip around her with his free arm, taking more of her weight. "We need bandages. I can feel it soaking through already. And we need to get you off your feet, lying down. Quickly."

She twisted, trying to see behind her. "I can't go home like this. If Steven were to find out, I would never hear the end of it."

The brothel they'd passed would have beds. He shuddered at the thought of taking her in there.

From a few blocks away came the repeated clanging of ships' bells, announcing the time. Eight bells. Midnight.

Ships. Or at least one ship in particular. Nick should

have arrived on last night's or this morning's tide. Which way to get to his ship's berth?

Miss Parnell looked up at him. "I have an idea."

Alistair raised his eyebrows in a silent question.

"I know someone who may be nearby, with bandages, who would not ask any questions."

"In slip number seventy-three?" He hid his smile at her shocked expression. "Can you walk, or shall I carry you?"

"Yes—ouch—I can still walk."

He watched her take a few halting steps, her jaw clenched, her chest heaving from the effort. Now that the urgent need to flee had eased, her body was protesting the insult of the injury.

He tossed the blood-soaked handkerchief into the gutter, swept her up in his arms, and strode for the docks.

"Put me down." She pushed against his chest.

"Speed is more important at the moment than your independence." He wished he could see her face, hidden beneath her bonnet's brim.

"I only needed a few more steps to work out the stiffness, that's all. This is entirely unnecessary."

He paused to shift her to a more comfortable position, the warm weight of her soft, curvy body against his chest, and resumed walking. "Just put your arm around my neck and enjoy the ride."

Still she resisted.

"You are in danger of pouting, Miss Parnell." He'd enjoyed their closeness last night up on the roof, his arm wrapped around her while she was tucked inside his coat, and hoped for an opportunity to repeat the experience.

This wasn't what he had in mind, but he might as well make the best of a bad situation. "It's not like you've never been in this position before."

She drew breath to protest.

"Three nights ago? Hotel balcony?"

Several strides later she heaved a great sigh and wrapped her arm around his neck. Her warm scent of rosewater wafted up. Did she realize she was running her fingers through the hair at his nape? He'd kiss her, if her bonnet wasn't in the way.

"At least my skirts aren't bunched in my lap this time," she muttered into his cravat.

"No, this is much more decorous." Though there was still a chance they might encounter his father again, even in this seedy neighborhood.

A prostitute with her customer barely spared them a glance, but two sailors seemed intent on mischief until Alistair scowled at them.

He kept walking. Miss Parnell rested her head against his shoulder, which was pleasant and made it easier for him to see where he was going, but she'd stopped talking, which was worrisome.

He turned a corner, and ships stretched out on the riverfront as far as the eye could see, disappearing into the darkness, the skeletons of their masts raised toward the stars.

"Not far now." His breathing was more labored, but he had no intention of letting her down. He kept walking.

She patted his chest, her hand sliding under the folds of his cravat and staying there. "Your heart is beating so fast."

"It would be easier to carry you slung over my shoulder, but I thought you might object to that."

She giggled. "I 'preciate your concern."

His stomach knotted at her uncharacteristic response. He walked faster.

They passed hulking shadows looming in the darkness, one dock after another, progress toward their goal agonizingly slow. Perhaps they'd have been better off hailing a hackney and taking her home after all.

At last he recognized the hull a few slips down, and realized they were only a few yards shy of their goal. Thank heavens.

"Ahoy, *Wind Dancer*," Alistair shouted when they reached the brig's mooring ropes. Miss Parnell lifted her head from his shoulder.

Several faces appeared over the railing. "Who goes there?" one called.

"Jonesy, is the captain aboard?"

The first mate held his lantern high. Alistair stepped forward into the weak circle of light it cast. Miss Parnell shielded her eyes.

"Aye, my lord, that he is." Jonesy turned his head and passed instructions to another crewman.

Miss Parnell pushed at Alistair's chest. "Let me down. I just needed to rest a few minutes."

Reluctantly, he set her on her feet, holding his arms out to either side to catch her should she stumble, like a day-old foal. She swayed but steadied herself with a hand against his shoulder.

Nick's tall bulk appeared at the railing. "What's amiss?"

"Nicky!" Miss Parnell called out.

Alistair looked down in surprise. Only Nick's sisters got away with calling him by that pet name, and they usually received a growl in response.

"Charlie? That you?" He motioned his first mate over. "Hell's bells," Nick muttered. "Lower the gang board!"

She wobbled for a step or two, but limped up the board as soon as it was secure. Nick met her at the gangway and swept her up in a hug that lifted her right off her feet.

Alistair tamped down a sudden flare of jealousy. He'd known that Nick and Steven were acquainted, so it stood to reason that Miss Parnell was also acquainted with his roguish friend. But just how well were they acquainted? They were still unabashedly embracing, in full view of the crew. To make matters worse, Jonesy and a few other crew members had gathered close, offering words of welcome and pats to her shoulder.

Just as Alistair was ready to throttle his friend, Nick set Miss Parnell back on her feet and held her at arm's length, and the crew stepped back.

"What're you doing here, Charlie? Where's Steven? What's wrong?"

"Nice to see you, too, Nick," Alistair muttered.

Nick finally looked beyond Miss Parnell. "What the devil?"

Alistair caught Miss Parnell's gaze. "For someone who wouldn't ask questions, he's certainly got a lot of them."

She rested one hand on the railing for support. "Much as I've missed you, Nicky, I need your help."

"That much I'd guessed, lass." He ran a hand through his black hair. "What do you need? Money? Transportation? An alibi?"

Alistair shook his head. "Bandages. Brandy. And some privacy." He pointed at Miss Parnell with his chin.

"Charlie?" Nick swept her with his gaze, and walked in a tight circle around her. "What have you got yourself into this time?"

"'Tis just a scratch."

He gestured for Jonesy to hold the lantern closer, and Nick touched her skirt in back. "That's a bloody big scratch on your a—"

"A scratch that's still bleeding." Alistair strode forward. "Can we go below already?"

Nick held out his arm to assist her, but Alistair picked her up again and strode for the aft hatchway, Miss Parnell voicing a protest the whole way.

He set her on her feet inside the captain's cabin, but kept an arm around her to steady her.

Nick quickly lit the lantern over the table in the center of the small space. "We dropped Norton off at Southampton this morning on our way in so he could visit his mum, but I can send one of the crew to fetch another surgeon."

Miss Parnell shook her hand. "A surgeon won't be necessary. I'm sure it's just a scratch. I can take care of it myself, given some bandages and a little privacy."

Nick harrumphed. "Well, I'll at least send someone to fetch Steven. Is he at home?"

"No! I mean, that won't be necessary, either. No need

to bother him. And he's not home, so don't send anyone—you'll just frighten Aunt Hermione."

Nick narrowed his eyes, and Alistair kept his mouth shut.

Jonesy arrived seconds later, carrying cloth bundles and a basin of steaming water. "Bandages and a sewing kit, Cap'n."

Another crewman arrived with lengths of fabric, and more men filled the narrow passageway behind, trying to catch a glimpse of the proceedings. Nick ushered in the men with supplies and slid the door shut on the gawkers.

Alistair swept his gaze over the cabin, which was dominated by a bunk, a drop-leaf desk, and two chairs set at the table in the center. Five people in the cramped quarters seemed three too many.

Nick took the cloths and shook them out, revealing a silk dressing gown in scarlet and another in sky blue. He held them up to Miss Parnell. "Too long," he said, and tossed the red one back to Jonesy. "Blue's always been your color, sweetings," he said, draping it over her shoulder. "All right, everyone out. Hand me your dress when you get it off, Charlie, and Jonesy will work his magic on the bloodstains."

Alistair pointed at the silk draped over the first mate's shoulder. "Dare I ask how you came to possess such feminine attire on board?"

"Not in front of the children." Nick clapped his hands over the ears of a crewman who looked old enough to be his father and pushed him out the door. He gestured for Jonesy to step out, then followed.

Alistair was the last to leave. "Do you need any help?" he asked.

Miss Parnell untied her bonnet and tossed it on the table. "I'm sure I can manage just fine, thank you."

"I'll wait out in the hall, then." He pointed over his shoulder. "Call if you need anything. Anything at all."

She made shooing motions.

Reluctantly, he shut the door.

Nick glanced around to make sure they were alone in the passageway, and slapped his hand on Alistair's shoulder. "So, how did Charlie get the scratch?"

It was not his place to divulge any of her secrets. "We were unwanted guests at an impromptu gathering." He leaned closer to the cabin door, listening for any sounds of movement. Or distress.

Nick nodded, and stroked his gold earring. Before he could continue to ask awkward questions, they heard a muffled thud from inside the cabin and a not-so-muffled curse in a foreign language. Nick cocked his head, listening. "Portuguese. That's my girl," he said with obvious pride. "Taught her that one myself."

"*Your* girl?"

"Oh, don't get your drawers in a twist." He gave Alistair a considering stare. "Just what are you doing with Charlie?"

Nick would find out soon enough anyway. "We are betrothed."

"You? And Charlie?" He glanced between Alistair and the closed door. "I didn't know you two had even met."

Another thud came from inside the cabin. Alistair waited a few seconds but heard no curse.

He opened the door a crack and poked his nose in. Miss Parnell was on the floor in a puddle of gray velvet, not so much as a single blond curl visible amidst the tangle of fabric.

"Do you require assistance?"

"Apparently," came the disgusted reply.

He stepped in, shut the door in Nick's face, and tried to find an edge of the fabric. He found what seemed to be the bottom of the skirt and tugged upward.

"Stop! My hair's caught on the buttons."

"Forgive me. I've never acted as a lady's maid before." Alistair knelt beside her. First he had to find her hair amidst the mass of velvet, then work the silky strands free of the buttons. Almost a quarter of her skirt was damp with blood, making the already heavy fabric especially weighty. He heaved the mess toward the door, where it landed with a soggy *thwap*.

Once freed, Miss Parnell tried to sit up, but grimaced in pain and went back to lying on her side, arms wrapped around her drawn-up knees. Her hair was a tangled mess, nothing of her neat chignon remaining, with curls spilling about her shoulders in a golden cloud. She had kicked off her shoes, leaving her covered only by her black stockings and once-white shift. The crimson stain spread obscenely from her left hip down to the back of her knee.

Presented with unmistakable evidence of his failure to protect her, Alistair sucked in a steadying breath. "The shift has to come off, too."

"I know." Her voice was tight with pain and embarrassment.

He rubbed his hands together and tried for a brusque

tone, hoping that would ease her discomfiture. "Right, then. Sooner begun, sooner we're done." He pulled the blankets down to the foot of the bunk and turned back the sheets. Once more he knelt beside Miss Parnell. "Relax, and let me do all the work."

She nodded.

He grasped her under the arms and carried her to the bunk, setting her on her feet where she could lean against the wall for support, her back to him. "I'm going to pull your shift over your head, and then while you get into the bunk facedown, I'll get the bandages and such. All right?"

Her face went even paler than before, and she was biting her bottom lip.

He rested his hands on her shoulders, gave her upper arms a reassuring squeeze, and leaned close to whisper. "I'd promise not to peek, but it would make things even more awkward if I can't see what I'm doing."

She didn't laugh at his jest, but at least looked a little less grim. "Just hurry up and do it already."

"Your wish is my command."

It was only as he bent down to grasp the bottom hem of her shift did he remember she was not wearing stays. Once he removed her shift, nothing would hide her from his gaze. Nothing but her stockings, which offered little protection for her modesty.

Waiting was only going to make it more difficult. For both of them.

He swallowed hard, grabbed the bottom hem, and tugged it up and over her head.

He tried not to look at her intriguing freckles, sprinkled across her shoulders, back, legs, and other areas no man should see before her wedding night.

He balled up the shift and tossed it onto the dress, and turned his back to retrieve the bundle of bandages from the table. He waited a few seconds after he heard the creak of wood as she got on the bunk, to give her a chance to settle, before dropping to his knees beside the bunk.

Crimson smears stained the creamy skin of her back, across her backside, and spread in a rivulet down her left thigh. Some of the blood had already dried, while more oozed from the torn flesh, a deep gash as long as his index finger running at a forty-five degree angle, halfway down her left cheek.

He'd had only one task to perform tonight, to protect her. He clenched his fists.

He forced a cheery tone into his voice. "Well, the good news is, the bullet grazed you. We don't have to dig it out."

"Thank God for small mercies." Her voice was muffled by the pillow that she grasped with both arms. Gooseflesh had risen on her skin, and there was a fine tremor shaking her body that had nothing to do with embarrassment.

He needed to hurry, get her covered, get her warm. But he'd never personally tended to anything worse than a nosebleed or a cut from shaving himself. What to do first?

Warm. Covered up. Right.

He wrung out a cloth in the hot water and washed her with one hand, immediately drying her with a towel in the other. He draped the blue dressing gown over her back as soon as it was clean, doing his damnedest not to linger over her smooth, soft skin.

Blood had dripped onto her left stocking, so he untied the garter and slid her stocking down her shapely calf and off her delicate foot. It seemed almost sacrilegious to wad up the black silk, but it was the only way to toss it onto the pile of velvet and cotton near the door.

With the blood cleaned off her thigh, he arranged the sheet to cover her legs and right side and then adjusted the dressing down, so her only exposed flesh was the wound itself and immediately around it, an area smaller than the palm of his hand. He pressed a clean cloth to it, to stop the bleeding, which had already slowed considerably.

Miss Parnell had remained quiet while he worked, her eyes closed as though she wasn't in a mortifying situation if she couldn't see it, but now she looked at him over her silk-covered shoulder. "Thank you."

A hundred replies raced through his mind, from the serious to the sublime. "Your freckles are safe with me," he finally said.

That must have been the correct response, as she gave a tiny answering smile.

The cabin door slid open and Nick entered, neatly stepping over the pile of clothing without jostling the tray he carried. "Candied plums, brandy, cheese and bread." He set the tray on the table and lit the lanterns in the gimbals beside his desk and the bunk, tripling the light in the small cabin. "Get her to eat something sweet first, then a little cheese and bread."

"*She* can hear you just fine," Miss Parnell ground out.

"No need to speak about her in the third person. And I don't want any sweets."

"You were shaking and you're still pale, Charlie. Trust me, you need to eat." He poured a small glass of brandy and held it up in one hand, a brown bottle and spoon in the other. "Pick your poison. Laudanum or brandy?"

"Is that the good stuff, or rotgut?"

Nick looked affronted. "My best brandy, smuggled straight from France."

She gave a resigned nod. "That should help ease the sting."

Nick knelt on the floor at the head of the bunk with the glass. "Here you go, drink up."

Alistair picked through the medical supplies while Miss Parnell downed a few swallows of brandy.

She coughed and pushed the glass away. "No more."

Nick shrugged and tossed back the rest of the glass. Alistair considered asking for a shot for himself, but he needed to keep his head clear and his wits about him. Nick refilled the glass and brought it to him.

"No, thank you."

"It's not for you, you dolt." Nick pointed at the open wound, where Alistair still had his hand pressed. "That would be an especially nasty place to develop an infection. Have to make sure it's clean." He knelt beside Alistair and peeled back the bloody cloth, seemingly unperturbed by the deep gash marring her perfect skin. "Afraid it needs stitches, Charlie."

Miss Parnell groaned.

"I'll just get—"

"You're not going to touch me, Nicky."

"What? Why not?"

She stared at Alistair. "Can you do the stitches?"

He gulped. "I made do without a valet while at school, and sewed on my own buttons."

"Close enough. Please get on with it. I'm still cold."

He nodded, and held a needle to the lantern flame.

"Really, Charlie, you know I've had a lot more experience at stitching up flesh than Alistair here."

"Yes, I do know. I've seen the jagged scar on Steven's arm. Pardon me for not wanting similar handiwork on my arse."

Nick harrumphed and folded his arms.

Alistair threaded the needle.

"That's not fair. We were at sea during a storm. I can't help it if the ship was being tossed about on the waves. Would you rather he'd bled to death?"

"Steven loves his scars. Thinks they're very manly." She turned back to Alistair. "Are your buttons neat?"

Wordlessly, he removed his coat and held it out for her inspection, featuring the section where he'd sewn three buttons back on.

"Divine. Get out, Nicky."

"But—"

"I love you dearly, Nicky, but if you don't get out right now, I may have to hurt you."

He sputtered one more protest.

Alistair rolled up his shirtsleeves. "You heard the lady. Go."

"I still have my knife, Nicky."

He heaved a long-suffering sigh. "I suppose having

your fiancé do this is best." Nick scooped up the soiled clothing, but lingered near the door.

Alistair was ready to reach for Miss Parnell's knife himself. "Will you leave already?" He needed to get this over with before he lost his nerve, or did something unforgivable.

Nick stepped out but stuck his head back in. "Make sure she eats something before you let her pass out," he said before closing the door.

As if Alistair had any control over what she did.

"Finally." She turned her gaze back on him. "One more thing before you use the needle." She licked her bottom lip. "I think I need a little more Dutch courage."

"Of course, Miss Parnell." Alistair refilled the brandy glass and brought it to her. "Anything else?"

"Formality seems a bit silly under the circumstances. You should probably call me Charlotte."

"Not Charlie?"

"I'm going to strangle the next person who calls me Charlie."

He smiled. "Then we have much in common, since I have often felt the urge to strangle Nick." He helped her rise up so she could drink. "You should address me as Alistair, then."

She coughed, but didn't let him take away the glass until she had downed all the brandy in it. "I'm ready, Alistair. Let's get this over with."

He made sure he had all the supplies close at hand. Looking at the assortment of instruments and bandages and powders reminded him of two years ago, when a surgeon had treated his father after a duel. Intrigued by the science of treating the wound, a gash on the arm from a pistol ball, Alistair had bombarded the surgeon with questions. He'd never expected to actually put the knowledge into practice.

He worked as quickly and smoothly as he could. His stomach clenched in sympathetic pain with every strained gasp and muffled yelp, but Charlotte did not ask him to stop. Nor did she ease her white-knuckled grip on the pillow.

By the time he finished, her face was as white as the pillowcase, her breathing ragged. His wasn't much smoother. He pressed a square of folded cloth over the neat row of ten stitches, a long strip of cotton in his other hand, and pondered how best to apply it.

"I need you to rise up a little so I can wrap this around you." He guided her with his hands on her hips, and did his best not to let his touch on her silky skin cross over to a caress. With enough clearance between her and the mattress to slide his hand beneath her, he wrapped the strip around her twice to hold the bandage in place and tied it off. She slumped down to the mattress, shaking and pale.

"The worst is over, Charlotte." He draped the dressing gown down the length of her back and helped her work her arms into the sleeves.

"For tonight, at any rate."

"How's that?"

She pushed up to her knees, closed the gown around herself and tied the sash with shaking hands. "For the next fortnight at least, every time I try to sit down, I will be forcibly reminded of my failure tonight." She gave a slow shake of her head.

"A setback, certainly, but not a failure." *He* was the only one who had failed tonight.

She put her hands on her hips. "How do you figure that? Not only did I not get the snuffbox, I'm no longer certain who does possess it. Did the smoking man find it before Toussaint interrupted him, or is it still hidden in Toussaint's study?"

He rested his hands on his hips. "A sword is not a sword until it's been tempered in fire."

"Fire, eh? Well, I've certainly been branded." She held her hand out, and he grasped her icy fingers, helping her slide off the bunk until she stood beside him on unsteady legs. She let go of his hand to wrap her arms around herself, shivering.

Alistair hurried to drape his coat over her shoulders. "Nick was right. You need to eat something."

"N-Not hungry. Where's a roaring f-fire when you need one?"

"Three bites. You eat three bites, and I'll find more blankets."

She picked up one of the candied plums from the dish on the table and stared at it. "I usually try to avoid sweets. I'm stout enough as it is."

Alistair paused in the act of rifling through the chest at the foot of the bunk. Though he had no siblings of his own, he was well acquainted with Nick's five sisters and their constant concern about their figures. He shook out the blanket and closed the chest lid.

"At the risk of being ungentlemanly, I remind you that I have seen your figure. Quite recently, and at close range, in fact." He removed his coat from her shoulders and draped the blanket around her instead. He drew the edges together in front, over her chest, and tilted her chin up. He waited until her gaze rose to meet his. "So you can be assured that I speak with some authority when I say that your figure is lovely and perfectly proportioned just the way it is."

Her rosebud mouth formed a silent *Oh*.

He wanted to lean in and kiss her. He went so far as to raise his hand to cup her downy soft cheek, but slid his fingers through her shimmering hair instead, taming the wild sun-kissed curls, removing the last of the hairpins. Her eyes closed and she stayed perfectly still, almost purring, letting him smooth tendrils back from her face, the curls tumbling down her back, sliding across the silk dressing gown.

At last, her hair danced around her shoulders, just as he'd envisioned when they sat in the dappled shade of the elm tree in the corner of the garden, the first day they'd entered into their agreement.

Had that been only two days ago? Now he couldn't imagine his life without Miss Parnell in it.

He wrapped his fingers around her wrist and guided her hand to her temptingly curved mouth, until the sugared plum pressed against her parted lips and her eyes flew open. "Eat, Charlotte."

She obediently popped the plum in and chewed. Her eyes widened. "This is good." She reached for another, and Alistair selected one for himself.

"Bread and cheese, too. Don't forget." He sliced the cheese into smaller, bite-size pieces and fed one to her.

She accepted it without comment, though she looked vaguely surprised.

Alistair was rather surprised himself. He'd never before felt the inclination to feed somebody else, but now it seemed the most natural thing to do. He fed her another piece, and allowed his thumb to linger on her full lower lip.

The tip of her moist pink tongue darted out and touched his thumb before retreating.

He cleared his throat. "Good, that's three bites. Do you want any more? Food, that is."

She graced him with a crooked smile. "Actually, I'm famished. I was too excited to eat much at dinner."

Alistair pulled out a chair from the table. "Then you should sit down and—" He briefly squeezed his eyes shut. "Sorry." He sliced off some chunks of bread, arranged them within easy reach of the cheese and plums, and refilled the brandy glass. "You *stand* here and eat, and I will clean things up."

He gathered the soiled linen and other supplies he'd used in dressing her wound and set them on the floor by the door.

The bloody water sloshing in the basin and the bloodstained cloths mocked him. If he'd gone over the gate first, it would have been him injured instead of Charlotte. It *should* have been him. He should have been able to protect her. That was the whole purpose for him coming along tonight.

He'd failed her, utterly.

She clutched the blanket closed with one hand. The

hand she ate with shook, and the edges of the blanket danced from her constant trembling.

He stepped up behind her and wrapped her in his embrace, rubbing her arms through the blanket. "Getting any warmer?"

She leaned her head back onto his shoulder and graced him with a tipsy smile. The brandy glass was empty again. Since she'd had the first two glasses on an empty stomach, she was likely well on her way to being foxed.

Probably just as well, though he'd rather she didn't have to deal with a hangover in the morning, on top of her injury.

"There's no fire, so I suppose you'll have to do." She spun in his embrace, wrapped her arms around his waist, and rested her cheek against his chest. "Mmm, much better." She burrowed closer.

He ran his arms up and down her back, still feeling the tiny tremors wracking her body. "You should lie down, bundle up with more blankets."

She shook her head. "Bed's cold. You're warm." She splayed her hands against his back and pressed her body tight against his.

He tried not to inhale her enchanting rosewater scent, tried not to think about her ripe curves pressed against his hard planes. Especially now that he didn't have to imagine what those curves looked like, or even felt like. Under ideal circumstances he'd have been in no hurry to cover up her smooth-as-satin skin, would have traced the freckles with his fingers, and had her gasping from laughter, moaning in pleasure.

He squeezed his eyes shut. Logic was the way to go.

"Your bare foot will be warmer tucked between the blankets than standing on the cold wooden decking." At the very least, he should successfully protect her from catching a chill.

"Mmm, per'aps you're right." She eased her grip on him, took a step toward the bunk, and swayed.

Alistair caught her before she could fall.

She giggled. "I think I should have eaten *before* drinking the brandy." A hiccup escaped, which made her laugh again.

"Definitely time for you to lie down." He guided her to the bunk and helped her settle on her uninjured right side, and tucked the blankets around her.

As he drew back, she caught his cravat and tugged him close again. "You're a gen'leman, right? So I can trust you not to take advantage of me."

He'd have been insulted she even had to ask were it not for his baser instincts clamoring to be let out. "Of course."

"Good. Climb in." She patted the mattress beside her.

Chapter 11

This must be how Adam felt when Eve offered him that damned apple. "I really don't think that's appropriate." Alistair had everything under control, but only because he was no longer in physical contact with Charlotte.

"We passed 'appropriate' when you had your hands on my bare arse." She patted the mattress again. "Please. I'm cold."

He could no more deny those guileless blue eyes than stop breathing. But get in bed with her?

He was a gentleman. Not a scoundrel with the self-restraint of a two-year-old, like his father. He could keep his baser instincts in check. "Let me just take off my shoes."

He slipped them off and then padded in his stocking feet to the lantern over the table and blew it out. He extinguished the lantern by the bunk, too, leaving just the one lit over by the desk. Lamps out on the wharf were now visible through the window, and cast shadows across the cabin. After a glance down at his silk waistcoat, he took it off and hung it over the chair back, on top of his coat. With another moment's consideration, he untied his cravat and added it to the collection of his clothing.

"You're stalling."

Her quiet accusation struck him to the quick. He slowly turned to face her. "Generally, when a man contemplates getting into bed with a woman, it is under different circumstances than this, with a very different intent."

"But I'm cold." She held the blanket to her chin. "I need you."

When was the last time the independent Miss Parnell had uttered those three words to anyone? He slid into the bunk beside her.

He arranged the blankets to cover them both on the narrow mattress that was never intended to sleep two, and stiffly lay on his back. "Have enough room?"

"You're too far away. C'mere." She wrapped her arm around his waist and tugged him closer. Once he'd complied, she pushed his arm out of the way so she could snuggle against his side, tucked her icy feet against legs, and rested her cheek on his chest.

Silence reigned in the semi-dark cabin, broken only by the distant call of a night watchman or a clanging ship's bell.

"Your heart is beating faster than a galloping horse."

"No," he lied, "that's yours you hear pounding. Mine

is as steady as if I'd stayed home and read improving sermons all evening."

She giggled, and he felt the tremor all the way down to his knees. Cautiously, he wrapped his arms around her, trying to share the warmth of his body and nothing else.

"Mmm." She burrowed even closer and tightened her arm around his waist.

She was injured, cold, and under the influence of pain and brandy. He should not be tempted.

Try telling that to certain parts of his anatomy.

She had nubile curves that begged to be explored, soft and rounded in all the right places, and a mouth made for kissing.

He stroked her hair, smoothing the silken strands from the top of her head down her back. Her hair ended just below her shoulders, and the wool blanket wasn't nearly as soft against his fingertips, but he kept stroking, all the way down to her waist. And stopped there.

That should be safe.

"That's nice."

He kissed the top of her head. "Try to sleep."

"You'll still be here with me when I wake up?"

He patted her back. Definitely not a caress. "Not going anywhere."

Soon she stopped trembling. Her iron grip on his waist slackened and her breathing evened out.

What a night of firsts. First time he'd treated a bullet wound.

First time he'd spent the night with a woman in his arms without making love to her.

First time he'd seen Charlotte's naked body, and heard her pant and moan. For all the wrong reasons.

First time he'd ever been on a spy mission, for that was most certainly what Charlotte had been on tonight.

She hadn't stated it so bluntly, but she had apparently been working as one with her brother. For years.

By accompanying Charlotte, he had acted as a spy as well.

He didn't feel like a spy. He certainly bore no resemblance to what he expected of a spy. Weren't they roguish-looking fellows, almost but not quite fitting in with polite Society? Like Nick or Blakeney, or the two men who'd also been after the snuffbox before Nigel stole it from them. Who were they working for? He'd have to discuss that with Charlotte when she woke up and her head cleared.

Then again, Charlotte didn't look like a spy, either.

But the war was over. There wasn't any real spying to be done anymore, was there? The assignment given to Steven, which Charlotte wanted to complete on her own, was nothing more than restoring a stolen object to its rightful owner.

It was retrieval, not espionage.

But how often was a pistol fired in a simple retrieval operation? He heard again the sharp report of the pistol, the grunt of pain when Charlotte had been hit. How she had bravely said nothing, though it must have hurt like the devil.

But she was safe now, asleep in his arms. He'd failed to keep her safe in Toussaint's garden. He wouldn't fail her now. He'd stopped the bleeding, and she was no longer chilled.

He must have dozed off, for the next thing he knew, Nick was leaning over him. Silent, unmoving. Unnerving.

"What?" Alistair whispered.

"How is she?" Nick whispered back, his brow furrowed.

Alistair shifted his arms just enough to check that he could still do so. He didn't move any farther, not wanting to disturb his living, breathing, Charlotte blanket. Yes, she was still breathing, still warm. He opened his mouth to reply.

"She's sleeping," came her muffled voice from the vicinity of his chest. "Go 'way."

"Ungrateful wench." Nick gave a broad grin with his softly spoken words. "Kick a man out of his own cabin, force him to sleep in a hammock among the riffraff crew, and—"

"Bugger off."

Alistair nodded. "What she said."

Nick pulled the blankets up to Charlotte's chin and tucked them around her. "I'm going now, but only so that you'll name me as godfather to your first child." Nick picked up the detritus by the door and left them in peace again.

Alistair's thoughts raced, even as Charlotte's breathing slowed, indicating she had already slipped back into sleep.

Their first child?

The very idea ought to terrify him. Their engagement was a sham, just a cover to enable the spy to do her work, and for his father and grandfather to leave him out of their feud and let him continue his astronomical observations in peace. But he'd done precious little of his own work since he'd begun helping Charlotte with hers.

She was close to attaining her goal. As soon as she retrieved the snuffbox, they could end their fake engagement and part ways.

Alistair tightened his arms around her. He didn't want to let her go. Not now, not in the morning, and certainly not once she had the snuffbox.

He didn't want their engagement to be a fake. The only satisfactory ending to their betrothal would be their marriage.

At some point during this crazy day and night, his feelings had shifted from being intrigued, amused by, and attracted to the curvy blonde, to something much deeper, less transitory. Something permanent.

She murmured in her sleep.

"You're safe, I've got you." He kissed the top of her head again. "And I'm not letting you go."

She snuggled more securely into his embrace and was still.

Her eyes still closed, Charlotte awoke to a rumbling beneath her ear. A snore.

A very quiet snore, to be sure, hardly more than loud breathing, but definitely a masculine snore.

And the reason she heard it so clearly was because she was lying atop the snoring man, her ear pressed against his chest. Not just lying next to or beside him, but directly on top of him.

Such a position yielded quite different sensations from that of dancing with a man, even waltzing. His heart beat steadily beneath her ear. His arms wrapped snugly around her, enveloping her in a cocoon of warmth and security. The fine wool of his breeches and stockings brushed against her bare legs. Bare?

She slid one leg to the side, with the intent of sliding off him before he awoke, and gasped at the sudden pain in her backside. She froze, and the pain eased.

Then again, perhaps she'd just stay right where she was. Her companion tightened his hold around her and murmured in his sleep. She gulped.

Good heavens, had she drooled on him?

Her eyes flew open. Daylight streamed through the small window in Nick's cabin.

She was aboard the *Wind Dancer.*

Lying on top of Viscount Moncreiffe.

Memories of everything that happened the previous night came crowding back, and her cheeks flooded with heat. Mortifying. Last night had been utterly mortifying. Not to mention painful.

Instead of a simple in-and-out excursion to collect the snuffbox, she'd shown herself to be incompetent, bested by Toussaint *and* the two smoking men. Nick and Moncreiffe had had to come to her aid as though she were a weak damsel in distress. And in so doing, she'd been laid bare before his gaze. Literally.

It was just a body. Everyone had one. It shouldn't bother her that Moncreiffe had seen more of her flesh than even her current maid had. No stays to hold up her bosom, no empire gown to hide her thick waist, and most humiliating of all was that he'd had to clean and stitch the wound on her bottom.

Oh, and how delightful, they were to be informal and address each other by first name now.

Nobody had actually fired a pistol, she'd so blithely said when he expressed his concern the other night. Her words had came back to literally bite her on the a—

The snoring stopped. His arms relaxed a bit. Should she move now?

There was a knock on the cabin door. "I'm coming in," Nick announced.

She should sit up. She should not be seen like this, in such a compromising position.

As if sensing her intent, Alistair tightened his arms around her again. She pulled the blanket up over her head.

Nick slid the door open and poked his head in, his eyes closed. "Are you both decent?"

"Nothing to see, Nick." Still thick with sleep, Alistair's voice was a rich rumble in Charlotte's ear.

Though the blanket covered her, she still needed to breathe, and was forced to pull the blanket back just the tiniest bit.

Nick tilted his head to stare at Charlotte, whose cheek was still pillowed on Alistair's chest, until she felt like shouting *What?* at him. Most disturbing was that she couldn't read his expression. He knew that nothing untoward had happened last night between her and Alistair, despite current appearances to the contrary. Didn't he?

"I let you snooze as long as I dared. The tide and wind have shifted, and I can't wait any longer or it will take us three days to get out to the Channel. You have ten minutes to disembark, or stay on board for the trip to Dorset."

"I hear Dorset is nice this time of year."

Charlotte drew breath to protest.

Alistair patted her back. "Kidding."

Nick draped her clothing over the back of a chair. "Your dress is still warm from hanging before the galley fire. Might be a bit damp in some places yet, but the shift is dry. Jonesy managed to get the blood out, and Tucker stitched it up all nice and neat."

"Not to be ungrateful, but he didn't use the same supplies he uses for repairing the sails, did he?"

"The thread came from the same source as the dressing gown you're wearing. Trust me, even your maid will have a hard time spotting the repairs."

"Thank you."

"You can thank Tucker. All I did was spend the night in a hammock. Again." He pulled out his pocket watch. "Nine minutes." He shut the door with a thump.

Alistair pushed the blanket down to her shoulders. "I'd forgotten how grumpy he can be in the morning."

"Me, too." She could delay the inevitable no longer. She lifted her head and found Alistair looking at her with narrowed eyes.

"You know what Nick is like in the morning?"

"Well, of course. Sometimes it would take a week or more to get where we were going." If she had a suspicious nature, she might have thought Alistair was jealous.

"How's your head?"

She blinked. "My head?" The place where she'd been shot was considerably farther south.

"You drank brandy on an empty stomach last night." He rubbed one hand up and down her back, reminding her that only a thin layer of silk separated her skin from his.

She had trouble concentrating on his words. His light brown hair was tousled as though she'd run her fingers through it, and stubble darkened his jaw. The top three buttons of his shirt had come undone, letting her glimpse the hollow of his throat and the top of his chest. Did his skin feel as smooth as it looked? She watched in fascination as his throat worked when he spoke.

"Do you feel any ill aftereffects?"

She took a moment to take stock. Aside from a sharp twinge of pain when she tried to move her left side, she felt as refreshed as if she'd spent the night in her own bed. "Just a little soreness. 'Tis nothing." She shouldn't have lifted her shoulders quite so far to answer. Sometime during the night the belt had come untied on the dressing gown. More of her bust was visible than in her most daring gown. The fine linen of his shirt was the only thing separating her chest from his.

Alistair followed the direction of her gaze. He cleared his throat. "Well, time is ticking away." He sat up and slid sideways in a neat maneuver that quickly got them both standing up, still chest-to-chest. He rested his hands at her waist to steady her.

"We should probably check the bandage. Make sure it hasn't slipped, that the bleeding didn't start again."

He wanted to examine her, in the light of day, with no

brandy in her system? She coughed. Her hand slid down to her hip. No dampness. The cloth binding was still in place. "That's not necessary. It feels fine."

He raised his brows.

"I'll be home within an hour or so. I'll have my maid take a look then."

He didn't look quite convinced. "If you're sure."

"I'm sure. I'll remind her who pays her wages, and she'll keep a still tongue."

"Very well." He stepped to the side to the table to retrieve her shift.

Charlotte quickly closed the gown around her and tied the belt. There was no dressing screen in the cabin for her to hide behind. Should she ask Alistair to step out?

Oh, what was the point? He'd seen everything already. Had to have.

While she debated, he came back, her shift scrunched up in his hands.

"I'll slip this over your head, while you slip off the dressing gown."

Humor and brazenness were the only way to go. "Gaining more experience as a lady's maid, my lord?"

He winked at her, and raised the shift over her head. Somehow they managed the maneuver with a minimum of awkwardness, and Charlotte breathed a sigh of relief. He also helped her with her dress, and she pulled her snarled hair to one side as he stood behind her to do up the buttons. His touch was light and sure, nothing overtly seductive about it, but she couldn't suppress a shiver when his fingers brushed her skin, or again when his warm breath tickled the fine hairs at her nape.

Instead of stepping aside when he finished the last button, he bent down. "Nick was right, Tucker did an amazing job. I can't find either of the tears."

He was examining her backside? She ought to tease him about making a habit of this, but she couldn't get the words out. She held perfectly still.

"Think you can manage your stocking by yourself?" He held out the scrap of black silk.

"I'll have to. You won't be there to take it off tonight." Good Lord, had she actually said that out loud?

He grinned, and reached for his waistcoat.

Standing still wasn't bad, but every movement reminded her of last night's folly, as muscles and flesh protested the insult. She had to move, though, and hope she could work out some of the soreness before encountering Steven. She carefully perched on the edge of the chair and gained enough leverage to pull on her stocking, feeling the pull of the stitches with every motion.

By the time she'd tied her garter, Alistair stood in front of the mirror above the desk, adjusting the knot in his sadly wrinkled cravat. "It would never pass Brummel's inspection, but it will have to do until I get home." He ran his fingers through his hair, trying to give it some order.

"There should be a comb in the top left drawer." Now, where had she kicked her shoes off to last night?

"That wasn't a lucky guess." Alistair gestured with the comb.

Charlotte shrugged. "Nick's a creature of habit. His shaving gear is in that drawer, too, but we don't have time for you to borrow his razor." She spotted her shoes under the table. If she stood beside it and stretched her right leg, she might be able to reach them with her foot and drag them out without having to bend down.

"You've spent a lot of time in here, haven't you?"

The odd note in Alistair's voice made her glance up from the battle to retrieve her shoe. His jaw was tight and his blue eyes bore right through her. Jealousy? Maybe it wasn't her imagination after all.

"Well, any time I've sailed on board, he's insisted I stay in here at night. It took us almost two weeks to make the Channel crossing the first time, when I was fifteen. I remember I was very cross he wouldn't let me sleep in a hammock like the crew."

"A girl of fifteen? I should hope not. Did Steven guard the door each night?"

"No, he was still in France. He sent Nick to fetch me after my mother died." One shoe at hand, but the other remained stubbornly out of her reach.

Alistair got down on one knee in front of her, retrieved the shoe with no difficulty whatsoever, and reached for her ankle. She put a hand on the table to steady herself as he lifted her foot to his bent knee and slipped the shoe on her foot.

"So a friend of the family came to escort you to your new guardian?"

She had trouble following the conversation, with his large, warm hand wrapped around her ankle. Why couldn't she have been shot down there? He was welcome to touch her leg or ankle anytime he wanted. "Well, he was a friend of Steven's. I thought my cousin Marianne was going to swoon when she saw Nick at the door. She'd never seen a man with a gold earring and long black hair in a queue before. Thought for certain he was a pirate, even though Bath is inland."

"I'm sure Nick did everything possible to foster that impression." Alistair wound the shoe's ribbon around her ankle and gently tied it. Such graceful fingers he had. "You weren't inclined to swoon, too?"

She gave a rueful smile, remembering how silly she had been around Nick at first. "He is handsome and dashing, everything a girl daydreams about, and while he can be quite charming, he can also be a bully and overly protective. Almost as bad as Steven, in fact. Quite ripped the wool from my eyes."

"Nick, a bully?" His twinkling smile said she wasn't the only person Nick had tried to intimidate.

"My aunt only let me go with him because he'd brought one of the handkerchiefs I'd embroidered for Steven as a birthday gift, along with his letter asking for me. Plus, he knew our secret phrase. But if she'd known Nick was really taking me to the Continent, she would never have allowed me to leave, no matter how difficult her own troubles at the time."

They finished dressing while she talked. With a last glance around, she grabbed her bonnet and limped out to the passageway. She stopped at the bottom of the ladder leading to the top deck, staring up at the daunting prospect.

"Anything wrong?" Alistair said behind her.

"I'd never before noticed how steep these steps are, or how far apart."

He settled his hands on her shoulders, a comforting gesture. "I'll carry you."

While being carried in his arms again certainly held appeal, she had to decline. "I'll have to climb the stairs to my bedchamber. Best I get used to it now."

He rested his hand against the small of her back, and said not a word of complaint at her sluggish progress up the ladder. Though she couldn't suppress an occasional unladylike grunt, she bit her bottom lip to keep from crying out. She'd made a cake of herself last night while he'd cleaned and stitched—she wouldn't do it again.

Daylight poured down the hatch as the door was flung open. "There you are," Nick said, leaning in. "Thought you'd changed your mind about staying on board."

"We still have at least a minute to spare, Nicky." She heaved herself up the final few rungs and at last stood on the deck, the welcome breeze cooling her heated cheeks and the sweat trickling down her back. "Where are you off to this time?"

"Dorset, since we're almost out of cheese, then on to the Isle of Skye." He tucked her arm in his and led her to the gangway, Alistair right behind them. "But do I need to cut the journey short? I wouldn't want to miss your wedding." He beamed at her, though there was an edge to the smile when he shifted his focus to Alistair.

She might be able to bluff her way past other men, but Nick had always been able to see right through her. "We haven't set a date yet." Which was true, so there was no reason for him to doubt her. Alistair's posture stiffened beside her.

It was not her imagination. There was definitely an undercurrent between the two men, which was odd since they were friends, and she was friends with both of them.

Nick was like another big brother, while Alistair . . . there was nothing brotherly about Alistair. Last night they had been almost as intimate as lovers.

She glanced between the two men again. Could it be? She stretched up on her tiptoes to plant a kiss on Nick's cheek. "I'm so glad you were in port last night. Don't know what we would have done otherwise."

Alistair definitely narrowed his eyes at her action. He brought his hand up, not for a friendly pat on her shoulder, but a possessive hold against her neck, right where it sloped down to meet her shoulder. His thumb rubbed slowly against her nape, back and forth, like the swishing tail of a cat preparing to pounce. Not on its prey, but against a rival tomcat.

He *was* jealous! She bit her lip again, this time to keep from smiling. She didn't want to be the source of discord between two friends, but couldn't help feeling a tiny thrill of feminine satisfaction.

She should not be thrilled. This would only complicate matters. They were together only so she could complete the assignment and prove to Lord Q she could be a spy in her own right. She did not need the complication of a romantic involvement.

It was probably nothing more than leftover emotions from their forced intimacy last night and this morning. Alistair undoubtedly felt that he'd saved her life, or some such rot.

Her injury hadn't been all that serious. Uncomfortable, certainly, but being shot in the butt had proved one could not actually die from embarrassment. Nor did she have the ability to faint on command, since she had certainly *wanted* to pass out, especially when both men had been scrutinizing her posterior.

"You be sure and keep me apprised of your wedding plans." There Nick went again, as though he was saying something to Alistair beneath the words. "I changed my schedule to be there for Tony and Sylvia—I'll change it again for you two." He tipped her chin up and pushed her bonnet back to drop a kiss on her forehead, as he did every time she left his ship.

She smiled at the little ritual, straightened her bonnet, and looked at Alistair. "Your friends in Dorset?"

He gave a tight nod. "We'll let you know when there's anything to report, Nick." He guided her to the gang board, which Jonesy had lowered while they'd been talking.

She whirled back to Nick and gestured for him to lean close. "I also wanted to thank you for your self-control," she whispered.

He frowned in puzzlement.

"Not one gibe from you about 'turning the other cheek,' or any other puns. Remarkable restraint."

He grinned. "I'm saving them up for later, when the sting isn't quite so fresh."

Just one more thing. She lowered her chin so she could look up at him through her lashes, a trick that often got her whatever she wanted. "Since everything turned out fine, you don't need to tell Steven about this."

Nick turned serious. "I'll be back within a fortnight. I expect you to do the right thing."

Well, no problem there. She'd need less than one week to retrieve the snuffbox, end her fake engagement, and be off on her next assignment from Lord Q. It was easy to nod agreement.

Alistair put his hand at the small of her back then and guided her down to the dock.

"Fair winds and following seas," she called.

Nick waved, and the crew cast off the mooring lines and prepared to get under way.

Alistair tucked her arm in his and they made their way through the crowd of dock workers, fishermen, and costermongers swarming the waterfront in the early morning mist. His possessiveness now was to keep her from being jostled and accosted, rather than marking her as his territory, she was sure.

"Oh, for heaven's sake," she muttered.

"Beg pardon?"

"I just realized what was going on between you two back there. Nick thinks you've compromised me."

"Well, of course—"

"No. You did nothing wrong. Nothing happened between us." Well, that wasn't entirely correct. He'd seen her in a way that no one ever had, at least not since she was out of leading strings. "True, you, ah, touched me in places that no man ever has before, but it was a medical necessity, and not done for lascivious purposes."

"But we were alone together all night. Regardless, I've decided that we should—"

"There's no reason for you, or Nick, to think you have to go through with our engagement. The original terms of our agreement still stand. At the end of the Little Season, if not sooner, we'll simply tell everyone we do not suit, just as we planned, and go our separate ways."

He patted her hand but did not voice his agreement.

She tugged him to a stop and waited until he was looking directly at her. "Are you listening to me?"

"I heard every word you said, Charlotte." There was an earnestness to his gaze and a glint of determination that made her take half a step back. "Let's get you home, shall we?"

They resumed walking toward the busy intersection. He still hadn't agreed with her, a fact she found quite annoying. She was about to press the issue when he spoke again.

"Is the soreness getting any better?"

"Walking is getting easier, at any rate." There was still a painful pull in the vicinity of the wound, making it difficult to concentrate on anything but putting one foot in front of the other.

After he hailed a hackney, she considered kneeling on the floor rather than sitting on the bench, but eyed the detritus on the floor with distaste. Kneeling on the bench seemed too precarious as the coach lurched into motion. She gingerly perched sideways on the bench.

"I wish there was some way to make this easier for you," Alistair said, breaking the silence. "I could procure a bottle of laudanum."

She shook her head. "Makes me feel like my head's stuffed with wool. No, I'll be fine. If it gets too bad, I'll just do like my aunt does, and have a nip of brandy in my tea."

They soon neared her home. "Shall I have the driver go 'round the back, so you can sneak in through the mews?"

She returned his smile. "That won't be necessary. Steven probably got home just a few hours ago and is sound asleep by now, and my aunt rarely rises before ten. No need to skulk about in my own home." She glanced out the window. "But we don't need to give the servants any fodder for gossip, so drop me off at the same place where we met last night."

Within a few minutes Alistair was assisting Charlotte out of the coach. "I will call for you this afternoon and we will . . . well, not go driving." He looked around the square. "We will go walking in the park." He gestured at the tiny park in the center of the square. "After last night, we have much to discuss."

His expression was far too serious for Charlotte's comfort. Undoubtedly, he had arguments as to why he felt her virtue was now compromised and he felt obligated to do the so-called honorable thing. Since he'd given her several hours notice, surely she could come up with a convincing argument as to why he was wrong.

"Yes, we do." She turned to leave, but he caught her hand and raised it for a kiss. Tingles raced up her arm at the intimate contact of his lips on her bare skin. She tugged free and left before he could see the heat stealing across her cheeks.

She felt his stare following her all the way to the town house and up the stairs, until she closed the front door behind her.

She leaned against the door for a few moments to regain her composure. Silly reaction, just silly. If she wasn't careful, she'd soon be as much a goose as Marianne.

Her solitude lasted mere seconds, as maids and a

footman crossed the hall in pursuit of their duties. She took a deep breath and began the painful climb up the stairs. It would take a little bit of convincing, but Nick would not press the issue, and she felt certain she could bring Alistair around to her way of thinking. If nothing else, she'd point out how unsuitable she'd be as a duchess. She was not going to marry him. She was going to get back the snuffbox.

She was halfway up the second flight of stairs when the drawing room door was flung open and Steven stomped into the hall, fists on his hips. "Charlie, where the hell have you been all night?"

Chapter 12

~~⁓⁓ᗡᗡᗞ⁓⁓~~

She schooled her expression to one of polite inquiry. "I thought you were going down to Lost Wages. What happened?"

"Don't try to change the subject. I want to know where you've been."

She mirrored his posture, planting her fists on her hips, and raised her chin. "Since you chose to ignore my theory, *again*, I followed up on the lead myself."

Instead of appearing suitably chastened, he looked more incensed. "*What* lead?"

One of them had to remain cool-headed. Since she had been proven correct, she could afford to be magnanimous. "About Sir Nigel having the snuffbox."

His eyes widened in horror. "You spent the night following Nigel?"

"Of course not. It only took a little while to confirm

that the coach I saw the snuffbox thief get into the previous night belongs to one of Sir Nigel's known associates. They're conspiring together."

He scowled. "And the rest of the night?"

Yes, about the rest of the night . . . "When I finished, it was late, and since I was much closer to the docks than home, I spent the night on the *Wind Dancer*. Nick sends his best, by the way." It was getting disturbingly easy, this lying by omission.

Steven scrubbed his fingers through his hair. "Damn it, Charlie, this is London, not Paris, and the war is over. There are rules here, and Society expects you to abide by them. What would the duke think?"

Society, not to mention the duke, would no doubt frown upon her spending the night sleeping atop the viscount. Society and the duke need never know. "When did you start caring so much about the rules?"

A maid walked down the hall just then, innocently going about her duties. Steven lowered his voice once she was out of sight, though his anger had not subsided. "You gave me a scare. You could have at least left a note."

"I didn't think you'd be home to see a note, and besides, I didn't expect to be gone all night. What happened at Lost Wages?"

He sighed, and gestured for her to come into the drawing room. "I'll have a breakfast tray brought up, and we can compare notes. Fair enough? Or did Nick already feed you?"

She shook her head. "He let me sleep until it was almost time for them to cast off." It was slightly easier to walk down the stairs than up, and she thought she was doing well.

Steven clamped his hand on her shoulder as she stepped past him in the doorway. "Why are you limping?"

She grimaced. "I . . . slipped and fell." She stopped short of offering any more details, since Steven would see through that as an obvious lie.

"Should I send for a doctor?"

She shook off his hand and headed for the fireplace. "It's just a bruise. I'll be fine in a few days." She held her hands out in front of the fire. She wasn't cold, hadn't been since waking up with Alistair, but this was a good reason to not sit down just yet.

To her relief, Steven did not press the issue, but instead rang the bell pull and requested a breakfast tray for two. They indulged in idle chitchat until the tray had been brought and they were alone again. Charlotte gingerly perched on the edge of the sofa and poured tea for both of them. "You first."

Steven scowled after taking a sip, but Charlotte knew his bitterness was not because of the tea.

"You were right. Jennison, the gaming hell manager, did have several snuffboxes for us to choose from, but not the one we were after." He removed the covers from the tray and dug into the eggs and ham.

She could gloat, but as she ate a bite of the ham, she was surprised to find herself wishing for candied plums. And cheese. Fed to her by Alistair.

It had to have been the brandy, not to mention the blood loss, that made her bold enough to touch her tongue to his thumb last night. With any luck, he too blamed her behavior on the brandy. Especially when she'd patted the mattress beside her and invited him to join her in bed.

Good heavens, no wonder he thought she was compromised. Her judgment certainly had been, though her virtue was still very much intact, thanks to Alistair's gentlemanly behavior. Had he been tempted at all? He hadn't even tried to steal a kiss, and had done everything possible under the circumstances to protect her modesty. Or did he think of her only as a partner in their subterfuge?

She realized she had been staring at the same forkful of meat, and Steven was staring at her. She cleared her throat. "So what did you do? Tell him none of the snuffboxes were to your liking?"

He shrugged. "We'd been playing for more than an hour before he arrived. We debated over the choices while we played, and it didn't take long to make it seem as though we'd lost too much to buy any trinkets. He wished us better luck next time." He took another bite. "Bow Street should have a jolly good time if they ever go in there—some really high-end stolen merchandise passes through the back room every night. And most items are small enough to fit in your reticule."

"So it's true, they have thieves all over the city selling to them?"

"Not the kind you'd expect. I saw Madame Melisande, and she appeared to be bargaining with Jennison over two vinaigrettes and a fan."

"She was buying?"

Steven shook his head. "Selling. It would seem her

favors as a mistress don't pay as well as she'd like, and this is how she keeps up appearances. Saw a couple of other women just like her as the night wore on, doing the same thing, not to mention a few dandies. Apparently those pink-and-yellow-striped silk waistcoats cost more than I thought."

He polished off his meal. "So. Your turn. Tell me about this lead you followed. Who's working with Sir Nigel?"

"Well, to begin with, I discovered his business partner Tumblety is actually our old friend Toussaint."

Steven slammed his cup to the tray hard enough to make the silverware dance. "I should have killed him when I had the chance."

"You almost didn't survive your last encounter with him." She'd now have a scar to mark her encounter with the traitor, just as Steven did.

Steven scrubbed his hands across his face. "All right. Keep going."

"There isn't much else to tell. I climbed up to the balcony to break into his study to get the snuffbox, but our friends from Darconia were already there, rifling his desk. I thought he would be at Lost Wages with you, but he surprised us all. The Darconians and I leaped over the balcony and the garden gate. They ran in one direction, I ran in the other, and stayed with Nick."

"You're supposed to be dancing at balls, not climbing balconies." He leaned back, stretched his arms over his head. "I should pay a call on Nick. It's been a while since he and I chatted."

She wasn't deceived by her brother's casual tone. She

made sure not to look away from his steady gaze. "That will be a bit difficult, seeing as he's halfway down the Thames by now. Said he'd be back in a fortnight or so."

Which was exactly how long she had to retrieve the snuffbox, jilt Alistair, and start getting her own assignments from Lord Q.

When the door knocker sounded at two, Charlotte was already in the foyer, tying the ribbons to her short-brimmed bonnet. The butler opened the door to admit Alistair, who stood on the threshold, hat in his hands.

As though he'd never before seen her, his gaze was riveted on her face, the way she imagined he studied a newly discovered astronomical object. After several heartbeats, his eyes drifted down, slowly traveling the length of her body and back up, his mouth softening.

The smoldering heat in his eyes startled her, and something intense flared deep inside her. Her pulse quickened, even as her hands stilled in the act of tying her ribbons.

"Allow me." Alistair's smooth baritone voice washed over her like a caress as he slid the ribbons from her nerveless fingers and tied a neat bow beneath her chin. His kid gloves were indeed soft as butter when he brushed against the bare skin of her throat.

If she didn't know better, she'd think he was besotted. Quite puzzling. She couldn't even attribute his reaction to the sight of her bosom, since she'd chosen a high-necked walking gown of Pomona green muslin with a matching spencer. She wanted no flesh on display, no visible reminders of last night.

If Steven saw them now, he'd have no doubt their engagement was the result of a love match. And if Alistair kept looking at her that way, she might come to believe it herself.

But Steven was still upstairs, discussing financial matters with Aunt Hermione. For whose benefit was Alistair playacting the smitten suitor?

He held one arm out for her and gestured over his shoulder. "Shall we, my dear?"

She gave herself a mental shake, and placed her hand in the crook of his arm. "Farnham, should anyone inquire, I'm just going for a turn about the square."

"Very good, miss."

They were quiet on the short walk to the park in the center of the square and past its gates. She felt a twinge of envy at the sight of a governess with her two young charges, happily seated as they all were on a bench beneath the elm tree. It would be days before she could sit comfortably.

"Shall we keep walking?"

She sighed. "That's probably for the best."

He waited until they were past the children and their governess and had relative privacy. Goodness, now he looked so serious, as though he'd recently received bad news. She felt a hint of apprehension.

"Last night could have gone quite badly," he began.

Last night had certainly been no stroll through the park, for at least one of them. She refrained from expressing her sarcasm aloud, willing to let him get off his chest whatever was so important.

"You escaped with a relatively minor injury. Had his aim been better, it could have been . . . fatal." Alistair paused, as though the words caused him pain.

She was the one who'd been shot. All he'd had to do was run.

Oh, and carry her, and clean up the blood, and stitch her up. Though that couldn't have been all that pleasant—she'd had to stitch one of Steven's knife wounds once, and had cast up her accounts immediately afterward. Last night she remembered feeling grateful that Alistair had not felt the need to do the same.

He stopped beneath the shade of a massive oak tree, which had probably been growing since King Charles's reign. Alistair took her hands in both of his and led her off the path, closer to the tree trunk. She had no choice but to meet his steady gaze, his eyes seeming as if they could see right through her, looking as serious as a vicar at an open grave.

The last meal she'd eaten was a cold, heavy lump in her stomach.

"You must admit this task is more dangerous than you counted on. Too dangerous." He stroked his thumbs across the backs of her hands. "I want you to come home with me while you recover."

She immediately thought back to this morning and how pleasant it had been to wake up held in Alistair's arms. Warm, safe, protected. Cherished, even. But that had just been wishful thinking, a fleeting fancy. And the aftereffects of too much brandy.

She was sober and clear-headed now. "Do I really need to tell you how improper that would be?"

He gave an impatient shake of his head. "Not home here, in London. I mean home, in Keswick. The Lake District. My family's coach is well sprung, so your discomfort on the journey would be minimal. You could recuperate at Moncreiffe Hall in peace. Spend the nights with me up on the roof, studying the sky. Sleep late, and spend the afternoons going on long walks on the park grounds, or around the lakes. There are plenty of shops in the village, and Scotland is not far."

She took a moment to envision what he described, and shook her head to clear it of the folly. "That's—I think I'm flattered. Because I'm fairly sure you didn't mean any insult, suggesting an arrangement that would make it look as though I were your mistress."

"Mistress?" His brows rose in shock. "No, no. Blast, I'm making a muddle of this." He reached up to rub his forehead, her hand still tucked in his. He took a deep breath and dropped his hand back to a more comfortable level for her. "You and I, we're already engaged. I'm suggesting that we follow our engagement through to its natural conclusion."

She couldn't breathe. He couldn't be suggesting what she thought he was suggesting. He tilted his head, frowning at her in concern, and she remembered to inhale.

"The natural conclusion of our arrangement, my lord, is for me to jilt you. That is what we agreed upon, from the very beginning. For us to tell everyone we do not suit. Nothing has changed."

"Nothing changed? Everything has changed!"

"The only thing that has changed since last night is that Toussaint now knows at least two groups of people

are trying to wrest the snuffbox from his possession."
The fact that Alistair was now acquainted with the location of nearly all her freckles, or that she had spent
the night resting on his powerful chest and muscular
thighs—shown to great advantage in the buff breeches
he was wearing now—did not change anything, either.

He squeezed her hands. "You could have been killed
last night."

"But I wasn't."

A sound escaped his throat that sounded suspiciously
like a growl. "You stubborn woman. You do not comprehend the effect your death would have had on your aunt
or your brother, do you? Or on me?" He let go her hands
in order to remove his hat and run his fingers through his
hair, disheveling the light brown locks. "How could you,
when I barely comprehend it myself?" He put his hat
back on and stepped closer, one hand cupping her jaw,
his thumb rubbing across her cheek.

Charlotte fought the urge to lean into his caress.

"Let me take care of you, Charlotte. Once we are married, you won't have to worry about what Steven wants,
or proving yourself to Lord Q, or to anyone else. Apart
from what I stand to inherit, I've already come into my
trust fund, so your lack of dowry doesn't signify. I can
support you in grand style. We can be quite comfortable
together, you and I."

The touch of his hand was almost unbearable in its
tenderness, his words softly seductive. But he was asking
her to give up everything she'd ever hoped for, dreamed
of, planned for. Worked for. She could not give in.

"In the short, tumultuous time we have been acquainted,

I have come to care for you, Charlotte. A great deal more than I intended when we entered into our bargain. But there you are. And here we are." He sighed, his warm breath stirring the hair at her temples. "I cannot in good conscience allow you to continue to put yourself in danger. Abandon your quest, let someone else retrieve the snuffbox, and be my wife. What you're doing is far too dangerous."

Lulled by his caressing thumb, it took a moment for the full meaning of his words to sink in. "Abandon my quest?" Charlotte jerked backward out of his grasp, until she felt the oak tree at her back and could go no farther. She should have stepped to the side—she always made sure she had more than one way out of any situation. "I'll do no such thing. If you are worried about endangering yourself by association with me, I'll free you from our agreement right now. I'll go write the notice to the papers. By the day after tomorrow—"

"That's not what I meant, not what I want." His hands slashed through the air, erasing her words.

"Then what *do* you want?"

"How can I make you understand? What I want is—" He growled low in his throat, threw his hat to the ground, cupped her face with both hands, and kissed her.

He moved so swiftly she had no chance to evade him, had the thought even occurred. For all his speed and apparent anger, however, his touch was gentle, tender but thorough, trying to convey by touch what he couldn't express in words alone. His control had slipped free of its moorings, but was not without rudder or helm.

His full lips were soft and warm, fit against hers

perfectly. He smelled of shaving soap and spice, and a trace of licorice, but beneath those civilized scents was the hint of *him*, elemental Alistair. She wasn't sure which was more intimate, the press of their clothed bodies lying against each other this morning, or this direct contact now, his mouth to hers.

Blood sang through her veins, and her toes curled as she returned his kiss, powerless to stop herself, hungry for more though she wasn't sure precisely what it was that she suddenly craved. She grasped his lapel to pull him even closer, and reached one hand inside his coat and slid it down his chest, beneath his waistcoat, until she felt his heart thudding against her palm.

He lifted his mouth from hers, and she couldn't help a moan of protest, silenced when he began kissing his way across her jaw. He slid one hand to her neck, his thumb continuing to caress her, while his other hand skimmed down her shoulder to her waist and pulled her flush against him. Flush against the same firm, muscled body she'd felt this morning, now with his hard arousal pressing into her belly.

She'd seen evidence of male arousal before, a telltale bulge in a man's breeches or trousers, but had never actually felt it. She'd done this to Alistair. Had made the reserved scholar lose control, at least to this degree. A thrill coursed through her. What could she achieve, if she tried on purpose?

Eyes closed, she arched her neck when he began kissing her throat just beneath her ear. How did he know that kisses and gentle nips and flicks of his tongue on her neck would make her knees weak, would make her cling to him breathlessly? How did he know what would send sparks of pleasure shooting throughout her traitorous body, when she'd had no idea herself? Causing her to lose control just as she'd done to him must be his sweet revenge.

"What you do to me, Charlotte," he whispered against her throat, kissing his way across to lavish the other side of her face and neck with the same tender attention.

She tried to reply, to form coherent words, but the sound came out as a groan, and she clutched him tighter.

The sound of children's laughter and shouting encroached on the sound of her heart hammering in her ears. The children were playing just a few feet away, on the other side of the oak. She flattened her palms against Alistair's chest but couldn't summon the strength of will to actually push him away.

Thankfully he heard the children, too. He dropped his hands to her waist and pulled back a little, though he nuzzled her neck another few precious seconds, his ragged breathing puffing against her ear, sending fresh shivers all the way down to her toes.

He bent down to retrieve his hat, and Charlotte held her hand over her pounding heart. While his head was turned, she fanned her overheated cheeks.

Oh, my.

Alistair's kiss was even better than she had imagined. Passionate and all-consuming. "I was right," she said to herself.

He dusted off his hat and set it on his head. "Right about what?"

"About the way you would kiss."

The left side of his mouth quirked up in a crooked smile. "You've thought about kissing me?"

She patted her clothing to make sure everything was in its proper place. "Perhaps a little. In passing." She glanced around the park, hoping she didn't look as wanton as she felt. The two children she saw earlier ran past the tree, chasing a ball, laughing and shrieking. Their governess was not far behind.

Once they were out of sight, Alistair gestured for her to step forward, and he reached behind her to brush the leaves and bits of bark from her dress. He barely skimmed her injured left side, but his hand lingered on the right side of her derriere, smoothing down the fabric. She arched an eyebrow at him, but he maintained a look of innocence.

Two more people headed their way on the path, a young woman Charlotte recognized from a few doors down, accompanied by her maid.

By silent agreement, Charlotte took Alistair's arm and they began walking again.

"You're not going to succeed in distracting me," he began when they were out of earshot of anyone else in the park.

"I beg your pardon?" He thought *she* had been trying to distract *him*? Her lips still tingled from his tender assault.

"I won't be swayed from my original intent."

"Which is?"

"To persuade you to give up this dangerous quest of yours. I thought I could protect you, but I was proven wrong."

Her spine stiffened. "I have never sought your protection, or anyone else's. I have been endeavoring to prove, in fact, that I don't need anyone's protection. Nor do I want it. I'm perfectly capable—"

"Yes, I know, and I place the blame for that independent streak squarely on Steven's shoulders. He had no right to subject you to such a dangerous way of life, and you were too young to know any better." The arm not holding hers gestured wildly as he talked. "Now it's like opium to you. You crave the excitement, the danger. It's going to get you killed."

She dug her nails into her palm. Becoming loud and defensive would only make him think he'd proved his point. "I always choose my course of action very carefully, after gathering information to help me make the best decision. Before last night, I had never injured anything but my dignity. In five years of working in France during the war, I never sustained anything more serious than a bruise or a few scratches. Steven is the one with the scars and quick temper. He's the one who acts rashly."

"But you can't control the rash actions of others with quick tempers. People who have pistols, and are willing to use them." He halted again, and his somber expression gave her pause. "Someone tried to kill you last night. I couldn't stop him. The only way I can protect you is to prevent you from being exposed to that kind of danger in the first place."

Charlotte narrowed her eyes. There was more going on here than just his masculine need to protect the so-called weaker sex. Beating her head against a wall was never productive, and Alistair had certainly put up a wall when it came to this issue.

Time to go around, over, or dig beneath that wall.

"Who did you fail to protect last time?"

He staggered back half a step as though she'd struck him a physical blow. "Wh-What?"

"You're speaking with the voice of experience. You needed to protect someone, and somehow you failed. I want to know details."

He widened his stance and raised his chin. "It's not that simple. And you're trying to change the subject. We're discussing how your pursuit of a career as a spy is putting you in danger, and how marrying me will preclude the need for such a career."

She put her hands on her hips. "No, I think we're discussing your need to protect people, and I simply happen to be the current target of that need." Her instincts had always been right—it's why she'd been so successful, and unscathed. They weren't letting her down this time, either. "You have no objection to Steven being a spy. During the war, not once did you try to persuade your dear friend Nick that it was too dangerous for him to be a courier for the Home Office and sneak his ship through the blockades, to sail right past the noses of the French navy. It is only with me that you have a problem. Why?"

He wouldn't meet her gaze for the longest time, but at last he raised his hand to trail his fingers down her cheek in a tender caress.

"Who was she?"

He didn't answer aloud, but his eyes clouded with sorrow.

Her stomach clenched. She grasped his wrist. "How did she die?"

He paused, his hand still cradling her cheek, her fingers wrapped around his wrist where she felt his pounding pulse. When he at last spoke, she barely heard him over the whisper of wind in the trees.

"The axle broke, and her carriage plunged into a ravine."

She waited a moment to let the horrific images his words conjured settle. "Were you driving? Or in the carriage?"

"No."

She lowered his hand so she could hold it between both of hers. "Did you cause the axle to break?"

"Of course not!"

"Then how was it your fault, your failure to protect?"

His fingers tightened around hers. "I saw the crack. I knew the axle was damaged, but I said nothing."

Her breath caught. She chose her words carefully. "You don't strike me as someone who would intentionally allow another person to be hurt. You must have had a very good reason for not speaking up."

He shook his head and stared off into the distance.

"How long ago did this happen?"

He mumbled a reply, his eyes apparently still seeing the accident.

"I couldn't hear you." She cupped his strong jaw and turned him back toward her.

"Twenty years ago, this past spring."

Twenty years? "That would mean that at the time of the accident you were . . ."

"Five."

"And you've carried the guilt for her accident all this time? But you were just a child!"

"You don't understand." His anguished tone tore at her insides.

"Then help me understand."

He let out a shaky sigh and began walking. She fell into step beside him.

"It was not just my mother who died in the accident. My older brother and two little sisters were also traveling with her that day."

Charlotte's heart squeezed, forcing the air out of her lungs. She threaded her fingers through his, locking their hands together.

"They were going into the village, shopping. A trip we'd made hundreds of times. Thousands. But I was being punished for misbehavior the day before, and not allowed to go. I didn't say anything about the axle looking wrong, because I was again being disobedient in playing in the carriage house in the first place."

Charlotte struggled to find words that would offer him comfort. What could she say that hadn't already been said to him, undoubtedly many times over, during the course of the years? "You're right. The accident was your fault."

He jerked to a halt and gaped at her.

"At the country estate of a family as exalted as yours, I would expect that your family employed at least one coachman, if not several coachmen, who were responsible for the care and maintenance of all the vehicles. I presume there were also any number of grooms and undergrooms who were employed to care for the horses, harnesses, and other equipment. With all of those adults, clearly it was up to you, a child of five, to ensure that the coach was safe for travel."

His jaw closed with a snap. "You make me sound ridiculous."

"That is not my intention." She caressed his hand with her thumb, feeling his coiled strength, hoping to impart some of hers. "I understand, at least a little, the horrible tragedy that you're still trying to come to terms with, to have it make some sense. Don't you think I wish there had been something I could do when my mother became ill, or my father died? Steven is still trying to prove that he is a better man than his stepfather, but we cannot dwell on the past."

"We can't forget the past. It's what makes us who we are today."

"True, but being overly protective of me will not bring back your mother or siblings. And you're right, Steven *is* to blame for indoctrinating me into the life of a spy, but he trained me well. I have the skills and instincts to be successful at it, and nothing you say or do can change that, no matter how much you might wish it. I'm going to get back the snuffbox. You can't stop me. But you can help me, if you want."

The anguish was gone from his eyes, replaced by a grim determination that did nothing for her peace of mind. "You leave me little choice in the matter."

Before she could respond, she saw Steven's approach.

"Ah, there you are." He sauntered up to them, hands clasped behind his back, the image of a gentleman at ease. "Lovely afternoon for a walk, isn't it?"

The lines of tension on his face proved the image to be

false. Her emotions still near the surface from her conversation with Alistair, she tried not to immediately think the worst. "Is anything amiss?"

"Can't a fellow simply enjoy a little stroll in the afternoon?"

"Any other fellow, perhaps." She gave him a pointed stare. "You're not planning to chaperone us, are you?"

"Do you two *need* a chaperone?"

"Steven," she ground out.

"Afternoon, Blakeney," Alistair said, perfectly polite. If his emotions were still too near the surface, he was hiding them well.

Steven acknowledged the greeting with a terse nod. He stopped in front of Charlotte. "When you are free, I've received some news that may be of interest to you. I just wanted you to know." He spun on his heel and headed back down the path, out of the park.

"News concerning his part of the investigation?"

Charlotte nodded. "That would be my guess."

"Then let's not keep him waiting." Alistair began walking, heading back to the house.

Since their hands were still linked and Alistair showed no inclination toward letting go, Charlotte had no choice but to try to keep up.

"Oh, sorry." He slowed down.

"You should know that I told Steven about my attempt to retrieve the box last night, but I may have left out a few details."

"Details, such as the fact that you got shot?"

"And I may have omitted the bit about your participation in the night's events." She winced, and tried to read his expression.

He gave a small smile. "How did you explain away your limp?"

"Told him it's a bruise. Does this mean you're with me rather than against me?"

"I will always be with you, Charlotte."

Chapter 13

❦

A listair followed Charlotte into the drawing room, where her brother was in the process of requesting a tea tray. Another man paced before the fireplace, his enormous Roman nose presented in profile. He was dressed in a similar fashion as Blakeney—barely respectable—and had used half a bottle of Macassar oil to hold his overlong, dark hair in place. Upon noticing Alistair, the stranger raised his nose and eyed him with the same disdain one generally reserved for a mosquito.

Alistair felt just as welcome, but had no intention of leaving Charlotte's side.

Apparently realizing none of the men would sit unless she did so first, she perched on the edge of a straight-back chair, doing her best to hide a grimace of pain. Alistair pulled up a nearby chair.

"What is the news?" She leaned forward.

Steven and the stranger said nothing, pointedly staring at Alistair.

She gave a huff of impatience. "Alistair knows everything," she announced.

"Everything, *ma petite*?"

"Yes, Gauthier. Oh, I'm sorry, you two haven't been properly introduced. He is a friend of Nick's, so you can speak freely."

Alistair was slightly affronted that she hadn't referred to him as her fiancé. Perhaps she still hadn't accepted their betrothal was real? Clearly he had more work to do.

"News?" she prompted her brother.

Steven scowled at him, then handed Charlotte a piece of paper. "This is a copy of the note that was delivered to Lord Q's office a few hours ago. They tried to track down the author but could get no further than the street urchin who delivered it. Lad couldn't be more than nine or ten, and claims he was paid a shilling by a well-dressed toff. No reason to doubt his story."

She held it to the side so Alistair could read over her shoulder.

A certain letter has fallen into my possession, which I am sure you would prefer to have returned to your own safekeeping. I would be happy to restore this precious document to its rightful owner, and only ask a finder's fee of twenty thousand pounds in exchange. I'm sure you'll agree 'tis a trifling sum to pay to avoid the contents being printed in a newspaper.

It went on to describe where and when the money should be delivered, in three days' time.

Alistair gave a low whistle. "Doesn't want much, does he?"

"And we all know twenty thousand is just the beginning." Steven held his finger up for silence when the maid knocked and entered with the tea tray. He gestured for her to bring it to the table in front of him, sparing Charlotte the need to play hostess.

"I don't understand," Charlotte said as soon as the maid had curtsied and left again. "Is Lord Q giving you a new assignment before the other is completed?"

Steven shook his head. "Lord Q left out a few details when he gave me the assignment. Apparently this letter was hidden inside the snuffbox."

She tossed the scrap of parchment onto the table. "Why would the Home Office or the prince care if the contents of this letter became public knowledge? He already lives a life so scandalous, no one should be shocked by anything he's written, or that was written to him."

"*Ma petite*, that was another detail. Your Prinny, he gave the box to someone else. It is not his letter, not his secret that has fallen into the wrong fingers."

"Hands," Steven corrected absently.

Charlotte accepted a cup of tea from her brother. "Then whose secret is it? Who was the original recipient of the blackmail note?"

"We haven't been made privy to that information." Steven sat down again. "What matters is that we can't allow the contents of the letter to become public knowledge."

Charlotte took a sip. "Whoever he is, I wonder if he's the one who sent those two men to retrieve it? I thought they were from Darconia, but perhaps not."

Alistair noted that Steven had not offered him a cup of tea. "Dar— What?"

"Darconia," Charlotte said. "You need a magnifying glass to see their country on a map of the Continent. One of their female dignitaries recently gave the snuffbox to Prinny as a token of her affections, but it turns out the box was part of their equivalent of the crown jewels. Our plan was to get back the box, make a duplicate of it for Prinny, and return the original to the Darconians. Then everyone would be happy, Prinny and his paramour none the wiser, and an international incident averted."

Alistair got up and poured his own cup while Charlotte explained. He let her words sink in while he stirred the sugar into his tea. "Except the Darconians are an impatient lot, aren't they? Or they simply didn't trust that you would give them back the original."

She frowned at him. "Why do you say they're impatient?"

"Who else would have an interest in breaking into Toussaint's study before we got there last night?"

Gauthier had been lounging by the fire, leaning an elbow against the mantel, but he straightened at this. "You were with *ma petite* last night?"

Steven pinned Alistair with a glare. "And you couldn't stop her?"

Alistair rolled his eyes. "Are we talking about the same female who followed you through Paris alleyways in the middle of the night when she was still young enough to have belonged in the schoolroom?"

He waved his hand. "Right. What was I thinking?"

"I'm getting bloody tired of people talking about me as if I'm not in the room."

Ignoring Charlotte's indignation, Steven marched over to Alistair's chair. "Just a moment. You were with her last night?" His tone was deadly soft, deceptively calm. "All night?"

Having his bride forced to the altar by her irate brother was not the best way to begin a marriage. Alistair was going to have her, but he wanted her to come willingly. "We spent the night on Nick's ship, yes." He stood up.

Steven did not back away.

They stood nose to nose. "It was late when we left Toussaint's, and it was safer for her to pass the night on the nearby *Wind Dancer* than travel through neighborhoods that even during daylight hours are dangerous at best. Nick had her stay in the captain's cabin. That's the usual procedure when she's stayed on board, I believe?"

He was quite proud of the fact that all of what he'd said was absolutely true. His future brother-in-law didn't need to know about the omitted details.

Steven harrumphed and returned to his chair, but didn't sit down.

Gauthier was still standing at attention, staring at Alistair with suspicion. "How is it you know this Nick, this schoolboy who played at being spy?"

Charlotte rapped her knuckles on the table. "Gentlemen, can we stop all this silly posturing and return to the important subject at hand? The letter?"

A few heartbeats passed before Steven and Alistair sat down and Gauthier resumed his negligent pose, leaning on the mantel.

She nodded. "Does this attempt at blackmail really change anything? We still must reclaim the snuffbox. We just have to be certain to retrieve the letter that's inside it as well."

Steven crossed one ankle over his knee. "Getting it will be a damn sight harder now, since Toussaint knows people are after it. Did he get a good look at you or the Darconians?"

She shook her head. "I was in the dark, on the balcony. But he may be able to recognize the Darconian who was in his study."

"The other one stayed in the back of the garden," Alistair added. "Impossible for Toussaint to pick him out of a crowd. I was on the ground, much closer, and still couldn't see his features."

"Well, what shall we do now?" She looked expectantly at each of the three men in turn. "Steven, you and Gauthier could distract him, lure him out of the house tonight, and I could make another attempt to break into the study."

Steven shook his head. "He's probably already moved it to a new hiding spot. I'd wager a year's income that it's no longer in his town house."

Alistair wanted to check Charlotte's forehead for fever—she couldn't possibly be thinking of making another attempt. At the very least, it might pull out her stitches, undo all his work. Cause a scar. He leaned toward her and kept his voice low. "You're in no condition to climb."

She smacked him on the knee.

Steven's head jerked up. "You know how she got the bruise?"

"Going over the garden gate," he said without missing a beat. "The second time proved to be more problematic than the first."

"My bruise is of no consequence. Do you think Toussaint would hide the box at Lost Wages?"

"It's possible, poppet. Gauthier and I plan to go back to the gaming hell tonight and have a better look around. You, meanwhile, should stay home and rest, and perhaps take a long hot bath with Epsom salts."

Alistair tried not to wince.

"That would certainly be good for a bruise. Thank you for your concern, Steven."

"I'll let Aunt Hermione know you won't be attending the musicale with her tonight." Steven paused. "You're not faking this in order to get out of going to hear all that caterwauling, are you?"

She smiled and batted her eyelashes.

Charlotte chafed at her inactivity the rest of the day. She wanted to be doing something, anything, to get the snuffbox back, but reluctantly agreed with Alistair's logic in taking a day of rest to let her body heal. It pained her greatly to admit that he was right, and she was in no condition to climb a balcony tonight because of the royal pain in her backside. At least, the indirect cause was a royal article. The throbbing ache when she moved had increased to the point where she considered drinking brandy straight, and skipping the pretense of having tea in her cup.

At the least, she could distract herself by gathering intelligence, so the time was not entirely wasted. The footman she'd sent on an errand just before lunch had returned from Hookham's Lending Library with an armload of books on astronomy, as requested. Since she needed to lie still, she would put the time to good use and study up on the subject so important to Alistair.

Unfortunately, the footman hadn't been able to find a single book that even mentioned Darconia, so she'd have to rely on what she already knew about the country to try to predict what the smoking men would try next.

She'd been unable to conceal her injury from her maid, Molly, who'd noticed the tiny new bloodstains on her shift. She'd had no choice but to take the maid into her confidence about some things, after reminding Molly that she was the one who actually paid her wages, not Steven or Hermione.

On a positive note, she discovered that Molly's mother was a healer and had taught her daughter several useful recipes, including one for a poultice that Molly promised would draw out much of the soreness from Charlotte's wound. It was worth the indignity of lying on her bed and having the poultice applied continually throughout the afternoon and evening.

"Your surgeon did a bang-up job, my lady." Molly wrung out the cloths from the concoction in the kettle that had been heating on the hearth, and used them to replace those on Charlotte's posterior that had cooled. "Even me mum's stitches aren't this neat. You'll have hardly any scar a'tall."

Thankfully, Charlotte was beyond blushing at that point.

If she had to get shot, why couldn't it have been someplace more heroic, and less personal? Like in the shoulder, or even just a few inches farther down, on her leg?

Scar or no, Alistair was never going to see the results of his handiwork. Molly was perfectly capable of removing the stitches when the time came. The man had a warm body and a cool head in trying circumstances—not to mention being a fabulous kisser—but their relationship was going to end soon.

Charlotte thought back on her emotional conversation with Alistair in the park. He wanted her to abandon her quest, but failing that, insisted on helping her.

That would be fine, if that was as far as he went. How could she dissuade him from following through with the rest of his plan? They would never suit as husband and wife, not really.

For a moment, she allowed herself the indulgence of picturing the fantasy life he had described for her. She had never been to the Lake District, but had seen enough paintings and read enough descriptions to know she would love it there. Mountains and lakes, nights under the stars spent with Alistair. Shopping and riding, and more time spent in Alistair's company. Being his wife, and all that entailed.

Hearing the rich, mellow timbre of his voice. Watching him talk, his elegant long fingers and expressive hands—without them, he'd probably be speechless. Staring into his brilliant blue eyes, like a patch of clear sky after weeks of endless rain. They'd turned darker than sapphires when he'd kissed her this afternoon.

And, oh, how the man could kiss. Without dislodging any of her clothing or his, he'd managed to kiss away any vestige of her intelligence, kiss away all her resistance, and he hadn't even used his tongue. She'd overheard conversations, knew about such types of kisses. Until this afternoon she'd never thought they would be all that appealing. Now she thought differently.

If he brought that weapon to bear, she'd be sunk. She did not dare allow him a chance to even try such a tactic. An intelligent man such as Alistair would wait until he had her mindless with passion, lost to sensation, and then renew his attempts to convince her that life in the country, being his wife, was exactly what she wanted.

But such a settled life was not for the likes of her.

She'd spent the first fifteen years of her life living in the same house, in the same quaint town of Bath, and had never traveled more than a few miles from her birthplace. After her mother's death, she'd been taken in by her aunt, who lived just down the street, and who had recently lost her own husband.

And then Steven had sent for her.

The five years since that fateful day had been filled to bursting with one adventure after another. She'd crossed the English Channel several times, had sailed on everything from fishing smacks to Dutch galliots, and once even an eighty-four-gun brig of war. She and Steven had traveled through at least eight countries and stayed in several dozen different lodgings, their accommodations ranging from exquisite country estates to the most abject hovels where the rats were big enough to saddle and ride. Through it all she remained free, untethered, no ties to bind her to any one place.

During the worst of the deprivations, she took heart in the knowledge that what they were doing made a difference. They enabled British soldiers to avoid traps set by the enemy. They intercepted French supply wagons, and fed and armed Wellington's troops with the spoils.

Sometimes they waited and watched, sometimes they ran for their lives. But there was always something to learn, to do, somewhere to go. They'd never stayed in one place more than a few weeks.

Even now, when she planned to spend the entire Little Season in London, more of her belongings were still stowed in trunks than were put away in drawers and wardrobes. She could be completely packed and on her way with only a few moments' notice, ready to go wherever her skills were needed. She'd had a great deal of practice—many times, they'd been forced to leave their lodgings in the middle of the night, and she was allowed to take only what she could pack and carry herself.

Once her plan succeeded, she was perfectly aware that Society would consider her an oddity—a single woman, without the protection of a father, husband, or brother. No matter. She planned to keep on moving, to never stay in one place too long. Her time on the Continent with Steven had taught her to never become a creature of habit, to never have a predictable schedule, never take the same route twice in a row.

Alistair liked order. Predictability. He approached life with the same methodical manner that he applied to his astronomical observations.

No, they would never suit. Soon, even he would come to realize that.

Charlotte buried her face in the soft cotton of her pillow. Odd that she hadn't noticed before that the poultice stung so badly when first applied.

The next morning she was eager to hear Steven's report on what he'd found at Lost Wages, but Ned, his valet, said Steven hadn't come in until after dawn. Her half brother was still down for the count on his bed, snoring loud enough to rattle the windows.

Since Steven was even grumpier than Nick if awakened too early, she had a breakfast tray sent up to her room, and spent the morning enduring the application of more poultices. She still felt a twinge of pain when she sat down, but the improvement over yesterday's soreness was remarkable. A few more applications, and she'd be ready to take an active part in the investigation again. Tonight.

At lunchtime she went downstairs, determined to throw a bucket of water on Steven if he wasn't awake by the time she finished eating. The footman filled her plate, and she dug into the meal, alone.

A few moments later, heavy footsteps trod down the hall. Steven suddenly filled the doorway, smiling when he saw her, despite his still bloodshot eyes.

Her nose twitched as he entered the room, from the stench of gin and tobacco smoke that clung to his clothes as he walked by to take his seat at the head of the table.

"Have a good night, poppet?"

"I am much recovered, thank you. Did you have any luck?"

He shook his head. "Lost every hand I played. At least Gauthier didn't win, either."

She arched an eyebrow at him. "And your search?"

He thanked the footman who had just filled his plate and cup, and waved his dismissal. "I even chatted up the serving wenches, to no avail." He dug into his meal as though he'd had nothing more substantial than cheap gin since dinner last night. "I did get several offers to accompany them upstairs, though." He gave her a big closed-mouth grin, his cheeks puffed with a forkful of kidney pie.

She drank the last of her tea, refusing to think about what her brother did, or did not do, in the course of his work. "I tried to tell you it wouldn't be at Lost Wages. I think it's still at Toussaint's town house."

"Then we are in accord. Tonight, after Toussaint heads down to the gaming hell, Gauthier and I are going to search his study." He poured more tea for himself and re-filled her cup. "What are your plans?"

Aunt Hermione bustled into the dining room in time to hear the question. "She's going shopping with me, in preparation for us attending the Grishams' ball tonight."

Charlotte cast a worried look at Steven. She was *not* going to miss out on another night of trying to get back the box. He shrugged his shoulders in a stunning display of no help whatsoever. She scowled at him.

Seeing that there were no footmen available, Hermione filled her own plate and sat down. "Good afternoon, Charlotte. Good heavens, Steven, those are the same clothes you were wearing when you left last evening. Where did you pass the night, in the arms of a doxy?" Her nose twitched. "What kind of example are you setting for your sister? I do hope a bath and shave is the first thing on your agenda for the day."

Steven lowered his head, looking suitably abashed. "Yes, Aunt." He winked at Charlotte, who snorted into her teacup. Served him right.

Hermione had barely tucked into her meal when a footman scurried in, asking her to attend a small matter in the kitchen. The distant clatter of pots and pans being thrown, and muffled French curses, punctuated his request.

"I may have another headache this evening," Charlotte said as soon as Hermione was out of earshot.

"Why is that?"

"How else am I to avoid attending the Grishams' ball?"

Steven shook his head. "We need you to go with Hermione, to act as a distraction. You know how she feels about me playing man about town two nights in a row. If she doesn't have you there to fuss over, she'll wonder too much about what I'm doing. We can't have her poking her nose in and possibly getting hurt."

Charlotte drew breath to argue, then realized the futility of it. Steven could be even more stubborn than she was. She narrowed her eyes. "There was a time when you recognized I was invaluable as a distraction *on* the mission, not just to cover up the mission."

"But this is London, poppet. Things have changed. You're an engaged woman now." He grinned widely, as though taking sole credit for her changed status. "Go to the ball tonight. Dance. Flirt. Be a typical London miss, as you promised."

"Typical London miss, my arse," she muttered, but subsided as Aunt Hermione returned just then.

"There is a reason for the truism that French chefs are bad tempered." Hermione sat down and ate a forkful of kidney pie, her eyes closed in blissful appreciation. "But you must admit, the results are worth humoring him."

They ate the rest of the meal with companionable chit-chat.

Charlotte didn't mind shopping—she looked upon it as selecting elements for her costumes, rather than buying needless fripperies—but she was concerned about having to plead a headache again so soon, to explain her absence from the ball. Alternating alibis was much more effective, and less likely to arouse suspicion.

Hermione hustled her out to the hall in preparation for their shopping trip, while Steven stayed at the table for a second helping of everything.

"You'll never guess who I ran into at Hookham's when I was out this morning." Aunt Hermione accepted her gloves and bonnet from Farnham.

The door knocker sounded. Hermione kept her hands on her bonnet ribbons so that she could say she had just come in or was just going out, depending on her desire to receive the visitor.

Charlotte hid a grin. She and Steven weren't the only people in the house who practiced deception.

The butler opened the door, stepping aside to admit Alistair into the foyer.

Her heart gave a lurch and then started beating much faster than usual. She chided herself for this completely uncalled-for excited reaction. It had barely been one full day since she had last seen him, not weeks or months. Must have something to do with the way the sunlight streaming through the door lit his golden brown hair like a halo.

"No need to announce him, Farnham." She held her bonnet and gloves out in the general vicinity of the butler, since she couldn't take her eyes off Alistair.

"Very good, miss." The butler gave a regal sniff.

Alistair stepped forward, his hat in one hand at his side. "Have I come at a bad time?" The question was meant for either of them, though his gaze was locked on Charlotte's face. Or her lips, to be precise. Was he thinking of their kiss beneath the oak tree, too?

"Not at all, dear boy, not at all." Aunt Hermione thrust her bonnet and gloves toward Farnham and hurried over to Alistair. "That's what I started to say earlier, Charlotte," she said over her shoulder. "This is who I bumped into at Hookham's." She tucked her arm through Alistair's and led him toward the drawing room. "And I do mean that literally. Wasn't watching where I was going. Nearly knocked the dear man to the ground."

"You exaggerate, my lady. And it was entirely my fault. I was absorbed in my research, and oblivious to my surroundings, however beautiful."

"Oh, pish." Aunt Hermione gave him a playful tap on the arm.

Charlotte swore she saw a blush steal across the old gel's cheeks.

"As luck would have it, Moncreiffe is planning to attend the Grishams' ball this evening, just as we are," Hermione said, "and has agreed to take us up in his carriage. Isn't that marvelous?"

Charlotte met Alistair's amused gaze. "Yes, quite lucky." She could just imagine how the arrangement had come about. She loved Aunt Hermione dearly, but the woman could be as subtle as a falling wall of bricks.

Hermione looked worried for a moment. "You don't think you'll have a repeat of the headache you had last evening, do you?"

"Seems unlikely," Charlotte assured her.

The door knocker sounded again, heralding the arrival of Aunt Hermione's bosom bow, Mrs. Higginbotham, and her two daughters. They too were headed for shopping, but alas had room for only one more in their carriage. The two Misses Higginbotham looked at Alistair as though they'd very much like him to be the only one they had room for.

"You go with them, Aunt," Charlotte said, tucking her arm in Alistair's. "Moncreiffe and I will take a turn about the garden, and discuss details about tonight's excursion."

Aunt Hermione looked torn.

Steven emerged from the dining room just then, saw the visitors, and made a polite bow. Before he could escape upstairs, Charlotte called him over.

"Steven can chaperone us," she said brightly.

"I— What?"

"Oh, well, that's all right, then." Aunt Hermione

retrieved her bonnet and gloves from Farnham again. "Be good, children!" With a waggle of her fingers, she was out the door with her friends.

"You don't need to actually chaperone us, Steven," Charlotte said. "Go on and have your bath as you planned."

He paused, one foot on the bottom step. "I can see the garden from my bedchamber, you know."

Charlotte made shooing motions at her brother, and tugged Alistair down the hall, toward the garden.

"Are you sure you wouldn't rather have gone shopping with your aunt? I could come back later."

She shook her head. "By the time Aunt Hermione and Mrs. Higginbotham finish buying out the shops, the girls will be lucky if they don't have to ride up top with the driver. I would much rather tour the garden with you."

The last bit made him smile, a dazzling display of straight teeth and crinkled eyes that warmed her from the inside. "You seem to be moving much more easily today. Is your . . . bruise . . . healing well?"

"Yes, thank you. My maid knows a poultice recipe which has remarkable recuperative effects. I still feel a reminder when I sit down, however."

They were quiet again until they reached the terrace steps. "I wish to apologize, my lord," she said as soon as they were outside.

"Whatever for? And I thought we had agreed formalities were silly at this point, Charlotte."

Hearing his rich, mellow voice pronounce her name like a caress sent a delicious shiver running down to her toes. He'd left his hat with the butler, and the afternoon sun highlighted his golden brown hair, made his eyes as blue as the late summer sky. His full lips were curved in an inviting smile. She'd wager he'd taste of licorice.

She remembered again their kiss beneath the oak tree, and felt the sudden yearning to repeat it. If she reached up on her toes, she was confident he would meet her halfway.

For the sake of her sanity, she tore her gaze away from his mouth. "Apologize for this awkward situation in which my aunt has placed you. I know how persuasive she can be, and you were too much the gentlemen to tell her no."

"But I *was* going to attend the Grishams' ball."

"Truly?"

He nodded. "As soon as I learned that you were going to attend, yes."

A warm glow spread through her, and she felt something melting. Her good sense, no doubt. "You're willing to sacrifice another night of viewing, just to escort my aunt and me to a stuffy ball? Soon the moon will be rising too early, and you won't get nights this dark for at least another three weeks."

His look of pleased surprise was worth every hour she'd spent studying astronomy. The subject still didn't fire her imagination the way it obviously did his, but she understood his attraction to it—all that order and predictability to the night sky.

"Escorting you is an entirely self-serving sacrifice, I assure you."

"How is that?"

He tucked a curl behind her ear. "It affords me the opportunity to spend more time in your company, of course."

He trailed his fingers down her cheek, but after a furtive glance at the upstairs windows, dropped his hand to his side.

They'd spent the night together on a narrow bunk, yet he was still worried about doing anything that might give her family the wrong idea? How did she manage to be so lucky as to pick this particular gentleman on the street last week?

"I have a treat planned for you tonight. It's the main reason I finally accepted the Grishams' invitation."

"But you didn't even know I would be going, until just a few hours ago."

"All right, you caught me out. It wasn't planned especially for you—Lord Grisham does this every year—but I still think you'll enjoy it."

"Sounds intriguing. What is it?"

"You'll have to wait until tonight to find out." He touched the tip of his finger to the tip of her nose. "When your aunt said that you would be attending, I wasn't sure she was correct. I half expected that you'd still be intent on breaking into Toussaint's town house."

Her features twisted into a grimace. "I am to be the decoy tonight, so that Aunt Hermione does not suspect Steven's activities."

"While he gets to experience the fun and adventure, without you."

"Exactly!" She resisted the urge to stamp her foot only because Alistair seemed to understand her frustration.

"Then we will just have to make sure you have fun and adventure of your own tonight, won't we?"

Chapter 14

Charlotte was just descending the staircase at eight o'clock that evening when Alistair arrived. She knew her pale blue silk gown was flattering to her coloring and figure, but the smoldering expression in his eyes as he swept his appreciative gaze over her, head to toes, made her feel like she was a work of art.

As soon as she reached the bottom of the stairs, he raised her hand to drop a soft, warm kiss on her knuckles. "You look divine."

His touch and his smile sent her pulse racing, and his simple declaration warmed her as no effusive praise would have done. "You look quite handsome as well." His black coat and breeches, white shirt and stockings, were elevated beyond the ordinary by a waistcoat of sky blue silk. A sapphire stick pin winked from the folds of his snowy cravat.

According to the rumors that Molly had shared while getting Charlotte dressed, all Moncreiffe had to do was smile at a girl a certain way and she would swoon at his feet. Looking at him in the brightly lit foyer, with the light from the chandelier gleaming in his golden brown hair, the flash of white teeth when he smiled, she could easily believe the rumors to be fact.

Aunt Hermione came down the stairs next, attired in a regal gown of rich purple velvet that perfectly suited her silver-streaked golden hair.

"I am a doubly lucky man tonight," Alistair declared, and made an elegant bow. "I shall be the envy of all who see us." He dropped a kiss just above Hermione's hand.

"Oh, you silly man." Hermione let out a chuckle. "Do go on."

With a conspiratorial grin, Alistair complied. He showered both women with effusive compliments as he helped them into the elegant carriage and they started off, climbing the heights of absurdity and making them both giggle for a good portion of the drive to the Grishams' town house.

Charlotte enjoyed the silliness—this was a facet of Alistair she had not seen before—but found herself eager to discover what plans he'd referred to. She suffered through the receiving line and the wait to be announced into the ballroom, juggling her curiosity with annoyance at Steven and wondering what he was doing at that moment. Had he reclaimed the box yet?

A delicious shiver ran down her spine when Alistair leaned over to whisper in her ear. "Patience is a virtue, Charlotte."

She looked up, and almost melted at his mischievous smile. "Is it that obvious?"

"Only to me." He winked.

This flutter of anticipation in her stomach was entirely different from when she was about to embark on a mission, but no less intoxicating. She had racked her brain all afternoon, trying to think of what he had planned for this evening, and had come up blank.

At long last they completed the niceties of settling Aunt Hermione among the dowagers, and Alistair fetched her the obligatory cup of punch.

"Run along now, children." Hermione fluttered her fan toward the dance floor, where the musicians were striking the first chords of a waltz.

Charlotte gave her aunt a kiss on the cheek, then slipped her hand in the crook of Alistair's arm, and he led her out.

He spun her into the dance with just as much grace as she remembered from their first dance together, the same day that they had met by such unconventional means. Goodness, that had been less than one week ago. She had foolishly tried to play the simpering debutante with him, but he had seen right through her subterfuge. And he'd seen a great deal more since then.

She waited until they had settled into the rhythm of the waltz, moving together in perfect unity, before speaking. "Is the view to your liking as much as last time we danced?"

"I beg your pardon?" He affected a puzzled innocence, but she detected a knowing glint in his eye.

"My freckle. I noticed the first time we danced that it was of particular interest to you."

They both glanced down at the freckle in question, which was just visible at the neckline of her bodice. It served as a measuring stick of sorts, the point beyond which she would not allow her gowns to be cut any lower.

"I admit I found it quite distracting at first. But of course you're well aware of that, and use it to your advantage." His voice held no censure, just a statement of facts.

"A woman must use whatever weapons she has at hand. So to speak." It was not her intent to lead him on, and their relationship would end as soon as she had the box, but the words he'd used rankled. "You no longer find it distracting?"

He opened his mouth to answer, but apparently thought better of it and twirled her instead. When they faced each other again, he bent to whisper in her ear, his intimacy camouflaged by the steps of the dance. "A great many things about you drive me to distraction, Charlotte."

Another shiver danced down her spine.

He straightened into the proper position, the picture of propriety. Only his wickedly handsome smile remained.

She had to look away to get her emotions under control again. The rumors about him were proving all too true, and she feared she was in danger of swooning. That, or dragging him to the nearest darkened corner, throwing him to the floor, and discovering if he had any freckles of his own. She desperately needed something else on which to focus her thoughts. "About these plans for tonight . . ."

He shook his head. "My, you are impatient." He tightened his fingers on hers. "It's not for another hour or so. You should try to enjoy the dancing. Is not my charming company sufficient for your pleasure?" He lowered his voice to a husky purr on the last word and gave her a look so seductive, her toes curled.

Her breath caught, and released a few seconds later with a whoosh. This time she couldn't blame her breathlessness on Molly tying her stays too tight. She'd gone back to wearing the corset slip she'd favored in France, which did not offer quite as much support but allowed far more freedom of movement.

Alistair had given her fair warning when they kissed in the park, and she had foolishly forgotten his determination to carry through and make their betrothal real.

Now that she was firmly reminded that they were engaged in conflict, she should be able to enjoy their skirmishes without losing sight of her battle plan.

She did indeed take pleasure in the rest of the dance, relishing the feel of his hand at the small of her back, like a hot brand, the comforting strength of his hand holding hers, though they were separated by gloves. Dancing so close, she couldn't help but feel light and dainty in his arms, powerfully reminded of just how tall, handsome, and charming her fake fiancé was.

When the music ended, Alistair escorted her back to Aunt Hermione. She hid a flash of disappointment when he did not sit down beside her, but excused himself and disappeared into the swirling, colorful crowd. Grudgingly, she allowed she couldn't keep him to herself all evening long. They were allowed only one more dance together.

She did not have long to stew on the matter, as several gentlemen acquaintances came to request dances. All were polite, and probably handsome in their own right, but none compared favorably to Alistair.

By the time she returned from taking part in a stately polonaise, Alistair was chatting with Hermione, along with a small group of men and women. She recognized two of the party, Mr. Clarke and Sir Dorian, and guessed that the women beside them were also interested in astronomy.

Alistair quickly made the introductions, presenting her to Miss Davidson and Mrs. Lumby as his fiancée. She should be accustomed to it by now, but hearing him say the words still made her pulse flutter.

He turned to Aunt Hermione. "Our host, Lord Grisham, is also a member of The Royal Society, and has set up a special display for us. It should be ready by now."

"Off you go, then," Hermione said with a smile.

"Shall we?" Alistair held his arm out for Charlotte, and they followed the other two couples out of the ballroom and deep into the house.

Instead of going down the hallway and to another room as she expected, the group turned the corner and climbed the servants' stairs.

"Is this the pre-planned part of the evening?"

"Most assuredly." He squeezed her hand on his arm.

She couldn't make out the words in the conversations between the other two couples, but the general air of excitement was contagious. Her flutterings of anticipation increased.

They continued up, one flight after another, until they reached the door to the roof.

"This seems vaguely familiar," Charlotte whispered, remembering the last time she'd been up on a rooftop. "If you had warned me, I could have worn a warmer dress."

"Not to worry." There was a chair near the door, piled high with blankets. Each of the men grabbed one and draped it around their lady's shoulders just before they stepped outside into the crisp night air.

Alistair and Charlotte were the last in the hallway. Instead of draping the blanket from behind or beside her, he stood in front, and brought the edges of the blanket together just beneath her chin. His eyes grew serious. "Much better circumstances than the last time I did this."

She nodded.

"Your . . . bruise . . . did not make it uncomfortable to climb the stairs, I hope?"

She reached up to hold the blanket, resting her hands on top of his. She wished neither of them were wearing gloves. She'd become accustomed to his warm, bare touch, to the point of craving it. "Stairs are more comfortable than sitting, I assure you."

His gaze had remained fixed on her mouth while she spoke. "That's . . . good." His voice dropped to the barest whisper. He leaned forward, his head tilted to one side.

Her breath caught. She tried to moisten her lips but her mouth had suddenly gone dry.

Voices beyond the open doorway made him look up. He straightened. She clenched her fist in frustration.

He cleared his throat. "Shall we join the others before they wonder what's become of us?" He gave her a slow smile, and gestured grandly for her to precede him out the door.

A brief afternoon rain shower had washed the air clean, and the clouds had obligingly moved off. Stars glittered brightly overhead, with the moon not due to rise for several hours yet. The tallest parts of the London skyline were shown in silhouette, black voids against the backdrop of stars.

Down on the roof, she heard the hushed conversations far better than she could make out the pale blur of faces of the other astronomers. Miss Davidson laughed aloud at something Mr. Clarke said, but quickly covered her mouth with her gloved hand.

Here, five stories above the London streets, the canopy of stars seemed to call for reverent tones, as if they were in a giant cathedral.

Alistair took her hand and guided her to the center of the roof, where she discovered three telescopes had been set up, each about a dozen feet apart. A shuttered lantern marked the location of each tripod.

"This is an annual event," he explained. "Lord Grisham hosts a week-long star party at his country estate every summer. Lady Grisham insists on coming back to the city for the Little Season, so he plans a smaller gathering up here while she hosts the ball downstairs."

Charlotte heard a different voice then, deeper than

those of the other men in their group, though she couldn't make out the words.

"Let me introduce you." Still holding her hand, Alistair led her to the cluster of people around the telescopes. "Lord Grisham, may I present my fiancée, Miss Parnell."

"Pleased to make your acquaintance, so to speak, Miss Parnell." She could barely see the blur of his face, but heard the rustle of fabric and knew that he had bowed.

"Likewise, my lord." She curtsied, amused that they were keeping the formalities even though they were in almost complete darkness.

"Everyone, may I have your attention, please?" Lord Grisham said, raising his voice to a normal conversational level.

The other discussions immediately halted, and everyone took a step closer.

"Mr. Clarke's refractor is being used for the Messier Challenge tonight, Sir Dorian plans to use his for comet hunting, and Moncreiffe's is for viewing . . . whatever you please. There are chairs around the table as usual, and of course, a footman will be up with more refreshments shortly."

"Jolly good host," Sir Dorian said.

"As always," Mr. Clarke seconded.

"Which object are you on now?" That was Mrs. Lumby, who had accompanied Mr. Clarke.

"Number twenty-two," Lord Grisham replied. "And it's giving me a devil of a time."

"One would think it would get easier each time one located it," Alistair said.

"One would think that, yes," Lord Grisham growled.

There was a smattering of laughter, and the group dispersed to the various telescopes.

"That probably sounded like gibberish to you. Let me explain."

Charlotte shook her head, then remembered Alistair couldn't see her. "Not at all. I've been meaning to ask if you've ever attempted the Messier Challenge, or rather, how many times you have found all of the objects on Messier's list in one night of observations."

Certain that his silence meant his jaw had gone slack, she wished she could see his expression. When he still did not answer, she continued. "We are discussing the French astronomer, a famous comet-hunter, who made a list of all the objects he found in the night sky that were not comets, yes?"

"Yes." There was a flash of white as he gave a broad grin. "How many of the objects have you seen?"

"I'm afraid that all of my viewing through a telescope or spyglass has been aimed at things of a more earthly nature. I've only seen drawings of the objects in books."

"Then we must make haste to remedy such a glaring gap in your education."

He led her to the middle telescope, where Sir Dorian and Miss Davidson were debating the merits of equatorial mounts versus altazimuth mounts.

"Looking at anything interesting?"

Sir Dorian scratched his chin. "I think the last thing we looked at was M29, in Cygnus. Isn't that right, Miss Davidson?"

"Yes, but it was already moving out of the field of view, so you'll have to adjust the ascension and declination."

Alistair let go of Charlotte's hand to pull off his gloves before he bent to look through the telescope, and made a slight adjustment. "Yes, that's M29, an open star cluster in Cygnus, the southern cross." He guided Charlotte closer. "Take a look."

The excitement in his voice was contagious. She reached out, found the cold brass eyepiece with her hand, used it to guide the way so she didn't poke her eye on it, and looked through the lens.

All she saw was a collection of white dots. Very similar to the spots of light visible with the unaided eye, if she raised her gaze to the night sky. Just larger, and a bit brighter. No discernible pattern.

The disappointment was almost a physical thing. "How very . . . nice."

"Nice?" He sounded almost as disappointed as she felt.

"Exactly which of the white dots comprise the Messier object?"

There was a pause while he checked the aim of the scope. "In the very center. Do you see it now?"

She closed her left eye and looked through the eyepiece with her right eye. A cluster of white dots, in no discernible pattern. She tried looking with her left eye, and still detected no discernible pattern. "Perhaps I would recognize it if I had seen a better drawing."

He located two more of the Messier objects, but still all Charlotte saw were white dots. She listened in on the excited, hushed conversations around her while he found each object, and heard their enthusiasm as they shared the joy of each other's discovery.

All of this excitement, over random white dots?

"All right, let's try something simpler," Alistair said. "Look up, directly overhead. See the white trail of stars that covers so much of the sky, like steam rising from a teapot?" He stood beside her, shoulder to shoulder. Well, her shoulder to his bicep.

"Via Lactea." That was an easy one to remember. She'd been intrigued by the description of Sagittarius, the Archer, a constellation that resembled a teapot. Steam escaping from its spout poured across the sky, forming the Via Lactea.

He wrapped one arm around her shoulders and pointed with his free hand, directing her gaze to the south. "Look just above the horizon and you'll see Sagittarius. Can you make out the lid on the teapot?"

She had a sudden yearning for licorice. He'd apparently eaten a piece this evening, sometime after their waltz together.

Focusing on the sweet was better than thinking about the warm male scent of him now enveloping her, or the feel of his coiled strength pressed against her side, the way his fingers were slowly caressing her upper arm through the blanket.

He was still waiting for some kind of response to his question.

Right. Sky. She mentally drew lines between the indicated stars, and realized it truly did look like a child's drawing of a teapot. "Yes, I see it." She'd never taken the time to notice that before. Maybe there was something to this hobby after all.

Alistair let go of her to swivel the telescope and aimed it at Sagittarius. "Just above and to the right of the teapot lid is M8, known as the Lagoon Nebula. At home in the Lake District, it gets dark enough at night that you can see it with the naked eye. London has too many gas lamps."

Annoyed with herself for missing his warmth at her side, once more Charlotte bent to look through the telescope. She had no real hope of seeing anything of interest, and mostly made the attempt in order to placate Alistair.

Her breath caught. "I see something! It's like a cloud."

"Yes, a massive cloud of dust and gas. A nebula. Not a very romantic description for what you're seeing, is it?"

"Accurate, though." She studied the Lagoon through the telescope a moment longer, then straightened and tried to locate it with her naked eye. She stayed perfectly still, staring at the spot in space. There. Perhaps it was just her imagination, but she thought she saw the tiny white blob that marked the nebula. Success! She looked through the telescope again to confirm.

She began to understand what the astronomers found so exciting about their hobby. To find such intriguing objects in the vastness of the night sky was like solving a puzzle, or knowing a secret that most people were oblivious to, even though it was right there, over their heads. "What other things can we look at?"

"There's another Messier object, M20, about one degree north of the Lagoon."

She started to step back to let him move the telescope, but he rested his hand between her shoulders. "You can find it. Just tilt the scope up a tiny bit."

While she adjusted the instrument, she thought about the sextant Nick used for navigating. He had never let her touch it, never mind teach her how to use it. Steven, likewise, had been reluctant to let her use his spyglass. It was only after she won money in a card game and bought her own that he taught her some of the finer points of using one.

She'd known Alistair less than a week, and already he was willing to let her use his telescope. True, they were much more intimately acquainted then most people after a week—after years, for that matter.

She reached down to check that the bandage was still in place. There was still some soreness around the stitches he'd sewn so neatly, but tolerable as long as she didn't have to sit down or otherwise have any contact on her posterior.

"Everything all right?" he whispered.

She ignored the shiver caused by his breath in her ear. "Fine. Just making sure the bandage is still in place."

"And?"

"It is."

"Good," he murmured, and trailed his hand down her shoulder.

In some ways, she had been more intimate with Alistair than she had with anyone else. Ever. Or had ever planned to be. She hadn't decided yet if that was a good thing.

He made it difficult to concentrate, resting one hand on hers to help her adjust the telescope, the other rubbing slow circles between her shoulder blades. Thinking about the warmth of his hand, she moved the telescope too far, and saw nothing but random white dots again. But she refused to let him know he was distracting her. By alternating which eye she opened and closed, staring at the sky and then through the telescope, she started over again. She found the tip of the teapot lid, then over to the Lagoon, and then moved upward.

"It's another nebula, only smaller." She heard the pride in her voice, but didn't care. She'd been able to find and recognize the Messier object all by herself.

"Yes, you're right." He was obviously pleased with her progress as well.

She didn't seek or need his approval, but she couldn't help a thread of warmth winding its way through her at the note in his voice. The warmth was definitely from his words, not from the way he kept touching her. Did he realize he was massaging her shoulder? Flush with her success in finding the last object, she was eager to locate others. "What else?"

"How about the Andromeda Nebula? It's to the west, where Mars and the Pleiades are rising above the skyline."

She stood up and turned in a full circle, trying to locate the constellation also known as the Seven Sisters, without Alistair's assistance. She remembered one of the books showing them near Cassiopeia, which simply looked like a flattened W to her. She followed the bottom star in Cassiopeia, and soon had the Pleiades in the center of the eyepiece.

"The beauty of the Seven Sisters outshines Androm-eda, so one can only see the nebula with the aid of a telescope."

The staid scholar was speaking in poetic imagery? His voice was low and soft, near her ear. Any other man might use that tone of gravel-poured-through-honey for seduction, for reading a love poem, for issuing an invita-tion to his bed.

And he was touching her again. His hand ghosted across her nape, stirring the fine hairs. His bare fingers were stroking her exposed skin above the blanket, above her gown's neckline. He'd removed his gloves, enabling her to feel every callus on the pads of each fingertip. Surely by now he felt the goose bumps he'd raised on her flesh.

Why was he doing this? If she didn't know better, she'd think he was trying to seduce her.

Perhaps he was simply excited to have her share in something so important to him, a new convert to his hobby. The majority of their time together had been spent on her quest, the thing most important to her. For all the help he had given her, it seemed only fair to spend some time on his passionate interest.

She cleared her throat. "This one is shaped differently. It's more like a flattened circle."

"Mm-hmm. Andromeda has always been one of my favorites to study." His fingertips were studying the back of her neck.

She stared at the sky without the aid of the telescope, noting the relative location of Andromeda to the Seven

Sisters and Mars, fighting the urge to sway against Alistair, to lean in against his hard body. A white flare streaked above them, cutting right below Mars. "A shooting star." She couldn't help the tinge of awe in her voice.

"The Perseid meteor showers ended a few weeks ago, but we should still see quite a few meteors, if we stay up here long enough." Now his thumb and first two fingers were massaging opposite sides of her neck, close to the base of her skull. Knots of tension dissolved under his ministrations, but instead of feeling relaxed, a new kind of energy thrummed through her veins.

She forced her focus back on the sky. "Andromeda is nice. What's next?"

"Some people have devoted their entire life to the study of Andromeda. Or at least an entire night." His fingers dipped below the blanket, sliding down the slope toward her shoulder.

Her breathing hitched. "I'm not some people."

"I'm well aware of that." He paused, as though giving grave consideration to the selection of their next object, his fingers tapping on her shoulder. Not only could he not talk without using his hands, apparently they were required for thinking, too. "Have you ever seen a dolphin in the night sky? It's over near the Summer Triangle formed by Deneb, Altair, and Vega."

"Triangle? I should warn you, I was never very good at geometry."

He lowered his voice even further, a low rumble beside her ear. "I'm saving the math lesson for later." He slid his arm around her shoulders and turned her so they both faced west. He wasn't just beside her now—he'd turned at an angle, so her right arm was against his chest, his left leg behind her. She could lean to the side and rest her head in the hollow of his shoulder. If she wanted to do such a thing.

"See the brightest star, almost directly overhead?" His breath stirred the hair at her temples, raised gooseflesh in its wake.

He was the one who insisted on looking directly overhead—it wasn't her fault if that required her to rest her head on him. There were a great many stars overhead, more random white dots. But one of them did outshine all its neighbors. "Yes."

"That's Vega, one of the brightest stars in the sky. Think of it as being at the two o'clock position on the face of a clock. Delphinus, the dolphin, is between seven and eight."

She tried to follow the line of his pointing hand and not think about his hand on her shoulder, the heat from his body surrounding her, how his warm breath stirred the hair beside her ear. She wanted licorice.

"Do you see it yet? Some people think it looks more like a kite with a long tail."

"Oh! It's like a porpoise leaping out of the ocean."

He gave her shoulders a squeeze, and didn't let go. Their bodies touched, from shoulder to thigh. There wasn't room for a slip of parchment between them. "That's it."

Miss Davidson and Sir Dorian had drifted over to Lord Grisham's telescope, at least twenty feet away, the three engaged in an animated but still quiet discussion in their hunt for Messier objects.

Mr. Clarke and Mrs. Lumby were huddled around the other telescope, a dozen yards away, only the barest outline of their silhouettes visible. They could be doing anything.

She and Alistair could be doing anything.

It was difficult to focus on the tiny pinpoints of light overhead. Alistair's hand had left her shoulder and drifted over and up until his fingers stroked the hair at her nape, sending shivers of delight up and down her spine. She wanted to take out all of the pins, shake her hair loose, and let him run his fingers through it. His long, elegant fingers. What a man could do with fingers like that . . . Did he want to run his fingers through all of her hair, too? She shifted, and accidentally bumped her hip against his thigh.

Oh my. He wanted to do more than stroke her hair.

They weren't in a park, in daylight, and there were no children around.

Nobody could see them.

Off in the distance, Miss Davidson giggled.

Drat. Sound carried too well up here.

Obviously, Alistair knew that, and had gallantly been restraining himself. She should follow his example and do the same. Just because one wanted to do something didn't mean one should give in to that desire. Even if it was a once in a lifetime opportunity.

"Hungry?" Alistair whispered. "The footman should be up soon."

"I want licorice," she whispered back.

"Oh. My apologies. I should have saved you a piece."

"I only want a taste." She stretched up, reached her hand around the back of his head, and pulled him down for a kiss. His lips were warm, firm yet yielding, fitted perfectly to hers. And tasted divinely of Alistair and licorice. Tormenting him with a kiss was fitting retribution for what he'd been doing to her while making her see stars.

All too soon he pulled away. Before she could form a protest, he felt along her arm until he found her hand, twined his fingers with hers, and started walking. Not toward the rooftop door, not toward the refreshment table, but toward the far side of the roof. Where there were no lit lanterns. No people.

Trusting him to lead her in the darkness, she hurried along at his side, still clutching the blanket closed around her shoulders with her free hand. He squeezed her fingers and she squeezed back, butterflies of anticipation taking flight in her stomach.

Their kiss wasn't over yet.

On one hand, she felt chagrined that he had outmaneuvered her so neatly. With his near-constant touches and caresses over the past hour or more, he had chased her until she caught him by initiating the kiss. On the other hand . . .

Something big and black loomed up ahead, which soon turned out to be a chimney stack, well over seven feet high, more than four feet across. Alistair didn't stop until they had gone around to its far side, completely hiding them from view from the others, had anyone been able to see this far in the dark.

With a growl he backed her up to the brick wall. He planted his palms on the brick, on either side of her face, deliciously crowding her with his body.

"I thought I was going to go mad," he whispered, just before he swooped in and kissed her.

Chapter 15

Desperately needing to touch him, she tore off her gloves and stuffed them in his coat pocket, and gave her full attention to his pulse-pounding, toe-curling kiss.

She had been right. Right about Alistair's intentions, his desire for her, his apparent need to overwhelm her.

Yesterday he had been gentle and tender. Tonight, tenderness was replaced by a consuming, raw desire that left her gasping for breath, yearning for more.

He wrapped one arm around her waist, yanked her close. His other hand cupped her jaw, his fingers stroking her cheek, back and forth, in a slow caress, the way his lips were caressing hers.

She ran her fingers through his hair and cradled the back of his head with one hand in case he had any foolish notions about pulling away again. She sifted her fingers through his wavy hair, soft as silk, delightfully disheveled. Later, when they came back to reality, no one would suspect it had been her fingers going through it rather than Alistair's own.

The kiss changed. She felt the tip of his tongue stroking along the fullness of her bottom lip, moving up, asking to be let in. She opened her mouth, let him in, and all rational thought fled.

Stunned at first by the new flood of sensations, she held perfectly still and let him explore, and felt as much as heard his murmur of approval. He tickled the roof of her mouth, and she wrapped her tongue around his, sucking it farther in. He groaned, and she swallowed the guttural sound. She could still taste a hint of licorice, inextricably mixed with the taste of Alistair.

She saw stars, whether her eyes were open or closed.

It wasn't enough. Without fully understanding the need, she widened her stance and pressed against his hip. He seemed to know what she needed better than she did, and insinuated one long, muscled thigh between hers. She groaned and pressed even harder against him.

Before she could stop him, he slid the kiss to the corner of her lips and kissed his way along her jaw, to her ear. His breathing was delightfully ragged, warm puffs against the oh-so-sensitive skin of her neck.

"I know what you want," he whispered against her skin, his lips brushing her earlobe.

She shivered. "You do?" Good thing one of them knew. She tried to form a longer answer, but couldn't recall any words. Her heart pounded erratically, her breathing just as ragged as his, every sense attuned to what he was doing, saying.

He continued to explore the texture of her cheek, the curve of her jaw, with the fingers of one hand while his other hand slid down her chin, trailed along her neck to the hollow of her throat, where he could undoubtedly feel the flutter of her pulse.

He nodded, the motion brushing his jaw against hers, just a hint of stubble scraping her sensitized skin. "I've seen you watching me." He nibbled on her earlobe. "Seen the way you stare at my hands, at my fingers." He dipped his tongue just inside the shell of her ear, making her shiver again. "You want to know what they can do." He traced the curve of her ear with one fingertip. "What they feel like." Every word was spoken against her skin, his lips caressing her with every declaration.

She turned her head to make it easier for him to kiss his way over to her other ear, let his fingers continue to caress her. "Nice. They feel nice." Someday, she'd again be able to speak in words of more than one syllable.

He let out a low laugh, tickling her ear. "You want to know what they feel like against your naked skin."

She shuddered involuntarily at the image. His fingers were already against her bare skin, dancing along her collarbone, sliding the blanket from her shoulders, skimming the exposed skin just above the neckline of her bodice. Dipping down inside.

She gasped. "Yes. More."

He cupped one breast, the heat of his hand burning through her silk gown and cotton chemise, while his fingers caressed the curve above. She couldn't help letting out a sound distressingly akin to a whimper.

"Shh." He kissed both her eyelids in turn, then the tip of her nose. "Don't cry out." He kissed the underside of her jaw. "You don't want us to be interrupted, do you?"

Distantly, she heard the clink of glassware, the hum of conversation.

She shook her head, biting her bottom lip to keep from crying out again as Alistair tried to discover just how far down inside her dress his fingers could reach.

He kissed her on the mouth again, and gave her little nips that he soothed with his tongue. He swallowed her moan.

He kissed a trail down her neck, to the top curve of her breast, and kept going down, his cheek skimming against her silk dress, one hand skimming her ribs to her hip. She lost track of his other hand until she felt the cool night air stir against her legs.

Being tall and having long fingers also meant the man had long arms. Bent at the waist, Alistair had slipped his hand under the bottom hem of her gown and wrapped his hand around the stocking encasing her ankle. "Mmm, silk," he murmured from somewhere in the vicinity of her waist.

He slid his hand up her leg, slowly moving from side to side, up past her calf. He paused to explore the sensitive back of her knee, his fingers dipping into the slight indentation, his touch just firm enough to not be ticklish, before sliding upward again, her gown bunching on his arm as he went.

The air was cool, but all she felt was the heat of his hand on her leg, constantly caressing, raising her skirt as he brought his hand ever higher. She let her head fall back against the brick wall of the chimney stack, feeling almost giddy, beyond caring that this was much more than she'd bargained for when she'd kissed him.

He reached the top of her stocking and paused, his hand cradling the back of her bare thigh. She felt all four fingers, his wide palm, every callus, his thumb stroking back and forth just above her knee. She wished there was enough light for her to see it clearly—his strong hand on her bare thigh.

He raised her skirt even higher and bent down to press a hot kiss halfway up her naked thigh. And then another. And two to the other leg as well. Good thing she had a solid wall at her back to keep her from toppling over. She reached out and pressed one hand against the cool brick to keep her steady, rested her other on the fine wool covering his broad shoulder.

He straightened, keeping his hand on her leg, her skirt still bunched up on his forearm. "Do you have any idea," he slid his hand from one side to the other, "the effect you had on me," he skimmed across to the other leg, "when I caught a glimpse of these the other night?"

Well, no. She'd been so concerned with the practical considerations of climbing up to the balcony without her dress getting in her way, she hadn't considered how he might be affected by her actions. Or her inadvertent display of skin.

"Just a tiny peek of creamy flesh." His hand slid higher,

almost to the top of her leg now. "So soft." Most of her skirt was bunched on his arm, the gentle breeze brushing her bare legs.

What was he going to do when he ran out of leg?

She had trouble drawing sufficient breath into her lungs.

He kissed his way back up her throat, over her chin, skimmed the corner of her mouth, and up to her ear. "I'm going to give you what you want now." He nibbled the tip of her earlobe between his teeth, soothed it with his tongue. "I'm going to touch you."

What had he been doing all this time, if not touching her? Her skin was on fire from his touch.

He trailed his fingers across the front of her thigh, higher. To her center.

And cupped her in the palm of his hand.

She sucked in a shuddering breath.

Another meteor blazed across the sky overhead.

Holding her, his hand motionless while she adjusted to the shock of such intimate contact, he pressed his body against her side. He cradled the back of her head, his thumb brushing her ear, while his lips grazed her other ear when he spoke. "This is what you wanted, Charlotte. Every time you stared at my fingers, this is what you were imagining."

She moved her lips, tried to form a protest, but the only sound that emerged was a low moan.

He started to move his left hand, back and forth, brushing against the crisp curls between her legs, sending tiny ripples of pleasure throughout her body.

How could this be what she had imagined? She had hardly dared touch herself in such a manner, even in the privacy of her bath, let alone thought of someone else ever doing so. She had tried to imagine what he could do with his fingers, but her imagination was no match for reality.

He increased the pressure, molding his hand to her, massaging back and forth. Needing more, she spread her legs a little wider and started moving her hips, meeting each thrust of his hand.

"Yes, Charlotte," he whispered against her ear. "I know what you want."

Smug braggart, she thought without any real rancor, and thrust harder.

So intent on the sensations he was creating down below, she barely registered the way he caressed her cheek with the backs of his fingers. He captured her lips in another open kiss, at the same time his fingers spread the folds of skin below and slid between them.

He swallowed her gasp.

Slick with evidence of her desire, his finger slid in and out, while his thumb brushed against a particularly sensitive spot that sent sparks shooting along her every nerve ending.

"Don't cry out," he whispered against her mouth.

She heard the distant rumble of conversation, a reminder that there was nothing to shield her and Alistair from discovery but a chimney stack and darkness.

She tried to swallow back the sounds emerging from the back of her throat but was helpless to quiet down her harsh breathing. It became harder to draw air as he increased the tempo and pressure. Something started to build, deep within her.

"I want to bury myself inside you," he said at the same time his fingers did just that. "I want to plunge deep inside your moist heat, feel your warmth, until you envelop me entirely." His thumb brushed over the sensitive nub again.

She saw another blazing meteor, even though her eyes were closed.

"But I can wait."

Of his desire, she had no doubt, as he was still pressed against her hip, his arousal undoubtedly straining his breeches. Given that she was so much shorter than him, was there a crate nearby for her to stand on? Since her injury made her too sore to lie on her back, this was the best position for them to finish what they'd started. And she desperately needed to finish, whatever this was, whatever it entailed.

She opened her mouth to speak, to tell him, but his tongue dove inside in a hot, searing kiss that made her incapable of speech. Possibly for the next week. At least.

She tried to differentiate the sensations assailing her—his kiss, the fingers of his right hand gently, tenderly, stroking the sensitive skin around her ear, the very talented fingers of his busy left hand, his thumb fluttering over that little nub, until the little ripples of pleasure grew to waves big enough to drown her.

Unable to articulate her need, not even certain what her need was, she pounded on Alistair's shoulder, panting for breath.

"That's it." His hand thrust faster, harder. "You're almost there."

"More," she gasped.

She bucked against him, clenching his hair in her fist, clutching the back of his head, arching her back, pressing him even closer, until suddenly all the stars overhead exploded at once and rained fire down on her, burning her from within.

She clung to Alistair, her knees in imminent danger of collapsing.

Over the thudding of her heart she gradually realized he was whispering soothing nonsense in her ear, dusting her cheek and neck with light kisses, his breath stirring the hair that had come loose from her chignon.

She moved one leg, and realized Alistair had not yet removed his hand. Fine tremors still coursed through her body. Not trusting her voice yet, she unclenched her fingers and smoothed his hair.

He slowly, oh so slowly, slid his hand out from between her legs, setting off more tremors, and let her skirt slide down her legs, back into place. "Sweet Charlotte," he whispered in her ear.

Her breathing almost back to normal, she cleared her throat. "What's next?" Even to her own ears, her voice was unusually husky.

Leaning his forehead against hers, Alistair gave a soft chuckle.

"Isn't it your turn?"

He'd moved his hips back, no longer in contact with hers, so she was uncertain of his state. "I told you, I will wait."

The sound of carriages clattering past on the street below brought her back to the reality of their location, on Lord Grisham's rooftop. People stargazing just a few yards away, dancers whirling to music downstairs. Above, the stars still twinkled in their proper places.

"But what about you? That can't be all we're going to do."

"It is for now." He ghosted his fingertips across her cheek, ran his thumb over her lips. "I don't think you have a whisker burn, but we'll have to wait before we go into the light. One look at your kiss-swollen lips and anyone with two thoughts to rub together will know what we've been doing."

She traced his lips with her thumb. "You, too."

He kissed the pad of her thumb. "Me, too."

He'd outmaneuvered her, and she'd lost the skirmish. Soundly.

She didn't care.

Part of her mind—the part not busy reliving every moment, every touch and caress of the last few minutes, the logical part—recognized the strategy he'd employed just now. He'd renewed his argument for them to marry by giving her a sample of the delights to be shared between them as husband and wife. A carrot, rather than a stick.

Later, she would probably be annoyed with him for lulling her into his trap, irritated at herself for falling into it.

But right now, she still throbbed with remembered pleasure, and felt as mellow as if she'd had one too many glasses of wine. She was willing to concede his victory, but just in this skirmish. The battle wasn't over yet.

They stayed motionless for another few precious seconds, then with unspoken accord each began adjusting their clothing, setting things to right.

Behind them the rooftop door opened, spilling light. A footman in Grisham's livery appeared, balancing a tray in one hand and a lantern in the other. He set the tray on the table near Lord Grisham's telescope, bowed, and left again as quickly as he'd arrived, leaving everyone in darkness once more.

"Anyone care for a bite to eat?" Lord Grisham opened the lantern shutter just enough to illuminate the plate of cakes and a full decanter with seven glasses.

The other couples drifted toward the table.

Alistair took her hand and led the way back toward the group.

"You're just in time if you want to see M45," Mr. Clarke said as they approached the refreshment table. "Hurry up, though, or it will be out of the viewfinder range and we'll have to move the telescope again."

Alistair squeezed her hand where it rested on his forearm. "Thank you, but that won't be necessary. We looked at the Pleiades earlier."

Sir Dorian moved into the circle of light cast by the lantern. "Moncreiffe giving you a proper guided tour of the stars, Miss Parnell?" He popped a cake in his mouth.

She was thankful the darkness hid her blush. "He's been showing me quite a few stars, actually, as well as nebulae." She looked up at Alistair. "What was the name of the kite constellation again?"

"Delphinus."

She nodded, even though she knew Dorian could not

see her. "Yes, it's been a very educational evening."

Alistair made a strangled sound, and covered it with a cough.

After experiencing such a life-altering encounter only minutes before, the next half hour or so seemed surreal, spent in meaningless polite conversation with the other astronomers, eating bite-sized pastries, and observing the sky.

She saw several more meteors, though it all paled after the explosive ecstasy she'd experienced at Alistair's touch. He continued to take every opportunity to touch her, but now there was different quality to his contact—more possessive and reassuring, rather than seductive.

Soon Mrs. Lumby announced she was getting cold, and the others decided it was time to head back down to the ball. Their private star party was at an end.

Alistair made certain they were the last to enter the lit hallway, to make sure they had put everything to right before they were seen in public. He took the blanket that had been around her shoulders and tossed it onto the chair, then slipped her sleeves a little higher on her shoulders.

She straightened the folds of his cravat. "Think we'll pass muster?" She stared at his full lips, still reddened from their kisses. She couldn't look at his hands without blushing anew, heat curling through her insides.

He tucked a strand of hair behind her ear. "Try not to let your aunt get a good look at you. She probably wouldn't mind too much, under the circumstances, but there's no sense taking unnecessary risk."

He was determined to win her over, but wouldn't stoop

to taking the decision away from her. Her heart swelled. All adversaries should fight with such fairness.

One last thing—she dug into his coat pocket and retrieved her gloves. He still hadn't put his back on. She couldn't help staring at his fingers, especially those of his left hand.

Heat stole across her cheeks again at the remembered intimacy of where that hand had been, what he'd done to her. What he'd whispered in her ear as he did such marvelous things.

"Stop looking at me like that."

Guiltily, she glanced up. Seeing the sparkle in his eyes, she smiled. "Like what?" She batted her lashes for good measure.

"Are you intentionally trying to make it impossible for me to go back to the ball room?"

"I offered—"

"I say, did you two get lost?" Mrs. Lumby called.

Alistair rolled his eyes heavenward, then leaned over the stairwell. "Coming!"

"As I was saying . . ." Charlotte whispered.

"Hush." He gave her a gentle push toward the stairs, and they soon joined the group, and the dancing. They'd returned just in time for the last waltz of the evening.

Reluctantly, Alistair pulled his gloves on just before they entered the brightly lit ballroom. Much as he wanted to keep touching Charlotte, he didn't dare allow any skin-to-skin contact while his control was still so tenuous.

He'd had the best of intentions, the most innocent of intentions, when he'd taken her up to the roof.

He had to touch her, make sure she was beside him in the dark, make sure she really was safe. He'd woken up last night in a cold sweat, his heart in his throat, having dreamt that the pistol shot that wounded Charlotte's dignity had been fatal.

He'd tried to reassure himself of her safety by remembering the night they spent together after he tended her wound. Tending that had required touching. He'd done his damnedest to be a gentleman, to not take advantage of her moment of vulnerability, but visions of her naked flesh, the remembered feel of her soft skin, tortured him. Kept him awake long into the night, yearning for release.

Her breathless excitement at recognizing the object in the sky had been his undoing. He might still have resisted temptation, had she not requested the taste of licorice.

One kiss in the dark, and he was lost.

He needed to kiss her, to mark her as his own. Feeling the bandage around her hip brought him to his senses, to a degree. The first time they made love would be after their wedding, on a soft, comfortable bed, her injury fully healed. His own satisfaction could wait until then. But tonight . . . he needed to hear her sigh, gasp, pant and moan.

And she'd done all of that. Because of him. Because of the pleasure he'd given her.

He was not above reminding her of that, should the need arise.

Most women would not need coaxing to become his bride. But if he'd wanted most women, he could have wed years ago.

He wanted Charlotte.

He would make certain she wanted him.

Charlotte floated through the rest of the evening, barely noticing Miss Hewitt's dagger-like stare or Lord Durrell's lisping commentary on the other dancers as they moved through the minuet together. Most of the time she remembered to hide her cat-in-the-cream-pot smile, but it slipped free almost every time she locked gazes with Alistair.

She drifted to sleep that night still feeling the ghost of his touch, and awoke in the morning trying to grasp the tendrils of dreams that left her yearning for more.

Reality reasserted itself when she faced herself in the mirror, brushing out her hair. There could be no repeat of last night, at least not with Alistair. She had less than two weeks before Nick would return. He wouldn't intentionally rat her out, but Steven would undoubtedly press him for details about the night she'd spent on the *Wind Dancer* with Alistair.

She needed to have the snuffbox and be off working on her first solo assignment from Lord Q long before then.

After they ended their fake engagement, Alistair would be free to pursue whatever liaisons he felt so inclined. Plenty of women would be ecstatic to take her place in his arms.

As an independent woman, she could engage in similar discreet encounters with other men if she wanted, or perhaps even as part of her spy work.

She didn't feel the thrill of anticipation at the prospect that she expected.

Perhaps she just needed a good meal.

She had just sat down to breakfast when the front door opened and closed. Moments later Steven swept in and kissed her on the cheek, his expression somber. That was not unusual in and of itself, but he also lingered to squeeze her shoulders and pat the top of her head.

"What was that for?" She wrinkled her nose. He looked and smelled even worse than yesterday. "Find anything useful or interesting at Toussaint's?"

He sat down and ran his fingers through his hair, which was an improvement on its disheveled state. "Damnable business we're in."

Her heart skipped a beat. "Is Gauthier all right?"

"Oh, he's fine. Probably in better shape than I am, the old frog." He leaned back in his chair, his expression still serious.

"Steven, do not keep me in suspense like this."

"Sorry." He gave a rueful shake of his head. "We searched every inch of the town house last night. Found plenty that could make Toussaint swing at Tyburn, but no sign of the box we're after, so we went down to have another go at the gaming hell. There was a fight in the alley."

"And? There are lots of fights in the alleys in that neighborhood."

He let out a gusty sigh. "A man was stabbed to death."

She took a long drink of tea and said a quick prayer for the man's family. "That's terrible, but that sort of thing happens down there on a regular basis. Why is this one in particular bothering you?"

He wouldn't meet her eyes for a moment. "The victim,

Kolenka, was identified by a man claiming to be his friend. We think Kolenka was one of the Darconian emissaries sent to retrieve the snuffbox."

Charlotte sucked in a breath. "Do you think he's the same man who broke into Toussaint's study? That would be too coincidental to simply be a coincidence."

"You mean him being killed so near Toussaint's establishment, just two nights after breaking into Toussaint's study? No, I don't believe it's a coincidence, either." Steven leaned forward and clasped Charlotte's forearm, his blue-gray eyes intent. "How well did you see the intruder the other night? Do you think you'd be able to recognize him?"

"You mean, would I recognize his corpse?" She tightened her lips and tried to be logical about the matter.

Once she'd reached the balcony that night, she had taken a moment to rub her stinging hands after climbing the rough brick wall. She'd barely had time to register that there was a strange man in the room before the door to the study had been flung open. The only light was cast by the burning coals in the fireplace, but she'd been in the dark for the previous half hour or more, and her eyes had adjusted as well as they could.

"I only caught the briefest glimpse when Toussaint came in and the intruder turned toward me, before I leaned over the balcony to shout a warning to Alistair. Everything blurred a bit after that." She took a shaky breath. "But, yes, I think I may have seen enough to be able to identify him."

"That's my girl." Steven patted her arm.

Within the hour she was following her brother and

Gauthier down a dismal hallway in a nondescript building in the City that housed the coroner's office. With no
carpets or other furnishings to muffle the sounds, their
footsteps rang out on the tiled floor and bounced off the
walls. The walls might have been painted white at some
point, but they were now a dingy, sooty gray.

She refused to allow the gloomy surroundings to af-
fect her emotions. What she was about to do was part of
the job. An unpleasant part, an occasion she hoped was
rare, but something she had to be able to handle. Steven
and Gauthier had always shielded her from some of the
more gritty aspects of their work. This was her chance to
prove her sensibilities weren't the least bit delicate.

She pulled her gloves on tighter, glad she'd worn cotton instead of kidskin, as the fabric was better at ab-
sorbing the sweat from her palms.

The clerk leading the way opened an unmarked door,
one among dozens they'd passed, and gestured them
inside.

Charlotte took a fortifying breath, straightened her
posture, and crossed the threshold.

Weak sunlight filtered in through the high windows,
revealing several long, narrow tables, all but one of
which was empty. A workbench beneath the window was
cluttered with an array of jars whose contents she couldn't
identify and tools that looked like they belonged in a
torture chamber.

Aware that her brother and Gauthier were watching
her every move and flicker of expression, Charlotte determined she would show no emotion. After all, she'd
seen countless dead bodies before. An entire field strewn

with dead soldiers of several nationalities, the aftermath of a battle they'd failed to prevent. Blood and mud had clung to her skirts in equal amounts. She hadn't cast up her accounts then. She wouldn't do so now.

The clerk pulled back the sheet covering the body, revealing Kolenka's face and shoulders, his greasy black hair.

Charlotte's heart stopped, then started again at double its usual pace.

There was a world of difference between seeing dozens of anonymous bodies and viewing up close the corpse of one man whose name she knew.

Her feet felt rooted to the spot. Her breakfast threatened to reappear.

Soldiers going into battle were trained to fight, were fully aware that they might die before the day was out.

Had Kolenka known yesterday that he might die? Was he aware that his life was in danger? Had he even realized he'd engaged in battle?

"Well, poppet? Is this the same man who was in Toussaint's study?"

Charlotte forced air into her lungs and out again. She considered sitting down and putting her head between her knees, but refused to give in to the light-headedness. A few more deep breaths and she'd be fine. Even if the air in here was tainted with odors she didn't want to think about. "Can . . . can you roll him onto his side? I saw him from a different angle than this."

The clerk and Gauthier worked together to do as she asked, while Steven slung one arm around her shoulders and gave her a squeeze. She half expected him to rub his knuckles against her skull. The flash of memory from their shared childhood helped steady her.

She shrugged off her brother's arm, moved over to get a better angle, and tilted her head. For a moment she squeezed her eyes closed, to compare this sight against the mental picture from two nights ago, then opened them to take another long look. "You can let him go now."

Gauthier and the clerk let go, and the body rolled back onto the table with a dull thud.

One more thing, just to make certain. She leaned closer and took a tentative sniff of Kolenka's coat, averting her eyes from his blood-soaked chest. Her heart sank as the now familiar sharp odor of tobacco assaulted her senses. It was unlike any British blend of tobacco she'd previously encountered, far different from the cheroots Sir Nigel tended to favor. "Yes. That's him." She stepped back, toward the door. "Kolenka is the same man Toussaint caught breaking into his study."

"Merde," Gauthier muttered.

"Bloody hell," Steven echoed.

The clerk drew the sheet over the body, and the four living souls filed out into the hall.

"What now?" Charlotte concentrated on keeping her hands perfectly still at her sides, kept forcing air in and out of her lungs, and tried not to think about Kolenka. Had he left behind a wife and children? Or a mother? Sister?

"We have to make a report to Lord Q."

"Vraiment."

Charlotte looked up. "We're going to see him, at his office?" Though they'd made many reports to Lord Q over the years, she'd never actually seen him. Steven had always left her behind if there was a chance to deliver his report in person.

Steven shook his head. "We still can't risk being seen with him in the City. But an old friend of the family can certainly pay a call on us at home without drawing any attention. That was the other part of the message that arrived this morning—to expect him."

The ride home in the carriage seemed to take considerably longer than the ride to the City just an hour before. Aunt Hermione's town coach was better sprung than most hackneys, and the velvet squabs thickly padded, but having to sit back on the bench was less than comfortable, even after all of the poultices. Squirming only made it worse.

She stared out the window, searching for a tree, birds, flowers—anything living to replace the image of death that seemed etched into her mind.

She tried to analyze the situation dispassionately, the way she knew Lord Q would. Toussaint had identified the man breaking into his study, and either had him killed or killed him personally. He had personally wielded the knife that almost claimed Steven's life, and had escaped unscathed.

As a weeping girl of seventeen, Charlotte had been no threat to him.

Now, she was a woman of twenty, with a decade's worth of experience and training crammed into the intervening three years. She would wrest the snuffbox from Toussaint, see the letter restored to its rightful owner, avert the scandal that threatened to shake the foundations of the government, and prevent Toussaint from killing again.

Once home, the three adjourned to the drawing room. Steven retrieved parchment and ink from the desk, while Gauthier sharpened a quill pen, and Charlotte gazed out the window, watching children playing tag in the square's park, overflowing with trees and shrubs and chirping birds.

They went through the report carefully, each contributing the details they were most familiar with. Charlotte leaned over Gauthier's shoulder to read the final draft, and noted the embellishments their scribe had added. "*Mon ami*, you should write novels."

"But I already do, *ma petite*. You do not think this is my only secret life?" He winked at her.

They all looked up at the sound of a knock on the door.

Farnham entered and bowed. "A gentleman to see you, sir. He declined to give me his card." His intonation remained perfectly polite, but when he straightened from his bow, his nose was just a few degrees higher than usual.

Charlotte couldn't help a small smile. Since they were so unaccustomed to having servants available, perhaps they should have insisted Aunt Hermione engage the services of someone a little less highly recommended.

"Show him in," Steven said. "And please send up refreshments."

"Very good, sir." He clicked his heels and left.

"That poor man," Charlotte said. "I hate to think of all the times we have failed to live up to his expectations."

Her stomach fluttered with nervousness at finally meeting Lord Q. Perhaps she should have gone upstairs and freshened up when they returned home. But surely a man like Lord Q would be more concerned with actions and results than neatly combed hair? She tried not to think about the fact that her whole future could depend on the next few minutes.

Moments later, footsteps sounded in the hall and there was a bit of shuffling as the guest preceded the butler into the room.

Lord Q was much shorter than she expected. In fact, she and he could probably see eye-to-eye, a detail that she hoped boded well for her future. He looked the grandfatherly sort, with deep lines on his cherubic face that showed he smiled often. His white hair poked up in tufts, contrasting with his pink cheeks. She almost expected him to offer her a sweet.

Many men must have been caught off guard over the years, underestimating him.

He handed his hat and walking stick to the butler and said, "That will be all."

Farnham looked at Steven for confirmation before he bowed and left.

Lord Q glanced at Steven and Gauthier, then strode directly toward Charlotte, his hand held out. "You must be Charlie. I have been dying to meet you, my dear."

Chapter 16

Charlotte remained frozen for a moment, then curtsied and shook Lord Q's proffered hand. His grip was firm. Unlike most men she'd ever shaken hands with, he did not treat her as a delicate creature. Her estimation of him rose a notch.

She made sure her own grip was equally firm and confident in return. "To be honest, my lord, I wasn't even certain you were aware of my existence."

Steven made a small choking sound in the back of his throat.

Lord Q gave Steven a *tsk tsk*, and patted her on the shoulder. "The safety of our operatives is always our top concern." Still with his hand on her shoulder, he led her to the sofa and gestured for her to be seated. "We list in our reports only the names that are absolutely essential, but be assured we have long been aware of your contributions."

She couldn't be rude, so she perched on the edge of the sofa as gracefully as she could. She wished she knew him well enough to know if he was using *we* in the royal *we* sense, or referring to his associates at the Home Office.

With his compliment, she couldn't have asked for a better opening. "I'm so happy to hear that, my lord. That is precisely what I wish to discuss with you—my ongoing contributions."

"The end of them, you mean," Steven said from his chair by the desk.

By force of will, Charlotte resisted the urge to shoot her brother a dirty look.

"Your fiancé, he was none too happy the other night, I'm thinking." Gauthier had assumed his usual position by the fireplace, where he could keep an eye on both the door and window.

"You are engaged, my dear? My felicitations." Lord Q patted her knee. "I must admit I'm disappointed to lose an agent with such promise so soon, but it is to be expected. Young women such as yourself tend not to remain in the field for long."

Charlotte wanted to grind her teeth. This was not going at all according to plan. She glanced between her dear brother, whom she currently wanted to strangle, and dear Gauthier, who had been like an uncle. Regardless of their expectations for her future, she wanted to work for Lord Q. "Thank you, but felicitations are not called for. I am not truly engaged."

Lord Q's brows knitted. "I'm afraid I don't understand."

"What the hell do you mean, you're not engaged?"

"Mon dieu!"

Charlotte ignored the outbursts and kept her attention focused on Lord Q, who thankfully maintained the attitude of polite interest in whatever she had to say. Some of the trepidation about revealing her plans evaporated. "Steven has changed since we came to London, and for some reason expects me to forget all about what I've been doing for the last five years. I, however, have no intention of giving up the work. My so-called engagement is simply a cover that has enabled me to continue my efforts to recover the snuffbox."

Lord Q did not seem taken aback by this astounding revelation. "And your fiancé is aware of your activities? Aware that your relationship is a sham?"

That made it sound . . . sordid. There was nothing dishonorable in what they'd done. "Alistair was only too happy to enter into our subterfuge, and has benefited just as much as I have."

"But you spent the night with him!"

"He was there when you broke into the *cochon's* study."

She pressed her hands flat against her skirts to keep from balling them into fists. Lord Q was also ignoring the interruption, his attention still patiently focused on her. Bless him.

"I took Alistair into my confidence early on in our acquaintance. He has shown himself to be a worthy partner. He is also a school chum of the captain of the *Wind Dancer*, where we sought refuge for the night."

She noted the flare of understanding in Q's eyes, and

felt a surge of confidence. "He is well-suited to our work, my lord. He is fast on his feet, both mentally and physically, and most importantly has no wish to dissuade me from completing this task." She spared a glare for Steven. "Unlike others in this room."

Q nodded. "It goes without saying, you find him trustworthy."

She'd certainly trusted Alistair last night, when he'd held her in his hands. His magnificent, talented hands . . . She turned the direction of her thoughts before they betrayed her with a blush. "He is a gentleman who can play the rogue when needed."

Q nodded gravely. "I do prefer that my operatives work in pairs when possible, or threes, as you all have done so successfully over the years. Pairs tend to be more productive, have fewer casualties. The cover of a false betrothal, however, cannot be maintained indefinitely."

A maid knocked and entered just then, and deposited the tea tray on the table in front of Charlotte. After she left, several minutes were taken up by the ritual of passing the plate of cakes and making sure that everyone had a cup of tea to their liking.

Her mood was boosted by the fact that Lord Q had not dismissed her intentions out of hand. She need only decide what to do when her engagement with Alistair ended, as it must inevitably.

She paused, the teacup halfway to her mouth. End her engagement to Alistair.

That had been the plan all along, of course. Nothing had changed. There was no reason to follow it through to the conclusion Alistair envisioned—their marriage. He did not truly want to be a spy, and she did not truly want to be a wife.

Not even Alistair's wife.

Not even with the potential for a lifetime of heaven-shattering experiences like last night. Not even to an open-minded man brave enough to let her drive his phaeton, someone charming enough to make her and Hermione giggle like silly schoolgirls.

She resolutely ignored the lump that formed in the pit of her stomach.

Steven gave their report to Lord Q to read while they were all munching on cakes and sipping tea.

From the thunderous expression on her brother's face, she knew he would try to continue the conversation again later, in private. She determinedly concentrated on the delicious pastry in her hand. At least, she assumed it was delicious. It may as well have been made of ash.

Lord Q set aside the report. "The first question we must address, gentlemen, and Miss Parnell, is how to proceed in regards to the snuffbox and letter." He refilled his teacup. "You are confident the items are not at Toussaint's gaming hell?"

"*Oui.*"

"We managed a rather thorough search, even before the altercation in the alley."

Charlotte set down her unfinished cake. "If I were Toussaint, I would now take the item from wherever it was hidden last night and move it to the gaming hell."

Steven shook his head. "He thinks he's got rid of the only outsider who knew it was at his town house. He'd believe the town house is the safest place to keep it."

"But someone has tried to break in there already," Gauthier said. "The one place no one has disturbed so far is the home of his partner. What is the little rat's name?"

"Sir Nigel," Charlotte offered. "I don't think Toussaint would trust him enough to let him keep it. If I were Toussaint, I would want such a valuable item on my property, perhaps even on my person, where I could keep a close eye on it."

Steven shook his head. "No, I agree with Gauthier. Our best option now is to search Sir Nigel's lodgings. No one would expect such a valuable item to be kept there." He looked to Gauthier. "I think we should do a bit of exploring this evening, don't you?"

"*Certainement.*"

Charlotte folded her arms. "Guineas to green beans it's not there. I still say it's at Lost Wages."

"Both theories have merit," Lord Q interjected, before the conversation could degenerate into a sibling squall. If he was about to take sides, they were prevented from learning his choice when the drawing room door opened.

"Ah, there you are, Steven." Aunt Hermione bustled in, untying the ribbons to her bonnet as she walked. "Mrs. Higginbotham was so disappointed you were not in attendance at the Grishams' ball last night. Please say you'll—" Now that her bonnet was off she noticed the other men in the room and came to a halt, her expression frozen. The men jumped to their feet.

"Good afternoon, Aunt. Do you remember—"

"Lady Marwood, may I say you look just as ravishing as the last time I saw you."

"William!" She patted her hair into place and hurried toward Lord Q with a seraphic smile lighting her face such as Charlotte had never before seen. She half expected her aunt to fling herself into the old gent's arms. "Yes, you may, and there's no need to stand on ceremony."

Lord Q raised Hermione's hand for a courtly kiss.

Steven's jaw worked several times before he managed to get out a syllable. "I wasn't aware you two were so well acquainted. Indeed, I wasn't even sure you would remember him."

Hermione sat on the sofa and patted the spot beside her. Lord Q obediently sat down. Everyone else shifted until they were seated also. Charlotte gratefully moved to a straight-back chair, where it was easier to perch on the edge of the seat. "True, our first meeting was not an auspicious occasion, God rest your father."

Charlotte's puzzlement must have shown.

"I'm afraid I'm the one who was charged with the task of bearing bad news when Sir Blakeney's ship went down and all hands were lost," Lord Q explained.

"William's been such a dear, keeping in contact with me and your mother, Charlotte, seeing how we got on. Until she remarried, of course. He paid several calls on Marianne and me after Helena passed on, but alas, you'd already left to live with Steven in Scotland."

"Yes. Glasgow was marvelous." Since she'd only spent a week there in her entire life, she turned her attention to Lord Q before Aunt Hermione could ask any questions about her supposed five-year stay there. "I wasn't aware your association went as far back as Steven's childhood."

Hermione nodded. "Thank goodness I was visiting Helena that fateful day, or she'd have had no one to comfort her but her baby boy."

Steven cleared his throat.

"I do believe you are embarrassing the boy," Lord Q said, looking not the least apologetic.

Charlotte bit her bottom lip to keep from grinning. If she had a laugh at Steven's expense, he would make her pay for it later. There was already plenty of retribution in store for her deception.

"Madame Marwood, are you enjoying the season's entertainment?"

Charlotte sent a silent thank-you to Gauthier for steering the subject back to a more neutral topic.

"I must say, it is an entirely different experience now that my little Marianne has been successfully launched. There is but one task left for me, and that is to see my niece blissfully settled. Fortunately, we are already well on our way to that happy ending." She beamed a smile at Charlotte.

"How nice for you." Lord Q shifted his adoring gaze from Hermione to raise an eyebrow at Charlotte.

She gave a slight shake of her head. Hermione knew nothing about Steven's true vocation, or Charlotte's, and she intended to keep it that way. Forever, if possible.

Distantly, she registered the sound of the door knocker. Should she lay the groundwork for the end of her engagement now, give some hint that the ending in store was not the one Hermione envisioned?

Steven had included her in the most recent developments in the investigation, but only because he'd had no choice. His thoughts on the subject of marriage—specifically hers—had not changed. But as long as they were all gathered like this, he could not express his displeasure at her deception.

Farnham tapped on the open door. "Excuse me, madam, sir." He turned to Charlotte. "A gentleman caller for you, miss."

Hermione practically clapped her hands together. "Oh, show him in, show him in!" She gave Charlotte a guilty glance. "Do forgive me, dear, I got carried away. Such a charming young man. I can hardly wait until he's officially part of the family."

For the second day in a row, as though thoughts of him had conjured him, Alistair stood in the doorway. Hermione hustled forward and drew him into the room.

"Sir William, may I make known to you Alistair, Viscount Moncreiffe. My future nephew-in-law."

The men exchanged bows.

"William has been a friend of the family since Steven was in leading strings," Hermione confided to Alistair sotto voce. "I believe you already know Steven and his friend Monsieur Gauthier," she continued, louder. Alistair nodded a greeting to Steven and Gauthier.

"This is your Alistair?" Lord Q threw Charlotte a glance before he strode forward, hand extended. "I haven't seen you since before you went off to Cambridge, lad. How are you?"

"Quite well, sir, thank you." He looked a bit perplexed to have his hand pumped so enthusiastically.

"I was just sharing a bottle with your father last week, and he was telling me about a paper you presented to The Royal Society. He's quite proud of you, you know."

Alistair closed his jaw with an audible click. "To be honest, I didn't think he was listening when I mentioned the presentation. I was discussing it with my grandfather."

Charlotte was extremely thankful she was already sitting down. Never in a million years would she have guessed Alistair and Lord Q were already acquainted.

Then again, it shouldn't be that surprising that Lord Q was acquainted with the family of a duke, given the relatively small size of the ton.

This could work in her favor. Since Q was already acquainted with Alistair's family . . . On second thought, his father, the Marquess of Penrith, was an unreliable sot, being primarily concerned with lifting skirts and emptying bottles. Surely Lord Q wouldn't paint Alistair with the same brush as his father?

Lord Q sat back down on the sofa, obligingly beside Hermione, leaving only the chair next to Charlotte for Alistair. "Ah, yes, the old feud between Penrith and Keswick. The way you've managed to keep the two from throttling each other all these years, you could have a promising career in diplomacy."

Alistair ducked his chin in a charming display of modesty. "I completely understand their urge to throttle each other, sir, since I often share it." He smiled at Charlotte, looking at her through his lashes. She fought the sudden urge to throw her arms around him and ask if they could go somewhere private and share a repeat of last night.

Hermione cleared her throat.

Lord Q gave a guilty start. "But I'm sure you didn't come calling here today to reminisce about your family with me."

"No, I . . ."

"Have you come to discuss a date with Charlotte?" Hermione looked as eager as if she were to be a bride. "If we are to make all the necessary wedding arrangements, we will need to set a date. Soon."

"Date? Right. Yes. Yes, I came to discuss things with Charlotte." Alistair ran his finger between his neck and cravat, as though it were suddenly too tight.

Oh, blast well-meaning relatives. "Shall we go for a turn about the garden?" Charlotte didn't even look to see if Alistair followed.

She didn't need to see, as she could feel his presence behind her like a physical thing. Almost as tangible as his presence had been in front of her, last night, up on the roof.

Not wanting any maids or footmen to overhear their conversation, they were silent on the trip to the back of the house. And just because they would be alone was no reason to lose her head. She needed to stay focused on the snuffbox. Tonight presented a perfect opportunity, too good to pass up or allow herself to be distracted, yet again, by Alistair.

Walking with Charlotte at his side, Alistair debated the best way to broach the subject of their betrothal. Convincing her that they should marry because he had compromised her had already proven unsuccessful. Even after their interlude on the roof last night, he doubted she would see things any differently.

Perhaps it was a simple matter of bribery.

Not with jewelry. Even though his grandmother's sapphire betrothal ring was a dainty thing of beauty, perfectly suited for Charlotte's petite hand, and currently tucked away in a jeweler's box in his coat pocket, jewelry was not the way to her heart.

Not with social ranking, and its accompanying wealth and power. Becoming his viscountess, with the prospect of becoming a marchioness and eventually a duchess, was not the lure to Charlotte that it was to the likes of Miss Hewitt. Charlotte's life in France, so soon after the reign of terror, had inured her to such trivialities.

No, the way to her heart was through her mind and body. She was a woman who craved excitement, who needed to take action rather than wait for others to do so. She needed—and deserved—respect and acknowledgment for the unusual skills she'd cultivated and put to use. And she was most definitely a sensual creature, who had taken great delight in physical pleasure last night.

All he had to do was go along with her being a spy, and remind her that last night had been a mere taste of the veritable buffet that awaited her in the marriage bed. *Their* marriage bed.

Once they stepped outside into the garden, Alistair reached for her hand, then thought better of it—too many windows overlooking the garden—and tucked it into the crook of his arm.

He was searching for the proper words to begin this all important conversation when Charlotte tugged him to the farthest corner of the garden.

"We have to go to Lost Wages tonight," she said, her voice low and urgent.

"We do?"

She nodded vehemently. "Steven and Gauthier have been wrong on every guess as to the whereabouts of the snuffbox. Tonight they're going to search Sir Nigel's lodgings, but I believe Toussaint has moved the box back to Lost Wages. He killed Kolenka last night, or had him killed, but Toussaint knows someone else was trying to break into the study the same time Kolenka was there, so he won't keep the snuffbox at his home. We need to—"

"Stop. Back up. Who's dead?"

"Kolenka."

She appeared reluctant to elaborate, so Alistair gave her a "go on" gesture and waited patiently, schooling his expression to hide his growing horror.

"He's one of the Darconian emissaries sent to retrieve the snuffbox. He was killed in what was supposed to look like a robbery, but it happened too near Toussaint's gaming hell to be a coincidence."

"And how do we know he's the one who broke into Toussaint's study?"

"I recognized him." Her voice had gone quiet, but she threw her shoulders back and lifted her chin. "I went down to the coroner's office with Steven and Gauthier this morning and . . . examined the corpse. It was him, the same man I saw in Toussaint's study."

He was impressed by her bravery, and completely horrified by what she'd gone through.

"So we need to search for it at Lost Wages. Tonight, while he still thinks no one suspects him of being the blackmailer."

"We? You're including me? Willingly?"

She had the grace to look embarrassed. "I just told Lord Q a few minutes before you arrived about how well we work together. If you don't want to go, I'll understand."

He was getting dizzy from the succession of revelations, like a mouse being batted back and forth by a cat. "Sir William is Lord Q? And you told him that we've worked together?"

Alistair needed a moment to reconcile his preconceived notion of a spymaster with the image he'd had all these years of his father's friend. Hmm. Sometimes he'd wondered if Father was really as drunk as he appeared to be.

Then he took a moment to ponder the implications of his father's friend being aware that Alistair was acting as a spy. Q certainly wasn't going to tell Father. "Whatever gave you the idea I wouldn't go? I told you, Charlotte, I will always be with you." He caressed her cheek under the guise of tucking back a stray lock of hair, knowing she reacted to such a stroke the way other women did to a much more intimate caress. "If I didn't, you'd simply go anyway, by yourself."

She closed her eyes briefly, fighting an almost visible battle between pleasure and determination as he trailed his finger down her throat. She blinked at him. "Well, of course I would. Steven has stopped listening to me, and he's even less likely to listen to me now that he knows our engagement is a fraud. Since he won't search Lost Wages, I have to."

He dropped his hand to his side. "You told him about the engagement? Thank you—now I understand why he gave me such a scathing look when I arrived." Alistair ran his fingers through his hair. This had all been entirely too much to take in during such a short stroll through a garden. "I take it Aunt Hermione has not been disabused of her illusion?"

"About us? It's going to break her heart, but no, I haven't told her the truth yet."

He fingered the ring box in his pocket. "We don't have to break her heart, you know. We do work well together." He made sure that Charlotte was looking directly at him, and deliberately stroked his index finger along his upper lip.

Her sudden indrawn breath proved his reminder of last night had not been too subtle. He would much rather have given her a kiss, but his instincts screamed that they were being watched.

Charlotte jerked his arm as she started walking again, racing an unseen foe around the garden's perimeter. "The most unobtrusive way for us to get into Lost Wages is for you to be a young buck out on the town for the night, and me to be your mistress."

"My *what*?"

"Well, what other sort of woman could accompany you to a place like that? It makes perfect sense. You'll have to make a show of being there to gamble. Not too large a purse, though, or you'll be too tempting a target for thieves. The coin won't be a problem for you, will it?"

She went on, planning their foray for the coming evening with great enthusiasm and excitement.

Tomorrow, with the snuffbox in their possession, would be soon enough to finish the conversation he'd intended.

Tonight they were going to search the office of a man known to have killed at least once already.

The ring could wait.

Chapter 17

As they'd agreed, Alistair called for Charlotte that evening in a hackney, picking her up at the same corner as before their attempt to break into Toussaint's study.

Had that only been three nights ago?

Then, she'd been dressed in demure dark gray, her blond curls concealed by a bonnet. Tonight she wore a blood red cloak over a matching scarlet gown cut low enough that her charms were in danger of spilling over the top. A curly black wig completed her disguise.

As she walked toward him, into the swaying light of the coach's lantern, it also became apparent she was not wearing stays. Rouge darkened her cheeks and eminently kissable lips. His groin tightened. No one would recognize the proper Miss Parnell in this costume.

Charlotte, with her blond curls and fresh beauty, was

the picture of innocence, while this creature was temptation on two legs. He wanted both versions. In his bed.

"Promise me you'll burn this dress after we're done tonight," he said as soon as she settled beside him on the bench and the carriage was on its way.

"You don't like it?"

"I like it very much, and I like what it lets me see. Problem is, I don't want anyone else seeing."

She laughed. "That's the point. Men look at this," she waved in the general direction of her exposed décolletage, "and don't see this." She pointed at her face.

"And why is that a *good* thing?"

"Because, silly, they won't remember my face, or notice if I'm looking at them or across the room. It's perfect."

Perfectly distracting. She had a point. "And that is all we are doing tonight—looking. If we find the snuffbox, Lord Q can send somebody else to take it out of there. Toussaint has already killed once. I don't want him aiming at you." He didn't want Toussaint in the same country, let alone the same building, as Charlotte.

She shifted on the bench. "He already aimed at me once, and didn't exactly miss."

His heart contracted painfully at the memory. He rested his hand possessively on her knee. "Don't give him a second shot. If he's there, we're leaving. Is that clear? I won't take the chance that he might recognize you, even in this getup."

She gave a murmur in response that he chose to interpret as acquiescence.

They rode in silence for a bit, Alistair's hand still on her knee. The single lantern inside the coach cast enough light for him to see the growing excitement on her face. He could almost feel it thrumming through her body, just as it was thrumming through his. The adventure, the anticipation—heaven help him, he craved it just as much as she.

She cleared her throat. "Are you prepared for the way we will have to act tonight?"

He noted she still had not clearly acknowledged or agreed with either of his directives. At least she hadn't disagreed, either. "Act what way?"

"As though we are love—as though I am your mistress."

He grabbed her around the waist, eliciting a squeak of surprise, and gently settled her on his lap, careful of her stitches. "Like this?" He wrapped his arms around her, to steady her against the sway of the coach.

She had applied more perfume than usual tonight. He nuzzled her neck just beneath her ear, where he knew it made her quiver with delight, and inhaled attar of roses, much heavier than the light rosewater she generally favored. It had become his favorite scent. He had become intimately acquainted with all of her scents, especially the delicious musk of her arousal. Just thinking about it was sending his blood south.

She kept her back straight as a poker. "Do you normally have your mistress sit on your lap?"

Since he'd never kept a mistress, he almost laughed, but realized in time what a mistake that would be. "The only woman I want on my lap is you," he whispered in her ear.

She might be keeping her back stiff, but she couldn't hide the shudder that coursed through her as his lips brushed her skin.

Last night she had been incredibly responsive to his touch. It would be so easy to repeat the experience, right here in the coach. Just slide his hand beneath her skirts, up her silken thigh . . .

This was a monumentally bad idea. The motion of the coach had Charlotte coming into contact with parts of his anatomy that had no business having any contact with her until after their wedding. Sweet torture.

He should move her back to the cushion, but couldn't bring himself to end his delightful torment.

"It's all right," she suddenly said. "I know it's something men don't have a great deal of control over."

Ah, damn, she had noticed. "Boys may have little control," he said, pulling her closer. If she didn't bend, she was going to break. "But as a mature man, I assure you, the only time this occurs is when I'm with you, because I want so desperately to . . . be with you." He nuzzled her ear again, remembering how she had shuddered in response. He knew exactly where and how to touch her, to elicit which sort of reaction. After they were married, he'd take her where she could be as vocal as she wanted, unlike last night when they'd both struggled to be quiet, to not draw attention.

She sighed and snuggled into his embrace.

A moment later she surprised him by nuzzling his ear,

sending an unexpected shiver down his spine when she whispered against his skin, "Don't cry out." She nibbled on his earlobe, snaked an arm around his waist, and dipped her fingers just inside his breeches.

He grinned at the remembered admonition, and reflexively tightened his grip around her waist. Her dark red velvet gown invited his touch, exploration. He wanted to pull off his gloves and slide his bare hand over the soft fabric, caress the gentle curve of her hip, cup her breast, slide the low neckline even lower, and . . .

Just as he was about to toss aside all his good intentions and toss her skirts, the coach rocked to a halt.

He shut his eyes and drew upon the dregs of his willpower. "We're there."

"No," she whispered, and kissed him just beneath his ear. "We still have a long way to go."

Damn reading the banns, he was going to carry her straight to Scotland, marry her over the anvil, and have their wedding night above the blacksmith's shop.

Just as soon as they retrieved the snuffbox, or she'd never forgive him.

He'd never been so reluctant to remove a woman's arm from his waist. "Time to go to work, Charlotte."

"What?" She sat up so quickly she almost tumbled to the floor. "Oh."

He assisted her to her feet before he climbed out. The driver had stopped right by a mud puddle, so Alistair lifted Charlotte out of the carriage and carried her to the stone steps leading into the tavern, shouldering aside the people clustered about the entrance. He heard a few ribald comments directed their way, and overheard one woman negotiating fees and services with her customer. He wanted to cover Charlotte's ears. She, however, was eavesdropping.

He paid the driver, tucked Charlotte's arm in his, and sauntered into the raucous, smoky interior, feeling an altogether different sort of excitement from just a few minutes ago.

He loved astronomy, and had been studying the night sky most of his life. But no matter what secrets of the universe he unlocked, none of it made a difference in anyone's day-to-day life—at least, not in any tangible, practical way. Getting back the snuffbox, and the damning letter hidden inside, was tangible. Would make a difference.

This was exactly the type of seedy tavern his father was likely to patronize, one that the duke would never enter. Serving wenches hurried to and fro in the taproom, ale and other beverages sloshing out of the tankards they carried, nimbly avoiding the occasional pinch or slap from the crowd of disreputable-looking male patrons. Several men had platters of food on the table in front of them, a doxy sitting on their lap, or both. Most of the women wore gowns that made Charlotte's look positively prudish.

"This way," she whispered, and guided him through a doorway in the back. They passed the kitchen, where steam and the savory scent of food wafted out, past the door to the keg room, and down a dimly lit hall. Soon, the clatter of coins being tossed amidst more raucous laughter became audible.

Under the guise of nuzzling her ear, Alistair stopped

just inside the doorway of the main gaming room, which was filled with tables, chairs, gamblers, and more serving wenches. "The snuffbox is not likely to be in here."

"No, it's more likely to be in the office, the wine cellar, or even the kitchen. And there are rooms upstairs that can be rented."

"All of which, I'm sure, were thoroughly searched by Steven and Gauthier. What do you propose to do differently than they did?"

"Succeed."

Alistair threw his head back and laughed. "Shall we begin, my dear?" he said loudly, and staggered toward the nearest table with an empty chair.

Charlotte slipped into the role-playing without missing a beat. "By all means, my lord, let's spend your coins."

Her giggle was pitch perfect, but she didn't need to sway her hips quite that much.

Once he was seated, she stood behind him, carding her fingers through his hair as he gave a cursory greeting to the other men at the table and ordered a glass of wine each for himself and Charlotte.

"Fresh blood," said the white-haired gent to Alistair's right.

"More import'ly, fresh money," said a man with an enormous red nose to Alistair's left. He hiccuped.

A third man, who looked young enough to still be at school, rapped his knuckles on the table. "Deal again, damn you!" Beads of sweat stood out on his upper lip.

Alistair placed his bet, and the dealer, a buxom, heavily rouged woman who might still be in her thirties, dealt him into the next hand of *vingt et un*.

Over the next hour, he won as much as he lost, which required more concentration than he had known he was capable of, what with Charlotte toying with his hair, whispering in his ear, and at one point even perching on his knee.

Thanks to his friend Nick's tutelage back in their school days, Alistair was able to spot the markings on the cards, which almost made the game fair again. The other three men continued to drink as heavily as they played, and the number of empty bottles on the table grew. Alistair sipped at his one glass.

The noise level in the room rose concurrently with the quantity of alcohol consumed and the lateness of the hour. More than one man slipped out of the room, a giggling *fille de joie* on his arm. Some didn't even make it all the way out the door before reaching into the girl's bodice or under her skirts.

"That's Mr. Jennison, the manager, buying stolen goods," Charlotte whispered in his ear. She tilted her head, pointing out a man with three chins and just as many fobs hanging from his garish green waistcoat, who sat down at a table in the back corner.

As Alistair watched, Madame Melisande entered and sat down opposite Jennison, and spread her fan out on the table. The two launched into a spirited conversation conducted in low tones, until Jennison pushed a few coins across the table.

Leaving her fan on the table, Melisande got up and moved to a gaming table, sitting directly beneath the chandelier. Alistair had never before noticed how similar her build was to Charlotte's. His fiancée might have modeled her daring dress and glossy black curls on the French courtesan's, but Charlotte could never mimic the hard look that marred Melisande's once-beautiful features as she scowled at Jennison, or the avaricious gleam in her eyes as she cast her wager.

Setting them apart even further, Charlotte had chosen a luxurious scarlet silk cape to go with her dress, rather than the more cheaply made black cape adorning Melisande's shoulders.

Jennison tucked the fan into the cabinet behind him and turned his attention to the young man who'd just sat down and pushed a fob across the table.

Alistair nuzzled Charlotte. "Looks like he's begun his night work."

"Now would be a good time to take a look at his office."

At the end of the next hand, Alistair made a show of stretching, and patted his belly. "Time to get rid of some of this wine, eh what?"

Charlotte obligingly clung to him as he staggered out of the room and into the hall.

"The men's necessary is in there," said one of the serving wenches, pointing over her shoulder. She blew a strand of red hair out of her eyes. "Or them's rooms upstairs, what can be had for a shilling an hour."

"Thank you." Alistair didn't have to fake the lurch to the side, as Charlotte stepped behind him the instant she'd spotted the wench, almost knocking him over.

As soon as they were alone in the hall, Alistair backed her up against the wall, planted his hands on the stained wallpaper on either side of her face and leaned in as though for a passionate encounter. "What's going on?"

"That was Ginny. When I talked to her here last week, I was wearing this same costume, but told her I wasn't in this line of work."

"And you didn't want to disappoint her, let her know that you've become a fallen woman?"

As he'd hoped, Charlotte laughed. "She's already threatened to throw me out on my arse once."

"Well, we can't allow that to happen. It would hurt considerably more now than it would've last week." He glanced up and down the still deserted hall. "Which way to Jennison's office?"

"This way, I think."

Several doors opened out onto the corridor in which they stood. When Charlotte would have opened them, Alistair pulled her back, shaking his head. He peeked into what turned out to be a storage room, the men's water closet, and a private gaming room, before finding Jennison's office. Several other doors, farther down the hall, went unexplored.

The office was devoid of people but far from deserted. The usual accoutrements of desk, chairs, sofa, and cabinets were cluttered with what looked like the contents of an entire town house. There was a narrow path to a massive oak desk, past trunks overflowing with china and silverplate. Dozens of candlesticks, from simple to garishly ornate, some even with candles, covered every available surface. Several glass-fronted cabinets lined the far wall, their shelves filled with everything from marble busts to diamond brooches glinting in the candlelight.

Charlotte lit another of the candles from the banked coals in the fireplace and held it aloft, revealing even more household goods.

"It would require days to search all of this." Alistair turned in a circle, taking in all of the possible hiding places for something as small as a snuffbox. "Weeks."

She kept her voice low, as he had. "We don't dare stay any longer than a few minutes." She set the candle down on a clothes press, lying on its side, and started rummaging through the chest of drawers next to it.

They both froze as footsteps sounded in the hall, then relaxed at the sound of masculine giggling and the footsteps receding up the stairs.

"We have to be methodical about this," Alistair said, almost to himself. A bookcase nearby was loaded with small personal objects such as fans and fobs. "Could it be that simple? Hidden in plain sight?" He lifted the candle to illuminate the items in the back. He pushed aside hair combs and crystal scent bottles, revealing at least a dozen snuffboxes. "Are any of these the one we're after?"

Charlotte eased a drawer closed, scurried over and stood up on her tiptoes to peer at the shelf in question. After a moment she dropped down to her heels and shook her head. "None of them are gaudy enough."

She wandered toward the oak desk, trailing her hands over the objects she passed—a pile of beaded reticules, somebody's family portrait in a gilt frame, a silver tea service—and sat in Jennison's massive leather chair.

"Comfortable?" Alistair cocked his head to one side.

She propped her feet up on the corner of the desk and

crossed her ankles, unintentionally gifting him with an extensive view of her black silk stockings. "Have to think like Toussaint." She tapped her chin with one finger. "These are all stolen objects. Items that Toussaint and Sir Nigel have bought and intend to sell. Or are they? Is there something here that stands out?"

Alistair took another look around, and this time paid closer attention to the several *objets d'art*. "Well, I doubt Shakespeare ever wore a bonnet like that." The white marble bust on the top shelf of a bookcase was capped by a cheap straw bonnet decorated with an unseemly number of peacock feathers.

Charlotte dropped her feet to the floor. "Can you reach it?"

"You think it's hidden under the bonnet?" Alistair stretched up, and staggered back a step with the bust in his arms. The bonnet fell to the floor. "It's definitely not inside the bust." The solid marble had to weigh nearly two stone.

"No, I suppose not. Just someone's bizarre sense of humor. Like tying a cravat on Caesar over there. I don't think cravats were fashionable in ancient Rome, do you?"

Alistair lifted the bust back onto the shelf and tossed the bonnet up. It landed at a jaunty angle, dipping low over Shakespeare's left eye.

"Unless . . ." Charlotte leaped over a stack of Wedgwood dinner plates on her way to the bust of Julius Caesar, displayed behind glass on an upper shelf in a cabinet against the far wall. She tapped on the glass, pointing at the marble figurine. "In Paris, Toussaint once used a hollow bust of Bonaparte to hide a cache of stolen jewels."

He joined her at the cabinet and raised the candle high, shadows dancing over the cabinet's contents. "What makes you think Caesar isn't as solid as Shakespeare?"

She grasped his wrist and brought the candle even closer. "See the indentation beneath the cravat, all the way 'round the neck? The head comes off, and the neck is hollow, maybe even the entire chest." She tried to turn the handle on the glass door. "Locked." She grabbed the silver teapot and swung it back like a cricket bat.

Just as he was about to catch her arm and protest, she set it down again. "No, too loud," she muttered.

"Key's probably in the desk." If it was there, and the snuffbox was hidden inside a hollow bust, he would concede she'd been right—men were indeed boringly predictable in hiding their valuables.

"You look for it. I've got another idea." She reached under her wig, retrieved a hairpin, and bent toward the lock.

Alistair stepped over a pile of waistcoats, heading for the desk, but froze at the sound of footsteps in the hall. He darted his gaze around the room, looking for a second exit, or something big enough for them to hide behind. Would Jennison remember how many candles he had left burning?

The footsteps were steady, not those of a drunk, and still headed their way.

Only one exit. He grabbed Charlotte and they dove into the wardrobe. He eased the door closed just as the hall door slammed open.

"Greedy, conniving bi—" There was a crash as Jennison, Alistair presumed, kicked over the stack of dinner plates. Desk drawers opened and slammed shut, followed by the muffled clink of coins.

Alistair struggled to hold perfectly still in the cramped confines of the wardrobe, a task made monumentally difficult by having Charlotte tucked in his embrace, bent over. If she didn't stop wiggling her bottom . . . Oh. This position couldn't be comfortable for her, either. He hoped none of her stitches had pulled loose.

"Pay her some more, the frog says," Jennison said in a mocking voice. His boots crunched over the pottery shards. "I'll show him, and his French tart." The door slammed behind him.

Alistair waited a moment, listening to make sure they were actually alone in the office again, before letting go of Charlotte and opening the wardrobe door. Once he had straightened and popped a kink in his back, he helped her climb out.

"We need to get out of here, before somebody else comes in," he whispered.

"Right. Just let me get . . ." She headed for the bust of Julius Caesar.

Alistair grabbed her hand. "Not on your life. We agreed. Toussaint is here, so we're leaving. Since you've figured out where it is, Sir Will—Lord Q can send somebody else to retrieve it."

"But I'm so close!" She glanced back at the glass case.

"I know, but so is Toussaint. He could come in here any moment. Don't take any foolish risks. Lord Q is a fair man, and will give you credit for locating the box."

He caressed the side of her neck. "The important thing is to get you out of here safely."

He hated to see her shoulders slump in defeat, but felt relief that she saw the wisdom in his decision. Careful not to disturb the teetering stack of teacups, he lifted her up and over the broken plates, opened the door a crack, and peered out. He saw the swish of a black cloak as someone entered the room across the hall, two doors down. Noise emanated from behind several closed doors and drifted down from the staircase at the far end, but the hall itself was deserted. Grabbing her hand, he darted out, pulled the door shut behind them, and wrapped his arm around her waist as befitting a properly besotted sot with his mistress.

As another couple emerged from the private gaming room, giggling and groping and heading for the stairs, Alistair bent to nuzzle her ear. "We accomplished our objective for the evening. The sooner I get you home and away from this place, the better I will feel."

"Just one thing before we go. It's a long ride home." She spun on her heel and headed back, past Jennison's office, and went in through a door on the opposite side of the hall, the same one into which the black cloak had disappeared.

Alistair started to follow her until he spotted the *L* carved into the door. She should be safe in the ladies' water closet. Even here.

Shouldn't she?

Charlotte shut the door to the ladies' withdrawing room and leaned against it, her heart pounding. There was no way on God's green earth she was going to get this close to the snuffbox and simply leave it behind.

Sounds of rustling fabric reminded her she was not alone—someone was in the curtained alcove, attending the call of nature. The other woman had hung her thin, worn black cloak on the peg near the door.

Black. Charlotte glanced down at her red cloak, which she'd worn less than a dozen times.

She opened the door and peeked out. In the time-honored tradition of all men waiting for women, Alistair was pacing the length of the hall. She ducked back as he made his turn and softly closed the door.

The other woman, whoever she was, shouldn't mind a trade too terribly much, since she was getting a better cloak in exchange.

Alistair felt ridiculous propping up the wall. He paced up and down the hall, drawing a puzzled look from the serving wench who passed by. How long could it possibly take her? He strolled to the stairs and actually climbed to the next floor, then turned around as though he'd forgotten something, and strolled to the other end of the hall.

On the second round he thought he heard a hall door open, but when he looked, they were all still closed.

On the third round he spun at the sound of a door opening, but saw only the bottom edge of a black cloak entering Jennison's office before the door clicked shut.

Charlotte pulled the hood of the black cloak over her head and peeked out the door. Alistair was halfway down the hall, his back to her.

She pulled the door closed behind her and darted across the hall, into Jennison's office. One minute. That was all she needed. One minute, and one hairpin.

After she had the snuffbox in her reticule, she'd swap cloaks again and meet Alistair in the hall, as though nothing had happened.

She hurried over to the glass cabinet and bent to the lock. Her hands were trembling so much she almost dropped the hairpin. "Steady on," she muttered, and took a deep breath. She glanced over her shoulder, listening. Nothing but Alistair's even tread out in the hall.

Sweat trickled down her back and beaded on her upper lip, but she didn't take time to swipe it off. It took a few twists and a second hairpin, but finally the lock clicked open. She slid the glass door aside, grabbed Caesar by the ears, and tugged off his head.

Yes! She plunged her hand inside Caesar's neck, feeling the cold marble, smooth metal, and something beaded. First she pulled out an enameled cosmetic case, then a purse filled with clinking coins. She reached in again.

On the third try she withdrew a snuffbox—the most gaudy snuffbox she'd ever laid eyes on. The silver box, just big enough it didn't quite fit in the palm of her hand, was studded with gemstones of every shape and color, set in random order, with abstract designs etched into the silver. She flipped open the lid, and her heart did a triumphant somersault at the sight of the piece of parchment folded into a tiny square.

She grinned from ear to ear, resisted the impulse to dance a little jig, and tucked the box into her reticule.

She was just putting Caesar's head back in place when the knob on the office door turned.

Alistair scrubbed his hands through his hair. Women could certainly take an age at their toilette, but surely Charlotte would not want to linger in the water closet of a gaming hell? Especially knowing that Toussaint was on the premises.

Perhaps he'd missed her when he had climbed the stairs, and she was even now awaiting him in the taproom, impatiently tapping her toe. Fending off unwanted advances. He strode toward that end of the hall, and collided with a man just exiting the gaming room.

He was as tall as Alistair and a couple decades older, but with a heavier build, an enormous nose, and a ruddiness in his cheeks that could have come from too much alcohol or from physical exercise. Though large, he was certainly not fat.

"Beg pardon," they both muttered at the same time, and stepped apart.

Alistair took another step to the side, dodging the three-chinned man who barreled out of the gaming room next—Jennison.

"But, Monsieur Toussaint, I have already paid that French tart what the fan was worth."

Alistair froze.

The hair on the back of his neck rose, and he clenched his fists.

"I don't care," Toussaint said with a dismissive wave, continuing down the hall. He stopped with his hand on the doorknob to the office. "Pay her more." He slammed the door behind him, and Jennison returned to the gaming room, muttering under his breath.

His heart racing, Alistair glanced into each of the open doorways on his way out to the taproom, anxious for a glimpse of Charlotte's scarlet cloak.

The taproom was even more crowded than before, a sea of unwashed bodies in various states of inebriation and undress, with the scent of burnt mutton wafting over it all, drifting out from the kitchen.

No Charlotte.

To hell with the niceties, he was going to barge into the ladies' water closet.

He had just taken a step when he heard a roar of outrage, quickly followed by a crash and a slammed door, then a string of colorful French oaths bellowed by a healthy set of lungs, barely muffled behind a closed door.

Several people pushed at him to get out into the hall, to see the source of the outcry. Alistair shoved back, pushing his way to the front of the pack.

"*Allez au diable*, Parnell! I should have drowned you in the Seine when I had the chance!"

Alistair turned the corner just in time to see the edge of a black cloak disappearing at the top of the stairs. His blood froze at the sight of Toussaint raising a pistol, aimed at a retreating woman's back. Clad in a scarlet cloak.

"No!" he screamed, surging forward.

Toussaint fired.

The explosion of the pistol in such a confined space was deafening, and shattered Alistair's world.

She pitched forward, the red stain darkening her scarlet cloak, spreading from between her shoulders, and was still.

Chapter 18

"Putain," Toussaint muttered, glaring at the body. "Should have drowned you in the river, like a sack of kittens, instead of wasting powder and shot." He finally noticed the crowd in the hallway. "She was a thief! No one steals from me and gets away with it. She—"

Alistair smashed his fist into Toussaint's nose.

The Frenchman staggered, blood spurting, staining the walls and Alistair's cravat, but did not go down.

He wouldn't give the whoreson a chance to fire again. Putting all of his weight behind it, all of his fury and pain, Alistair hit him again, an uppercut to the jaw that whipped Toussaint's head back. Toussaint slammed into the door frame and crumpled to the floor. Unconscious or dead, Alistair didn't much care.

In the hush that fell over the assembled crowd, he dropped to his knees beside Charlotte's motionless form.

The scarlet cloak covered her scandalous dress, the hood drawn up to conceal her dark wig.

The bloodstain on her back had stopped spreading.

No heartbeat to pump the blood.

He stretched out one hand to her shoulder, surprised that it did not tremble. He remembered her mischievous blue eyes, her distracting freckle, her stubborn streak. He wanted to throw his head back and howl.

Howl to vocalize the pain of his lost dreams of his life with Charlotte, the life they were supposed to share. All the hopes he'd only just begun to harbor for their future. Gone.

He'd failed to protect her.

All of his strength, his determination, wealth and power, vaunted lineage—it meant nothing. He'd failed to protect the woman he loved.

As a helpless child, he couldn't save his mother and siblings.

He was a mature adult now, far from helpless, and still he'd failed.

He pulled off his gloves and rested his hand on her shoulder, as he had done so often. She lay still, as though peacefully sleeping, but the warm, sticky blood on his fingers shattered the illusion. Swallowing back the lump in his throat, he leaned across to caress her downy soft cheek one last, final time. Whisper in her ear what he should have said while she still lived.

The curve of her jaw was different.

This wasn't Charlotte.

He jerked back as though burned, then pulled down the hood of the cloak.

Melisande.

This wasn't Charlotte. Charlotte wasn't dead.

He lurched to his feet, scrubbing his hands through his hair, oblivious to the blood on his fingers.

Charlotte was alive.

He started breathing again. He sagged against the wall, weak with relief. Poor unfortunate Melisande, but Charlotte was alive.

Where was she?

The crowd had started chattering, discussing whether they should send for the Watch or not. Perhaps they should just throw the thief's body into the river?

Alistair searched their faces, looking for Charlotte's familiar gamine features among them, her blue eyes and rouged lips. Not there.

He pushed his way through the crowd until he could open the door to the ladies' water closet and step inside, ignoring the shocked gasps.

"He's gone daft," one woman muttered.

"Oi, mate, the gent's room is down that way," a gruff voice offered.

There were mirrors and wall sconces, curtains and stools, wall hooks and dressing tables—everything one would expect in a ladies' water closet, but no ladies.

No Charlotte.

Damn it, where was she? His stomach clenched anew.

He pushed his way out into the hall and searched the crowd again.

His gaze fell on Melisande, still lying on the floor in a pool of blood. Wearing a scarlet cloak.

Charlotte's cloak.

When he'd noted Melisande in the gaming room before, she'd been wearing a black cloak.

From the corner of his eye he'd seen someone in a black cloak scampering up the stairs just before Toussaint fired. Before that, he'd seen a black cloak entering Jennison's office.

Charlotte must have switched cloaks while Melisande was occupied in the water closet.

Damn Charlotte's impetuous, impatient hide.

Upstairs, he opened every door, poked inside every room, ignoring the outraged complaints from the occupants.

Still no Charlotte.

But there was an open window at the end of the hall.

He leaned out. No one in their right mind would willingly go out onto the steep, tiled roof in the dark, made slick from the steady drizzle falling from the sky.

No one but an astronomer. Or a female spy.

He banged his hand against the window casing, adding to the throbbing pain from when he'd hit Toussaint.

At least now he knew how she had made her exit.

He went back downstairs, stepped over Toussaint's prone form into the office, and checked the bust of Julius Caesar.

The glass case stood open and Caesar's head was shattered on the floor, revealing the bust's hollow neck. Empty.

No snuffbox.

Alistair slammed the cabinet door shut, and the glass splintered into a thousand shards.

She'd agreed. He'd said they were here to look. It was

too dangerous for them to remove the snuffbox. They would let Lord Q send somebody else to get it.

But Charlotte had taken the box anyway, and now Melisande was dead.

He hung his head in defeat.

Charlotte hadn't actually agreed with him. She'd kept silent.

He lifted his head, stared around the room.

What now?

She had the snuffbox. Would she rush home, in a hurry to show it off to Steven, rub his nose in the fact that she'd been right, he was wrong, and she'd succeeded where he and Gauthier had failed?

As Alistair stepped through the doorway, Toussaint groaned and struggled to sit up. Alistair plucked the pistol from his limp grip, smashed the butt into Toussaint's jaw, and strode down the still crowded hall.

Everyone scrambled out of his way.

Halfway to the town house Charlotte shared with her aunt and half brother, Alistair reconsidered, and shouted different directions to the driver.

The coach dropped him at the requested address, and Alistair marched up to the front door of an elegant town house in Mayfair.

What if Sir William was not at home? Or worse, what if he had company?

It was after midnight. Would Charlotte wait until tomorrow, deliver her prize during respectable calling hours?

Certainly propriety would force her to wait until morning. He snorted. Charlotte, wait? That would be like a rooster trying to hold back the dawn.

He raised his hand to lift the knocker. Behind him, the jingle of a harness alerted him to the arrival of another coach.

Charlotte hopped out of the coach, paid the driver, and trotted up the path toward Lord Q's front door.

She'd done it! She'd successfully retrieved the box *and* the letter. Lord Q couldn't help but be impressed with her skills. Now he'd offer her continued employment, with or without Steven. She would be able to fend for herself, and not be reliant on a husband, father, or brother. She wasn't condemned to the life of a social butterfly like her mother, silly and useless. Like her father, she'd serve the crown, save lives. Make a difference. Do the work she loved. Be independent.

Live life exactly the way she wanted. On *her* terms.

She'd had a moment of panic when Toussaint surprised her by entering the office. She'd crouched down and hidden behind a painting. When his back had been turned, going to his desk, she'd jumped up and darted out. He saw her just as she went out the door, and bellowed her name in rage.

Her heart still beat wildly at the memory. She'd never ascended a flight of stairs so quickly. The back of her neck prickled, but he'd shot wide of the mark and missed her entirely.

She hadn't even torn Melisande's borrowed cloak when she climbed out the window, skittered down the roof and drain pipe, and jumped to the ground. Hailing a hackney several blocks away had proven to be the most difficult part of retrieving the snuffbox.

But she'd succeeded!

A shadow near the town house door detached itself from the wall, stepped into the puddle of light cast by the lantern beside the door frame, and revealed itself to be Alistair.

He'd no doubt be upset she had gone against his wishes, and miffed that she'd left Lost Wages without him, but surely he would bear no grudge when he realized she'd succeeded? She offered a smile in greeting. "I knew you'd figure out where to meet me."

His fingers were stiff at his sides, as though he was forcing himself not to curl them into fists. "How could you?"

She recoiled from the controlled fury in his voice.

Oh, what a wealth of meanings to which that question could refer. There were tight lines around his mouth and a particularly deep furrow between his eyes. Tension rolled off him in palpable waves.

Her grin faltered. "I'm afraid you'll have to be more specific."

"We were going to wait. Let Q send somebody else to actually retrieve the snuffbox. You would have still been given credit for locating it." He stepped so close she had to tilt her head back to an uncomfortable angle to still see his face.

She swallowed. "I couldn't take the chance Toussaint would move it. The last time I just waited and watched, like you wanted, I watched someone else make off with the box right out from under my nose. I couldn't let that happen again."

"Melisande is dead, because you couldn't wait." He gripped her shoulders.

"What?" Her body struggled with the simple act of remembering to breathe.

"Toussaint killed her. Because she was wearing your cloak. He shot her, screaming your name."

Her hand flew to cover her mouth in horror. *"Sacre bleu."* She'd only switched cloaks so Alistair wouldn't recognize her when she snuck across the hall into Jennison's office.

"Do you have any idea what I went through, thinking it was you that Toussaint shot? How I felt when I saw you lying in a puddle of blood?" He was practically shaking her, his fingers digging painfully into her flesh.

"I'm sorry." Her voice broke. "You must know I never meant for anyone to be hurt." Not Melisande, and certainly not Alistair.

He abruptly let go and stepped back, his face now a rigid mask.

She stumbled, caught her balance. "I read the letter in the coach." She patted her reticule, where she'd hidden the snuffbox. The slight bulge was still there. "You have no idea how high the stakes were on this. Q was not exaggerating when he said the monarchy could be in jeopardy."

"I don't give a damn about the monarchy just now."

Neither did she. Not really. Someone had just died in her place.

She was going to be sick. She needed to put her head between her knees.

The front door opened and a footman in blue livery and a periwig leaned out. "Who goes there?"

Charlotte gathered herself and stepped around Alistair, who did not move. "I—" She cleared her throat and tried again. "I've brought an urgent message for the master of the house."

"Couldn't be all that urgent, standing out there flapping your gums like that," the footman muttered. He stepped to the side and gestured for Charlotte to enter the foyer. "I'll see if he's at home," he said in a normal tone, obviously accustomed to people paying calls at all hours.

Charlotte half expected Alistair to stalk off into the night, but he followed her into the foyer.

She'd never before been unnerved by his silence. She didn't dwell on that, since she was busy dwelling on the fact that Toussaint had now killed twice because of the damn snuffbox.

Fortunately, the butler soon arrived, and gestured for her to follow him into a well-appointed study. "The master will be with you shortly." He gave a perfunctory bow and left.

Charlotte headed directly for the fireplace, feeling a chill from without and within. The cloak she'd switched in the ladies withdrawing room was much thinner than her own, hardly capable of warding off a midsummer breeze. She feared, however, the thickest sable wouldn't be able to dispel the chill now coursing through her bones.

Alistair stood before the dark window, hands clasped behind his back, his profile that of a carved marble statue.

She'd gained the snuffbox, but had she lost Alistair? She'd planned from the start to move on from him, but always expected they'd part under amicable terms.

She held her hands out to the crackling blaze, glowing like the fires of hell, and cast about for some comment with which to break the silence. None was forthcoming.

Just as she was about to make some inane observation regarding the weather, Lord Q entered the room. He was fully dressed and his white hair neatly combed, despite the lateness of the hour, as though he was just going out or had just come in. Or expecting callers.

"Yes, miss, how can I be of—" He stopped when he recognized her beneath the artifice. "Miss Parnell? And Moncreiffe." He gestured for them to be seated. "Has something happened?" His expression remained polite but neutral, prepared for good or bad news.

Alistair remained motionless by the window.

Charlotte stayed by the fire, for all the good it was doing. Something happened? She wasn't sure where to begin.

"Blakeney and Monsieur Gauthier?" Lord Q's brows drew together in concern.

She shook her head. "They're fine, as far as I know."

"Then . . . ?"

Right. The reason she came here. The objective she'd attained, at such a high cost. She dug the snuffbox out of her reticule. The gems on the box sparkled under the light cast by the chandeliers overhead.

She held the gleaming box out to Lord Q on the palm of her hand. "I believe someone's been looking for this."

Here it was, the moment she'd been working toward,

planning for—the pinnacle of her success, the linchpin of her future.

This wasn't how she'd pictured it. She always thought she'd feel elation at this moment. Not this . . . emptiness.

Lord Q's face broke into a huge smile. "Certainly is an ugly thing of beauty, isn't it?" He took it from her hand and sat at his desk to examine the box more carefully. He unfolded the parchment tucked inside and held it up to the light. "I'll have to confirm with . . . the owner . . . but it appears this is the original letter." He beamed at Charlotte. "Excellent work, Charlie."

"Thank you, sir."

He refolded the paper and tucked it back inside. "I assume you had something to do with this also, Moncreiffe?"

Alistair shook his head. "I take no credit whatsoever for its recovery."

Her stomach plummeted to the vicinity of her shoes. "Oh, but I couldn't have done this without your help." She glanced over at Lord Q. "He was an invaluable partner."

Lord Q shifted his gaze between the two of them, perplexed.

"I'm afraid its recovery was not without incident," she explained. She swallowed a lump. "There was a . . . casualty. Toussaint fired at me, but his bullet struck someone else. A Frenchwoman, Madame Melisande."

"She's dead." Somehow, Alistair's flat, wooden tone was even more disturbing then his controlled anger of earlier.

"Toussaint shot her, eh?" Lord Q pushed aside what turned out to be a false bookcase, revealing a safe. He quickly opened it, tucked the snuffbox inside, and concealed it again. He dusted his hands off. "Well, I've always been of the opinion it was simply a matter of time before one of them turned on the other."

Alistair whipped his head around to stare at Lord Q. "Turned?"

"We've been aware for some time that she was feeding him information, eavesdropping at parties to gather intelligence."

"I thought she was just a thief, supplementing her income from being a mistress." Reflecting on all the times she'd watched Melisande when the Frenchwoman had the snuffbox, Charlotte now saw her actions in a whole new light.

"Well, there was that, too." Lord Q poured three glasses of brandy from the sideboard. "Our operatives had to take care that she didn't pinch their valuables when they were letting her overhear their conversations."

Alistair accepted the glass. "You were feeding her false information, which you knew she would then give to Toussaint?"

"Brilliant strategy, if I do say so myself." Q handed a glass to Charlotte, and kept the last for himself. "But it couldn't have lasted too much longer. Toussaint would have added up his misfortunes, each of his plans gone awry, and come up with the common denominator."

"Information from Melisande."

"Precisely." Lord Q gestured at Alistair's cravat. "That's her blood, I presume?"

Charlotte had missed seeing it until now—his once-snowy linen marred by crimson splotches.

Merde, he had been standing close enough when Melisande was shot to be splattered with her blood? Her chest hurt from the stab of guilt.

Alistair glanced down with a look of disgust and shook his head. "Toussaint suffered a nosebleed after he shot Melisande. Possibly a broken jaw." He rubbed the knuckles of his right hand. "Probably a concussion, too."

Lord Q murmured his approval, while Charlotte looked at Alistair, really looked at him, and saw a different man. Not the staid scholar, not the playful lover or the passionate astronomer, but a man more than capable of defending himself.

He was tall, with a trim but muscular build. For all the sedentary hours he spent observing the night sky, it was obvious he spent an equal number of hours engaged in physical pursuits—she'd felt the muscled contours of his chest and thighs. When he'd carried her to Nick's ship, she was the one panting for breath, not Alistair.

And he'd injured Toussaint, thinking she'd just been killed.

Would he ever forgive her?

Lord Q tugged on the bell pull, and requested his carriage be made ready. He came back to the center of the room and raised his glass. "A toast, to the successful completion of your first mission without your brother. May it be the first of many."

Charlotte forced a smile in return. Lord Q saw her as an operative in her own right, not as her brother's assistant. She'd achieved her goal.

The brandy burned like acid going down her throat. Alistair did not drink.

It wasn't her fault that Melisande was dead. Engaged in the line of work that she was, such a fate was always a possibility, and Melisande had to have known that. Just as Charlotte knew she had risked mortal danger in getting back the snuffbox.

"If you don't mind my asking . . ." Alistair began.

Lord Q raised his eyebrows.

"Just what is so damn important about that letter?"

She glanced at Lord Q, who nodded. "It's a *billet doux*, from a man." She set down her glass.

"Men in love are idiots. What is so remarkable about this particular love letter?"

At his harsh words, she turned to the fireplace so he wouldn't see her wince. Was he referring to the letter writer being an idiot, or was it more personal?

Did he regret their time together? Perhaps he was even now cursing that day on Bond Street when she'd hooked his arm with hers.

But if it was personal, that meant . . . She glanced back at his proud, handsome profile, and felt the color drain from her face. She had not meant to engage Alistair's emotions when she'd suggested their mock betrothal. But if his emotions were *not* involved, would he have been as tender and passionate last night when he'd coaxed her to the heights of sensual pleasure?

Even more disturbing, would she have responded so

willingly, with such intensity, if her own emotions were not equally engaged?

Oh, this was going to muck everything up. Even worse than it already was. She dropped onto the sofa with an unladylike thump.

Lord Q sat on the other end of the sofa and crossed an ankle over his knee. "The recipient is also a man."

Alistair blinked. "Unusual, but since neither the writer nor the recipient was the Prince Regent, I fail to see how this endangered the monarchy."

"The punishment for sodomy is death. The letter's recipient is . . . well, let's say he holds high office, and leave it at that." Q took another sip of brandy. "If his preference in companionship were to be bruited about, even as a rumor, he would be forced to resign amidst a scandal that could jeopardize the stability of our government. Incidents like the machine-smashing at the mills in Loughborough this summer could become commonplace. Hundreds, perhaps thousands, of lives could be lost in such unrest."

The butler tapped on the door. "Your carriage is ready, my lord."

Lord Q nodded, and the butler left. "It's been a very long evening for you, Charlie. The excitement will soon wear off, and you'll be wanting to seek your bed. My driver is at your disposal."

Still dazed by her personal realizations, she stood and murmured something appropriate.

Alistair scrubbed the heels of his hands over his eyes. "I'll see that she gets home safely."

"Very good of you, Moncreiffe."

Moments later, Alistair helped her into Lord Q's elegant coach. His touch was polite, and completely impersonal. None of the lingering caresses or touches that she had come to expect, come to crave.

Other than issuing her direction to the driver, he remained silent. Seated on the bench opposite, he wouldn't even look at her in the dim confines of the coach, but stared out the window at the blackness beyond, broken only by the occasional street lamp.

Steven would have begun shouting at her the moment they were alone. Her brother might see a different future than what she envisioned for herself, but she always knew where she stood with him.

Finally, she could stand the silence no more. "Speak to me. Chastise me, rail at me for going against your wishes, blame me for Melisande's death, just say something. Anything."

"I love you."

Her mouth fell open.

He looked at her then, more pain in his blue eyes than she had ever before seen.

"I love you and respect you, and wanted to be your partner. I wanted to make our betrothal real. Get married. Grow old together. But your actions tonight made it clear that you do not feel the same way." He leaned forward to tilt her jaw shut with one finger, and sat back. "You don't want a partner. You don't respect me. You only wanted me as a distraction. I do not want to be used in such a way, any more than you wanted your brother to use you."

His words hung there between them, like an extremely low cloud that had moved in, made the air too thick to breathe.

The devil of it was, he was right. She had been guilty of treating Alistair with the same callous disregard that made her want to throttle Steven. She shrank back into the squabs, wincing, struggling for the words to say that would make things right between them again.

She had pictured their life together in the Lake District, and known it was not meant for her. She was independent, untethered. She had already made the decision to be alone. There was no reason for her heart to ache, to feel a raw pain in the back of her throat that she knew was the prelude to tears, just because he had been the one to utter the words aloud, with such finality.

"I'm sorry." Sorry that she had caused him anguish, sorry for the future they would never have.

"I know." He returned to gazing out the window.

His words continued to echo in her thoughts, each accusation pummeling her like a physical blow.

"Now that you've succeeded in your quest, I'll expect to read the notice in the papers day after tomorrow." He addressed the windowpane. The anger had drained from his voice, leaving it as flat as the glass.

"Notice?"

"Announcing the end of our betrothal. That's been part of your plan from the beginning. No need to change it."

His calm acceptance only made her feel worse.

The coach stopped, and Alistair helped her out. He followed her to the brick column beside the path to the town house door, deep in the shadows, and spun her to face him. He brushed the backs of his fingers down her cheek in a familiar gesture, achingly sweet. Tears stung her eyes.

He leaned forward and kissed her, tender and gentle, then straightened abruptly, as though he hadn't intended to kiss her. "Good-bye, Charlotte."

She tried to speak but couldn't force the words past the lump in her throat. She cupped his strong jaw and ran her thumb along his lush lower lip. One last time, a memory to last the rest of her life.

Then she turned on her heel and ran up the steps and into the house before he could see her tears.

The night seemed to go on forever.

Farnham had informed her Steven had not come home yet, so she couldn't even share the evening's high point with her brother, to distract herself from the incredible low.

She tossed and turned, even tried counting sheep. But instead of sheep, she saw stars. The same stars she'd seen on the rooftop with Alistair. Remembered his whispered endearments, the touch of his hands, the warmth of his kisses.

Gone from her world forever.

She must have fallen asleep at some point, because she awoke to sunlight streaming across her room. She rolled over, giving the sun the cut direct.

There was no reason to jump out of bed. She had accomplished her mission. Now she need only wait until Lord Q gave her another assignment. If she wanted to lie abed all day, that was her business.

She spotted the stack of astronomy books on the floor beside her bed, and squeezed her eyes shut.

Sometime later, there was a scratch at the door, and Aunt Hermione leaned into the room. "Charlotte, dear, aren't you coming down to breakfast?"

She poked her head out from under the blankets. "Not hungry."

"Hmm. Steven hasn't come down yet, either. I wonder if that naughty boy stayed out all night again?"

The door clicked shut, and Charlotte pulled the blankets back up over her head, blissfully alone once more.

She threw them back and sat up. Sir Nigel had not been at the gaming hell last night. Had he been home when Steven and Gauthier were searching his town house?

Spurred by her worry, she got up and dressed.

This was a good day, she told herself as she dragged a brush through her hair. A great day, even. Last night she had attained the dream that she had worked toward so hard, for so long. The empty feeling inside had to be hunger.

Time to rub her success in her brother's face. Surely he had come home by now? She forced a smile and went downstairs for breakfast. She was going to eat kippers and eggs, and Steven was going to eat crow.

But Steven wasn't there.

"Still haven't seen him yet this morning," Aunt Hermione replied when asked. She peered at Charlotte over the rim of her teacup. "Are you feeling quite the thing? You look a little peaked."

"I may have stayed up a little too late last night. I'll have a lie down this afternoon, and be fine."

"See that you do. We don't want you run ragged before your big day." Her eyes sparkled. "When is the big day? That is what you were discussing with Moncreiffe yesterday, was it not?"

Charlotte winced. She could delay no longer. It would only hurt worse. She rested her hand on Hermione's forearm. "I'm so sorry to have to tell you, but . . ."

"Yes?"

She couldn't do it. Bad news should not have to be digested before lunch. "We haven't set a date yet."

The butler entered just then. "This message just arrived for you, miss. The delivery person said it was urgent, but did not wait for a reply."

"Thank you, Farnham." She took the folded vellum and glanced at the seal, half hoping it was from Alistair. The *T* in a fleur de lis made her blood run cold.

"A love note from your intended?" Aunt Hermione batted her lashes, her smile teasing.

Charlotte forced air in and out of her lungs, and pasted a smile on her face. "If you'll excuse me . . ."

"Of course, dear."

She forced herself to walk, not run, and shut herself into the drawing room before she broke the seal.

You have something of mine. I have something of yours. Shall we trade?
    Don't keep me waiting.

Toussaint had signed the note with just an elaborate *T*.

She paced the length of the room. She'd left her heart in Lord Q's coach last night, but had left nothing behind at the gaming hell except her cloak. She certainly didn't wish that to be returned, so to what could Toussaint be referring?

She pounded up the stairs and threw open the door to Steven's bedchamber.

Ned, his valet, dropped the stack of cravats he had just folded. "Yes, miss?"

"When was the last time you saw Steven?"

He glanced at the clock. "Just before ten."

It was only half past ten now. She sagged against the door frame in relief, her hand to her heart, and tried to catch her breath.

"Ten last night, that is. He hasn't come home yet."

Now was not the time to panic. There could still be a simple reason for Steven to have not come home yet, one that had nothing to do with Toussaint. She cleared her throat. "I need you to go over to Gauthier's lodgings, see if he is there and if he knows Steven's whereabouts."

Ned bent to pick up the cravats.

"Now, man! Make haste!"

Ned dropped the cravats and darted out the door, almost knocking over Charlotte in his rush.

More pacing would accomplish nothing but wear a path in a perfectly innocent Aubusson rug. She certainly didn't want to go downstairs and risk encountering Aunt Hermione.

What to do?

There was a good chance that Ned would come back with the news that Steven and Gauthier had searched

Sir Nigel's town house last night, found nothing, decided to drown their sorrows, and were sleeping it off at Gauthier's flat.

No, she didn't really believe that, either. Steven rarely overindulged in drink, and never while he was working on an assignment.

She had to do something, anything, and do it *now*. She returned to her own bedchamber and changed into a heavy velvet dress in verdant green she hadn't worn since they left France. Made by a very special modiste, the dress had all sorts of useful slits, pockets, and linings. Charlotte set about filling them.

She strapped on both of her knife sheaths, after making sure the knives were clean and sharp. Checked that the small pistol Steven had given her two years ago was loaded, and tucked that into its hiding place, along with pouches of extra shot and powder.

One pistol was not enough. If Toussaint had hurt Steven, she was going to need a lot more weaponry.

Since they hadn't wanted to arouse her new maid's suspicions, she had allowed Steven to store most of her arsenal of weapons in his room. She grabbed her parasol that concealed a sword, peeked into the hall, saw that no servants were about, and darted back down to his bedchamber.

Both of Steven's pistols were gone, though hers were still there. She finished arming herself and checked her appearance in the mirror. Nothing looked out of the ordinary, but she felt at least two stone heavier than usual. It was a wonder she didn't clank as she moved.

Ned returned, gasping for breath, his face ashen. "So sorry, miss, but Gauthier's man says he ain't been home since last night, either."

She had been expecting to hear as much, but it was still a blow. She closed her eyes and took a deep breath. "Thank you, Ned." She grabbed Toussaint's note on her way out.

"I'm very sorry, my dear," Lord Q said, giving Charlotte's shoulder a consoling pat a short time later. "Blakeney is one of my best operatives. But you know the department's official policy. We do not negotiate. I cannot make an exception, however much it pains me to say that."

She had not really expected him to hand over the snuffbox. She'd come mainly as a professional courtesy, to let Lord Q know—

No. She wouldn't even finish the thought. No harm was going to come to Steven.

For half a second she flirted with the idea of knocking out Q with her parasol, breaking open his safe, and making off with the snuffbox. But Q's butler stood at the open doorway. He was no aged family retainer, but a burly bear of a fellow still in his prime. More servants casually lingered between her and the exit points.

"I understand, sir." The sad thing was, she truly did understand. If word got out that the Home Office could be coerced in such a way, no telling what havoc would ensue.

"I suggest that you go home and trust in your brother's skills, that everything will turn out all right."

If he patted her one more time, she would not be held responsible for her actions.

She folded the vellum and tucked it up her sleeve again. "Thank you, sir. Good-bye."

He gave her what was probably supposed to be a reassuring smile as she left.

She exited the town house and stood on the sidewalk, watching the coaches go by on the street as if everything in the world were perfectly normal.

Toussaint had Steven at his mercy. Steven would not have succumbed easily to being captured. Given their history, Toussaint would take great delight in inflicting the most pain possible. He would want revenge for the way Steven had thwarted him in Paris.

If she had not stolen the snuffbox last night . . .

No. Her success and Steven's capture were unrelated. In fact, Toussaint would probably have already killed Steven if he didn't need him alive to use as leverage in bargaining.

Alive didn't mean unharmed, though. Steven was likely in a great deal of pain by now, possibly injured. Might even be dying.

She fought down the rising panic and pushed aside images of hideous tortures being inflicted on her only brother. She needed to be logical, to focus. She had to rescue him. Now.

But how? A stealth attack? Sneak into the gaming hell and surprise Toussaint? The note had not offered a specific address, so he must mean for her to come to Lost Wages.

He would not be alone.

Neither should she.

But Lord Q was withholding his help. Gauthier was unavailable, since he, too, was in need of rescue.

She'd thought she wanted to work on her own. She'd forgotten that Steven rarely acted alone—he usually worked with Gauthier, or her, or another of Q's operatives.

She needed someone, too. Someone who could think fast on their feet. Someone who would not be intimidated, no matter what they faced.

There was only one man who could help her.

But would he be willing? She didn't deserve his help, but perhaps he'd do it for Steven's sake.

Swallowing down a great lump of dread, she gave her coachman directions.

Minutes later, a lofty butler escorted her into an elegant salon befitting the home of a duke. And a marquess. And a viscount.

All three were present.

Three generations, living together under one roof.

Despite their many disagreements over the years, the duke had not booted out his son, the marquess. Despite the many disagreements, Alistair had not abandoned them to their mutually bitter fate, but remained on hand, still attempting to be their peacemaker.

Standing here in their salon, she felt the connection to their past, the weight of their shared history, as an almost tangible thing. But it was not oppressive—more like the weight of favorite blankets piled on the bed at night to keep away the winter chill. Comforting. Reassuring.

Something she did not have. Had not even noticed the lack until now.

Tears pricked at her eyes.

She'd had her chance to gain this kind of connection for herself, and had given it up. Had given up Alistair.

Seeing him again was almost as painful as having to ask for his assistance. At the moment, though, he appeared disinclined to so much as help her across the street. She took a steadying breath and stared into the youngest pair of blue eyes in the room. "I need your help, Alistair."

Chapter 19

All three men had risen to their feet, with varying degrees of ease, when she entered the room.

His grace, the Duke of Keswick, stood up with the aid of his walking stick, and an audible creak.

The Marquess of Penrith tossed aside his newspaper and rose with an unsteady lurch that indicated, despite the early hour, the half-empty bottle of brandy at his side had recently been full. "Thought you said the chit told you to bugger off," he said in a loud aside to Alistair.

"Father," Alistair growled. He had been seated behind a desk, quill pen in hand, and eyed her with an unnerving wariness.

Keswick thumped his walking stick. "How may we be of assistance, Miss Parnell?"

Alistair tossed down his quill. "You have at least a

dozen names, sir, but I don't recall any of them being Alistair." He stepped out from behind the desk, toward Charlotte. "You were saying?"

The three gazed at her expectantly.

"I, that is . . . might we speak in private?" She struggled to keep her hands flat at her sides, not fisted or fidgeting.

"Sure you don't need a chaperone?"

"Enough, Father," Alistair growled.

"Right, sod off," Penrith said cheerfully. He sat down and opened his newspaper with a loud rattle, raising it high to cover his face.

Alistair rested his hands on his hips. "I think we said all there is to say last night."

She shook her head. Keswick was still unabashedly eavesdropping, and Alistair appeared as immovable as an ancient oak. "Toussaint has Steven," she said in a rush. "He wants to trade for the . . . box."

Alistair remained frozen, though his eyes seemed to be thawing.

Keswick glanced between her and Alistair but made no move, made not a sound.

The ticking of the clock seemed abnormally loud.

"My brother is being held hostage by a man who has already killed twice this week. Steven's life is in danger. I have a chance to save him. But I need help."

Alistair still made no move to come toward her. "I assume the box is not available to trade?"

She nodded.

"That is unfortunate." He appeared to be studying the frieze above and beyond her shoulder.

"I'm not asking for my sake—I know I don't deserve that—but I thought you'd be willing to help save my brother's life."

He did not reply.

She rubbed her hands over her eyes. This was a mistake. Of colossal proportions.

And she had no one to blame for her predicament but herself. She could bloody well find a way out on her own. "Sorry to have disturbed you, gentlemen." She turned, blindly heading for the door.

The newspaper rattled. "By Jove, boy, you're not going to let her leave, are you?"

Even before Penrith finished speaking, a hand grabbed her shoulder, spun her back, and pulled her close. Alistair wrapped her in his warm, familiar embrace, and she melted against his chest.

She closed her eyes, inhaled deeply of his spicy scent, with the hint of licorice, and felt a sob escape.

"We'll get him back," he murmured, rubbing a hand up and down her back.

She sniffed back any other tears and tried to gather her self-control.

"What do you want to do? What did . . . your employer . . . say?"

Still conscious of the two other men in the room watching and listening to the proceedings with great interest, she reluctantly took a step back from Alistair and cleared her throat. "He says he's very sorry, but is unable to offer any assistance in the matter." She tried to prevent any bitterness creeping into her tone.

Alistair nodded. "I thought as much. Have you formulated a plan?"

He led her to the sofa, where there was a tea service and a plate half full of biscuits on the low table. Once she was seated, Alistair beside her, Penrith and Keswick both pulled up chairs to form a small circle.

His grace poured and thrust a cup into her hands. "Drink up, lass, and explain what's amiss."

She felt a bubble of hysteria working its way to the surface. She was glad to be back in Britain after five years abroad, and couldn't believe she'd almost forgotten the way Brits seemed to think a cup of tea was the cure for anything. She drank deeply to swallow the bubble.

"Toussaint, did you say?" Penrith tossed back the dregs of brandy in his glass. "So, your employer would be Sir William, then."

Charlotte choked.

Keswick thumped her on the back with such vigor she nearly pitched onto the floor. "Don't be so shocked. Boy's not as cupshot as he seems. Usually."

Charlotte had trouble reconciling this statement, since the "boy" in reference was at least in his fifties, his once-brown hair turning white at the temples.

"Always wanted to try my hand at spying." Penrith poured a splash of tea into his brandy glass.

"Oh, don't start that rubbish again, you nodcock."

Penrith ignored his father. "Alas, William keeps saying my face is too notorious." He heaved a great sigh. "Despite that, I've met Toussaint a time or two myself. Nasty bugger. Cheats at cards." The last sentiment was expressed in a tone that clearly conveyed Penrith's opinion that cheating at cards was a hanging offense.

"She and her brother have had run-ins with Toussaint before," Alistair said.

Penrith steepled his fingers. "So, William is leaving young Steven to twist in the wind, while Toussaint thinks up inventive ways to inflict pain on his captive."

She shuddered at the image he'd conjured.

"What do you intend to do about it, Miss Parnell? I don't imagine you came here merely to sob on my grandson's waistcoat, and Sir William wouldn't employ the sort of miss who expects others to solve her problems."

It had to be a good thing, having a duke and a marquess on her side. Both Penrith and the duke were waiting patiently—not just feigning polite interest, unless they were gifted thespians. They actually wanted to hear what she had to say.

She sat up straighter. "I don't have the item Toussaint wants to trade, but I thought I could bluff him with something similar."

"You think to fool him with a substitute?" The duke rubbed the carved handle of his walking stick.

"Only for a few minutes, to distract him. While I have his attention, I'll need someone else to sneak in and free my brother."

Alistair looked directly at her for the first time since sitting down, his eyes sharp and assessing.

She met his stare, unwavering. "I need a partner."

Alistair hardly dared breathe. Perhaps he'd been hasty last night when he'd given up on Charlotte as a lost cause. Or perhaps she was a faster learner than he'd given her credit. Sufficient motivation could overcome almost any obstacle, make any difficult subject easier to master. Was Charlotte's affection for him sufficient motivation to change her ways?

He'd almost groaned in frustration when the butler showed her in. He'd already imagined her in his bed, her golden hair splayed on his pillow like a halo. He didn't need to see her here, in his home, in the flesh. Presented with reality, he'd steeled himself against the pain that stabbed through him at seeing her again.

But now there was a tiny spark of hope. She had a plan that required a partner, and she'd come to him. She recognized she had a greater chance of success by working with someone than she did working alone.

Granted, there was likely no one else to whom she could turn. Aunt Hermione was a sweetheart, but hardly equipped to handle the situation that Charlotte now faced. And he was well aware that she had chosen her wording with great care. She was counting on his guilt about being unable to save his own siblings to help her save hers.

Her attempt at manipulation didn't upset him—he'd probably do the same if their roles were reversed.

It wasn't concern for her brother's life that moved him. It was the realization that she was determined to do her damnedest to save Steven, even if it cost her own life. He couldn't allow that. As angry as he'd been with her last night, he still needed to know that she walked the earth.

Her single unshed tear had sealed his fate. Holding her in his arms once more had been heavenly torture.

And now he was committed to carrying out her plan, even though it was probably the last thing they would ever do together.

He held his hand out toward his grandfather. "Your snuffbox, if you please, sir."

The duke's eyebrows rose. "That's a very special blend, made exclusively—"

"Hand it over. You can keep the snuff. I just want the box."

"Ah. No cause for concern, then. It's merely a family heirloom handed down from my great-grandfather to me, someday destined for you. Or at least, it was." Keswick removed the box from his pocket, took a pinch of snuff, and tipped the rest into the last clean cup on the tray before handing the box to Alistair.

The handsome silver box was inlaid with sapphires and diamonds, arranged in the familiar shape of the family crest. Penrith squinted as it changed hands. "I suppose a fake might fool Toussaint for a moment or two, from a distance. Especially if the light is poor."

Alistair placed it in Charlotte's palm and closed her fingers around it. "Now tell us about your plan."

With the unexpected assistance of his father, who insisted on taking part in order to exact revenge for a long-ago crooked card game, Charlotte altered her plan as they discussed it.

Scarcely an hour later, the duke waited nearby in his coach, a sheet draped down to conceal the crest on the door. Bandages and other medical supplies were on board, as well as his grace's favorite surgeon, who'd literally been dragged from his bed to join the excursion—who was going to say nay to a duke?

Alistair huddled with Charlotte in the doorway of the chandler's shop next door to the gaming hell while they waited for the marquess to return and report on his reconnaissance.

"I need to tell you something." She clasped her hands together, something he knew she did only when struggling to contain her emotions. "This morning I came to a very unpleasant conclusion."

His heart skipped a beat. He stepped closer, shielding her from the view of a group of sailors sauntering past. He meant to keep his voice carefully neutral but couldn't resist whispering in her ear. "Before or after Toussaint's note arrived?"

Her rosewater scent teased him, even as she licked her lips and closed her eyes. "I—"

"Come along, children." Penrith staggered past, seemingly only the judicious use of his walking stick keeping him from falling to the gutter in a drunken stupor.

Stifling a curse for his father's bad timing, Alistair tucked Charlotte's hand in his and followed after, though not too closely. Penrith had liberally sprinkled Blue Ruin on his cravat, and left an odiferous wake.

He turned the corner into the alley and plopped down on an overturned whiskey barrel. "All right, here's what we've got." Though he slumped with the boneless posture of the thoroughly inebriated, his words were clear and his eyes bright as he looked between Alistair and Charlotte. "The serving wenches and pot boys aren't paid enough to be loyal, so I don't think you'll have to worry about them. Toussaint is in the main gaming room, along with Sir Nigel and Mr. Jennison, and two men at the back table who are not playing cards because their hands are tied to their chairs. One of them bears a striking resemblance to you, Miss Parnell, or at least he did before his eye was blacked."

"Steven's alive!" Charlotte grabbed Alistair's arm and sagged against his side. He wrapped his arm around her in a reassuring squeeze while she took a moment to collect herself. "The other gentleman, does he have a rather large nose?"

Penrith nodded. "Gauthier?"

"They're all in the same room at once." Alistair realized he was stroking her arm when his father raised a sardonic eyebrow. He stilled but didn't let go. "This should make our task easier."

"How did you manage to see all this without arousing suspicion?"

"No one pays any attention to a drunkard." Alistair spoke slowly, wondering just how often over the years his father had been sober when he seemed inebriated.

Penrith tapped the tip of his nose with his finger and winked. "Now let's go save your family, miss."

They parted company outside the tavern entrance of the gaming hell. Penrith entered first, loudly calling for a tankard of ale, damn it.

Charlotte watched Alistair dart to the corner of the brick building and climb up the same drain pipe she had climbed down last night. If someone had closed the window that Penrith had opened on his first foray into the structure, would he still be able to get in without attracting too much attention?

A doxy strolling by glanced up and followed Alistair's progress. An appreciative smile lit her care-worn face. Charlotte couldn't help a tiny smile herself at his display of masculine strength and agility, not to mention the way his breeches delineated his backside as he climbed.

Once up on the roof, he made no effort at stealth, instinctively following a truism she had learned early on in espionage. Act like you're supposed to be doing whatever it is you're doing, and most people won't question your actions. He reached the window, gave her a little wave, and climbed inside.

She wanted to be the one skulking about, sneaking down the stairs, tiptoeing down the hallway. Wanted to be the one to cut Steven and Gauthier free of their bonds, be the one to rescue them, see the astonishment and relief on their faces.

But the painful truth was, it was best if she did what she had done most often—be a distraction. She could keep Toussaint's attention longer and get him to talk to her more than he would to anyone else, which would improve the odds of their plan's success. She could provide Alistair the most time to free Steven and Gauthier.

After counting to ten, to give Alistair and his father a chance to get into position, Charlotte sauntered into the tavern, through the taproom and to the back hall. It was much less crowded than last night, with a few men stretched out on benches or the floor by the fire, sleeping off the prior night's merriment.

The door to the gaming room was ajar. She could sneak in, catch Toussaint and his minions unawares, and rescue Steven and Gauthier all by herself. She could hold Toussaint at gunpoint and coerce him into doing her bidding. It would certainly be a sight to see him forced to cut his own prisoners free.

But that was not the plan. She had a better plan, and a partner. They had a greater chance of succeeding by working together.

And she never made the same mistake twice—she'd learned her lesson after last night. Instead of acting impulsively, she should have talked with Alistair. Despite her taking advantage of him on many occasions, he'd come through for her every single time—been the best partner one could ask for. If she hadn't been so obstinate about getting the snuffbox on her own, she probably would have been able to pick the lock and get the box safely while he kept watch out in the hall.

But instead she'd acted brashly, and committed the cardinal sin of treating him with the same casual disregard of which Steven was guilty of treating her.

Penrith sat on the floor in the hall, slumped in a passed-out lump against the wall. At the top of the staircase she could just make out the toe of Alistair's boot, off to one side.

Right. Time to raise the curtain on their little drama.

"Toussaint!" she called out, relishing the very unladylike bellow. Giving vent to the mix of anticipation, fear, and exhilaration racing through her blood helped her slow her breathing to an almost normal rate. "Show yourself!" She had her hands in her pockets, feeling the cold metal of the snuffbox in one and the reassuring butt of a pistol in the other.

She'd never actually shot anything but paper targets pinned to bales of straw before, but she'd make an exception for Toussaint. Without hesitation. He'd already killed twice, and no telling how badly he'd hurt Steven this time. Her brother already bore a knife scar from their last encounter.

From the doorway of the main gaming room, Sir Nigel poked his head into the hall. "Have you brought it?"

"Where's my brother?" She planted her feet wide, chin out, shoulders back.

"He's here, he's alive. For now. Did you bring it?"

Breathe. In, out, in, out. "I want proof."

Nigel disappeared back into the gaming room, but left the door open. "She wants proof he ain't dead."

She heard some mutterings and shuffling in the room, then a grunt of pain.

"Don't give it to him, Charlie! Leave!" quickly followed by an "Oof."

Hearing the pain in Steven's voice, she strangled the urge to cry out. Focus. She slipped her finger around the pistol trigger.

Sir Nigel poked his head out again. "Good enough? Now let's see the box."

Charlotte withdrew the box from her pocket, just far enough to let the light glint off the silver corner. "I'll only give it to Toussaint, and only after Steven and Gauthier are released. Unharmed."

Nigel scratched his jaw. "That might prove difficult, depending on your definition of unharmed."

She refused to flinch. Steven certainly wasn't comfortable, but he hadn't sounded like he was in agony. She wouldn't think about the fact that she hadn't heard Gauthier's voice yet. Keeping her gaze locked on Nigel's, she pushed the box back in her pocket, out of sight, and gave a nonchalant shrug.

Nigel withdrew again, muttering as he went.

She flicked her gaze down to Penrith, who was still slumped against the wall, an empty tankard clutched in one hand. Nigel had hardly spared him a glance.

Just as the butterflies threatened to take flight in her stomach, Nigel stepped out into the hall, moving aside to make room for Toussaint.

She clenched her teeth to keep her mouth from falling open.

Toussaint's nose was obviously broken, with deep bruises beneath both eyes, and another dark, mottled patch along his jaw. His bottom lip was split and grossly swollen. His squint could be caused by swelling from the broken nose, or painful sensitivity to light because of a concussion.

She wanted to whistle appreciation at Alistair's handiwork. Instead she determinedly kept her gaze on Toussaint's damaged face so she wouldn't draw attention to Alistair, who was currently creeping down the stairs, inching toward the gaming room. He rolled his hand, gesturing for her to keep them talking.

She pointed at Toussaint's injured face. "Did one of your little birds say no to you?" Baiting a man about his sexual conquests—or lack thereof—was so easy, it almost seemed unscrupulous. But Toussaint didn't play fair, so she wouldn't, either.

When she lowered her arm, she slid her hand into a different pocket, this one filled with a dagger.

Toussaint's eyes narrowed even farther. "Box." Movement of his lips was barely perceptible, and his jaw moved not at all.

"I'm sorry, I didn't understand you," she said brightly. "Could you repeat that?"

If looks could kill, she would have exploded on the spot under his furious glare.

"He said you should give him the snuffbox. Now." Nigel edged out a little farther into the hall, his hand held out.

"Really? You heard all that, expressed in only one syllable?" She held her hand to her chest in mock amazement. One more step, and Alistair would be able to slip behind them into the gaming room.

Toussaint gave an inarticulate growl.

"His jaw is broken," Nigel said, poorly disguising a snicker of amusement at Toussaint's predicament by coughing into his sleeve. He gave Toussaint a sidelong glance, and returned his attention to Charlotte, serious once more. "This has gone on long enough, miss. Give me the box, I'll release your brother and the Frenchman, and we'll all walk away with what we want."

Alistair was in. She kept her eyes on Nigel, but inside she was hopping up and down in excitement.

She lifted the corner of the box out of her pocket, just far enough to make sure Nigel and Toussaint focused on it and not the muffled thud coming from the gaming room as Alistair made his presence known to Jennison. "I'm not so sure I want to do that. The gemstones alone on this box could support me in grand style for the rest of my life. Not to mention what I could do with what's inside it."

Nigel's brows knitted together. "You'd sacrifice your brother and friend?"

"Well, I—"

The sound of flesh striking flesh made everyone in the hall look toward the gaming room.

As Nigel and Toussaint turned, Penrith suddenly swung his foot, taking Nigel out at the knee. The two struggled on the floor.

Toussaint hardly spared them a glance, intent on getting back into the gaming room, his expression even more thunderous than before.

Knowing she couldn't overpower him physically, Charlotte threw her knife. It pinned Toussaint's sleeve to the doorjamb.

He growled something that may have been a slur on her parentage, and reached for the still-quivering dagger handle.

She retrieved more throwing knives from her pockets and let one fly. It caught the open flap of his coat, just below his navel, though she'd been aiming for his other sleeve.

"The next one will be lower," she promised. She drew her arm back but did not release the knife.

His eyes were narrow slits as he stared at her, his chest heaving with impotent rage.

Penrith finally managed a clean blow, and finished off

Sir Nigel with an uppercut to the jaw. Nigel went still.

Charlotte glanced at the two on the floor. When she turned back to Toussaint, he had his hand on the knife handle, trying to extricate it from where it pinned his sleeve to the wall. She pulled her pistol and cocked it. "Please, do keep trying to free yourself."

Toussaint's eyes widened. He froze.

Penrith climbed to his feet, dusted himself off, and retrieved his walking stick.

Steven and Gauthier tumbled into the hall just then, a little worse for wear with bruises and cuts. "Told you she was great guns," Steven said, rubbing his red, raw wrists. Careful not to get in the way of her pistol, he leaned in to kiss her cheek.

Her gun still steady on Toussaint, she gave Steven a one-armed hug.

"Certainement, une femme formidable." Gauthier gave her a peck on the other cheek.

Alistair emerged then, a knife in one hand, rope in the other. "Shall we put these to better use?" He held up the ropes that until recently had bound Steven and Gauthier.

"Excellent idea." Steven grabbed one and leaned close to Toussaint. "I'm hoping you'll resist," he growled.

Toussaint sniffed and looked away.

Charlotte kept her pistol trained on Toussaint while Steven trussed him up and Gauthier bound Nigel's hands.

"Don't forget Jennison." She kept her gaze trained on Toussaint, but noted with pride the triumphant smile lighting Alistair's face.

"Oh, he won't be going anywhere, anytime soon." Alistair shook out his right hand.

"What shall we do with this rubbish?" Steven indicated Toussaint, and nudged Nigel's foot with the toe of his boot.

"Last night he wanted to throw Charlotte's body into the river." Alistair studied Toussaint's injured face as though considering where best to add more damage.

Toussaint flinched.

At the reminder of the emotional anguish Alistair had suffered when he thought she'd died, her heart constricted. How could she make it up to him?

Steven's brows rose. "Poppet?"

"I'll explain later." She suddenly realized all five men present—Nigel didn't count, since he was unconscious— were looking toward her. She was, however temporarily, in a position of authority. They were willing to listen to her.

The first thing she wanted to do was give back a family heirloom. She dug the snuffbox out of her pocket and handed it to Penrith. "Would you please return this to his grace, with my thanks?"

Penrith tucked the snuffbox into a coat pocket. "Perhaps." He winked at her.

"You borrowed a *duke's* snuffbox?" Steven gave a low whistle.

Sir Nigel, on the floor at their feet, groaned.

She gave him a considering glance. "The Bow Street Runners would be interested in the office full of stolen goods." From the corner of her eye she noted Toussaint relax slightly. "But I think we'll send for our mutual friend instead. I'm sure he has a few questions he'd like to ask of Monsieur Toussaint."

Toussaint paled.

"That won't be necessary, my dear." Lord Q stood in the doorway of the taproom. As he spoke, half a dozen men surged forward and collected Sir Nigel and Toussaint. "The Home Office does indeed have a few questions."

Steven jerked a thumb over his shoulder, toward the gaming room. "Don't forget Jennison."

Charlotte stared at Q and lifted her chin. "I thought you said you could offer no help."

"Officially, I cannot. *Un*-officially, however, I came to see if acquaintances were in need of assistance." Lord Q stepped aside to allow his men to walk past, Nigel slung over one man's shoulder, Jennison slung over another who bore a strong resemblance to Q's butler, though he was not in livery. Two others herded Toussaint. "But I see you already have matters well in hand." He gave Steven and Gauthier an appraising stare. "You two should see a doctor."

"What great luck we happen to have one on hand." Penrith grabbed both men by the shoulder and led them out. "His grace will be eager to hear about all that transpired last night. However did you manage to allow yourselves to be captured by Nigel?"

"The same duke who loaned his snuffbox?" Steven gave Charlotte a glance over her shoulder as he left the hall.

"Oh, yes. He brought his personal surgeon, just for you two." Penrith clapped Steven on the back as they disappeared into the taproom.

Lord Q watched them leave. "Excellent work, Charlie."

"Thank you, my lord, but I could not have succeeded without my partner." She gestured toward Alistair.

"You two work well together." Lord Q beamed his approval.

It was probably the last time they'd work together, but Charlotte didn't have the heart to say so out loud.

No. She raised her chin. She wasn't going to give up again as easily as she had last night. She wasn't going to give up Alistair, even if it meant the end of working for Q.

"Well." Lord Q cleared his throat. "I'll see that she gets home safely, Moncreiffe." He spoke directly over Charlotte's head.

"Of course." Alistair turned, as if to leave.

"Wait!" She clutched at his sleeve, hating that she sounded so desperate. "We're not done. The conversation we started at the chandler's shop next door?"

"Oh, that."

Even with his disinterested tone, she refused to give up without a fight. "I won't need your assistance, my lord," she said to Lord Q without taking her eyes off Alistair.

"If you're sure?"

Alistair kept his gaze locked on hers. Was that a twinkle in his eyes? "Certain. Good day, sir."

Lord Q left.

There were more voices in the taproom, and people scurrying down the hallway.

"I think we had more privacy in the doorway," Charlotte grumbled, stepping aside as a couple pushed past, headed for the stairs.

Alistair led her to the private gaming room. After checking to make sure the room was unoccupied, he pulled her inside and shut the door. "You were trying to tell me something earlier." He adopted a neutral expression of polite interest.

He had to have an inkling of what she was going to say. Didn't he? Drat him, he was going to make her say it aloud, in excruciating detail.

Nothing ventured, nothing gained. She stood straight and tipped her head back to look directly into his eyes.

"Last night, I gained everything I thought I wanted, but in doing so, I realized I had lost what had become most important to me."

"Oh?" He linked his hands together. "What would that be?"

She swallowed and took a deep breath. "You."

"Me." He ducked his chin and stared at her intently.

She nodded vigorously. "In the week and a half we have known each other, you have done the most horrible thing, something I thought impossible, would never, could never, happen."

"Horrible?" A spark lit in his eyes. She hoped it was humor.

She babbled on, eager to get it out before she lost her nerve. "You've made me think about being a wife—your wife—and made it an attractive proposition. So appealing, in fact, I . . . I would give up working for Lord Q." The words rolled off her tongue as though they'd been there all along, just waiting for a chance to be heard. "That is, if you meant what you said in the carriage last night."

He wasn't smiling, but at least he wasn't walking away from her in disgust. That had to be a good sign.

"I said a lot in the carriage last night. You'll have to refresh my memory."

She smoothed her hands on her skirt, drying her palms. "Much as it pains me to admit it, you were right. I used you. I convinced myself we were both benefiting from the arrangement, but last night I went beyond that. I used you most abominably. I did not respect your wishes or trust your instincts, and relied solely on my own."

Was he simply allowing her to continue to dig herself deeper into a hole? She plunged onward. "I've realized that, had I thought of you as a true partner then, and had I behaved as a partner, we may have been victorious without a casualty. As we were today."

She studied his expression, trying to read his reaction. All her skills at reading people failed her. His handsome face remained frustratingly impassive.

"I did notice that you didn't march into the room and try to free Steven and Gauthier by yourself. Remarkable restraint."

"I was confident you would succeed if I did my part."

He tilted his head to one side. "So, you're saying you've changed? You're not the impetuous woman you were last night?"

This was not something she could dip her toe into—she had to plunge in, even if she was over her head. "Changed so much, in fact, that I'm willing to give up being a spy in order to be your wife. If you'll still have me."

"Why?"

Why? A million reasons tumbled through her thoughts, both trifling and profound. "Because I don't want to go another day thinking I've lost your respect. Because I want to spend my nights gazing at the stars with you." She took a deep breath. "Because I love you."

He continued to study her.

Her heart sank. She hadn't exactly expected tearful smiles from the viscount, but his non-reaction made her insides twist and shrivel. "Put me out of my misery," she whispered.

A lock of hair had come loose from her chignon, and he tucked it behind her ear. He slowly trailed his finger down her cheek and along her jaw. "No. That's not what I want."

He wanted her miserable? She supposed she owed him that, after the appalling way she'd treated him last night. She found it difficult to swallow past the lump in her throat.

He slid his hand around the back of her neck, pulled her closer and pressed his lips to hers in a tender kiss. "I find I've had a change of heart." He kissed her again.

The kissing was killing her. She pushed on his chest when he leaned in for another. "Please clarify."

"I don't want you to give up being a spy."

She realized she still had her hands on his warm, muscular chest, and had slid one down inside his waistcoat. She dropped her hands to her sides. "I see."

"No, I don't think you do. You see, I also want you to be my wife."

Euphoria was almost within her reach.

"That's the change of heart part. You'll be my wife, and we'll both work for Lord Q. I'm sure he can find us assignments that will suit our complementary skills." He reached for her hands and held them snugly in his. "I think we've both learned something since last night, something very important. I fell in love with a woman who tackles life head-on, rather then some simpering miss who worries about her wardrobe and social standing."

Exhilaration swept through her, and flooding warmth made her toes curl. She allowed him to tip her head back, and closed her eyes as he kissed her neck. "And what did I learn?" Oh my, the man knew how to kiss.

"You could have tried to rescue Steven and Gauthier by yourself," he whispered in her ear. His lips brushed her skin as he spoke. "But you knew you had a better chance of success by working with someone rather than alone." He walked her backward, until her spine touched the wall. "A partner who acknowledges and respects your skills." He kissed the corner of her mouth. "As I do."

"True," she murmured, and tugged one hand free in order to cup his jaw and move his mouth into proper position for a full kiss.

He groaned his approval, and wrapped one arm around her waist, the other holding the back of her head, enveloping her in a cocoon of passion.

"I'm still not a patient woman," she said, sliding her hand down his muscular chest, past his trim waist, and lower. "I don't think I can wait until we're married before we finish what we started on the roof." She closed her hand around him, through his breeches.

His breath caught, and released in a hot rush against her neck. "We'll have to work on teaching you patience." He bunched her skirt up in his hands and started sliding it up her thighs. "Later . . ."

Epilogue

Moncreiffe Hall, the Lake District
One month later

Feeling the afternoon sun on her face, Charlotte rolled over in bed, away from the intruding light. She reached out her arm, blindly patting the mattress beside her. Empty.

She opened her eyes and squinted at the bed canopy and curtains, still startled to see the deep indigo and rich mahogany.

Molly, her maid, scratched on the door. "Beg pardon for the intrusion," she said, "but a note has just arrived for you. The messenger said as how it was urgent."

Charlotte stretched, luxuriating in the feel of the soft cotton sheets against her bare skin. "Slide it under the door, please."

A piece of folded vellum slid across the floor.

Alistair, who had been standing at the now-cold breakfast tray, bent over and picked it up. "It's from Lord Q, addressed to both of us." He ate a bite of licorice and held the rest of the piece out to her.

She shook her head, letting a lazy smile of appreciation stretch across her face as she watched him. Early afternoon sunlight gilded his bare skin, turning the light dusting of hair on his powerful thighs and muscular chest to burnished gold.

"Read it later. Come back to bed." She stretched again, letting the sheet fall away from her naked torso.

He slid in beside her and kissed her beneath the ear, his arm snaking around her waist. "Excellent idea," he murmured, his lips brushing her skin.

She gave herself up to his ministrations, but a few minutes later sighed in frustration. "He has the worst timing. Now I'm worried I will think about the letter's contents at a most inopportune moment."

He sighed, a warm, gentle puff in her ear. "It's a good thing I'm secure in your affection for me. Otherwise I might be concerned about the amount of time you spend thinking about another man."

"He is our employer." Her sudden gasp had nothing to do with said employer and everything to do with Alistair's tongue.

Without interrupting his exploration of her skin—a freckle hunt, he'd called it a few mornings ago—Alistair reached for the note beside the pillow and handed it to her. "What's so urgent the old man couldn't give us time for a decent honeymoon? We've been gone less then a week."

She broke the seal and read it, though it took her much longer than usual since her concentration was elsewhere. "Seems he has another assignment for us."

"Mmm."

She shivered in appreciation of what Alistair was doing, and slid her fingers through his hair. "Doesn't he know we're in the midst of watching the Orionid meteor showers?"

Alistair traced lines between her freckles with his fingertips, and followed the path with scorching kisses. "That's only at night, Charlotte."

True. She had the best of both worlds now, even though it would be hours before she'd be able to speak again in words of more than one syllable. Nights spent under the stars with Alistair, mornings and afternoons sleeping in his embrace, exploring the delights of the marriage bed. Which left their evenings free, to work for Lord Q if they chose.

"But you make me see stars, day *and* night."